War of the Fae
Book Three

Darkness & Light

Elle Casey

All names, places, and events depicted in this book are fictional and products of the author's imagination.

No part of this publication my be reproduced, stored in a retrieval system, converted to another format, or transmitted in any form without explicit, written permission from the publisher of this work. For information regarding redistribution or to contact the author, write to the publisher at the following address:

Elle Casey
PO Box 14367
N Palm Beach, FL 33408

Website: www.ElleCasey.com
Email: info@ellecasey.com

ISBN/EAN-13: 978-0-9866071-6-6

Copyright © 2012 Elle Casey
All rights reserved

First Edition

Dedication

To Grace, my baby pixie in human form.
Do Momma a favor, lovebug ... don't ever lose your pixie playfulness.

Other Books by Elle Casey

War of the Fae: Book One, The Changelings
War of the Fae: Book Two, Call to Arms
War of the Fae: Book Three, Darkness & Light
War of the Fae: Book Four, New World Order

Clash of the Otherworlds: Book 1, After the Fall
Clash of the Otherworlds: Book 2, Between the Realms
Clash of the Otherworlds: Book 3, Portal Guardians

Apocalypsis: Book 1, Kahayatle
Apocalypsis: Book 2, Warpaint
Apocalypsis: Book 3, Exodus
Apocalypsis: Book 4, Haven

My Vampire Summer
My Vampire Fall

Wrecked
Reckless

War of the Fae
Book Three

Darkness & Light

Elle Casey

Chapter One

MY BEST FRIEND TONY'S HAND rested on my shoulder, sending a sense of peace into my heart - which is no small accomplishment, seeing as how at this particular moment I was locked in a potentially epic battle with none other than Ben, the Dark Fae fire demon who right now looked like a creature sent straight from hell. Tony saying he wanted to stay with me and that we didn't have to be apart anymore was the best news I'd had in two months, since I'd changed from human to fae. Now all I had to do was figure out how to handle the flaming terror standing in front of me with a firebomb in his hands.

"Ben, he doesn't want to go with you! He's coming with me!" I thought the roar of our two opposing powers would make it difficult to hear, but apparently there was no need for me to yell, because Ben answered me in a perfectly normal tone of voice, and I understood him just fine.

"I heard him. But I don't believe he's making the decision with all of the information he needs. It's only fair that he go into this with full disclosure, don't you think?" He arched his eyebrow at me patronizingly, making me feel small and stupid.

I hated feeling small and stupid, and I *especially* hated when it was Ben making me feel that way. His answer was unsettling too, because I didn't want Tony to think I was hiding anything. I knew the truth, and I had already given it to Tony before Ben showed up. We were the good guys, the Light Fae; Ben represented the bad guys, the Dark Fae. There was really nothing else to tell.

It was obvious this guy Ben knew something about the use of psychological warfare. He probably invented the term a hundred years ago or something. You never could tell the age of a fae from the looks of him. On the outside, he was a seriously, amazingly awesome-looking human guy of eighteen. On the inside, he was probably a three hundred and fifty year old, ugly ass fae serpent, using a spell to mesmerize me into thinking he was hotness personified. I didn't even know that there were such things as fae serpents - but he *could* be one. He was that slithery.

I gave my head a mental shake, forcing myself to stop focusing on his looks. I was pretty sure the rule I had for human guys went for fae guys too - namely, that the better looking they were, the crappier they acted towards girls and the shallower they could be. Seriously ... why would a guy bother to develop a decent personality when everyone just handed him everything he wanted in life just because he was gorgeous? *Focus, Jayne.* I had to ignore his beautiful face ... concentrate on the blackness of his soul and how much I despised him for trying to steal Tony from me.

"Tony knows everything. I already told him before you came in, uninvited and unwanted, I'd like to add."

Ben broke his gaze away from me and looked at Tony. "Did she tell you that she's going to force you to fight in a war? That you're going to have to kill people?"

Tony's hand left my shoulder, making me instantly uneasy. I'd just spent thirty minutes convincing Tony he needed to go with me and that everything would be okay. But I knew he didn't like the idea of

War of the Fae: Book Three

violence, and apparently, so did Ben.

"Tony knows enough to make a good decision, which he already did. So why don't you just get the hell outta here so we can be on our way?"

"Um, Jayne?" came Tony's scared voice from behind me. "I ... I really don't want to be part of a war ... "

His voice trailed off, but I knew what this meant. I had to do something to salvage the situation as best I could - and quickly. I fixed Ben with the angriest look I could muster past my fear. "Power down, asshole, so we can talk about this without blowing up the neighborhood."

"I will if you will," he said, eyebrow raised again, this time in challenge.

Man, is he ever good with the eyebrow thing. I eased off on my hold over The Green, letting it know I wanted it to go back through the ley line below Tony's house and down into the earth, where it rested when I wasn't calling it up and using it to do my bidding. The red glow that had amassed itself in Ben's hands got lighter and dissipated up his arms and around the back of his body. Soon we were both standing there looking like regular teenagers again. No more glowing and no more roaring or humming. I glanced at the guys to my left and right - Finn, Jared, Spike and Chase. They all visibly relaxed from their fight-ready stances, but still seemed wary.

"I don't trust him," said Finn.

"Me neither," said Spike.

Chase remained silent - as usual - holding onto my injured pixie friend, Tim, who Ben had pretty much just fried in midair with a laser beam of fire. My other daemon friend, Jared, was also quiet. Even so, I knew they didn't trust Ben any more than I did.

"Well, I trust him," said Tony.

Elle Casey

I looked at Tony with frustration. "Dammit, Tony, what the hell? I thought we went over this."

"No, you're right, we did. I'm not saying I'm going anywhere with him or not going with you. I'm just saying I trust him. He's been nice to me, Jayne, and he hasn't done anything to hurt me. And apparently, he could have if he had wanted to." He looked up at Ben, giving him a nervous smile.

This was so typical of Tony, giving someone the benefit of the doubt, even when that someone was a friggin, pixie-roasting asshole.

"Listen, Tony, I get it that you felt abandoned when I stayed in the forest and you came back here ... "

Tony started to interrupt, and I was fairly certain what he was going to say, so I held out my hand to shut him up.

I continued, " ... and I know you don't remember being there, but you *were*, and I'll be happy to prove that to you when we get back. But we need to go." I looked over at Ben again. "You may trust him, but we sure as hell don't; and I have a friend to take care of." I gestured with my head to Tim, lying in Chase's hands, his blackened stump of a wing sticking out from his side.

"He's breathing," said Chase.

"Well, thankfully he's unconscious, because I know for a fact that having a wing taken off is painful - I'm sure having one *burned* off is excruciating." I shot Ben a look that conveyed what a piece of shit I thought he was.

Tony looked at Tim and got a sick expression on his face.

Ben was going to ignore my comment, but then he noticed Tony's face too. "Tony, you need to understand - pixies are very dangerous. They may seem small and cute, but he was coming over to attack me. I was only defending myself."

Tony looked at me for confirmation, making me feel

War of the Fae: Book Three

uncomfortable. Why was I having to defend my tiny, currently inert friend who had only been trying to save us?

I faced Ben angrily. "Tim, as you've conveniently forgotten, was only protecting us. From you!"

"I was no danger to any of you. I did nothing. You're the one who issued the threats."

The further this conversation went, the worse I felt. Somehow Ben was turning everything around to make me look like the bad guy in this whole thing. I knew my face was expressing my frustration, and as I looked at Ben to respond, I saw him smile smugly. Asshole thought he had me up a tree. "Don't stand there and act like you're mister honest guy. You never told Tony you were fae, and you never told him your true intentions, either." I looked at Tony and continued. "Ask him, Tony. Ask him why he didn't tell you. You trusted a guy who was lying to you and hiding things the whole time he was getting to know you."

Just then there was a banging on Tony's door.

"Tony? Do you have someone in your room?"

Tony got a panicked look on his face. "No, Mom! It's my music!"

"Well, turn it down. It's way past your bedtime."

Finn snickered but had the decency to look chagrined when I shot him a dirty look. All we needed was for Tony to think we were laughing at him. Sure, his mom was clueless and obviously nearly deaf, but that wasn't Tony's fault.

I whispered to the group. "Listen, we're not getting anywhere with this. Besides, there's no point anyway. Tony's coming with us, and we need to go." I looked at Tony, my eyes begging him. "You're still coming, right?"

"Yeah, I'm still coming. But I want to hear what Ben has to say, first. He's my friend, Jayne. I know you don't like that, but that's how it is. I owe him the chance to give me his side of the story."

Ben smiled. "Tony is a fair person. He's always been willing to listen. Maybe you could take a minute to listen too, Jayne. You might be surprised to hear what I have to say."

"*Pfft*, not likely."

Jared stepped up, his hands held out in a gesture of peace. "Why don't we take this outside or somewhere we can talk." He glanced at Ben and then me. "Neutral territory, a place where everyone would feel comfortable."

Ben nodded.

I looked around and everyone else seemed to think it was a good idea. I was more in favor of just getting the hell out of there and never looking back, but I had to be fair to Tony. I didn't want him leaving here thinking I had anything to hide.

"Fine. Where?" I asked.

"How about the all-night diner, over by the school?" suggested Tony.

We all nodded.

Two seconds later, Ben's form faded. "See you there," was the last thing he said before he disappeared in a puff of black smoke and wind.

I looked at Tony, whose eyes were bugging out of his head. I sneered. "Yeah. You trust this guy. Fucking demon fae or whatever he is." I shook my head, walking to the window and looking out, confirming that Ben wasn't there anymore. I wondered how far he could go with that disappeary-smokey thing.

"You guys go ahead and wait for us outside. I'm going to help Tony get some stuff together." I looked at Chase. "Please be extra careful with Tim. I'm going to see if I can find something to put him in."

Chase nodded in acquiescence before following the others,

War of the Fae: Book Three

climbing out the window wordlessly while Tony and I watched.

Once we were alone, I turned to him. "You need to pack a couple things - just what you can't live without. There will be clothes and stuff for you there."

"For me where?" asked Tony, not moving.

"At the compound. Where we live."

Tony looked distressed but said nothing.

I took his hand lightly in mine. "Listen. Here's the deal. Once we get there and you get a full tour and know everything that's going on, you will have the choice to stay or go. You had that chance once before, and you chose to come home. I think it's because you didn't know everything then. Now I can make sure you know it all. I'm pretty sure once you do, you'll decide to stay."

"So I can come back if I decide I want nothing to do with this stuff?"

I shook my head in frustration. "Yes. But Tony, you're not going to. Ben being here is proof of that. Either way you're getting involved. You're either going to come in voluntarily with us, or you're going to get dragged in by Ben. You're important to him for some reason that he isn't telling us. And you're important to me because you're my best friend. You *are* going to end up Light Fae or Dark Fae ... and I want you to be Light Fae, with me."

"What about Tim? I thought he was your new best friend."

I smiled. "Jealous?"

Tony smiled slightly. "No. Not much."

"Well, you have nothing to worry about; no one can take your place in my heart. You're going to love him, though. Just be glad you can't hear him."

"*You* can? How?"

"Witch's spell. I'll explain about that later."

"Why don't I want to be able to hear him?"

"Let's just say pixies are gassy."

Tony got a disgusted look. "Oh, geez."

"Yeah. Tell me about it. Come on, let's pack. What do you want to bring?"

Tony looked around his room, walking over to pick up the picture of him and me in a frame, broken as a result of him launching against the wall the other day. I had seen him throw it when I visited his room traveling through the Gray with the help of my friend Gregale, a gray elf. That was when I really knew how much trouble Tony was in. Watching him cry tears on that picture and then hurl it into the wall had just torn me up inside.

He pulled the broken frame apart and took the picture out, tucking it into his back pocket and tossing the rest in the trashcan. He reached down and picked up a sweatshirt from the floor, tugging it on over his head as he walked over to sit on the edge of his bed and pull on his boots.

"Do you have something I could put Tim in?"

Tony gestured towards his closet with his head as he bent over to tie his bootlaces. "In there."

I went over and opened the door, pushing junk aside until I found an old shoebox. Then I went to his bed, grabbing the pillow and pulling the pillowcase off, using it to line the inside of the box to make it more comfortable.

Tony stood and walked over to his desk, pulling a piece of paper out of his printer. "I'm gonna leave my parents a note."

"What are you going to tell them?"

"That I'm leaving for a while and I'll call them later."

"Tell them you'll send them an email. We have computers there but not phones."

War of the Fae: Book Three

Tony shrugged. "Okay." He finished his note, folding the paper and putting it on his pillow. He pulled up his covers so the bed looked neater. His dirty clothes went next, kicked into a pile in the corner of the room. Tony looked around, throwing up his hands and letting them drop to his sides.

"Ready?" I asked. "Got your passport?"

"I guess so ... and yeah. I have it." He went to his desk drawer and pulled it out, shoving the little book in his back pocket after finding it between a pile of papers.

"Good. Come on." I wanted to get the heck out of there before he changed his mind.

We climbed out of the window and went to the edge of his porch roof, using the fence nearby to get to the ground. The guys were waiting for us in the front yard.

I walked up to Chase and held the box out. "Pixie me."

Chase carefully lowered Tim inside.

I looked down at my little buddy who was still out cold, covering him as gently as I could with the corner of the pillowcase. "Hang on tight, Tim. I'm gonna get you back so Maggie can fix you right up." I received no response, so I put the lid on and used that brief moment of fumbling around, trying to get it to fit on right, to fight the feelings of despair that had welled up. I sniffed and cleared my throat, shoving that lump that was there down deep into my gut. I could not go into this showdown with Ben feeling all weepy and weak. There was no downplaying the seriousness of this meeting. I was fighting for Tony's life. There would be time for crying over Tim later - when I had all my guys on a plane and we were headed back to the Green Forest.

Chapter Two

WE WENT INTO THE DINER and joined Ben at a big round table in the back corner. A waitress came over and took our drink orders before leaving us alone.

I looked at Ben expressionlessly. "You wanted to talk. So talk."

"Thanks for coming."

I shrugged, refusing to play his nicey-nice games.

Ben shook his head in bemusement. "This doesn't need to be a fight, Jayne." He looked at Jared. "Jared, tell her."

I looked at Jared curiously. *How does Ben know Jared?*

Jared's eyebrows raised. "I'm not telling Jayne anything. She's smart enough to see the truth in front of her. Say what you have to say so we can leave. None of us are interested in your Dark Fae propaganda."

"I could call the nonsense you spout propaganda, too," Ben responded, calmly.

Finn, my redneck green elf friend, never one to keep his opinion a secret for long, spoke up. "As far as I'm concerned, you could start with explainin' why you shot Chase in the back with a poisoned arrow last month, aimin' for Jayne."

Ben raised his eyebrow sardonically at Finn. "I have no idea what you're talking about."

I laughed bitterly. "Oh, wow, this is a surprise. Ben's going to use denial as his big strategy to convince you to go with him, Tony." I looked at my friends. "Someone please tell me why we're wasting our time here."

"Jayne," Ben said forcefully, "I was not responsible for whatever happened to you or Chase; but believe me, I will find out who is and take care of it."

"Well, forgive me if that doesn't make me feel all warm and fuzzy inside." *Well, not much anyway. Wait a minute ... what?* I gave myself another mental shake. *Shit. Stop looking at him like that. He is the enemy.* This was ridiculous - I couldn't even trust *myself* around this guy. We needed to get the hell out of here. He was worse than Spike on the sexy scale. I glanced over at my incubus friend in time to catch his knowing smile and glimmering red eyes. Friggin Spike was detecting my amped up feelings again. *Dammit.* I glanced over at Tony and he was giving me a funny look now, too. *Double dammit.* I forgot he could feel my vibes. Pretty soon everyone at the table was going to be all hot and bothered if I didn't get a grip on myself.

"Ben, let's just get down to the bottom line here. I'm taking Tony back to the Green Forest with us. You can't have him, plain and simple. You'll just have to figure out your whole world domination scheme without including him as part of your army."

Ben smirked. "World domination? That's hardly my agenda." He turned to address Tony. "Tony, you know me. Am I the world domination type?" He didn't wait for answer. "No, I'm not. Now, do I believe that I have something to offer the world? Yes. I have ideas - good ideas - that would benefit all of us. And when I say 'all of us', I mean both fae and human alike."

Tony's eyes widened at that but he remained silent, studying us and listening carefully to the conversation.

"At least he's admittin' there's fae in the world now. I call that a step in the right direction," said Finn.

I couldn't resist adding, "Told you he was a liar."

Ben sighed. "I never lied to Tony. I just didn't tell him facts that weren't relevant to our relationship."

"Ha! That's a joke. You have a reason for coming to our school and befriending Tony, out of everyone you could have. And don't try to say it's because you really love West Palm, either."

Ben shrugged. "Tony is an extraordinary person. You of all people should know that."

"I *do* know that. Better than you do, because I don't *want* anything from Tony, other than his friendship, *unlike you.*"

"You seem to have me all figured out, Jayne. So tell me - what exactly do I want Tony for?"

He had me stumped with that one. The fact was, I really didn't know *what* he wanted Tony for. I had to wing it if I was going to get out of this whole thing and get back home.

"Tony's special. He somehow fits into your plan for killing all the humans and taking over the world."

Ben laughed. And not just a little. A lot.

"What? Killing humans is funny?" He was so pissing me off right now, acting all callous.

He calmed down enough to speak. "No, it's not funny at all. What *is* funny is your characterization of my grand scheme. You don't seriously believe that stuff do you?" He looked at our faces, seeing nothing but hard stares in return. "Really? You guys think that?"

I raised my eyebrow at him, not saying a word. If he was going to deny it, he had a lot of convincing to do. An arrow in the back was pretty hard evidence that his kind had little sense of fair play.

"You see, *this* is the problem with believing rumors and letting history dictate our future," said Ben, now clearly frustrated. "I have no intention of killing off all the humans, and I don't know where you got that information. Why would I do that? More than half of our fae population needs humans for one reason or another."

I looked at Tony. "Yeah, orcs *eat* humans. They're Dark Fae."

"Listen, there are plenty of Light Fae who eat humans too. And orcs are not technically Dark Fae anymore since they live in the Underworld - but that's not the point. The point is that no one wants to kill off humans. Our plan is really quite simple. The Dark Fae want to assert their place in society. No more skulking around in the dark, hiding who we are." He looked at each one of us, advocating passionately for his plan. "Together, we could all take a stand and demand our fair share. Why should we live as monsters and outcasts? We are who we are. Our natures are *from* nature, so why should we continue to be demonized by humans?" He gripped the edge of the table and leaned in towards us. "We *shouldn't*. And that's where we're coming from. We want all the fae on board, Light and Dark, so we can engage the world leaders and make the integration happen."

"Exactly," said Jared. "So you want to announce to the humans that the fae are here to stay and oh, by the way, don't be afraid, but we are going to eat some of you." Jared shook his head. "Yeah ... that'll work."

I was with Jared. I couldn't believe this guy's arrogance. He really thought that just because he'd come up with a plan, it was a good one and everyone was just going to follow along.

Ben shrugged. "I'm not saying it'll be easy or accomplished without bloodshed; but it can be done. And it will." His last sentence was said with such intensity, I felt a trickle of fear up my spine. I was hoping he wasn't going to ignite again. I wasn't ready for a showdown

War of the Fae: Book Three

in the middle of the diner, and I'd already almost lost one friend to his fire today.

"There aren't enough of you Dark Fae to take a stand against humans," said Jared.

"That's why we need you Light Fae to join us." He smiled as if he was our new best friend.

That was the point when I started laughing. I looked around our table as I tried to keep my guffaws to a minimum level, worried about attracting too much attention from the few late-night diners nearby. My friends were smiling at my amusement, even Chase; Ben, however, wasn't. The more I laughed, the more pissed he became.

"What is so funny?" he asked through gritted teeth.

"Oh, nothing. Just that you think the Light Fae are going to join you in your little invasion."

"They *will* join us."

I got serious quickly. "Like hell we will."

"Those who are not *with* us are *against* us."

"Sounds like a threat," said Spike, his eyes smoldering dark red with tendrils of black mixed in.

"Take it however you want. It is what it is."

I pushed my chair out, standing up and taking my shoebox with Tim in it under my arm, resting it on my hip. "I've heard enough. No point in wasting any more of our time." I looked at Ben pointedly and held up the box a little. "Thanks to you, I have a friend in need of medical attention. Already a fae casualty in your little war against the humans."

Ben stood angrily, bumping the table and jingling the ice in our water glasses. "I have no war with the humans - only those who refuse to see reason and get with the program."

"Your program," I said angrily.

"Yes."

"Screw that and screw you too, Ben."

Ben looked at Tony. "Tony, I really wish you would reconsider and come with me."

Tony stood slowly. "I know, Ben, but I'm sorry. I need to go with Jayne. I really wish you had told me some of this before."

"Would you have believed me?"

Tony thought about it for a second. "No, probably not. But you could have tried."

"That's exactly the point I've been trying to make here, Tony ... everyone." Ben looked around the table, beseeching all of us. "If I had told Tony the truth, would he have been my friend? No. He would have thought I was nuts and refused to hang out with me. All of us fae have to go through life pretending to be something we're not. We have to move from place to place over the years so people won't notice we aren't aging as fast as they are. We cannot make friends with non-fae for fear they will find out our secret and turn us in to the cops or mental hospitals - or worse. All I want is to be able to live as a fae, out in the open."

"All you want is something you can never have," said Jared, disgusted. "Let's go, guys."

He walked out, Finn and Spike right behind him.

I handed Tim's box to Chase. "Go ahead. I'll be right there."

Chase leaned in to whisper in my ear. "I'm not crazy about leaving you here with him."

I squeezed his arm and nodded, letting him know I'd be fine. "Go." I turned to Tony. "Tony, I'll meet you outside, 'kay?"

Tony looked worriedly from me to Ben. "Don't do anything stupid, Jayne."

I shoved him gently. "Shut up. I never do stupid stuff. Well,

War of the Fae: Book Three

almost never. I'll be there in a minute, just go."

Tony left us, glancing back once on his way out. I knew exactly what he was thinking, but I had no intention of launching a green power bomb at Ben's stupid head, much as I might have wanted to.

Ben and I stared at each other for a few seconds. Now that everyone was gone and it was just the two of us, the chemistry there was undeniable. This was the first time we had ever been alone together. I had intended to lay down the law with him and tell him in no uncertain terms that Tony was off-limits forever, but all of that went right out of my head when he looked at me.

He slowly walked from behind his chair, coming over to stand in front of me, and I looked up to meet his eyes. He was taller than me by several inches and his dark hair was in striking contrast to his green eyes. Holy batballs, he was gorgeous, in a seriously dangerous sort of way. He made your typical bad boy look like a saint. He probably had every single girl at our high school drooling all over him. And while I might have been fully aware of how good he looked, that didn't mean I was going to start acting all girly stupid around him.

"You wanted a private word?" he said, amused.

"Why is that so funny?"

"It's not. It's just that I was waiting for the threats to start, but all I'm seeing now is a little fae girl, sweating."

I frowned, reaching up to wipe the perspiration off my upper lip. "It's hot in here."

He smiled. "If you say so."

"Listen, I'm not interested in whatever little fae games you're trying to play with me right now. You can lay off the glamouring or mesmerizing or whatever else you call that shit you're doing."

He held up his hands in a gesture of innocence. "I'm not doing anything. Whatever you have going on right now is all you."

"*Pfft*. Right. Whatever. I just wanted to tell you that Tony is with me. Like, *forever*. You need to stay away from him and tell your Dark Fae friends to stay away from him, too; if anything happens to him, I'm coming after you ... and only after blowing up everyone you care about."

Ben looked at me with a touch of anger on his face. "That's a pretty big threat for such a young and inexperienced fae girl like you. I'm not so sure you can back it up."

I put every ounce of outrage I felt over the idea of something happening to Tony into my eyes, so Ben wouldn't doubt my sincerity for a second. "Trust me, Ben, I can. Whatever it takes. If something happens to Tony, I will bring you down and take you out, even if it means taking myself out in the process."

Ben moved closer - so close I could smell him. *Dammit*, he even smelled good.

"And who protects the big, bad Jayne Blackthorn?"

I cleared my suddenly constricted throat. "That's Jayne Sparks to you, asshole. And I don't need protection."

Ben leaned down a little, looking directly into my eyes. "I think you do."

"Fuck you, Ben." I said, pushing him away, hard. When my hands touched his chest I felt the heat going into them and up my arms. I wondered briefly how he went through this human world all the time not setting things or people on fire.

Ben smiled, looking down at the spot on his chest where I had touched him. "I'm letting you leave with your friends and Tony to show my good intentions. I was serious when I said before that I'd like to have you with me too, Jayne. Together, you and me, we could be unstoppable." He stared down at me, flames burning in his eyes.

I looked at him like he was nuts. "Keep dreaming, fire boy. I'm not interested."

"Something about you tells me otherwise. I can sense a heat coming from you, even though you have a remarkably cool touch with those hands of yours."

"Yeah, well that giant head you have precariously balanced on your shoulders is plenty powerful enough to cool me down, believe me." I walked away with my back straight and my head up, tossing my hair and yelling over my shoulder, "Stay out of my forest, asshole!"

I caught the look on his face before I turned back. He was smiling bitterly, his eyes narrowed at my retreating form.

Chapter Three

I STRODE OUT OF THE diner and walked up to Chase, taking the box with Tim inside from his hands.

"Ready?" asked Jared, searching my face. "Everything okay with Ben?"

"Yep. I told him to leave us the hell alone. Let's go."

Jared pulled out his phone to call for a taxi.

Spike sidled up and nudged me. "Things got a little hot in there, eh?"

"Shut up." I grinned, refusing to rise to his bait but unable to stay totally stern about it.

Spike smiled. "You know, incubi are really good at helping people ... work off their energy."

"Oh, yeah?" I asked, not bothered by the suggestive look on his face, even though his timing wasn't exactly the best. He never quit. Sometimes it was annoying, but tonight, for some reason, it gave me sense of security. After feeling the uneasy chemistry flying between Ben and me, the relaxed sexiness of Spike seemed like a much easier thing to manage.

"Yeah. You should let me show you what I've learned." He wiggled his eyebrows up and down at me. "I've heard I'm pretty good."

I frowned at him with my eyes but my mouth stayed in a semi-grin. "*Ew,* Spike. No bragging about your sex life. That's just gross."

"I'm not talking about sex - although, I've had no complaints there either. I'm talking about what I do as an incubus. My ... special talents. I think you could use them right now."

"Right *now,* right now?" I asked, curious about what he meant. *Is it something he can do while we're walking?* I was confused.

He laughed. "No, not right this second. But when we get back to the hotel ..."

I slapped him lightly on the arm. "Thanks, but I have roommates and too much on my mind. Maybe when we get back to the forest you can ... uh ... show me your stuff."

Spike smiled, rubbing his hands together. "Oh, goody. It's a date. I promise, you won't be disappointed."

I laughed to myself, enjoying his enthusiasm. He was never discouraged; no matter how many times I rejected his overtures, he always came back making more of them. There was something to be said for undying affection.

I walked over to Tony. "So, are you completely freaked out, or what?"

He smiled gently. "I am pretty freaked out. But I'll survive."

I put my arm around his waist. "I'm so friggin glad you're here with me, Tones. I was lost without you."

He put his arm over my shoulders. "Me too. It was a lot ... quieter without you here."

"That must've sucked."

"Yep. Sure did." Tony looked over my head at the guys who were standing a few feet away, near where the taxi would soon be. "So, what's next?"

War of the Fae: Book Three

"Well, we have a couple hotel rooms downtown. I think we're going to stay there for the rest of the night, what's left of it anyway, and then get on the plane tomorrow."

"Did you already buy tickets?"

"No, we don't need to. It's a private jet."

Tony nodded slowly. "Nice."

"Yeah. You've been on it before. You just forgot."

"That's just so weird for me to believe."

"Yeah, I know. I'm sorry about that. Maybe when you see some of the stuff, your memory will come back."

"I don't know. Even after seeing that little guy fly around, I didn't remember anything."

"Yeah, but you remembered Spike's teeth. And you'd never met Tim before, so there's no reason why he would trigger any memories."

"Why was that? About the teeth, I mean? That's kinda weird, isn't it? ... That I'd forgot all that other stuff but remember his teeth?"

I didn't really want to talk about this, but Tony remembering stuff was a good sign, and I wanted to encourage it. "Yeah, well, see I ... uh ... was ... *am* ... a little obsessed with Spike's smile and his teeth. And what with you vibing me all the time and knowing sometimes what I'm feeling or thinking about, well, you were kind of exposed to a lot of me staring at him, thinking about him ... you get the picture."

Tony was nodding. "I guess that makes sense. I was still vibing you, you know. When you were gone."

"Oh yeah? Like, what did you feel?"

"Various things. Anger a lot at first. Then surprise and happiness. The last few weeks I got a lot of happy vibes. Also feelings like you were proud - of yourself, I mean." He looked at me intently. "I know you're happy there. That's one reason I was willing to give this a shot. It has to be something special to have helped you get over ... that stuff that was going on at your house and to make you feel good again."

Just then the taxi pulled up, saving me from that embarrassing conversation.

"Come on, let's go to the hotel."

Luckily, Jared had told them to send a van-sized taxi, so we all fit in without a problem.

"So what's the plan?" I asked after we were all inside the van. "We sleeping here tonight?"

"No. We need to get back right away. I've arranged for the plane to take us out tonight."

"Ain't it a little late?" asked Finn, yawning.

"Yeah, it's late; but it's better to fly at night. We can sleep and try to get ahead of the jet lag."

"Where exactly are we going?" asked Tony.

I opened my mouth to respond and then realized I didn't really know the answer to that question. I mean, I knew it was the Green Forest, but I doubted that name existed on any human map.

"Yeah, where are we going, exactly?" I asked.

"I'll tell you later," said Jared, motioning to the taxi driver, indicating his desire to keep our location secret from the outside world.

Spike spoke up. "What time will we arrive there?"

"After our drive from the airport? About three or four in the afternoon, give or take."

Good. That would give me enough time to visit with Maggie in the woods and get Tim fixed up.

We arrived at the hotel and rode up the elevator to our rooms. We had to retrieve our stuff that we'd left there. It seemed a shame to not even use the rooms we'd already paid for, but I was anxious to get back. A part of me was worried that Ben's easy release of Tony and me was some kind of scam that was going to come back and bite me on the ass.

"Aren't you going to be too tired to deal with all this stuff - with me, I mean - when we get back?" asked Tony, as we walked out of the hotel lobby with our bags on our backs, Tim's box tucked under my left arm.

"Are you kidding me? I get up every day at oh-five-thirty, thank you very much."

"Wow. That's impressive."

"Tony, you are looking at a very finely tuned, warrior fae machine." I gave him a bicep curl with my free arm for effect. "I get up at the crack of my ass dawn and work until I drop at the end of the day. Just like everyone else. Just like *you* will." I gave him my most brilliant smile and tweaked his nose, for the sole purpose of annoying him. I hadn't mentioned that little tidbit of waking up insanely early before, so it was kinda fun to share it now - get him back for making me panic around Ben, thinking for a couple of tense seconds that he was going to change his mind and stay behind.

Jared walked up to me, nodding at Tony who was now scowling playfully at me. "Jayne, can I talk to you in private for a minute?"

"Sure. Tony, go wait with Chase, would you?" I knew I could count on Chase to look out for him, just in case Ben decided to make an appearance.

"What's up?" I asked when we were well away from the group.

"I just wanted to talk to you about the issue we still have with bringing Tony back with us. We really haven't discussed it. I figured before there wasn't any point unless we actually convinced him to come."

"Okay. Shoot."

"You remember the rule, right? That once a candidate has refused to become a changeling, he can never make the change?"

My ears were burning with fear and a touch of anger. "Yeah, I remember. They're just going to have to change the rule."

Jared shook his head slowly, looking down at the ground. "I don't think you should plan on that happening."

"Well, what the hell did we come all the way out here for, then?"

Jared shrugged. "It was better than leaving him to Ben."

"Ben would have let him change," I said accusingly. "He would have forced it on him. So if the Dark Fae would do it, why won't the Light?"

"I don't know why the rules are what they are. I just know this council in particular is set on following them. They're very traditional. They don't make change easily."

"Well, they can sit with their thumbs up their asses all day for all I care. Tony is making the change or else."

"Or else what?" asked Jared, searching my eyes.

"Or else I'm leaving with him."

Jared sighed in resignation. "Well, let's hope it doesn't come to that."

"Yeah. Let's do that," I said bitterly. *Friggin council*. They weren't going to decide for me what Tony and I did. I'd had enough of adults in my life making stupid decisions that affected me negatively. If they couldn't see reason, I'd ... I'd ... well, I wasn't sure exactly what I was going to do, but whatever it was, it wouldn't involve me blowing off my friend ever again.

Jared and I walked over to the shuttle that had parked in the valet area in front of the hotel.

"Don't stress over it too much," he said. "I'm sure it'll all work out."

"Yeah."

War of the Fae: Book Three

Jared opened the door so we could all climb in.

"Hey, Jared?"

"Yeah?"

"Thanks. For all this, I mean. For helping me get Tony back. I owe you one."

Jared smiled briefly. "No problem." He climbed in last, closing the door behind him.

I was sitting next to Tony in the front row of seats. I reached over and took Tim's box from him. "How is he?"

"Still out," said Tony.

I lifted up the lid gently, pulling back the piece of pillowcase that was covering Tim's frail body. I glanced up to make sure the shuttle driver wasn't watching me in the rearview mirror before whispering, "Tim ... Tim? Can you hear me?"

I heard a tiny moan in response, but his eyes stayed closed.

"Listen, Tim ... we're going to get you on the plane in just a few minutes and back to the forest. I'll get Maggie to take care of your wing right away, okay? You're going to be alright."

I got choked up looking at him. He was so pitiful lying there with his broken and blackened wing. *Fucking Ben.* Somebody needed to zap him good - show him what it felt like to have an appendage seared off like that. *Jerk.*

I covered Tim up again and looked out the window, slipping the lid of the box back on. Ben was going to pay for what he'd done and for what he'd tried to do. I was going to make sure of it.

Chapter Four

WE WERE ON THE PLANE and heading back to the Green Forest within thirty minutes. I had strapped Blackie - my most amazingly awesome dragon tooth weapon - back onto my leg, and felt much more secure with its threat there for the fae world to see. Tim still hadn't really moved much, only moaning from time to time to let me know he was still alive ... barely.

Tony took everything in stride, picking a window seat where he could watch the lights of the runway go by and then the sleepy cities twinkling beneath us until we were out over the ocean and in the clouds.

I slept in the comfy, reclining, soft leather seats, trying not to worry overly much about Tim. I was fairly confident that Maggie, the witch in the Dark Fae forest, could fix him. She knew everything about bad shit happening to fae and how to dose it up, and she especially loved pixie wings, so something told me she'd be an expert at getting a bad one off. At least, I hoped she would be. The fact that she lived in the Dark Forest was a bit disconcerting, but I'd spent enough time with her as she trained me to use the underground ley lines to summon my power to know that she was decent - a little prickly and unconventional, sure, but willing to help a clueless changeling like me in exchange for a green mushroom now and again. I was pretty sure I was getting the better end of that deal.

I fell into a dreamless sleep, listening to Finn's snores and Tony's even breathing beside me.

*****

An hour before we landed, Jared sat down across the table from Tony and me.

"Hey. I thought maybe you'd like to go over your plan for bringing Tony back to the compound." He looked across the aisle at Chase, Finn and Spike and said in a raised voice, "Hey! Guys! Wake up and get in on this."

They all sat up drowsily, pushing the buttons on their seats to put them in their upright positions. Ivar walked over and joined us too, sitting in front of Chase, next to Spike. Even though Ivar and I didn't see eye-to-eye on the appropriate way to treat guests on a private jet - me being of the mind that drugging them unconscious is rude - I was glad for his support. He was an ogre, and if nothing else, visually intimidating.

"So, Jayne, tell us what you're thinking about for bringing Tony back."

All eyes were on me, waiting expectantly for my brilliant answer.

I picked Tim's box up from the side of my seat and put it on the table, so if he was conscious at all, he'd hear the conversation. "Uh, I really didn't have a plan, actually."

Spike smirked, and Finn rolled his eyes. Chase looked at me expectantly. Tony seemed still half asleep, a little bit in a daze. The expressions I saw on Spike's and Finn's faces made sense, but Chase's was unexpected. Maybe he had some ideas.

"Why are you looking at me like that, Chase? What're you thinking?"

War of the Fae: Book Three

He shrugged. "Just waiting for you to come up with something. You always do, and it always seems to work out one way or another."

"Thanks for the vote of confidence; I appreciate it, even if I'm not sure I agree. I'm not messing around, though ... I really don't have a plan this time. I just want to get him in there, get an amulet on him, have him speak the words that start the change, and then, I don't know, get him a room and a trainer from his race." I looked around at my co-conspirators, smiling weakly. "It would all work so smoothly if there was no council in my way."

"That there's the problem. There *is* a council, an' they're gonna be P.O.'ed," said Finn. "Don't get me wrong - I'm willin' to shoulder the blame with you an' all, but I'm thinkin' you oughta be prepared for a little kickback from the rifle you done shot here, sneakin' off to the U.S. of A. and bringin' Tony on board."

Finn's colorful phrasing made me smile. "When you put it like that, it doesn't seem all that bad."

"Well, it is," said Jared, all seriousness. "We went against the council's direct orders. They're not just going to say 'okay, we'll let him change' and it's over. They're going to say no - and probably a few other things we don't want to think about right now."

I looked at Tony's face and was distressed to see that he was catching on to the problem. He looked as worried as I felt.

"Yeah, what we need to do is figure out where we go after they say no," said Spike.

"Okay, well, I have an amulet here on my finger, and I'm sure between us we can remember the words that have to be said. I'll just do it with him myself."

Ivar was shaking his head slowly, a frown on his face. He looked at Jared.

Jared lifted his eyebrows but said nothing.

"What, Ivar?" I said, impatiently. "Speak up or forever hold your peace."

Ivar answered in his deep, gruff voice. "Deliberately disobeying a fae law earns harsh punishment. It has always been so."

"Oh yeah? Like what kind of harsh punishment?"

Ivar grunted. "You can ask Anton about that. He has suffered the punishment."

That was a surprise. Dardennes not following orders? I probably shouldn't have been surprised at that. He'd pretty much told us to go on this trip, even though the council had said that Tony couldn't come back. Hopefully, he had assumed the council would be lenient with us and wasn't just selling us out.

"Well, since Dardennes isn't here to ask, and I think we need to know how deep the shit is that we're jumping into, maybe you can tell us the basics."

Ivar and Jared shared looks once again. Ivar nodded to Jared who let out a deep breath before beginning.

"Anton Dardennes used to be with the Dark Fae." He waited while everyone let that sink in. I had heard that piece of information before, but my understanding was that he'd had a change of heart and defected over to the Light Fae side.

"They have a council like ours, only it's of course made up of Dark Fae. He was given an order which he refused to follow, doing instead what he thought was right; and to punish him, they banned him from the Dark Fae."

Whoa. So he didn't leave voluntarily? That was big news to me.

"He got kicked out?" asked Finn, shock in his voice.

"Essentially, yes."

"And you guys just took him in and gave him a seat on the Light Fae council? That's pretty generous," said Spike, sarcastically.

War of the Fae: Book Three

"And trusting." I couldn't believe they could be so lax with their security, letting a Dark Fae run the Light Fae show. Sounded first-class stupid to me.

"It was a long, long time ago - hundreds of years now - and Anton has proven himself worthy many times over. If he wants to tell you the story himself someday, that's his prerogative. I'll just say one last thing about it - he was ejected from the Dark Fae for choosing to do something that was Light Fae in principal. He had refused to do something I'm sure none of us would ever consider being involved in."

"What?" asked Finn.

"Like I said, if Anton wants to tell you, he can. It's not for me to do that. But I trust him and so do all the other council members - fae who are impossible to fool."

I always knew there was something a little strange about Dardennes. Now I knew what it was. He had Dark Fae blood running around in those veins of his. I could see that he was Light Fae now - I mean, he had given me the gift of changeling status; but that didn't necessarily mean he had lost all of his connection to Them. I was going to be watching him a little closer now, and if the looks on my friends' faces told me anything, they were too.

"So what's to stop them from throwing all of you ... us ... out of the Light Fae for breaking their law and coming to get me?" asked Tony worriedly.

Jared gave him a half smile. "That won't happen. First of all, it wasn't a law that we not go pick you up. That was a directive they gave to Anton, that *he* couldn't come get you. So he didn't violate that directive because he didn't do this. *We* did. And the council never gave us that directive. As far as they know, we don't even know it was issued, since it wasn't done in front of a general assembly."

Tony nodded his head slowly, still with the same worried

expression on his face. "So what law are we breaking then?"

"None. That's the good news and why I agreed to go on this mission. But the law we *want* to break is the one saying you cannot become a changeling once you have refused the change."

"Does it matter that I don't remember refusing it?"

Tony would have made a great lawyer one day, except that he lacked that necessary ability to go for the throat in the name of winning - although he does go for the throat with an axe when his life is being threatened. I'd seen that firsthand when we were battling orcs in the Green Forest during our changeling test.

"No." Jared shook his head firmly. "The law was created knowing once you refused, you would be erased. That doesn't matter to them at all. This isn't like the law you're used to. There are no loopholes."

"Alright," I said, "so now that we know we're totally screwed, does anyone have any suggestions?"

All I saw were blank faces looking back at me.

"Okay, then - the way I see it, I have only one option left."

"What's that?" asked Spike, suspiciously, raising a glass of water to his lips and peering at me over the rim as he took a sip.

"Blackmail."

Spike choked, sending droplets of water all over the top of the table in front of him and onto Finn.

"Shit on a stick, Spike! What in the *hell* is your problem?!" yelled Finn, wiping his arm off and shooting Spike a dirty look.

Spike wiped his mouth with the back of his hand and used his sleeve to wipe off the table, sweeping his arm back and forth. "Sorry about that, dude. My bad. Just wasn't expecting that answer."

"I'm not so sure that's the best plan we can come up with," said Jared, dryly.

"Jayne ... " said Chase, a warning in his voice.

"Listen, from what I can see, we don't have a choice. There's a law that says we can't change him. The council is going to say no. We can't go against the law and do it ourselves or we'll get kicked out. The only thing we have left is brute force. I'm going to tell them that if they don't change him, I'm leaving. We'll see just how valuable I am to them."

"I'm not sure you should challenge them like that," said Jared.

"Do you have any other ideas?" I asked, frustrated that all he could come up with was what *not* to do.

He hesitated for a few seconds, then surrendered. "No. I guess not."

"Fine. Then that's my official plan. Blackmail it is."

Jared looked at Ivar beseechingly. "Tell her Ivar. Tell her what a bad idea this is."

Ivar shrugged. "Sounds good to me."

I smiled. "Thank you, Ivar."

He clarified. "Either way it works. Either she gets kicked out or Tony gets brought in. We can't lose."

My mouth dropped open in surprise. Was he friggin kidding me? That was his idea of support? Then I saw the corner of his mouth lift, ever so slightly. "Ivar?" I said, disbelieving my eyes. "Did you just mess with me? Like, make a totally cutting joke on me?"

Ivar shrugged.

I kicked him under the table while smiling back at him. "Bite me, you big dumb ogre."

He lifted his eyebrows at me, tilted his head to the side and shrugged again.

"Now *that's* funny," said a highly amused Finn.

"Yeah," agreed Spike, "you had me goin' there for a second."

Tony just sat there with a bemused expression on his face, probably trying to figure out our group dynamics. I should've told him to save his brain cells. There was no figuring out this wacky bunch with conventional human logic.

I turned my attention back to the group. "Ivar's right, though," I said. "Either way. You're either going to get a new changeling, an *awesome* one, or you're gonna be short one ... an *awesome* elemental, thank you very much, *ogre*." I scowled at Ivar, trying to keep a straight face, but not really succeeding.

"Well, they ain't gonna be short just one fae, I can tell you that," said Finn. "The green elves do not abandon Mother."

I glared at Finn. "Don't fucking start with that shit again, Finn."

"I'm jus' sayin' ... "

"What's he talking about?" asked Tony, perking up. "Did he just call you a mother?"

"Never mind. Just focus on looking either adorable or badass, so the council will say yes to my request to change the law." The thought of me standing in front of that table full of council members, who sat there like arrogant judges in a courtroom, caused an idea to pop up into my head. I was technically asking for a change in the law or an exception to be made; and there was one guy who might be able to help me.

"Finn, can you contact one of your elf buddies from here?"

"Dunno. Never tried. Whatcha got in mind?"

"I need to talk to Gregale right away, as soon as we land. I know he's a gray elf, but maybe one of the green elves can get a message to him."

"I'm willin' to try. Hold on a sec." Finn closed his eyes and sat quietly for a few minutes.

Spike leaned over and talked in a hushed voice. "So, what are you thinking Gregale can do?"

I noticed Finn's eyes opening.

"You'll see." I looked at Finn. "So? Did it work?"

"Yeah. I'm able to reach Robin. He has the strongest abilities, being our leader. What do you want me to tell him?"

"Tell him I need to speak to Gregale as soon as we land and that it's a top priority. Tell him I'm calling in my favor. He'll know what that means."

"Okay. Just hang on a sec." Finn closed his eyes again and came back to us a minute later. "It's done. Robin is going to find him and deliver the message."

"Awesome."

"That's about as good as texting," said Tony, smiling in wonder.

"Yeah, but way cooler." I smiled back at him. The more times we were able to show him the benefits of being fae, the better chance I had of making him more comfortable with his choice of coming with me. I'd decided to ignore Tony's statement earlier that he was still thinking about it. I knew once he had the whole story, he would want to be a changeling. I just had to convince the council that it was a good idea.

Chapter Five

I TRIED NOT TO FREAK myself out thinking about the council's angry reaction, choosing instead to focus on Tim and his more immediate need. Just before we got off the plane, I pulled Jared and Chase aside.

"Guys, I need to get Tim to the witch before I do anything else. Jared, when we get to the compound, can you keep an eye on Tony and make sure he stays away from the council until I get back? It'll be less than an hour."

Jared nodded. "Yeah. But hurry up. I won't be able to keep them in the dark much longer than that."

I nodded my agreement. "Chase, you want to go with me?"

"Of course." He took my bag from me so I was left holding just Tim's box in my hand.

We got into the van that was waiting to drive us back to the Light Fae compound. Niles - or the commando dwarf as I liked to call him - was in the driver's seat. Usually wherever you found Ivar, you could find Niles close by, but he was never on the plane. Maybe he was afraid of flying. I noticed for the first time that this van was equipped with special pedals so he could reach the accelerator and brakes. *Sweet.*

After driving for almost an hour on a mostly empty highway, several smaller country roads, and eventually dirt roads through the forest, we arrived at the compound. Chase and I rushed out of the van ahead of the others and darted through the trees on the pathway that led to the compound doors.

Standing at the entrance was Becky, my best water sprite friend and the only girl I hung out with at the Light Fae compound. There were a lot more male than female fae around here. I learned from Becky that many of the females lived outside the compound, choosing the forest as their home instead. Apparently, the compound was more like some sort of headquarters - few fae resided within its walls, aside from us changelings and the council members. Leaders of the different fae races or warrior groups frequently stopped by to visit with Dardennes or deal with fae business, but they left before nightfall usually.

"Hey, guys! I see you brought Tony with you." She ran up and gave him a hug, not even caring that he stood there as stiff as a board not recognizing her. "Welcome back, Tony." She turned to me, asking, "How'd it go? I figured it was going okay since no one contacted me and asked for intel on what the old dudes were up to." She grinned at all of us, waiting for our story.

She was supposed to keep an eye on the council and teleport over to warn us if necessary. She was able to do being a water sprite fae; they used the moisture in the air to travel from place to place. Becky hadn't been sure how far she could go, so I was kind of glad we hadn't needed her. Last thing I wanted was my fae friend floating out in the ocean somewhere because she'd overestimated her abilities.

"It went okay, but we had a little problem with a Dark Fae that was there. He hit Tim pretty bad. I need to get him over to Maggie, ASAP."

War of the Fae: Book Three

I went through the door to the compound, Chase holding it open for Becky and me.

"Can I go with?" she asked, obviously excited about the idea. She'd never actually met Maggie before.

"Sure, but we need to hurry. I don't want the council seeing Tony until I'm back." I walked backwards to speak to Tony. "Tony, hang with Jared. I'll be back soon."

I waited until he agreed and then turned around, walking quickly down the hallways and pulling ahead of the rest of them, imagining the door with the gargoyle on the center of it the entire way. All of the hallways in our compound were spelled with witch magic so that it seemed as if they were just one long corridor. We had to imagine the door we wanted for the pathway and the right door to appear. Someone who hadn't been to the compound before would never be able to find things, simply because they couldn't imagine what they looked like. It wasn't a perfect security system, but it was pretty good. It impressed the hell out of me, anyway. It had taken me a couple days to figure out how to use it correctly.

Soon we were in front of the door with the gargoyle symbol, and Chase opened it for us. We ran through the forest as fast as we could, while I tried like hell not to jostle Tim too much. We finally reached the base of the super huge tree with a door on the front of it that was Maggie's house.

Tim had introduced me to this crazy witch a month or so ago. He knew Maggie very well, but he refused to tell me how he knew her. When Chase had been struck by the black magic spelled arrow that had been meant for me, she was the only one who knew the right brew to bring him out of his coma. Ever since our first meeting, which had culminated in Tim sacrificing one of his tiny, green wings as a trade for Chase's remedy and me eating a spelled leaf that enabled me to hear

Tim talk, snore, and fart, I'd been going out to see her and work on my training, learning how to better manage my power over The Green.

Maggie had this nutball idea that in order for any of her brews to work, they had to have something green in them. Whenever Tim and I came across green mushrooms or other nasty green things in the forest, we collected them for her and then brought them over. She and I had an odd friendship. She yelled and growled at me the entire time I was there, and then always managed to offer me cool and insightful advice. I never really knew if she was Dark or Light Fae, but it didn't stop her from teaching me a lot about my power and how to use ley lines to tap into it. She had a ley line running in the earth beneath her house - she used it to amp up her spells.

Even though she was as ugly as sin and mean as a snake, I still liked her. She did her own thing and didn't give a shit what anyone thought, and that was something I could admire. Tim liked to tease me and say that she and I were a lot alike, but only when he was far out of arm's reach. Tim knew I'd never hurt him, but I was not above messing with him by doing things like holding his wings still so he couldn't fly, blowing raspberries at him which tended to drench him in spit since he was so small, or breathing heavy-duty garlic breath in his face - bad breath of dragon-sized proportions. I was capable of meting out seriously noxious torture against my little friend. Did I feel bad about this now, as he sat there all burned up and suffering? No. *Well ... okay ... maybe a little.*

I knocked on the door three times. That seemed to be the magic number around here for doors. No more, no less. In Maggie's case, if you knocked more than three times, it made her cranky as hell. More cranky than usual, in other words.

"What?!" a voice yelled from within.

"Open up, old lady! I have an injured pixie out here who needs your help."

The door opened a crack and a cloudy eye peeked out. Then her head moved and a black eye took its place.

"That's better. Who is that with you?"

"Chase, my daemon, and Becky, my friend."

"Lie!" spat Maggie. She's like a fae lie detector or something. She detests lies.

"Bullshit! She's my friend."

"Truth! But the other part ... lie!"

"Chase being my daemon?"

"Yes!"

I was confused by that. Of course he was my daemon, my protector. That was his job, and he took it seriously. That was how he ended up with an arrow in his back in the first place. But I didn't have time to argue semantics with her right now.

"Whatever. Just let us in. I have Tim with me." I held up the box for her to see.

The door opened and she beckoned us in, croaking out, "So? What else did you bring me, hmmmm? Anything green perchance?"

"No. I've already brought you a buttload of that stuff. I need your help this time with nothing in return."

"Nothing in life comes for free. You must offer me a trade to fix your friend." She peered into the box I had opened for her. "Hmmmm. A pixie wing, perhaps ..." She smiled her nearly toothless grin at me, making me cringe. The few teeth she had left were brown and rotten-looking. I hated making her happy because her smile was truly nauseating.

I looked at her in disgust. "He's practically dead from having one wing burned off, and you want to take his only good one? Are you sick in the head?" I kind of already knew the answer to that question, but it didn't hurt to point it out, even though she didn't take the hint now and never had in all the other hundred times I'd mentioned it.

Maggie shrugged her shoulders, shuffling away. "Up to you ... " Then she started humming her favorite tune, breaking out in lyrics I knew only too well, but now enhanced with an extra line she came up with just for the occasion. *"Green things, green things, beautiful lovely green things; pixie wings, green and sparkly things, oh my lovely green things."*

"You're batshit crazy, Maggie, you know that?" I turned to my friends, speaking quietly as she puttered behind me. "I don't know what to do."

Becky peered into the box. "Oh, ouch. That looks so painful." She looked at me, concern marring her features. "She's going to take the bad, burnt one off, right?"

"Yeah, I guess so."

"So will he be able to fly with just one?"

"No, he has to wait for the other one to grow back."

She shrugged slowly at me, a questioning look on her face that was shared by Chase. "Well, if she took both of them off, would it make a difference to Tim? I mean, to him being able to fly and do the stuff ... I don't know ... that pixies do?"

I thought about it for a second, Maggie cackling behind me. The old hag was probably listening to everything we said.

"I guess not. But how pissed is he going to be when he wakes up and finds himself wingless? ... And realizes it was me who gave his wing away?"

"He did it for you once before," reminded Becky, gently.

"Yeah, but that was different. He volunteered. This would be me *taking* it."

"To save his life," said Chase. "He will understand."

War of the Fae: Book Three

I thought of going out into the forest to try and find something else green to trade, but I knew Maggie had scoured this part of the forest and picked it clean. I was only able to find her green things in Light Fae territory, far from here. And Tim didn't have enough time for me to go looking; his breathing was getting shallower by the hour.

I turned to her, frustrated. "Fine, you old bat. His good pixie wing for a *complete* healing. Deal or not?"

"Deal!"

"And you have to promise they'll both grow back - that's part of the definition of complete healing."

"I said *deal!*" she screeched at me.

"Shit, okay, okay - don't get your undies in a bunch." Good lord, I hoped she wore undies. I shuddered as I fought to get those horrific images out of my head.

She shuffled over and grabbed at the box. I held it up above her head. "Easy now. This is my friend. I expect you to treat him carefully." I gave her my most threatening look. "Hurt him, and you have me to deal with."

She cackled at me. "Truth!"

I rolled my eyes, shaking my head. "What is *with* you and the lie detector shit, anyway?" I lowered the box and gently handed it to her.

"Wait outside."

The other two didn't argue. They got out of there in a hurry, the door slamming behind them.

Maggie didn't even look up at me. "What do you want?" she demanded in a softer voice.

I wasn't sure exactly. I just looked at the box with Tim in it.

"Get out," she said in gentle tone. "I'm not going to hurt your precious pixie, even though he deserves it, believe me." She walked over to her kitchen table, setting the box down next to her black brew pot.

"What's that supposed to mean?"

She raised her eyebrow at me as she threw pinches of various things from nearby canisters into the black pot on top of her table.

"Tim has not told you of our previous ... liaisons?"

"No. He doesn't like talking about whatever relationship you used to have."

"Guilt!" she barked out.

"What did he do?"

She snorted. "Do you mean, what did he *try* to do?"

"Okay, sure. What did he *try* to do then?"

She stirred her concoction, eyeing it carefully.

"He tried to *pixie* me." She shouted the word pixie as if it was totally unbelievable that he'd try something like that. But I could totally see his reasoning. If anyone needed a good cheering up, it was Maggie.

I raised my eyebrows at the news, though. I knew pixies liked it when other fae were happy and dancing all over the place, which is why they pixied them if they weren't - sort of in a misdirected sense of giving the gift of happiness. Only, it would eventually drive the person mad and they'd end up dying from it, so it was more a curse than a gift. The pixies didn't quite get that part, but I'd convinced Tim it was true.

"Actually, I can see why he'd do it."

She scowled at me. "Truth. Explain yourself."

"Well, you seem kinda grouchy all the time, even when you're happy. I'm sure he was just trying to cheer you up."

"You truly believe this, I can see. But that was neither his purpose nor his motivation. He was trying to steal from me."

That didn't really sound like Tim. He was mischievous, sure, but he wasn't a thief. "What was he trying to steal?"

"A pixie."

"A pixie?"

"I do not repeat myself."

"You had a pixie ... and he was trying to free the pixie ... is that it?"

"The pixie was my willing captive. And yes, he was trying to steal her."

"Why?"

"You'll have to ask him. I don't read pixie minds. Wouldn't want to." She went over to her shelves, pulling down two canisters and setting them down on the table, muttering, " ... Empty-headed pests."

"Did he know the pixie?"

"Of course." She opened one of the jars and pulled out a pinch of something that went into the pot, causing a puff of smoke to rise up.

"Why 'of course'?"

"I suppose most people know their mates."

And that was when I found out for the first time that Tim had a girlfriend or maybe even a wife. But who was she and where the hell had she been for the past month? And why hadn't Tim mentioned her before?

Chapter Six

I WENT OUTSIDE AND JOINED the others while Maggie did her thing on Tim. After about a half hour, she came out of the door holding the box in her hand. Tony's pillowcase was still in there; Tim was now lying on top of it, wingless.

The sight of him with no wings and two mangled stumps where they should have been made me feel sick to my stomach. He looked like a regular man who'd been shrunk down to dragonfly size and then struck with a horrible illness. His skin was white, not its normal pink, and he didn't look like Tim at all.

"Is he going to be okay?" I asked hesitantly, trying not to show the weepiness I felt inside as I looked at him. He was obviously still very sick.

"We had a deal. He will live."

"What are you gonna do with his wing?" asked Becky, before she realized she was actually talking to a crazy witch about using body parts in weirdass magic. Her eyes bugged out, and she snuck a scared look at me, probably searching for assurances that she wasn't about to be cursed.

The old witch leaned in towards Becky with a sly grin on her face. "Would you like to see?"

Becky tittered nervously as she answered. "Uh, heh heh, no, that's okay. No thanks. But it's so nice of you to offer ... "

"Humph," said Maggie as she turned, shuffling towards her door.

Becky breathed a sigh of relief, her eyes crossing with the stress of what might have happened.

"Thank you, Maggie," I called out.

All I received was a cackle in response.

We got back to the compound as fast as we could, luckily encountering no one on the way. We split up at my door, promising to meet outside my room in ten minutes.

I put Tim in our room, gently laying him face down on his bed with his head to the side so he wouldn't suffocate in his pillow. I covered him with his tiny quilt, doing my best to spare the spot on his back where his wings used to be from suffering any additional pain. It was so weird touching his tiny body like that. I was worried I was going to break him.

His entire bedroom set, a miniature duplicate of mine, sat on top of my dresser. I wrote a note and put it on the floor next to his bed, telling him we'd be meeting with Dardennes - the head of the council - and the council members. I wrote as tiny as I could to make it easier for him to read. I knew he'd be mad when he woke up, because without his wings he'd be stranded in my room. But it was safer having him on the dresser at this point because being on the floor and as puny as he was made it too likely he'd get stepped on.

I opened my top dresser drawer a little, the second drawer a little more, the third one even more and finally the last one all the way. If Tim really wanted to get down, he'd be able to by climbing down the stairs I'd just made; but I was hoping he'd stay put until I got back. Last time he lost a wing, when he voluntarily gave it up to save Chase, he was in serious pain for a couple days, and it took a month for the

War of the Fae: Book Three

thing to grow back. So even though I doubted he'd climb down, I wanted him to know he had the option. Tim was tiny, but he could get mighty cranky when he wasn't happy. He had a condition I termed 'pixie complex' which meant he had a chip on his shoulder about being little - kinda like Napoleon, but much worse.

Someone knocked at my door, interrupting my fussing over my roommate. I opened it to find Gregale standing there alone. I grabbed his arm and pulled him in, shutting the door quickly behind him.

"Hello, Jayne," he said, flustered by my casual attack on his person. He was a gray elf, very intellectual, and not used to having much physical contact with other fae. Plus, I had once purposely burned him with my weapon, the Dark of Blackthorn - otherwise known to me as Blackie - the dragon fang that was currently strapped to my leg; so he was always a little distrustful around me. I couldn't blame him, even if I did end up giving him the notoriety of being the only gray elf ever to be burned by The Dark of Blackthorn and then healed by The Green.

"Hey, Gregale. I need your help. Desperately."

"So I gathered," he said wryly.

"I'm in big trouble, and you're the only one I know with the brains to get me out of it."

I could tell he was trying not to preen, but his attempts were mostly unsuccessful. "That must be some pretty big trouble you're in."

"I don't have time to give you the long version. I'm going in front of the council in about five minutes. They're going to accuse me, I think, of breaking some fae laws. I'm not even sure what they are, but I need you to help me get off, number one, and number two, get the council to see reason and allow my friend Tony to become a changeling."

"Wow. That's quite a tall order, especially when I have only five minutes to prepare. Perhaps you'd like me to work out a plan for world peace over dinner?"

"Stop screwing around, Gregale, I'm serious."

"So what exactly have you done that needs my help so emergently?"

"Geez, is that even a word, Gregale? Shit, never mind. What happened is, I took the private jet and went to my hometown and stopped a Dark Fae from taking my friend Tony, and then I brought him back with me. In the process, the pixie, Tim, got his wing burned off by that Dark Fae. He's recuperating now." I gestured to his tiny bed.

"What Dark Fae did this to him?" Gregale was bending over, looking at Tim's white face.

I pulled back the quilt so he could see the burned nub. Gregale caught sight of it and flinched, his face showing disgust.

"A guy named Ben. He was able to pull Fire into his hands and use it against us. I think he rode the wind too. He appeared in a breeze that blew through the window. I think he's some kind of demon. He mesmerizes people, too." I nodded to convey the seriousness of my accusations. I was pretty sure about that mesmerizing part.

Gregale got a scared look on his face. "This is serious. *Very* serious. I need to involve the other gray elves."

"Okay, but first you have to help me! I don't want to go to prison and Tony can't be sent back. Ben will take him."

"What was Ben doing there? Do you know?"

"I'm not sure. I thought he'd just recently moved to town, but I saw a picture I had from a year ago, and I think he was in the picture. If I'm right, then he's been hanging around my hometown for over a year, watching Tony and me. As soon as I was gone, he moved in and became Tony's best friend. He said stuff to try and turn Tony against me. He took over his life."

"Did he attempt to make him a changeling?"

"No. That's the weird part."

"Do you know anything about his motivations? Did you speak to him?"

"Yes, I actually had a sit-down with him in a restaurant. He told us a few things about his plans and his philosophies about humans. I don't know. I'm too freaked out to remember all of it now; but my friends were there too. They can tell you more."

"So, it's not just you who needs my help; it's all of them. All of your friends joined in this little escapade of yours."

"Well, yeah," I said, suddenly flustered, "but this whole thing was my fault, my plan. I'm not going to let them take the fall for it."

Gregale nodded as he thought. Then without a word, he turned to leave.

"Where are you going?"

"I must look into some things and speak to some colleagues. I will see you at the assembly that's been called."

He walked out of the room, shutting the door behind him.

I stood there in the middle of my bedroom, wondering if involving Gregale had been a wise move. We had started out as enemies when I'd first arrived, when I had called him a traitor after overhearing part of a conversation he was having with another fae. He didn't appreciate me almost letting Tim, the very dangerous pixie, out of the bell jar where Dardennes had him imprisoned. At the time, I didn't know that pixies could take out an entire community of fae with their slap-happy pixying stuff, but neither Gregale nor any of the other fae seemed to know that Tim didn't realize his pixying wasn't appreciated. So after we got our differences ironed out and were assigned to train together, we'd reached a form of friendship, mostly based on mutual admiration of the other's talents. I had shown Gregale the power of The Green, and Gregale had shown me that gray elves were not only very intellectual and very involved in planning the strategies of the impending fae conflict, but they were also able to travel into the Gray, the space between our world and the Otherworlds - known to humans as Heaven and Hell, but known to us fae as the Overworld and the Underworld.

Another knock came at my door. I opened it to find all of my friends waiting there, Jared out in front.

"Come on. Anton is getting the council together. We need to go."

I took one last look back at Tim, adjusted Blackie on my leg, and joined them in the hallway. "Let's go then." I nodded at Spike, Finn, and Chase. Becky smiled at me and blew me a friendly kiss. She was always so damn happy, even when I was practically being led to the gallows.

I followed Jared's lead, walking next to Tony. Tony kept wiping his hands on his jeans and stealing glances at me. I grabbed his hand and squeezed it. I didn't trust myself to talk then; I was nervous too.

Jared led us to the big doors that I knew led into the assembly hall. This was the biggest room in the compound that I'd been in. It was big enough to hold most of the fae who lived in and around the place. There was one elevated head table in the front that was now occupied by members of the council. All of the other tables were arranged in a semi-circular fashion, facing the head table and the space in front of it.

I had stood in that space before, when I first arrived at the compound. That was just after I had caused nearly thirty elves to go temporarily into la-la land after zapping them with the energy I had called up from The Green. I had done it in self-defense when the elves attacked me - under the influence of some Dark Fae witch we never successfully identified - so ultimately my time in front of the assembly of fae didn't end up with me going to jail or whatever. But from that day forward, a lot more fae got involved in my training and the questions about who I was and who I might be swirled around.

These questions remained unanswered, though. I was either just another fae girl, an elemental with a supernatural connection to the elements of Earth and Water, or I was *The* Elemental, the one they call Mother - the one I had always referred to in my human life as Mother Nature. She was someone they'd been waiting for, for like two thousand years or something. This idea - that I, of all people, could be this amazing, long lost fae goddess - was pretty unbelievable and ridiculous if you asked me; so I just functioned under the assumption that I wasn't her. I was just me - a girl who needed to help her best friend Tony find his place in the whole fae mix.

The horn that tells everyone in the assembly hall to shut the hell up started blowing, and so they all quickly found their seats and came to order. My friends and I walked up to the back row of seats, standing in the center aisle. The chamber was packed with no places left to sit. There was no point in sitting down anyway; I knew we were going to be called to stand in the front.

Dardennes gestured with his hand for us to come forward. For now, it was just Tony, Chase and me. Chase was good like that - never letting me go in front of an angry mob without him. Until today, I had just assumed that was part of his job, since he was my daemon, my warrior protector. But when Maggie said that it was a lie, and she was pretty much never wrong, it caused me to have some doubts. Right now, though, I had bigger problems to deal with, so I put that out of my head as stress to unglue over later.

Tony and I stood in front of the council, Chase behind us. The crowd went silent, with only the little sounds of people moving in their seats left to be heard.

Dardennes spoke, loud enough so everyone in the room could hear. "The council and fae have gathered for this general assembly to hear the charges against you, changeling Jayne Sparks. The council has been informed that at some point in the days prior to this, you left the compound with Jared Bloodworth and returned with Tony, a former changeling candidate who previously refused the change."

"Yes," I said, my voice ringing out around the room. The acoustics in this place made it possible for sounds to move in circles or something, because I could even hear my voice behind me now.

An old man on the council who I didn't know spoke next. "Who gave you permission to do this?"

I glanced at Dardennes whose face revealed nothing. He hadn't technically given us permission to do anything, even though he'd been pretty clear he wanted it done. But I wasn't going to throw him under the bus. He'd made it possible for me to rescue my friend, and I owed him for that.

"No one. I did it myself."

"You did *not* do this yourself. You had *help!*" he accused angrily, banging his fist on the table.

"Well, someone flew the plane and drove the cars for me, but they weren't involved in my plan to get Tony. I used them."

There was some grumbling behind me from the gathered fae, but I ignored it. I had done what was right, and I wasn't going to apologize for it. Even Ivar, the fae I liked least in this room, was getting a pass from me. No one was going down for this one, but me.

"You willingly dragged other fae into your scheme to take an action that this council has forbidden."

"I wasn't aware that I'd broken any laws."

War of the Fae: Book Three

At that moment there was a disturbance by the doors. Several fae were moving around, angry looks on their faces.

"What is the meaning of this interruption?!" demanded my questioner, his cheeks now assuming a mottled red color.

I saw Gregale's face emerging from the crowd at the door, and breathed a sigh of relief. If I was going to have any help at all, it had arrived. Hopefully, he had good news. I took Tony's hand in mine and squeezed it, not letting go. He squeezed mine back, and I noticed it was cool and clammy.

"Excuse me, council members, fae community," said Gregale, pausing to nod in their respective directions. "I am Gregale, of the gray elves. I have come to stand as Reasoner for the changeling, Jayne."

There was a bit of grumbling at the head table, the old man who was questioning me obviously not happy about this. I took that as a good sign. The fae in the audience whispered among themselves.

Gregale reached my side, and I leaned over to talk quietly in his ear. "I hope a Reasoner is like a lawyer."

Gregale looked at me quizzically, but I decided now was not the time to explain the concept or make the translation.

Dardennes cast a look out to the crowd, immediately quieting things down.

"Has the changeling been accused of violating any fae laws?" asked Gregale to the council.

"Not yet. We were getting to that," said the old man, sarcastically.

"Oh. Please forgive me. By all means, continue."

"Why thank you, gray elf. We appreciate your graciousness."

Gregale's face went a little red. I wasn't sure what the protocol was around here, but it looked like maybe Gregale had just put his foot in it. *Great. My lawyer was Vinny in 'My Cousin Vinny'.* I just hoped he could get the same ultimate results.

"The changeling Jayne has admitted to taking the jet to her hometown and bringing her friend Tony back with her to our compound. He is a human boy who has previously declined the change."

Gregale leaned over and whispered in my ear. "So far, no laws broken, just bad choices."

I rolled my eyes at him. He sounded like my mom.

"The law is that no human shall be given a second chance to make the change, once that opportunity has been declined."

There were a few comments from the assembly that sounded like agreements. Some of the fae apparently really liked that rule. *Selfish bastards.*

"May it please the council, the human Tony has not been changed, therefore, this law has not been broken."

"Correct. But we understand that Jayne intends to break this law," challenged the councilman.

"Intent to do something is not a violation of the law, technically speaking, sir." Gregale cleared his throat, obviously not entirely comfortable with being confrontational.

I smiled. Gregale was kicking ass. I could tell the old fart on the council was getting pissed. I leaned over and spoke quietly to Gregale. "I want them to change the law. I want Tony to be a changeling."

Gregale leaned in to whisper a reply. "There is very little chance of that happening. That is a very old rule and has been on the books for hundreds of years."

"Well, it's time for a change. We have a war coming. Tony is a resource. He's either ours or theirs. Ben has made it clear he wants Tony. If we don't have him with us, he will be against us." I put my hand on Gregale's sleeve. "And if he goes, *I* go."

Gregale's eyes opened wide in shock. "You don't mean that you

War of the Fae: Book Three

would leave us?"

"Yes, I do mean that. I'd go Dark Fae all the way and wear the damn t-shirt if it meant saving Tony's life. I can't look out for him if he's there and I'm here. We stick together. We're a team."

Gregale shook his head, looking at the floor.

I couldn't tell from his expression if he was pissed or sad. I was probably asking for the impossible, but I didn't care. This was how it was for me - black and white. If they weren't with me, they were against me. It was scary to think I was quoting Ben's words now. I'd made some friends here, that was true. And I didn't wish any of them ill will, and I'd never do anything to hurt any of them. But, if I had to choose between them and Tony? It would be Tony every day of the week and twice on Sunday.

"Ladies and gentlemen of the council," Gregale nodded to the council members and then turned and faced the assembled fae. "Ladies and gentlemen fae ... the changeling Jayne would like to put forth a petition - a petition to change the existing law as it relates to the humans agreeing to accept the change and become changelings."

Everyone immediately began talking out in the assembly, some of them pretty loudly. I noticed several council members leaning left or right to confer with their neighbors.

"What does she propose, exactly?" asked Dardennes. He was watching me closely, his expression giving nothing away.

Gregale leaned over to me. "I think it's best that you do the talking on this one."

I cleared my throat and began, nervously, still holding onto Tony's hand while facing the council. "It's true that Tony has once decided not to become a changeling. He was then erased and sent home. But after he was sent home, he was contacted and befriended by a powerful Dark Fae by the name of Ben. I knew there was something wrong, so I went back for him. Even though only a month had gone by, this fae had already exerted a lot of influence over Tony. Ben and I faced off, and Tony agreed to come with me." I turned to face the assembled fae. "You have to let him make the change. If he leaves here, Ben will take him over to the Dark Fae. He'll be lost to me forever." My voice caught on the last word. I couldn't help it. The idea of losing Tony? *Too much.*

An older woman on the council spoke up. "We have all lost loved ones to the Dark Fae. We cannot save them if that is the choice they make."

"But this isn't his choice!" I argued back. "He's choosing the Light Fae as his family! But we're denying him that choice."

"He had his chance and he rejected us!" yelled someone from the crowd. Some other fae cheered him on, obviously agreeing.

"He didn't reject the Light Fae, you idiot - he rejected the fae in general. He's a pacifist. He doesn't like war."

Gregale touched my arm and whispered loudly, "You may want to refrain from insulting those whose support you seek."

I whispered back, "I feel like I'm talking to a bunch of children."

"Be patient," he counseled. "The fae fear change. It has caused many deaths in our world."

I sighed, turning halfway so I faced both the council and the assembled fae. "Listen, I'm sorry if I insulted you guys. It's just that you have to understand - Tony is my best friend. He's like a brother to me. And like it or not, laws or not, he and I are going to be together. He understands now that war is inevitable. He has new information he didn't have before, and he has decided to join us."

The old man on the council stood up. "You flout the laws of the Light Fae! You stand here in front of our assembled body and tell us you intend to break our laws, and then expect no consequence? You

War of the Fae: Book Three

are a foolish changeling!"

"No!" I yelled back, turning to face the old man. "I am not saying I'm going to break your stupid, antiquated, useless law! I'm telling you that if you don't change this law, I'm outta here! You can take your stupid amulet," I grabbed at the ring on my finger, pulling and tugging to get it off, "and shove it up your ass!"

I finally got the ring off and held it in front of me. The crowd that had become very rowdy and vocal in their displeasure, dropped into dead silence when the ring suddenly began to glow.

Chapter Seven

I SPOKE AS IF NOTHING weird was going on, the green glow from my ring beaming up to hit the stone ceiling above us, bouncing off and illuminating the entire room with a soft green light. "You have the opportunity to welcome Tony into our Light Fae community. To do this you must revise the law and allow him to accept the change, even though he declined it once. Make no mistake ..." I ran my gaze over each of the council members and then back at the assembled fae. "If you keep the law as it is, I will leave this place and never come back. I will gladly become one of the Dark Fae, if you show me today that they want Tony and me more than you do." I looked at them in disgust. "I don't stay where I'm not wanted."

I turned and tossed the ring to the council, not caring who it went to, the glow immediately turning off as it left my hand. Céline, the silver elf who was the first to train me and the one who initially interviewed me when I was still living a human life in Florida, reached up and caught it in mid-air. She looked down at it with an expression of disbelief.

My finger felt light where the amulet had previously sat. The ring was a heavy, pyramid-shaped crystal, set in sterling silver with gold prongs. It was the amulet that had been used to change me from human to fae. Everyone else had returned their amulets after speaking the words that started the transformation, but Dardennes had told me to keep mine. I felt a little naked without it on now. I wondered if the ring was what kept me linked to my power, so I reached out tentatively to The Green to check. I was relieved to find its welcoming hum still waiting for me, wanting to connect. I didn't indulge myself, though, because I had a grand exit to make.

"Come on, Tony. Let's blow this friggin popsicle stand." I walked towards the aisle, pulling him after me.

"Wait!" yelled Dardennes, shouting to be heard over the ruckus created by a roomful of pissed-off fae.

I stopped and Tony ran into me. He whispered his apologies and backed up. I could sense Chase behind us, too. I was relieved to know that Dardennes wasn't going to just let me walk off alone with Tony dragging behind me. I turned to look at the council again.

"Jayne," he started, smiling patiently at me, "I don't think you realize what you are asking of this council." Several heads at his table were nodding.

"Oh, no," I said loudly, "believe me I do. I'm asking them to get off their crusty asses and wake up to what's going on outside these walls. But I can see they're too stuck in the past - too busy ignoring the obvious signs around them. That's fine ... whatever. I'll go somewhere where my talents and contributions will be appreciated."

That one really got them going, especially the old fart who was so critical of me. "She has absolutely *no* respect for this council or the Light Fae. Let her leave!"

"No!" came a voice from the back of the room.

I watched, stunned, as Jared came striding purposefully up the center aisle.

"You cannot let her leave. She is a valuable asset that we need on our side."

"Jared! What are you saying?" asked the old man, taken aback, speaking as if he'd been betrayed. Clearly, he was not happy with Jared getting involved.

"I'm saying that I've been out on the front lines, recruiting for the Light Fae, gathering candidates for the change. And I've seen firsthand that the Dark Fae are very busy doing the same thing. But they aren't being so selective, and they're building their forces a lot faster than we are. We need everyone we can get. So to let someone of Jayne's ... talents ... go? That would be a big mistake in my opinion. A mistake that would ultimately hurt us all."

"I agree," said Gregale, speaking up to be heard. "In fact, all of the gray elves agree. We have very limited resources. Although at first against the idea of changelings being involved in our efforts to combat the Dark Fae and their ever persistent attempts to force their agenda on our human friends, we have since come to change our minds on that score, in no small part because of the things Jayne has shown us that she and her friends are capable of. Without them, we would be missing a significant and vital portion of our arsenal."

My heart soared. Jared and the gray elves were important and respected fae. And they sounded smart as hell to me right now.

Then Robin of The Green, a green elf like my friend Finn, stood. "Council members ... fellow fae ... the green elves are unanimously in agreement. We do not want to face our Mother on the battlefield. We fight *with* her, not against her. We go where she goes."

Those words, spoken by the leader of the green elves, launched the biggest uproar this assembly hall had probably ever seen. Fae were springing up out of their chairs, shouting and gesticulating, the witches in the back waving their staffs above their heads threateningly. The council members sat there with shocked looks on their faces. A group of ogres moved up behind the council, standing there like impressive, scary-looking bodyguards, just in case any of the rowdy fae decided to get too frisky. I knew exactly what everyone was thinking: how could they possibly hold off the Dark Fae if all their green elf warriors were gone?

The green elves had just lobbed an old tomato over the fence. They were the mighty and noble warriors of the Green Forest. Without them, the Light Fae in this compound would be sitting ducks. I looked over at Robin, trying to put all of the thanks and appreciation I felt into my eyes. Then I decided I could do one better. I reached into The Green and grabbed a tendril of power, sending it over to my friend Robin, hoping he would feel it. I was pretty sure he did, too, because he looked stunned for a second, and then a smile broke out across his face. He faced me and placed his hand over his heart in a green elf salute. I nodded my head back. No one had officially called me Mother yet, but that didn't stop the green elves from thinking it was true. I wasn't going to argue with them about it now. I needed their support, and I wasn't above using The Green to get it. *A girl's gotta do what a girl's gotta do.*

I heard Jared's voice call out over the commotion. "The daemon Chase and I stand for Jayne. We go where she goes!"

The roars of the fae got even louder; it was like thunder echoing through the compound. Tony squeezed my hand and I returned the gesture.

Then Spike and his trainer Valentine walked up the center aisle, Finn following behind. Spike yelled out, "The incubi stand with Jayne! We also go where she goes!" They stopped in front of me, just at the end of the aisle.

Now the members of the council were standing, even the really old ones who were so hunched over they had difficulty looking at anything but the floor in front of their feet. Everyone was gesturing and shouting. I saw spittle flying out of the mouth of the old man who had questioned me.

I wasn't sure when it started exactly, but I soon became aware of the sound waves of an eerie call trickling through the anger around me, and the noise of the crowd became almost like an afterthought in my mind. Within seconds, the only thing I could hear - the only thing I wanted to hear - was this new sound. A song, maybe? A person's voice? I couldn't tell. It was pulling me in, making me want to listen.

I watched in a daze as a figure in white floated down the aisle towards me. All eyes turned to watch her advance. It was a woman. Her mouth was open and the bewitching song we were hearing was coming from her. I felt a hand on my arm and looked to see who was touching me. It was Chase - the only one who seemed to be unaffected by her voice.

"Jayne, it's the siren. Focus on my voice. Don't look at her."

The blueness of Chase's eyes, his strong grip on my arm, and then the serious tone of his voice snapped me out of my reverie. *What the hell?* I gave myself a mental shake to get the fog out of my brain.

The song stopped. The crowd that had been on the verge of rioting was now completely silent. You could have heard a marshmallow drop in that room. Standing next to me was the Lady of the Lake - a cunning seductress and one hell of a devious siren bitch when she wanted to be, as I had discovered on a couple of occasions.

She opened her mouth and everyone sat in stunned silence, waiting to hear what she would say. Her voice was nearly as spooky as her song.

"The sirens and the water sprites stand with Jayne. We go where she goes."

Becky then walked up the aisle to join us. The space in front of the head table was now filled to capacity. Voices were shouting again from the assembled fae in the audience, but they were singing a different tune now.

"The gray elves stand with Jayne! We go where she goes!"

"The silver elves stand with Jayne! We go wherever she goes!"

"The wood sprites stand with Jayne!"

"The dwarves stand with Jayne!"

And on and on it went, all of the fae races aligning themselves with my cause.

My heart was so full, I was afraid it was going to explode right there in front of everyone. Tears came to my eyes, much as I tried to hold them back. I quickly swiped them away hoping no one would notice. I looked over at Tony and noticed he had a sheen in his eyes, too.

He leaned in and whispered to me. "Now I get it, Jayne. I totally get it."

My life had gone full circle, from being an invisible nobody to being someone nobody wanted to be without. If I ever had doubts about being fae before, they were now completely gone.

I turned to look at the council, watching as they all took their seats. I pulled my shoulders back and lifted my head high, standing as straight as I could. I stared at the old man, the one who seemed to speak for the council, the sparkle of tears still bright in my eyes.

"So what's it gonna be then, Council? Can my friend Tony accept the change, or what?"

The old man looked to his left and right, receiving nods from each of the other members.

He turned to look at me, obviously pissed off but unable to do anything about it, and answered, "The fae have spoken. The council has heard their wishes. We hereby grant a special dispensation from

War of the Fae: Book Three

our law related to being offered a second opportunity to accept the change, but *only* for this potential changeling, Tony, and for no other. The council rests."

Chapter Eight

I HUGGED TONY TO ME as tightly as I could. I felt Chase's arms go around me and then Spike's and Finn's too.

"Hey! What about me?" came Becky's voice from behind us. I felt Spike let go and then the press of Becky's face between my shoulder blades a second later.

"Uh, thanks Spike," she said, her voice muffled.

I laughed with happiness. *I have awesome friends.*

"Come on," I said after a few moments, still patting Tony's back. "Let's go to Dardennes' office. That's where the amulets are."

The six of us reluctantly broke up our group hug to leave the room. Everyone was filtering out, occasionally looking back at us. The council members were long gone, always the first ones to leave.

"Hey, Gregale!" I shouted.

He turned on his way out.

"Thanks!" I said, giving him a thumbs-up and a ten-thousand-watt smile.

He looked down at his own hand as if he were going to return the gesture and then just nodded instead. The thumbs-up was probably just a little too human for him.

Ten minutes later, we were in front of Dardennes' door. Chase knocked three times and then pushed it open. Dardennes, Céline, and Ivar were inside, standing by Dardennes' desk.

Tony rubbed his hands together nervously and then down the front of his jeans again.

"Don't worry, man. These're the nice ones," Finn whispered in his ear.

Tony gave him a faltering grin.

"Please, come in," said Dardennes. "And shut the door behind you."

Spike was the last one in, slamming the door with too much force.

"Oops. Sorry about that. Guess I'm just a little excited."

I looked back and noticed that the red glow in his eyes was bright. I wasn't sure whether it was exhilaration from the assembly or Becky's hug that had gotten him going, but he was definitely feeling a liiittle too happy. I raised an eyebrow at Chase gesturing with my head for him to check Spike out. He glanced over at him and then back at me, rolling his eyes. He was on constant guard against Spike's amorous advances towards me. I didn't mind them - after all, Spike was hotness times two - but Spike didn't always wait for me to say yes before he got started; so Chase was Spike's cold shower in daemon form. They had a love-hate relationship.

Dardennes smiled at us as we advanced towards his desk. "So, we have a changeling candidate with us here today, yes?"

"A-*hem*, yes, sir," said Tony, nervously clearing his throat.

Céline smiled at him serenely, saying nothing. She and Dardennes looked like sister and brother - they both had silver hair and icy gray eyes. Their tunics were silver, which matched their looks perfectly. When they walked around in the human world, they wore silver suits too, but they didn't look tacky at all. They just looked extremely rich and a little bit intimidating. I didn't know if they were officially brother and sister, but they were both silver elves, so they belonged to the same race of fae. Whenever there were decisions to be made about us changelings, they were involved. Dardennes was the one who had given amulets to my friends and me, helping us begin our awakening from human to fae. He was also the one who had interviewed all of us and chosen us to come here in the first place. At first, I had blamed him for every bad thing that happened to me and my friends in the forest, but I learned to forgive him. Mostly.

Dardennes carefully lifted the lid of the box that I knew held the changeling amulets. He looked up at Tony and then down again at the contents before him.

"I have not had enough time to evaluate Tony as I would normally like. Let's see if this one works." He handed him the amulet I remembered Finn wearing - a wrist cuff.

Tony took it from him, looking at me as he put it on.

"How does it feel?" asked Dardennes.

Tony shrugged his shoulders. "Fine, I guess. Am I supposed to feel something?"

"Not necessarily. But no, I don't think this is right. Please give it back."

Tony took it off and returned it.

"Try this one." Dardennes handed Tony a ring.

Spike whispered in my ear. "That's the ring I used."

"I know, *shh!*" I whispered back. I was wondering why it was taking Dardennes so long to find the right amulet. I was starting to get nervous. I had thought this was going to be a mere formality, not a pain in my ass involved process.

"No, no, that's not right either. Let's try this one."

He handed Tony a necklace and took the ring back, putting it in the box with the others.

I looked at Chase, a question in my eyes. Chase nodded back, confirming this was the necklace that he had worn.

Dardennes and Céline smiled at the same time. "Yes, this is the one." He closed the lid on the box and clasped his hands together, looking at Tony. "Okay, young man, now is the last chance you have to change your mind. Are you certain that you want to become a changeling?"

Tony looked at them for a second and then turned to look at me. I knew he saw complete fear on my face - fear that he was going to walk away.

"Come on, Tony, don't do that to her again," moaned Finn. "*Shee-it*, she'll be unbearable if you ain't here."

Tony smiled. "So, you were a little difficult to live with?"

"You have *no* idea," said Spike.

"Trust me, Tony," said Becky, a smile in her voice, "it's better to just give her what she wants. Your life will be much easier that way. And so will ours."

I shot a dirty look at my friends. They acted like I was a monster or something. Just because I knew what I wanted and when I wanted it ...

Tony took a deep breath and reached out to grab my hand, turning to face Dardennes again. "Yes. I want to be a changeling. Let's do this."

I squeezed his hand back excitedly, unable to keep the huge grin from bursting out on my face.

Finn said, "Yesssss ... ," quietly behind my back. He and Spike were probably high-fiving each other.

Idiots.

Dardennes began the ritual. "Tony, please repeat after me:

War of the Fae: Book Three

I call to the fae blood that courses through my veins
I ask the fae magic to bring about the change
A fae I am
A changeling I will be
From this moment now
For all eternity."

Tony said the words, and I watched his face closely for any changes. They weren't physical ones, at least not for us, but when I changed, I felt something - like a tingle where the amulet was. It wasn't until several hours later that we noticed differences in our strengths and discovered abilities we had gained.

When he was finished, I waited a few seconds and then asked, "So, how do you feel? Different?"

"No, not really."

"Did you feel anything in the amulet?"

"No, I didn't. Is that bad?" Tony looked to Dardennes for guidance.

So did I, anxious that something had gone wrong or that something wasn't happening that should. Dardennes had always said that there was no guarantee that we were fae - just that we probably were, based on our performance during the test. I figured with Tony's supernatural-like ability to feel my vibes, that meant he was definitely fae, no question.

"It's different for everyone. Don't let it concern you. I believe you have made the transition." He looked to Céline and she nodded. "The only issue is ... well ... we aren't quite sure what type of fae you are."

Tony just stared at him blankly.

Well, this is a surprise. "So what the heck does that mean? I mean, what do we do from here?" I asked.

Céline answered, "He will be sent out to train with various groups until we see what skills manifest themselves."

"I want him with me," I said, matter-of-factly.

"That may not be possible," said Dardennes.

"Yeah, well, then he needs a daemon or something. My first day out at training some Dark Fae tried to turn me into a pincushion, and they've already shown how interested in Tony they are by enlisting Ben to try and win him over and become his best friend." *Pfft. As if that could happen.*

"Don't worry, Jayne, we will see to his security," said Céline.

"Forgive me if that doesn't fill me with the greatest sense of relief," I said wryly. Chase having been nearly turned into a cadaver not so long ago was kind of hard for me to forget.

"Jayne, it's okay," said Tony. "I'll be fine. I'm sure they'll take care of everything."

"There's a new daemon who just came in with one of the last changeling groups," suggested Chase.

"Who are you talking about?" asked Dardennes.

"Scrum."

"Scrum?" said a chorus of four voices - mine, Tony's, Becky's, and Finn's.

Dardennes nodded his head slowly, ignoring our surprise at this person's unfortunate name. "That might work. At least until we know what Tony can do for himself." He looked at Céline. "Could you please make the arrangements? Move the rooms and so forth? You can put Scrum on the other side of Jayne, and Tony one door down."

"Yes, fine. I'll take care of it." She moved to leave the room. "Ivar, come with me please." Then she looked at me. "Jayne, you did well today. We are very proud of you."

I didn't know why that made me so happy, but it did. "Thanks." I could feel my face burning a little.

The door shut behind her.

"Yes, well, you do know how to ruffle feathers, don't you, Jayne?" Dardennes raised an eyebrow at me.

I just shrugged in return, by no means giving him an apology. Desperate times called for desperate measures.

"You may take Tony to his new room shortly. Why don't you all go have dinner first?" he suggested.

"Best idea I've heard all dang day," said Finn. "I'm starvin'."

"Me too." Spike held out a bent arm. "Becky? Shall we?"

She laughed and went along, looping her hand through the crook of his elbow.

I took Tony by the hand. "Come on, Tones, you badass fae. Let's go get some grub."

Chapter Nine

"DO THEY EAT REGULAR FOOD here?" he asked as we walked out the door.

"That depends on who you're talking about," I said, looking at Chase.

"What?" asked Chase, genuinely in the dark about what I found so amusing.

"Nothing." I didn't bring up the fact that he ate meat off the buffet that was still moving and pretty much every other gross thing they offered here. I had vowed many meals ago to support his disgusting eating habits and huge appetite, because I was sure it was what kept him so huge and super muscular. No fae chick wants a wimpy daemon watching her back.

We got to the dining hall and filled up our plates, taking seats at our usual table that now had some other changelings sitting there, too. We were the first changeling group that had gone through the recruiting process, but there were many others who had come through since. They looked up to us, most of them afraid to even talk when we were around. I wasn't sure why, since we hadn't done anything to make them afraid - maybe our reputations preceded us or something. I *had* done a few messed up things on my first day, including putting

Céline into some state of suspended animation, not to mention doing pretty much the same thing to a whole group of thirty elves right after. Now that I thought about it, it was highly possible that they'd heard about everything I'd done and were a little afraid of me. But they didn't need to be. I could control my power over The Green now. Well, mostly anyway.

"So who's this Scrub kid?" I asked Chase, watching as he chewed a mouthful of mystery meats.

Tony watched him eat in fascination. He looked down at his own plate and then back at Chase's. Tony had a few slices of beef, a carrot, and some salad in front of him. Chase had squirming meat, meat that was motionless, a mountain of pasta, and a giant bowl of pudding. Three slices of bread were balanced on the side of it.

Chase pointed to a nearby table with his fork. There were a few changelings there; all of them looked younger than us. This was not promising.

"Which one is he?"

"The one in the brown tunic."

Oh, yeah. Duh. The daemon all wore brown tunics. We had changed back into our fae uniforms when we were on the plane, so it was easier to tell who was part of what race at the compound. Tony was the only one still in human street clothes. I knew there would be outfits waiting for him in his room by the time we got there. I wondered if it would be Ivar doing all the housework or if they would recruit a brownie to take care of Tony's room and stuff. I had one for my room. His name was Netter, and I paid him off every day with a token chocolate ball. He had no idea how easy they were to get and that they were no big deal to the rest of us. He thought chocolate balls were the food of the gods.

I looked over at the fae they called Scrum. He was sitting, but from the looks of it, he was several inches shorter than Tony. His body was shaped like a keg of beer.

"*He's* a daemon?" I asked, not believing my eyes.

"Mmm-hmm," affirmed Chase around his mouthful of food.

I watched as Scrum stood up, not realizing that his napkin, which was partially under his plate, had somehow gotten caught in his belted tunic. As he pulled away from the table, the plate went with him. The guys at his table tried to warn him, but his attention was caught by seeing Chase at our table.

"Oh, hey! Chase! What's up?" He moved one step closer, attempting to walk in our direction, but at that moment his plate left the table completely, spilling its contents all over Scrum's legs and his chair, crashing to the floor.

He stopped moving as the feeling of lukewarm mystery casserole and smooshed peas hit the material of his pants, quickly soaking in to reach his legs. He looked down at the mess. "Oopsy. How did that happen?"

"Chase," I said, instantly pissed and worried for my friend Tony's welfare, "you've got to be fucking kidding me. *This* is Tony's protection?" I was totally disgusted with Dardennes all over again. Just when he started acting cool, he went and did something totally screwed up like this - assigning a complete doofus to be Tony's bodyguard. I was trying to ignore the fact that it was Chase who had suggested Scrum in the first place and just focus on the fact that Dardennes had agreed to it.

Chase shrugged. "He's a good guy. He just needs a little fine-tuning."

"I'd say it's more like a lotta fine-tunin', if you ask me," said Finn, smirking. "Don't worry Tony - I'll keep an eye on things for ya. The green elves know how important you are to Jayne, and they wanna keep her happy."

"Maybe you'll do some training with me, Tony," said Becky brightly. "I'm a water sprite. Maybe you are, too."

"How will I know what kind of fae I am?" he asked all of us.

"Well, I can pretty much guarantee you're not an incubus," said Spike.

"Yeah, maybe we can figure out whatcha are by process of elimination," said Finn.

"How can you tell he's not an incubus, Spike?" I asked.

"Because, he's eating all that regular food, and I don't see any glow in his eyes."

I pulled Tony's shoulder so he was facing me. Looking into his eyes, I saw that Spike was right; there was no hot-blooded red stuff going on there. His irises were gray. I glanced at Spike's plate, noticing that he didn't have much food there. I'd never paid much attention to his diet before, but now that I saw he wasn't eating like we were, I wondered what he ate instead. I decided a split-second later that I didn't want to know.

"Tony, what color are your eyes normally?" I asked. I didn't remember them being gray. I was pretty sure they were normally brown. It was what made him look like such a sad puppy sometimes.

"Brown."

"Huh. That's what I thought," I said, thinking about what this might mean. I was going to have to ask Céline when I saw her again.

"Why?"

"'Cuz they're gray now."

"Really?" Tony looked at us, his head swiveling back and forth. "Does anyone have a mirror?"

"You have one in your room," said Becky, straining her neck to see his eyes better. "Yeah, you do have gray eyes now. Cute."

"Oh, Tony," said Finn in a high falsetto voice, "your eyes are sooooo cute now."

"Shut up, Finn. You're just jealous," said Becky, trying not to smile.

"Jealous of who? Tony? No way, lady. He's got Jayne attached to him at the hip. I ain't jealous o' that, no siree bob."

I smacked him on the arm. "Watch it, green elf, or I might forget we're friends."

"Ain't no chance o' that. You're stuck with me, Mother."

I grabbed a fistful of his tunic. "Call me that one more time and see what happens."

He held up his hands in surrender, laughing. "Okay, okay, mercy! I give up. You're the boss. I'll shut up now."

Tony smiled. I was glad to see that their teasing amused him and made him happy, even though it made me want to smack somebody. Those green elves calling me Mother made me a little nuts. The whole idea was too stupid to consider. I wasn't sure I was ready for that kind of responsibility or if I even wanted it. When I'd gone through the interview process to qualify for the fae test, and they'd asked me what superhero I wanted to be, I'd picked Mother Nature. I really hadn't thought too hard about what my life would mean if it were actually true. Now every time the subject came up, I'd think of a million other things I'd rather worry about - like the Dark Fae that were trying to steal my best friend Tony, for instance. Now that it wasn't so much of a problem anymore, though, I was probably going to have to start dealing with this Mother issue. *Ugh.*

Just then Scrum showed up at our table, covered in food stains and smiling like an idiot.

"Hey guys. What's up?"

Spike got up to leave. "Well, I'm gonna leave you kids to ... uh ...

whatever this is."

Finn joined him. "Yeah. Later. See ya'll at breakfast." He held out his hand to Becky. "Come on, girl. Let's blow this joint. I need some help with somethin'."

Becky eyed him suspiciously, taking his hand and standing. "If this is another one of your teleporting experiments, I'm not interested."

As they walked away I could hear him trying to convince her. "No, no, it's nothin' like that. This time I need you to show me ... "

I couldn't hear the rest of it, and I probably didn't want to either. Finn and Spike were always trying to figure out how to develop different powers they thought they might have. Neither of them was content with the amazing stuff they could already do, especially Finn. Becky could do things none of us could, and that drove him crazy. I was fairly certain Finn and Spike had made some sort of pact to become Super Fae or something stupid like that. *Guys.* They were all the same - little boys in big bodies.

Scrum stood there looking nervous, waiting for someone to acknowledge him.

I sighed. "Hey. So, I hear you're the new daemon on the block."

He shifted from one foot to the other, back and forth. "Yeah. I guess so. I'm with Chase."

Chase's eyebrows lifted, but he kept on eating.

"How do you like it? I mean, so far?" asked Tony, smiling at him.

"Oh, it's cool. Being a daemon is ... pretty awesome." He looked at Tony's shirt, his eyebrows screwing up in confusion. "Hey, what kind of fae are you? Your clothes look ... well ... not fae."

Wow. And it only took him half the dinner hour to notice that. Apparently 'observant' wasn't on the list of this daemon's qualifications. He must be pretty low on the totem pole to not have been a part of the assembly from hell. I thought everyone had been there.

"I was just made a changeling. Less than an hour ago. No one knows what kind of fae I am yet."

"Huh. Is that normal? All the guys who changed with me, Dardennes and them kinda knew what we all were, even before the change."

Tony shrugged. "Don't know. It's all new to me."

"What kinda stuff can you do?"

I interrupted. "Hey. He said he didn't know."

"Oh, bonkers, I'm so totally sorry. I talk too much. People say that all the time. I mean, now fae say it all the time."

"Bonkers?" *Did my ears fool me or did he really just say that?*

He looked sheepish. "Yeah. I'm not allowed to swear."

"Says who?" As far as I knew, there were no cuss-word police around here; otherwise, I'd be doing hard time by now.

"My grandma. She died just a little while ago, may her soul rest in peace for all of eternity. She was a stickler for the rules. No swear words and no elbows on the table." He looked embarrassed. "And a few other things I hate to tell you, but also no farting except in the bathroom ... "

"Holy shit, dude, too much information!" *Damn*, what was this guy's problem? Was he mental? Now I was really starting to worry about Tony again.

Chase was trying to keep a straight face but was failing badly. I nudged him to get him to quit. This guy was full-on annoying and Chase's smile was just pissing me off more. Now I was good and cranky, and this kid was gonna have to suffer the consequences.

"Listen, if you're going to be hanging around, you need to get one thing straight: if you give me a headache, I'm gonna kick your ass. And vomiting your personal stuff all over us ... is giving me a headache."

Tony's eyes bugged out of his head. "Jayne, chill. He's just nervous."

I looked at the daemon kid, and he did seem like he didn't know whether to run, cry, piss his pants or all three.

I instantly felt bad. "Listen, Scrub, I'm just tired and stressed and hungry. I'm sorry if I hurt your feelings. Just ... sit down and shut up for a few minutes, okay?"

His smile was right back on his face like it had never left. "Okay! It's Scrum by the way, not Scrub, but don't worry, I get that all the time. I'll sit right here with you guys. That's cool. I can be quiet. That's noooot a problem at all. I totally understand the headache thing. My grandma used to get them all the time. She'd send me to my room for hours and hours. That was the only thing that seemed to make her feel better. I think she liked the quiet, like you."

Chase kept eating, but placed his other hand over the one of mine that had balled up into a fist on the table.

"Breathe, Jayne," said Tony, a smile in his voice.

I looked at him. "Don't fucking start with me, Baloney head."

"What?" he laughed. "I didn't say anything."

Even if I slapped him right now, he probably wouldn't stop smiling.

"I'm happy that my misery makes you happy, Tony."

"Good. Now eat your dinner so you can show me my new room."

"Don't be so excited," I said as I shoveled a forkful of I didn't know what into my mouth. "It's a windowless cell."

I smiled at the look of horror on his face.

"But they're not bad, really," jumped in Scrub or Scabs or whatever the hell the kid's name was. "They're warm enough that you don't get cold, you get a nice quilt for your bed, ... "

I tuned out the rest of the crap that he was barfing out on us. I had a feeling I was going to have to do that a lot in the future with this doofus. My thoughts turned to my windowless room and my little friend Tim who I hoped was still sleeping through his pain.

"I'm gonna get some fruit for Tim," I said, standing.

"Who's Tim?" I heard the kid ask as I went to the buffet.

Minutes later we were all walking down the hall to my room, Chase leading the way. The Scabs kid kept talking and talking and talking. I couldn't figure out why he wasn't hoarse, if he talked like this all the time. And how the hell had he made it through the Green Forest and the changeling test? His talking would have alerted every single fae in the whole damn place, which meant he would have had a lot of fights on his hands. I made a mental note to ask Céline about his performance. Or maybe I could find one of the changelings that went through it with him who would tell me.

We got to my room, and I put my index finger in front of my lips. "Scabs, you need to shut the hell up now. I'm not playin'. I have a very sick pixie in here, and if you piss him off, he'll pixie-zap your ass."

His eyes got big and round, and he whispered, "Is that bad?"

"Yeah," I said, deadly serious. "It's *real* bad. It's worse than being killed and eaten by an *orc*."

He looked like he was going to have a stroke. I put my finger up to my lips again and raised my eyebrows, mouthing the words, *"Be quiet."*

While I was busy reprimanding and warning the new idiot daemon, Chase opened the door to the room and stepped inside. He was two steps in before I realized my mistake; but by then, it was too late.

Chapter Ten

"NOW YOU'LL PAY!" I HEARD the tiny voice yell, right before I heard Chase choking and gasping for air.

What the hell?

"Take that, you giant beast! Eat my dust!"

It was Tim's voice, but it had a definite manic quality to it.

"Tim! Stop! What the hell are you doing?!" I shouted, following Chase inside. I was so, so worried that eating Tim's dust was a very bad thing.

Chase was standing stock still in the center of the room.

I was afraid to move any closer because now I was far enough inside to see that Tim was awake and very, very cranky. His little tiny face was all flushed, and if my eyesight wasn't fooling me from this distance, he looked like he could very possibly be insane.

"Jayne!" he yelled, desperately.

"Yeah, it's me! What's wrong?"

"Someone took my wings," he cried frantically. "My wings! I'm completely grounded!"

"It wasn't Chase. Don't hurt him. It was a Dark Fae named Ben."

"Oh," he said, in a much calmer voice, looking at Chase and then me. "Well, that's ... inconvenient." His head sank into his shoulders, making him look like a turtle trying to go into its shell.

"In what way?" This seemed like a strange reaction to finding out your wings had been taken by the devil. I could have thought of much better words to use than 'inconvenient' - very creative ones in fact, with a liberal sprinkling of cuss words to really set the tone.

"Wellllll, uhhhh, I got a little panicked when I woke up and no one was here at first, and then that big beefcake came in with such a serious look on his face, and me here without any wings, sooooo..."

"Chase always has that look on his face; you know that."

Tim giggled nervously. "Not anymore, he doesn't."

I got a really bad feeling. "Chase, turn around."

Chase turned slowly to look at me, and I suffered what felt like a tiny heart attack. He had the biggest grin on his face he'd ever had, for as long as I'd known him, anyway. It looked freaky as hell.

"Chase," I whispered, *"what the fuck is wrong with you?"*

"Nothing!" he burst out, still smiling like a maniac. "Everything is awesome! Wow. I had no idea how great these rooms are. This is fabulous! This room, the bed, the dresser ... it's all real wood! Did you notice that before? I didn't."

He shoved past me out into the hallway, walking rapidly away.

"You know, he's totally right," said that daemon kid whose name I couldn't remember at the moment. "I've always thought the rooms were pretty nice. It's hard to get real wood furniture these days."

"Not now, nut brain," I said angrily. "Chase!" I yelled, going out after him. "Where are you going?"

"I have to go outside," he answered. "This place is too confining."

I ran back into my room. "Tim! What the hell did you do to him?"

Tim turned around, sheepishly circling his foot out in front of him on top of the dresser, looking down and avoiding my eyes.

War of the Fae: Book Three

"Tell me now, Tim, or I'm gonna ... "

"It's too late," he said softly. "You can't threaten to take my wings. They're already gone. And it's too late for Chase, too. I pixied him."

"You ... *what?!*"

Tim turned and looked up at me beseechingly. "I thought he was gonna kill me! I couldn't fly away! ... So I panicked a little."

I shook my head. "That's not *a little* Tim. That's a *lot*. You promised you wouldn't do this to anyone. And of all people ... Chase? Hasn't he suffered enough being my friend?" *First an arrow in the back, now this.*

Tim put his head down again. "I know. I'm sorry."

I looked at Tony. "Stay here with Tim. Don't let him out of the room."

I looked at the daemon goofball standing next to Tony. "You stay here, too. Don't let anyone near them."

Last, I looked at Tim. "Pixie anyone while I'm gone, and we're through. I'll put you under a bell jar myself. You understand me?"

Tim nodded, a tiny fart escaping in reply.

"Fuck me," was all I could think to say as I ran down the hallway in the direction Chase had just gone.

Chapter Eleven

I CAUGHT UP TO CHASE as he was leaving through the dining hall doors and into the never-ending corridor. I had no idea how many doors there were off of it or how big this compound actually was. Every time I thought I did, I ended up going out another door I'd never seen before or walking a longer distance than I had in the past. Normally, this phenomenon was just a curiosity. Tonight, it was a serious pain in my ass.

"Where are we going, Chase?" I asked, coming up behind him, totally out of breath. The guy had long legs and was in a hurry.

"Gotta get outside. Outside, outside, *outside!*" He did a little hop then; and of all the things Chase had done so far since getting pixied, that was the scariest. Chase is the coolest guy I knew - definitely the strong, silent type. He would no sooner skip around than I would stop swearing. It was one of those 'not in this lifetime' kind of things. But here he was doing it. And I'd been told by my very intelligent gray elf friend, Gregale, that a pixie curse was nearly impossible to break, and that if you managed to break one, the affected person was never quite right in the head after.

Please, please, please let someone have a cure. Sometimes Chase's stoicism got on my nerves, but I was pretty sure that this hyper happiness was going to be much, much worse. I might end up having to kill him to put him out of *my* misery.

Chase reached a door I had never seen before. It had a picture of a flower on it. Most of these doors had some unique symbol on them, which made it easier for us Light Fae to picture them in our minds - handy since that was how we made the door appear, both from inside this hallway and then again from outside the compound. Otherwise, it was just a blank spot on the wall or another place out in the forest.

Chase opened the door and ran out.

"Chase, wait, you idiot!"

He didn't go far. We were in a meadow, similar to the one I'd been in before with Gregale, where he'd told me my sharp stick-looking weapon - given to me during the changeling test - was none other than the fang of The Dark of Blackthorn. The Dark was a Dark Fae dragon, long slayed by some ancestor of mine. When I was using it against someone, it burned the shit out them with dragonfire - usually awesome, but totally useless against this current problem, so it stayed strapped to my leg.

I stopped running and stood at the edge of the grassy open space that was bathed in moonlight. I watched as Chase ran around in circles, spinning and laughing, smiling his damn fool head off. I could see pretty well at night in the forest, even without the moon, which had something to do with my connection to The Green.

I sat down in the grass. *Now what the hell am I supposed to do?* I ran through my options. I could reach out to Spike and he'd probably find me. As long as I was thinking sexy thoughts, he would likely pick up on them and show up so we could start making out. I wondered how many times I could use that trick to get him to come before he'd stop responding anymore. We'd never actually sealed the deal after one of my come-hither invitations. Every time I'd lured him in this way, I hadn't wanted him for sexual reasons, so I was always putting his x-rated intentions on hold.

I could also use The Green to bring Finn to me. All the green elves were hooked into my network that way. It wasn't as cool as the green elves' ability to send complete telepathic messages with actual words, but it was good enough for my purposes. The problem was, I didn't know who I should call in the elf network. Who could help us with this mess? Probably the healers in the compound needed to be called - but I'd already been warned by Dardennes that being pixied was practically a death sentence, which was why they had nearly shit themselves when I'd let Tim out of the bell jar. If I called them, Tim was going to get shipped out for sure. Now everything Dardennes and Gregale had said about the dangers of pixies was coming back to haunt me. *And Chase.* I looked out at him delighting in his happy frenzy and sighed. Maybe I could talk to him.

I got up and walked over to where he was jumping around, reaching out my hands to grab him and calm him down.

"Chase. Hey. Settle down for a second, would you? Come talk to me."

"I *am* talking to you, Jayne. Dance with me! Why are you just standing there? Can't you feel the vibrations? It's amazing. I can't stop moving. It's all through me! Do you know how much I've missed feeling this alive?"

He continued to whirl around, his arms stretched out to the sky. His face was beautiful, a big smile going from ear to ear. It was the first time I'd seen him look truly happy. It seemed somehow wrong that I was going to work really hard to get him back to his quiet, unaffected self. But I had to, because he wasn't going to stop this. He was going to keep blissing out until he dropped from exhaustion, and then when he got his energy back, he was going to get up and do it all over again. This process would go on for the rest of his life, and he's fae, so that's about a thousand years, give or take.

I was so busy scheming over how I was going to de-bliss Chase, I didn't see him coming up to me until it was too late. He grabbed me in his arms and twirled me around with him. He lifted me right off my feet, spinning me and spinning me, around and around, until I started to feel sick.

"Chase, put me *down* you fucknut!"

He refused. He just kept dancing and spinning. My arms and ribs were hurting where he was squeezing me.

"Let me go! You're *hurting* me!"

Still, he continued. I was starting to panic, squirming and trying to get away. He didn't realize or care that he was crushing me. I tried to get my mind away from the pain and nausea so I could reach out to The Green. As usual, its hum was just outside my mind, waiting to be invited in. Its welcoming touch embraced my body. The unpleasant sensations that Chase had created faded away, and I began to calm down.

I sent out a message through my link with the forest that I needed Chase to be stopped, so I could get away. Moments later, a group of vines raced over the ground from the nearby tree line to tangle themselves around his legs.

Chase kept trying to move anyway, but soon the vines overwhelmed him. I hadn't really thought the whole process through, obviously; that old adage 'the bigger they are, the harder they fall' took me by surprise. And, well, when they were as big as Chase, they fell pretty damn hard ... and when it was *on* me, it really sucked.

Chase went down like a ton of bricks, landing right on top of me. I grunted loudly as the air was pushed out of my lungs.

He giggled relentlessly. "That was a *great* idea, Jayne." He was

//War of the Fae: Book Three//

snuggling my neck, sending chills up my spine. "Mmmm, you smell good. Let's make love." He pulled at my tunic, trying to figure out how to get it off me. That was when I decided it was time to slap some sense into his crazy ass.

SMACK!

He looked at me with a pained expression. "*Ow*, that hurt." He pouted for a second and then smiled like a maniac again. "But it's okay, because I *forgive* you! Now help me get your tunic off. We can make love under the moon, Jayne; it'll be *magical!*"

I pushed him away as hard as I could, growling out, "No ... one ... is making ... love ... to anyone ... under the ... fucking *moon* ... shitforbrains ... "

I couldn't even get him to budge. He was two hundred and I didn't know how many pounds of frisky daemon that wouldn't be dissuaded from his romantic agenda. I hated to do it to him, but it was the only way I could get away.

I pulled Blackie out and touched his back with it. I heard a sizzle just before his scream.

"*Ahhhhh!!!* Ow, man, that *hurt*. Oooh, *geez*, that's a burner. Wow. Holy smokes, what's wrong with my back? I need to dance. Get me out of these weeds so I can dance the pain off!" He shoved me away so he could reach down and wrestle with the vines cinched around his ankles.

I rolled away from him and walked quickly to the edge of the meadow, sending a message to The Green that he needed to be held captive there until further notice. I had to find someone who could help him, but I didn't want Dardennes or any of the council members to get wind of this. They'd take Tim and banish him forever to a pixie colony somewhere and I'd never see him again. Plus, he was without wings right now, and it was partially my fault, so it wasn't right to let him go when he was grounded like that.

Chase started singing some old country song that was probably going to end up being stuck in my head for days. He sang pretty well, all things considered.

I tuned him out and tapped into the nearest ley line, reaching out to Maggie the witch. Once again, she was my only hope. I was afraid that I'd used up all my favors though, so I had no idea how I was going to compensate her for this second healing of Chase. I hated that I needed her help so soon after having just asked her to take care of Tim. I needed to find some other witch friends, especially since I'd now seen firsthand how handy they were to have around.

I felt Maggie's cranky energy out there, recognizing me. I sent her images of where I was and my problem, and then I waited. I got nothing back from her, but I wasn't really sure how this worked, so I just sat down, letting the link drop when all I had left from her was a dull hum. Maybe she'd come and maybe she wouldn't. I was going to give her an hour and then work on figuring out a Plan B.

While I waited, I sent a message across The Green to Finn. He was sleeping; I could tell by the low hum of his presence. I nudged him pretty hard and sent him images of the door in the hallway with the flower on it, hoping he'd understand that I needed him. He was the only one I knew how to contact this way. I had no link to Becky at all. With Spike I'd have to use sexy thoughts, and after being fondled by Chase, I wasn't in the mood. I liked Chase and found him pretty damn good looking and all, but not like this. Maybe some other time we could make love under the moonlight or whatever, but not when he was as crazy as a loon. Crazy was not sexy *at all*. This wasn't Chase, anyway. Someday, if he ever wanted to do that with me, I knew for sure he wouldn't say it like that. Right now he sounded like a guy in a really cheap and badly written romance novel. *Yuck*.

War of the Fae: Book Three

About ten minutes later, I heard the door open on the edge of the meadow and the sounds of footsteps and whispers. Soon the faces of Finn and Becky appeared out of the darkness.

I breathed a sigh of relief. "Thanks for coming, guys. Sorry to bother you so late."

Becky looked at me with concern. "What's up? Are you okay?"

"Yeah, I'm fine. But he's not." I pointed at Chase, lying on the ground, struggling valiantly to get free while giggling his head off.

"Is that ... ?" Becky asked, incredulously.

I sighed. "Yeah. It's Chase."

"What in the *hell?*" asked Finn, taking a step towards him.

"No!" I grabbed Finn's arm. "Don't. Just leave him be," I said, disgusted. "Don't get too close. He may try to make love to you under the light of the moon or something."

"Oh, hey! Finn! What's up, man?!" yelled Chase, interrupting us. "Come on over here and help me out, would ya? Wow, you look great. Is that a new haircut? Let's dance. I feel like dancing, don't you?"

Finn turned and looked at me in horror. "What in the sam hill happened to that poor guy? Cuz that ain't Chase. That's some kinda imposter, or Dark Fae voodoo goin' on there."

"No," I said sadly. "That's Chase. He got accidentally pixied."

Becky's hand flew to her mouth and her eyes grew wide. *"Oh, no!"* she whispered.

"Yeah. Tim did it. He was kinda still out of it from his wing removal and Chase surprised him, so he just ... I don't know ... *blammo*, pixied him. Chase has been doing this dancing and laughing shit ever since. I had to tie him up so he'd sit still and let go of me. You don't want to get too close to him right now, trust me."

"What was he trying to do to you?" asked Becky, tentatively, still in disbelief.

"First he just wanted me to join him in his fucked up dance routine which almost made me barf. Then he got a little frisky. Think Spike, but with big muscles and psychotic circus clown charisma."

Becky drew back her lips in a grimace. "Oh. Bummer."

"Yeah. He didn't get anywhere with it, but still. It's Chase. It just felt so *wrong*, especially because he's acting so ... different."

"Weird."

I nodded. She totally got it.

"So what the heck are we gonna do with him? Just wait it out all night, or what?"

I shook my head sadly. "There is no waiting it out, from what I hear. He's pixied for life unless Maggie can come up with something to help him. Otherwise, he'll keep doing this shit until he dies from exhaustion."

Becky got tears in her eyes. "Oh, my heaven. Oh, my *Water*. He's going to die from being pixied to death? What a horrible way to go."

"Come on now, Becky, we'll figure somethin' out. Don't go cryin'. We ain't gonna let ol' Chase just go 'n die on us. He's a strong guy, and Jayne's got her connection to The Green." Finn looked over at me. "Can't you just heal him, like you did for me and Becky during the test?"

It was true. I had been able to heal both of them from some pretty bad wounds they'd received from some cranky fae who were there in the forest to help us fail the test.

"I actually hadn't thought of that. I guess I can try. It might be better if we were all near an Ancient, though - one of the bigger trees."

"I'll go see what I can find. You girls stay here with ol' lover boy." Finn jerked a thumb in Chase's direction.

Becky came over and sat down with me, rubbing my back with her little hand. I wasn't not a large person myself, but she was positively tiny. She made me feel like a moose when she was near me. Right now I didn't care so much, though.

"Don't worry. We'll get this taken care of, one way or another."

"I called the witch. Maggie. I'm not sure if she's coming or not."

Becky shivered involuntarily. "I'm not her biggest fan, I have to tell you. She was just a liiiittle too happy to take Tim's wings off. It was creepy."

"I know. But if anyone has a remedy, it's her."

"I hate to think what's actually *in* that remedy though."

"Yeah. Me too. Probably newt balls or something."

Becky giggled. "You just said balls. Do newts even have balls?"

"Of course they do. I mean, I've never actually *seen* a newt's nads, but they must have 'em. How else would they make babies?" I smiled back at her. This was one of the more stupid conversations I'd ever had in my life, but at least it was getting my mind off my poor friend who was now singing something that sounded like *Moon River*, a song my dad used to sing, only it was the same line over and over and very out of tune. It was weird to me that Chase knew this old song.

Finn came back from the trees, jogging over to us and talking at the same time. "I found one. It's not far." He looked over at Chase. "Question is, how're we gonna move him from here to there?"

"Leave that to me," I said, linking up once again to my source of power. I imagined Chase being dragged behind us by the vines, and they began to do my bidding.

"Show us the way," I said. "Just don't step on the vines that are holding Chase."

Finn offered us his hands to help us get to our feet. We stood and followed him into the woods, Chase being dragged behind us. He'd probably suffer a few abrasions, but that was better than getting into another wrestling match with him. He was too damn heavy to carry.

Chase laughed and sang intermittently while he struggled against his bonds.

As soon as I saw the tree that Finn had picked, I knew it was the right one. It was *huge* huge. Almost as big as a sequoia. This forest was so strange. It had all kinds of trees in it, and not just the ones you would expect for the area. I knew we were in Europe ... France probably by my estimations of the time it took to get here from Florida, the climate, and the info I'd seen in the compound's computers. Some of the trees shouldn't be here, but they were. I shrugged it off as a fae thing. Pretty much anything I couldn't explain these days was chalked up to that catch-all explanation.

I asked the vines of The Green to tie Chase to the tree so he couldn't get away, and they dutifully complied. He was trussed up like a captive, and he didn't like it one bit. He was sweating with the exertion of trying to escape while also letting loose bursts of laughter and shouts of glee. His voice was starting to get hoarse.

I went over and knelt down next to him, being careful not to get too close. I looked over my shoulder, saying, "You guys might want to back up. I'm not exactly sure what's going to happen."

They each took five steps backward, saying nothing, just staring at Chase and me.

I looked at Chase, hating what I saw in his eyes and on his face. It was like love, desperation, and confusion all mixed together, and so not like him. It was as if there were an alien inhabiting my friend's mind.

"Chase, babe, I'm gonna try to heal you with The Green. I need you to sit still and just let it happen, okay?"

"Let's just dance instead! Or sing! We can sing together. Come on, I'll start. *Row, row, row your boat* ... okay, Jayne, now you do a chorus and we'll play off each other ... *row, row, row your boat* ... you go now ..."

I sighed; it was no use trying to talk to him. I got started, leaning towards the tree and placing my palms on its rough, brown bark so I could adjust my body against it, before assuming the tree-hugging stance. I found this was the best and purist way to commune with the life force that ran through this forest. I could connect with The Green from pretty much anywhere, now that I'd learned how to use and control my powers in training with various other fae, but tree hugging was still the best way to go about using my power when I needed it to be at level ten. There was just less effort required on my part, and I could focus better on what I was doing - or trying to do.

I spread my arms out across the tree, my left arm over Chase's chest. His back was against the tree, so now we were all connected together.

A voice came through the din of Chase's delirious singing and the hum of The Green.

"It's not going to work!"

I recognized the voice of Maggie, now standing behind me.

"I'm going to try anyway."

"Suit yourself. I'm leaving."

I disengaged myself from the tree, turning to face her. "No! Stay for a minute. Let me just try this."

She shrugged and stood still. "Don't take long. I need my beauty sleep. It's past my bedtime."

I turned back to business, ignoring the glaring error in her reasoning, since even with all her beauty rest, she was nothing less than hideous-looking. "Okay, Chase, here we go ... "

I closed my eyes, blocking out the rusty chorus of *Row, Row, Row Your Boat* as best I could. I sent out my request through this grand old tree that connected Chase and me to the energy linking all of the living and once living things in the Green Forest and out beyond. I asked for a healing to begin on my friend's mind - to help him find the old Chase and get rid of this ... thing ... or whatever it was that possessed him. I could feel the loving touch of The Green flowing through me and into Chase, but I had no idea if it was making any difference. I just kept it up until I thought it was all I could do, and then I gently let The Green go, thanking it for whatever it had been able to accomplish. A sigh escaped my lips when I once again found myself empty of The Green's loving force.

I pulled back from the tree, looking at Chase critically. He was quiet, smiling. That wasn't exactly a good sign. This was Chase after all, so the smile had me worried.

"Chase? You okay?"

His eyes slowly opened, his grin widening when he saw me. "That was *awesome!* Do it again! Please?! I feel so *energized* right now!" He struggled with the vines, a confused look on his face. "Why are these things on me? Can you help me get them off? I need to go dance."

Frustrated tears rushed to my eyes as I jumped to my feet. *"Shit balls!"* I yelled at no one in particular.

"I told you it wouldn't work," grouched Maggie. "Come over here, girl."

I turned angrily, stalking over to her while I explained. "Tim did this to him. It was an accident. If I can't fix this - if you can't fix this - they'll send Tim away to a leper-pixie colony and Chase to somewhere equally awful. Maybe they'll put him down or something, I don't know. I need both of them here. And *normal*. Tell me you can help," I pleaded.

"Pixies are dangerous friends to have."

"Yeah, well, it's too late for that advice now. I just need to know if you can make him better."

She shrugged. "He looks happy to me. Maybe he doesn't want to be better." She smiled shrewdly.

"Stop dicking around, you old bat. You know no one chooses to be pixied or to stay that way. He's going to kill himself with this kind of happiness."

She shrugged. "I can think of worse ways to die."

"Yeah," I said menacingly, putting my hand on Blackie, "so can I."

Maggie raised her eyebrow questioningly. "Are you threatening me?"

"Not exactly," I challenged back. "I'm asking you to help me. You're either going to do it or not - but tell me now and stop fucking around. I'm not in the mood."

"Truth!"

"You're damn straight it's the truth. So what's the deal? Can you help me?"

"Maybe. Pixie curses are tricky business. But it's not for me to help your friend. You need the healers in the Light Fae compound."

"Why? Why can't you do it?"

"You need an antidote made in a lab. It's new magic - not my specialty. You get the blood of Tim, the pixie who cursed him, and use it to make the reversal spell. I know the basics but not the actual process. You need a younger witch and an older witch, working together."

"Will it work? Will it make Chase ... normal again?"

"I don't know. Maybe. Maybe not."

I threw up my hands in frustration. "You're pretty much being no help at all here! I can't bring him back to the compound. They'll get rid of Tim for sure. I need you to fix him out here where they won't see."

Maggie started to walk away.

"Where are you going?" I yelled shrilly.

"To bed."

"But I need your help!"

"I helped you as much as I could. Now I'm going to bed."

"Arrrrggghhh!!" I screamed, wanting to tear my hair out.

Becky walked up to me, tentatively. "So ... what do you want us to do? Do you want to bring Chase back to the compound?" She rested her hand on my arm, its cool presence calming me a fraction.

Finn stepped up next to me too. "Sounds like that's the only solution."

"It can't be," I said, nearly weeping with frustration. "I just got Tony back. Now I'm gonna lose Tim? No," I shook my head, "it's just too much. He's injured. I can't let that happen."

"Yeah," said Becky, her eyes going over to Chase, "but you can't leave Chase out here, and there are no other options. He's too loud to hide. And how are you going to feed him? He eats like a horse."

Everything she was saying made sense, but I couldn't decide what to do. I really, really didn't want Tim to be punished for this. It wasn't fair. And I knew that expecting the council to be completely unbiased wasn't realistic. They were racist pixie haters, every last one of them, and I was sure they thought they'd already done me enough favors.

"Maybe I could be of assistance."

The voice came out of nowhere. I grabbed Blackie, pulling it out of the sheath on my leg. Finn's bow flew off his shoulder and into his hands, an arrow already notched. He was so friggin fast on the draw I hadn't even seen him move. If I wasn't so freaked out about a possible sneak attack, I would have been seriously impressed. Becky pulled a disappearing act, teleporting away to I had no idea where. *Man,* I was *so* jealous of that skill.

"Who's there?!" shouted Finn.

"My name is Gustav, but my friends call me Goose. And I am here in front of you, but I do not particularly like being shot or burned, so until you put your weapons down, I will stay in the Gray, thank you."

He had a light accent. It sounded German or something.

I looked at Finn and he shrugged at me. Neither of us put our weapons down.

"Do we know you?" I asked. I was stalling, searching my memory for a gray elf named Goose. I didn't know many of them, but Gregale had mentioned a few. I didn't recall a Gustav or a Goose.

"No. That is not likely," he said, a smile in his voice. He certainly didn't seem threatening, except for the fact that he was hiding himself from us.

"Do you live at the compound?" asked Finn.

"No. I live out here in the forest. And in the Gray."

"What the hell's he talkin' about, livin' in the Gray?" whispered Finn to me.

I leaned towards his ear and told him what I knew. "It's the space between this world and the Otherworlds - where the spirits live sometimes. I'm not exactly sure. Gregale took me there once to go visit Tony using astral projection. Gray elves can go there."

"Ah," said Finn, acting like everything I had just said made perfect sense, which it didn't. But it was the best I could do. The Gray was kind of a mystery to me too.

"If we put down our weapons, you have to promise not to hurt us," I said, trying to sound confident and not scared, conveniently ignoring the fact that anyone who wanted to harm us would have no problem lying to us about his intentions.

"If I wanted to hurt you, I could have already done that five times over. You are not the quietest fae in this forest, believe me."

He had a point there. "Yeah, well, we have a sick friend."

"I can see that. And as I've said - I may be able to help you with his little affliction. A pixilation problem, I'm guessing?"

Dammit. Now the whole compound was going to find out.

I lowered my weapon, reaching out and pushing on Finn's arm so he would put down his bow.

"Fine. Our weapons are down. Show yourself."

A shimmering appeared a few feet in front of us. First the form was just a gray outline. Then it became more solid. Standing there, wearing a blackish-gray tunic, was a skinny guy with a sharp nose and high cheekbones. He had blond hair like Chase but gray eyes like some I'd seen recently. *Whose eyes look like that?* I couldn't put my finger on it, and then he started speaking, so I instantly forgot what I was trying to remember.

"I am part of a group of witches and other fae who have recently found some success in treating pixilation. Perhaps your friend would be willing to come to our facility and participate in our latest study."

I looked at him like he was nuts. We were out here in the Green Forest, Chase tied to a tree laughing his fool head off, and this guy is talking about clinical trials? Was he mental? I was worrying that we had a total psycho on our hands and not the savior he was making himself out to be.

"Listen, Goose, I appreciate your little medical breakthrough or whatever, but this is not a joke. My friend needs help, and he's not interested in being a lab rat or whatever it is you're talking about. So unless you can really help him, I'm going to need you to get the hell away from us."

My hand itched to lift Blackie up and put it in his face, but I didn't want him disappearing again until I knew for sure he wasn't going to be any help. I was desperate - so desperate, I was talking to some strange gray elf who I'd never seen or heard of, out in an unfamiliar part of the forest in the middle of the night.

Goose smiled patiently. "No, he would not be a lab rat. Our study is beyond experiments with animals. We have actual fae participating now, who have found great success with our treatment."

Finn spoke up, unable to hold back his curiosity, "So, what is this treatment then? You jus', give 'im a shot in the butt cheek or somethin'?"

"No. We have witches on staff who have found the means to create an antidote ... much like the one described by your friend. Maggie, I believe, is her name."

"So what is the antidote like? What does it do?" I asked.

"It's a series of treatments, administered at various stages, until the pixilation is completely removed. The side effects are ... manageable. And temporary."

"Have you actually had a pixying completely reversed yet?"

Goose cleared his throat. "*A-hem*, well, not exactly. And the correct term is 'pixilation'. But we are very, very close. For thousands of years, various groups have worked on this solution, but for the first time, we have had major breakthroughs. It is quite exciting, really." He looked meaningfully over at Chase, his expression becoming serious. "Your friend needs us, that much is clear. And you shouldn't wait too long to decide what to do. The longer you wait, the harder it is to heal and the less chance there is of him coming all the way back from it."

I got a panicky feeling in my chest, and it was hard for me to breathe.

"Well, it sounds good 'n all, and not to be rude or nothin', but we don't even know who you are or where you're from. An' you're just expectin' us to hand over our friend to you and a buncha witches we don't know either? Huh-uh. I don't think so." Finn shook his head and frowned. "No siree bob. Ain't gonna happen."

Finn was right. As tempting as this sounded, I couldn't just give Chase to this guy like that. Not when we knew so little about him.

"He's right. Tell us what we need to know. Who are you and where are you from exactly?"

"I can tell you that I am Gustav. I am a fae ... of the wrathe race, as you can see by my tunic. I live in the Green Forest with others of my kind. And I am Dark Fae, if that makes any difference."

I looked at him, aghast. "Of course it makes a difference, you Dark Fae dumbass!" I immediately held Blackie up, noticing that Finn had beat me to it, already holding Gustav in his sights.

"Ah. So, you are Light Fae ... and newly changed if I am not mistaken. Do not worry, you have nothing to fear from me. I am merely a scientist at heart. Look ... " He held up his hands and gestured around him. "I hold no weapons. I have come in peace."

He certainly didn't look very threatening.

"You're Dark Fae. That makes you the bad guy," said Finn, matter-of-factly.

Gustav smiled. "I see they have the propaganda machine well-oiled and working soundly in the Light Fae camp. How unfortunate for you. Actually, young green elf, the world is not so easy to fit into categories, now is it? I suspect your friend was pixilated by a Light Fae pixie, yes?"

"Yeah. So?"

"Sounds to me as if *he's* the bad guy. Not me. I'm offering to help."

"But what do you want in return? That's the real question here."

I'd learned one very valuable thing from Maggie, who never even tried to hide the fact that it was her motto - nothing in this world came without personal sacrifice.

"So suspicious. So doubting. But I will give you your answers so that you will feel more comfortable - because it is true that I do this for selfish reasons. We have lost several of our brethren to pixilation. The more subjects we have from different fae races, the more opportunity we have to find the cure. We are nearly there. But we cannot ask fae to volunteer to be pixilated so we can continue our work. I travel the Gray looking for those who have had the misfortune to run into an angry or misguided pixie. That is why I am here and willing to help - even though you are, as we say over in the Dark Fae compound, the *bad guys*." He smiled at that, raising his eyebrow at us in a challenge.

It did make sense that he considered us adversaries.

Finn looked at me, shrugging his shoulders. "Makes sense to me."

"Yeah, me too. *If* he's telling the truth."

And that gave me the perfect idea. "Just wait one second, Goose. I want you to talk to a friend of mine."

I tapped into The Green through the nearby ley line again. I needed one more favor from Maggie, so I sent my message out: *Maggie, get your wrinkly old lie-detecting ass back here. I will owe you one.*

Chapter Twelve

A GROUCHY MAGGIE SHOWED UP not long after, joining the three of us under the branches of the Ancient tree where Chase remained tied.

"Maggie, I need you tell me if this guy Goose is telling us the truth. He's offering to help Chase, but I'm not sure if I can trust him."

She looked over at him and grunted, then looked back at me. "What is your offer?"

"I will owe you one favor of your choosing, if you do this for me."

"Anything I want?" a slow smile spread across her face.

I was a little uncomfortable about this opened-ended bargain, and a *lot* uncomfortable about that smile, but I didn't see any way around it. I had nothing else to give. "Within reason, yes."

"Whose reason?"

I rolled my eyes at her. She would have made a great lawyer in the human world. "I don't know ... an average fae's reason, I guess."

"Done." She nodded at me. Then she turned to face Goose. "Speak!"

"Tell her what you told us," I said.

Appearing intrigued, Goose began his story. "My name is Gustav and I am of the Dark Fae."

"Truth!"

Goose jumped, temporarily startled, but then he continued, "I am part of a group of witches who are working to heal those who have been pixilated."

"Truth!"

"We have found a cure."

"Lie!"

Gustav frowned at her and then looked at me.

"You have to be exactly truthful or she'll know."

"Ah," he said nodding. "Okay, we are nearly to a cure, and we have had many successes recently in finding it and successfully treating advanced pixilation."

"Truth!"

"And if I hand Chase over to you, you won't hurt him?"

"No."

"Lie!"

"Sorry ... What I mean to say is, the only pain he will endure, is that which is a side effect of the treatment. Otherwise, I intend him no harm."

"Truth!"

"And you'll let him go when he's done with the treatment or when I ask you to return him?"

"Yes, absolutely."

"Truth!"

"And you'll tell me the truth about how and where to find him?"

"Yes."

"Truth!"

I looked at Finn. "Can you think of anything else we need to know?"

Finn looked at him and said, "You have no other reason to help

Chase other than your scientific experiments?"

At this Goose squirmed a bit, taking a few seconds to answer. "My only interest in your friend, personally, is scientific."

"Truth!"

I looked at Finn and he returned my gaze, shrugging his shoulders. We were both satisfied enough to take the risk, apparently. I didn't feel as if I had any other choice.

"Thank you, Maggie. You can go back to bed now. Go get your beauty sleep."

She grunted and then shuffled off, disappearing among the trees.

I faced Goose. "Okay. You can take him to your lab. But I want your solemn promise that you'll take good care of him. He's very special to me." I tried not to think about how special he was because a lump was forming in my throat, making my voice rough.

"I promise you, I will do whatever I can to help rid him of his pixilation problem."

"And when will he be ready to come back home?"

"Assuming you can get us a sample of the pixie's blood? One week, if all goes well."

"One *week*? *Holy mess*, how in the heck are we gonna put off the council for a whole *week*?" asked Finn.

"I don't know. And how the hell do we get a sample of Tim's blood?"

I focused my attention back on Goose. "Okay. So how do we get you a pixie blood sample, and how do we get Chase home when it's all over?"

"Have your Light Fae healers take the sample - tell them it's for Maggie. Meet me back here with it tomorrow at noon. I'll return here with Chase in a week. Same time, noon. If I can get here sooner, I'll send you a message."

"How are you going to do that?"

"I will visit you through the Gray. Now that I know you, it should be possible to find you."

"How will I know you're there?"

Goose smiled patiently. "I've been told it feels as if the hairs on the back of your neck are standing up, and of course you will hear me when I speak to you."

"That pleasant, eh?" I smiled bitterly.

"I'm pretty sure it won't work inside the compound," said Finn.

I hadn't heard that before, but being a part of the green elves gave Finn access to a lot more security info than me.

"You are correct. But when you are outside, it will work. I will just keep trying, if need be, until I catch you out in the forest somewhere."

"Fine. So how are you going to transport Chase to your lab? And where is your lab?"

"I have already contacted some ogres who assist in our security details. They will be here shortly. And my lab is in the Dark Fae compound, here in this forest."

The fact that there was a Dark Fae compound here in the same forest was interesting, but I had other more immediate concerns to worry about. I decided I could mull over the Dark Fae compound issue later with my friends. Besides, Finn would probably know something about it.

"I'm going to have to release him from the vines or they won't come off," I explained.

"If you could wait until the ogres arrive, that would be best. A pixilated fae is hard to catch sometimes."

"Yeah. I noticed."

We heard a crashing through the nearby trees, and five seconds later two giant fae came walking up, stopping next to Goose.

"You called?" one of them said in a gravelly voice. He sounded so much like Ivar, it was uncanny. These ogres even looked a little like him - big heads with bulky eyebrow ridges that hung over small eyes, with thick necks and arms as big around as my leg. They were good fae to have around as security guys for sure.

Goose gestured to Chase. "Could you please deliver that fae who is tied to the tree over there to my laboratory?" He nodded at me. "You may release him now."

I quickly sent out a message to the vines that they could let Chase go. I didn't want those ogres tearing them away. I had never gotten any sign from The Green that breaking its vines or leaves off was painful in any way, but it still didn't seem right to let it happen when it could be avoided.

The vines retreated, going back to the trees and bushes they had come from.

Chase tried to get up, obviously planning to go run and dance some more, if the glee in his eyes was any indication. But the two ogres quickly put an end to those plans, grabbing him firmly by the arms. He struggled valiantly, twisting his body around as far as he could, trying to look back towards the meadow, all the while yelling for them to let him loose so he could go dance. He even invited them to go with him, which if it weren't so pitiful, would have been hysterical. I mean, Chase frolicking in the flowers with two ogres? - Hilarious and hideous, all at the same time.

"We will take our leave now, and I will see you tomorrow to get the blood," said Goose, giving us a slight bow as he began to fade into the Gray.

"Goose! Wait!"

He came back a little. "Yes?"

"What kind of fae are you again?"

"I am a wrathe."

I nodded. "Okay, thanks. See ya."

He faded into the Gray, disappearing completely within seconds.

"Why'd you ask him that?"

"Because I suddenly remembered where I'd seen eyes like his before."

"Where?"

"On Tony's face. Right after he changed."

"Oh shee-it. I didn't put two and two together, but you're right."

"Do you know what a wrathe is?"

"No idea."

"Me neither. Let's get back. Tomorrow we can ask Dardennes or Céline. Maybe even Jared will know."

We walked through the forest and then the meadow.

"So what're we gonna do about Chase bein' gone? What're we gonna say to everybody?"

"I don't know," I answered distractedly. "Let's go find Jared. He'll know what to do."

"Or he'll rat us out, and we'll all be totally screwed."

"Yeah, well, that could happen. But I have a feeling it won't. Jared does the right thing for faekind, even if it makes people hate him." I knew this firsthand because I had just recently gotten over my feelings of anger towards him that had started when he pretended to be a regular teen in Miami, rather than the fae recruiter he really was. But ever since he'd helped rescue Tony, he was off my bad list forever.

We arrived at the door to find Becky nervously waiting for us.

"Hey, guys ... where's Chase?"

"We gave him to some Dark Fae guy," I said. I was teasing her, enjoying her discomfort.

"What?" She looked at Finn for confirmation.

"Yep. Gave him up. Dumped his sorry butt."

"You guys aren't serious ... are you?"

I laughed a little because she looked so worried and sad, my sick sense of humor guiding me as usual. But I couldn't keep up the pretense. I was afraid she'd start crying. "Yeah, we did, but not like that. Just relax. Come with us to see Jared, and we'll explain everything. I don't want to say anything in the hallways, just in case anyone's around to overhear." I had no idea what time it was - it was late - but there were some fae night owls like Spike who might still be up and roaming around. "Anyone know where Jared's room is?"

"I do," said Becky, trying to act all casual but failing miserably when her voice caught.

I raised an eyebrow at her. "Oh, ya do, do ya?"

"Shush, it's not like that," she said, her face beet red.

Finn frowned. "Well, what is it like then, Becky?" He sounded like a parent.

"Jared's a good person. He's good to talk to if ... you know ... if you have questions and stuff."

Finn looked at her suspiciously, but I didn't care one way or another. If she wanted to hook up with Jared, it was her business. She was a big girl and could make up her own mind whether she wanted to get with a guy who was two hundred years older than her or whatever.

We followed Becky down the never-ending corridor until we reached the door she indicated as Jared's. She knocked three times, and he opened it, standing there fully dressed. He was apparently one of those night owl types.

His eyes took in the sight of all of us standing there. "Hey. What's up?" he asked cautiously, as if he weren't sure that he wanted to hear the answer.

"Can we come in?" I asked.

"Sure." He stepped back, giving us room to enter. After we were in, he shut the door.

These rooms of ours were very small, so whenever we gathered in one, we all immediately sat on the floor. Jared joined us there, hiking up one leg and resting his forearm on his bent knee in front of him.

"Jared, we have a problem. A big one. Is this room ... soundproof?"

"Yes. And there are no bug spells in it either."

"Bug spells?" Becky asked.

Finn quickly explained. "Witches can put a spell on your room that listens to whatever goes on there and reports it back to the witch."

That pissed me off and made me wonder whether my room was bugged. "How do you know if you have one?"

"Gotta have a witch come and do a scan."

"Mother*fucker*." I felt like I was never going to know all there was to know about being fae. They needed a school here or a manual, at least.

"You were saying?" prompted Jared.

"Sorry. Okay, so ... big trouble. It totally wasn't his fault, but Tim pixied, I mean pixelated, Chase ... " I kept talking fast, even though I could see Jared was practically shitting his pants angry, " ... so Chase got a little out of control and ran out into the woods, dancing and messing around. So we went after him and eventually tied him to a tree. Then this wrathe fae named Gustav came and offered to help with a new cure, and I made sure he wasn't lying by using Maggie the witch, who can tell if someone's lying, and he took Chase to his lab where he's going to fix him. But it's going to take a week, so we need

War of the Fae: Book Three

you to cover for Chase while he's gone; otherwise, Dardennes and the rest of the council will send Tim away. And right now he doesn't have any wings, and it really wasn't his fault, so it wouldn't be fair."

I stopped for a breath, anxiously studying Jared's face for his final reaction. His expression had gone from disbelief, to anger, to surprise, to something I now couldn't discern.

Chapter Thirteen

"WHAT ... ? ... HOW DID ... ? ... WHEN ARE ... ?" Jared ran his hand through his hair, frustrated. "What am I supposed to tell the council, Jayne? This community is too small. Someone missing for that long will be noticed. You know this isn't going to work."

"No, I don't know that," I said, testily.

Finn suggested, "You and Ivar go on recruitin' missions all the time. Why don't ya'll go on one and take imaginary Chase with ya?"

"I don't have any scheduled right now, and it takes a lot of coordination to get one going. I can't just throw one together like that. And the council is always involved; they'll know something's up. They'll want explanations that I won't have."

"Well, we have to come up with something. I just got one friend back; I'm not going to go and lose another one now. If they send Tim off to a pixie colony he'll never survive. He won't have new wings for a month at least. I don't even know if the one Ben burned off is going to come back." I hadn't voiced that concern to anyone before, but I'd been thinking it; and I figured it wouldn't hurt to lay it on thick right now. Jared needed convincing.

Jared got up and went over to sit down on his bed, looking down at us. "I'll do what I can to think of something, but right now, I'm coming up empty." He sighed loudly. "Come see me at breakfast. Nothing's going to happen tonight to change anything."

"Okay," I said, getting up and moving towards the door with Becky and Finn. "And thanks, Jared. I appreciate your help."

"Yeah," he said absently, his mind obviously still on our predicament.

Finn, Becky, and I stepped outside Jared's room and said our goodbyes to each other. They walked away, down the corridor in the opposite direction of my room. I imagined my door, and a few minutes later, was standing outside of it. I could hear the low murmur of voices coming from inside, which made me think about those bug spells again. I hoped I didn't have one in there.

"Hey, guys," I said as I entered, instantly pissed to see Scrubs sitting on my bed and Tony on the floor.

"Scrubs, get off my bed, you dumbass."

He jumped up. "Oops, sorry 'bout that. It's Scrum, by the way. Not Scrubs." He stepped over with exaggerated goofy tiptoe strides and sat on the floor near Tony.

"Tony, *you* can sit on my bed."

Tony smiled. "I'm fine here. What'd you find out?"

Tim was looking at me anxiously, and I frowned at him. Little shit was the cause of all of this. If he wasn't such a good friend I'd happily hang him out to dry. But he'd somehow found a way to get under my skin, so now I had to cover for his pixie ass.

"Chase is with the Dark Fae witches who are trying to work on a cure."

"What?!" yelled Tim. I was the only one in the room who could hear him. I'd taken a spell from Maggie so that I'd be able to hear his tiny voice, which was normally too small for humans to hear unless he was talking right down into an ear canal from half an inch away. Now

War of the Fae: Book Three

I could hear his voice like it was from a normal person.

"Yeah, you heard me right, you little punk. And tomorrow, you and I are going to the healers so they can get a blood sample from you. The Dark Fae need it for the cure."

Tim was shaking his head, fear on his face.

"Don't even think about telling me no, Tim. I'm not messing around with you. Chase can't be cured without it. You either cooperate and don't give me any shit, or I'm putting you back under that bell jar myself."

"Yeah," he said pleading with me, panic all over his face, "but do you know what a Dark Fae witch can do with a blood sample? And from a pixie?"

"No. And I don't want to know. Maggie said this guy we met in the forest was telling the truth. He can fix Chase - mostly fix him, anyway - so we have to do it. We're going to bring the sample to him tomorrow right before lunch."

Tim turned to face the wall, giving me a view of his angry back.

"Is there anything I can do to help?" asked Scrum.

"Just stay out of my way." I wasn't in the mood to babysit tonight.

"Jayne, he can help us, I think. He's been telling me a lot about his training and what goes on here at the compound."

I raised an eyebrow at that. This guy was such a klutz, it was hard to imagine him doing very well at any training. But he was a daemon, so he would at least know what they did on a day-to-day basis.

"Whatever. Scum, your room is next door to mine, that way," I jerked my thumb in the opposite direction of Chase's room. "Tony, yours is on the other side of his. Come on, I'll take you there."

"It's Scrum, not Scum. But okay, thanks. I guess they moved me."

He walked out into the hallway and opened the door to his room. "Goodnight, guys. It was nice meeting you, Tony. See you in the morning?"

"Sure, Scrum. Thanks for the orientation," said Tony, smiling. Tony was a sucker for misfits. I hated to think about what that said about me.

Scrum disappeared inside. I heard a banging and scraping sound coming from the room, which told me the kid had probably tripped and landed against his dresser, knocking it to the side. *What a dipshit.* How that guy could be a daemon warrior guardian was beyond me. I wondered if it was possible that they had screwed up somewhere letting him in.

Tony opened the door to his room, and I saw immediately that it was almost exactly like mine. I walked in and went to his dresser. The silver tray on top, the spot where he was supposed to leave tokens for his brownie, was a little different. It was also silver, but it had different scrollwork around the edges. I'd noticed the same thing in Spike's room the one time I'd been in there.

"When I went into my room for the first time there were clothes in the drawers for me." I opened his, and sure enough, it was full. The tunics were white like mine, and he had jeans for pants. How cute ... we were going to be twins. "You've got stuff in here, but I have a feeling these tunics are going to change."

Tony came over to look in the drawer with me. "Why? What's wrong with these ones?"

"They're white."

Tony looked at me. "Aaaand that's a problem because ... I'm messy, maybe?"

"No. Because I think you might be getting dark gray ones instead."

War of the Fae: Book Three

Tony gave me one of his looks. "Jayne, don't make me tickle torture you. Just tell me. I'm tired."

I rolled my eyes. "I met this Dark Fae guy tonight who's a wrathe."

"Is that the guy who's going to fix Chase?"

"Yes, exactly. Or he works with the witches who are doing it. His name is Gustav, or Goose for short. Anyway, he has the same color eyes as you. So it's not a definite or anything, but there's a possibility that you're a wrathe too."

"What's a wrathe?"

"I have no friggin' idea. I *do* know that they can do stuff in the Gray though, which is ... cool." Honestly, I didn't know if it was cool or not, but I wanted to give Tony something positive to think about. And if it was in his race to be a part of the Gray, I was sure it would be right for him, even if it wasn't my favorite place. I'd been in the Gray once, when Gregale took me on an astral projection trip to see Tony back in West Palm. I was so focused on getting to Tony, I didn't pay much attention to it, but I remembered it being cold and not a happy place. I also knew that the Gray distorted the way things looked - it casted a shadow that wasn't necessarily there. When I saw Tony through the Gray, he looked miserable and helpless, furious at me. He was kinda those things when we actually saw him in person, but not as amplified as the Gray made it seem.

"How will I find out about all this stuff?"

"During your training. And through talking to other changelings. I swear, most of what I know I learned through gossip or by accident. This ain't no Hogwarts, if you know what I mean. I'll talk to Dardennes about it tomorrow. I just have to figure out how to tell him I think you're a wrathe. We don't have any here that I've seen, so he'll wonder how I know."

"You said you could tell by his eyes? This Goose guy? What's that all about?"

"A lot of the fae here have physical characteristics that match their race. Like Dardennes and Céline, who are both silver elves, have those funky silvery-gray eyes. And when they do their thing, like ride the wind, their eyes go all wonky - swirling around and shit."

"They ride the wind? And their eyes swirl around?" Tony got a confused look on his face. "That sounds cool and gross at the same time."

I laughed, "No, their *eyes* don't swirl, dope. The *color* swirls around - like the wind is actually in their irises. But it's not like their eyeballs go rolling around or anything." I kept smiling, imagining the dignified Céline with googly eyes. Now *that* I'd like to see.

"How are you going to mention it to them?"

"I don't know. Maybe I'll have Jared do it."

Tony yawned. "Scrum showed me where the bathrooms for the guys are. Do you think I could take a shower before bed?"

"Sure. I do late showers all the time. There aren't as many girls around here, so I usually have the place to myself. Your clothes are in the dresser, towels in the bottom drawer. There are soap and shampoo dispensers in the showers. Your toothbrush and toothpaste stuff should be in the little cabinet by your sink." I pointed to the corner of his room. "Do you need anything else?"

"Just one of these," he said, holding out his arms for a hug.

I went willingly, pulling him into a super-sized squeeze. "Man, am I glad you're here." Tears welled up in my eyes, and I let them come. They were cleansing the anxiety from my soul. Tony was with me again, and once Chase was all fixed up and Tim had his wings grown back, all would be right with my world.

I could hear the smile in Tony's voice when he responded. "Me too, Jayne. Thanks for coming back to get me. I know I gave you a hard time, and I wasn't sure about all this, but I'm happy with my choice and very glad to be here."

"Ha!" I laughed, into his shoulder. "Like I'd leave you to Ben and his Dark Fae demon friends. I think not."

Tony pulled away from me. "Jayne, I know you pretty much despise him. And to be honest, his whole 'man on fire' thing kinda freaked me out. But I really think if you gave him a chance, you'd like him. He was really nice, and not just to me, either."

I shook my head. No way was I buying that load of crap. "Whatever, Tones. You always were good at overlooking people's faults."

"Like someone who swears all the time?"

"Yeah. Like that, smartass. I might cuss a little, but his faults are more like 'I'm an evil, fire-breathing demon' type of faults. Hardly comparable to a well-placed 'fucker' or 'shitforbrains'."

Tony laughed. "It's good to know that even though you're fae now, you're still the same Jayne underneath."

I smiled back at him. "That's right, baby. You're lookin' at the new and improved Jayne ... Jayne two-point-oh." I kissed him on one cheek and then slapped him lightly on the other. "Goodnight. I'll come get you in the morning. Don't wander these hallways, other than to go to the bathroom and our rooms, or you'll get lost; and I'm not sure how I'd find you."

He looked at me funny. "It's just a hallway, Jayne."

"Yeah. That's what you think."

I left his room without giving any further explanation, deciding that I'd let him try to show me the dining hall tomorrow. It was the best way I could think of to illustrate to him how clueless he was.

I went back to my room and walked over to my dresser where

Tim was in his little mini-bedroom. He was lying down on his bed, facing away from me.

"Tim, I know you're not sleeping. Turn over and talk to me."

He turned over in a huff, wincing in pain at the effect it had on his wing stubs but saying nothing.

"I'm super friggin' tired and not in the mood for any tantrums, so let me just say this: I'm going to do everything I possibly can to keep them from finding out about what you did and shipping you away to a pixie colony, Tim. I really am. But you have to help me. You promised me you wouldn't pixie anyone, and I put my reputation on the line, vouching for you. If they find out what you did, we're both busted. Do you get what I'm saying here?"

Tim pouted. "I don't need you to explain things to me like I'm a wee pixie."

"Well, apparently you do, since you unleashed your pixie powers on our friend, you idiot. So get over yourself and help me. Tomorrow we're going to suck some blood out of your lame ass self, and then you're going to help me come up with a plan."

"I already have one," he said softly, still refusing to let go of his pout.

"Well, what is it?"

"I'm going to turn myself in."

"Cut that martyr shit out and stop feeling sorry for yourself." I walked away from him in frustration. "You know what, Tim?" I whipped around to face him again. "If you weren't so small and wingless right now, I'd slap your ass silly. There are *no* pity parties allowed in this room."

"It's not a pity party," he said, weeping softly as he explained. "I went back on my word. My word is very important to me ... and so are you. I let you down. I don't even know why you'd still want me around ... " He choked and then sniffed, wiping his nose with the sleeve of his tunic.

So that was it. Tim was worried I wouldn't like him anymore. I sighed. "Tim. You know me pretty well by now. And you know I'm not the softest, lovey-doveyist girl in the compound. If you want someone to baby you and give you all kinds of pixie hugs, you'll have to talk to Becky. Right now I'm beyond tired and I'm super cranky, and all I want to do is sleep and wake up to find that this has all been a wicked bad dream. But at the end of it all, you need to know that I want to find you here in this room with me - still my roommate and still my friend. Now, until Chase is better, that's about all the warm fuzzy stuff you're going to get from me."

Tim slowly nodded, a tentative smile coming to his lips. "It's good enough for me. It's more than I deserve."

"Tim ... "

"Okay, okay," he held up one hand weakly, "no more pity parties. I'm going to sleep. I have two new wings to grow, you know. Not just one. Two wings. Two." He held up two tiny fingers.

"Oh, shut up. I'm glad she plucked that second wing off. Now maybe you can appreciate what Chase is going through."

Tim winced. "Low blow, Jayne. Even for you."

"Oh well. Deal with it."

I went over and threw back my covers, kicking off my moccasins. I collapsed into the bed, barely pulling the covers up before I started falling asleep.

"Aren't you going to brush your teeth first?"

"Aren't you going to shut the hell up before I come over there and shove you in a drawer?"

The only response I got was one of Tim's infamous pixie farts ...

"Wingless fucknut," I mumbled into my pillow.

He giggled, and it was the last thing I heard before falling into a dreamless sleep.

Chapter Fourteen

I AWOKE THE NEXT MORNING to a knock at my door. I got up and slogged over to open it, finding Spike standing there in the doorway.

"Ugh. What do *you* want?" I said, leaving him standing there and going back to my bed, crawling under the quilt and covering my head.

"What kinda way is that to greet your biggest fan?" I heard him step into the room and shut the door behind him. "I missed you yesterday. I came to see what was going on. I could tell you were upset, and you obviously still are now." Footsteps came towards my bed. "I've gotten zero sexy thoughts from you lately and that just isn't good. Everyone should indulge in a little sexy time each day. It's good for the soul."

I peeked out from under the covers and saw his eyes beginning to glow a little at the idea, as he sat down on the edge of my bed.

"My morning breath should be a cure for what ails you right now, my friend. So stay back." I held out my no-go hand in warning.

Spike took it from me and placed it on his lap. He jerked his head towards my dresser, whispering, "How's the little guy?"

"He's sleeping. And don't let him hear you call him 'little'. He pixied the shit out of Chase yesterday, and one fucked-up friend is about all I can handle right now."

"Whaaaat?"

"Yeah. I'm not joking." I sighed heavily, thinking of the big plate of steaming horseshit that was waiting to greet me at the breakfast table of my day.

"How come I always miss out on all the fun?"

I let go of Spike's hand and pinched his leg. Hard.

"Ouch! What was that for?" He raised his eyebrow at me. "You in the mood to play?"

I couldn't help but smile. "One of these days I'm going to take you up on your invitation. But not today."

He leaned in closer. "Why wait? There's no better time than the present." The red glow in his eyes got deeper and swirled around.

I deliberately closed my eyes. "Back up, or I'll unleash my dragon breath on you."

Spike laughed quietly. "As if that would stop me. You just say the word, Jayne, and I could take all your troubles away."

I opened one eye. "Can you really?"

Spike smiled sheepishly. "Well, they'd only be temporarily gone - you'd stop thinking about them for a while. But no, they'd still be there when you floated down off cloud nine."

"Still," I considered opening my other eye, "it might be worth trying one of these days ... to forget for a little while."

Spike stood in a flash and pulled off his tunic so he was standing there in just his black pants, his waist-to-neck-to-wrist colorful tattoos blazing out in all their glory.

I felt a shiver go through me. He was one beautiful specimen of a bad boy, that was for sure. I moaned in frustration. "Spiiiiike, put your shirt back on. I can't do this right now. I have too much shit to do and not enough time to do it all."

"I can be quick," he said, sitting back down on the edge of the bed, taking my hand and putting it on his chest. "It's better slow, but if you just need a quickie, I can accommodate." His face was all sexy seriousness now. His eyes were mesmerizing.

"Spike, I ... " I felt my denial disintegrating in the whirling madness I saw in those deep red depths. I wanted to drown in it.

Spike lowered his face to mine, drinking me in with his eyes. He was a second from kissing me, dragon breath and all, when there was a pounding at the door.

"Hey, Jayne!! It's me ... Scrum!! I'm gonna come in, okay? Don't get mad at me!"

And then the door flew open.

Spike sat up slowly, sighing. "Who the hell is this?" he asked tiredly, not even looking up.

"Hey, um, incubus guy. Sorry, I don't know your name. I'm Scrum, and you ... uh ... need to leave."

Spike raised an eyebrow at him and then looked at me. "Is this guy for real?"

Seeing Scrum's barrel-shaped body standing in my doorway snapped me out of my sensual fog. "What the hell are you doing here?" I demanded. I felt like someone had just dumped a bucket of cold water on my head.

Scrum looked uncomfortable. "I'm doing my duty. As a daemon." He looked at Spike. "I'm only going to say it one more time. You have to leave this room, incubus. *Now.*"

I smiled at the ridiculousness of this whole scene. I'd been two seconds away from engaging in something really *really* hot that was probably a big mistake, only to be saved by the kid who was named after shit that floated at the top of a dirty pond. This ... was my life.

"Thanks, Scum, for your help. But you can go now."

He sighed in frustration. "My name is not *Scum*. It's *Scrum*. As in the rugby move. And I'm not going anywhere until he does." He looked at Spike, his eyes narrowing. "You have five seconds to leave voluntarily. Otherwise, uh ... I will forcibly remove you."

Spike put his tunic back on. "I'd like to see you try." His eyes were glinting dangerously.

"Spike, please don't hurt the kid. Just go. I'm done here. I have to get up anyway." I moved the covers back to get out of bed.

Spike sat back down and put his hand possessively on my leg.

"Uh, Spike?" I said, noticing that he looked really serious.

"Okay ... ," said Scrum, stepping into the room, "if that's how you want it ... "

Spike jumped up, ready to attack. But Scrum beat him to it. I knew incubi could move astonishingly fast, but it didn't seem to faze Scrum at all. One second Spike was next to my bed, and the next, he was wrapped in a bear hug with Scrum at the door - Scrum being the bear and Spike being the huggee.

Spike was spitting mad, thrashing wildly against Scrum's body lockdown. Scrum held on, his face getting redder and redder by the second with the exertion. He backed slowly out of the room, fighting against Spike's struggling form. Once he was out in the hallway, he leaned back, squeezing Spike even harder. I heard Spike grunting and saw his face going whiter. It was already pretty pale, being that he was an incubus, but now it looked deathly so.

I jumped up from the bed, coming closer to them but staying back just a little. "You're hurting him! Put him down!" I yelled.

"Not until ... he ... surrenders," grunted Scrum.

Spike was shaking his head back and forth in denial, growling with what little breath he had left.

"Spike, just say 'uncle' or whatever!" I yelled, panicking. This Scrum kid wasn't messing around.

War of the Fae: Book Three

But it was too late. Scrum gave him one more extra squeeze, and Spike's body went limp. Scrum loosened his hold and let Spike drop until he was being held under Scrum's arm like a giant clutch purse.

I was in shock. "Did you ... ? Is he ... ?" I walked up closer to them, standing in the doorway now and staring at Spike's still form.

"He's not dead, if that's what you're worried about. I outwilled him. When he wakes up, he'll be fine."

"When's he going to wake up?"

Scrum shrugged the shoulder that wasn't holding Spike up from the floor. "When he admits I have a stronger will."

I looked at him like he was nuts. "When the hell is that going to be?"

Scrum shrugged. "Don't know. Whenever he decides to back down."

"But he's unconscious, you idiot! How's he going to back down?!"

"No, he's not ... not really. Just in suspended animation, kinda. Chase told me the incubi here in our compound aren't that stubborn. He'll be fine soon, I'm sure. I'll just go put him in his room so he'll be comfortable while he fights his inner demons. See you at breakfast."

With that, he walked down the hallway, lugging Spike under his arm, Spike's legs dragging and bumping pitifully across the stones behind them.

Tony's head was sticking out of his doorway, turning to watch Spike getting hauled by. "What was *that* all about?" he asked.

I shook my head. "I'll tell you at breakfast. Might as well get dressed and go. I'll be out in ten."

Five minutes later I heard Tony outside my door. I opened it so he could wait inside while I finished getting ready. I just had to put on a little eyeliner and mascara and then I'd be done. I'd just taken the fastest shower in the West, dressing in my standard white tunic and jeans. I glanced at Tony in my mirror to see that he was wearing the same thing as me. I wondered if he'd noticed yet that we were twins.

"I feel kinda funny in these clothes."

"Are you vibing me again?" I asked accusingly.

"Maybe," he said, a little defensively.

"Don't worry about it. Vibing is a fae thing."

"Well, if you remember correctly, I was doing it before I became fae."

"Yeah, well, I've always said you're special." I winked at him in the mirror.

"Do you guys have to be so loud?" grumbled Tim from under his quilt.

"Wake up, sleepy head. Time for breakfast. Gravy train's leaving."

"I'm skipping breakfast."

I pulled back his quilt and flung it on the floor. "No you're not. Get up. I'm leaving in two minutes, and I'm your pack mule."

Tim scowled at me. "Has anyone ever told you how bossy you are?"

"Yeah, anyone who's ever known me. Old news. Totally not interesting at all."

I grabbed the brush out of my top drawer and ran it through my damp hair. "You can brush your teeth after breakfast; come on." I turned my back to Tim and crouched down so he could climb on my shoulder, tossing the brush onto my bed.

I felt his light weight and then a painful tug as he grabbed a tiny fistful of hair.

"*Ouch*, you brat. Not so hard."

"*Thhhppbbbttt.*"

War of the Fae: Book Three

I sighed.

"What did he say?" asked Tony.

"Nothing. He just blew a raspberry at me."

Tony tried to hide his smile.

"Don't laugh. One of these days you'll be on the receiving end of one of his moods and then you'll see how much fun they are."

"Tony's not bossy like you. He's nice."

I shook my head, muttering under my breath. "Tim, I swear to all that is holy ... " We stepped out into the hallway, and I closed the door behind us. "Okay, Tony. Find the dining hall."

"What?"

"You said this place is just a hallway. So ... find the dining hall." I clasped my hands in front of me and twiddled my thumbs, waiting patiently.

Tony looked down the corridor one way and then the other ... and then turned and headed the wrong direction.

I laughed, reaching out to grab his shirt and pull him back. "That's what I thought. This way."

He followed me down the hall until we reached the breakfast room.

"I could have sworn ... "

"Yeah, I know. This place is spelled to confuse the shit out of you." I pulled the door open and entered the still quiet and mostly empty dining hall. "You have to imagine the place you want to be - picture it in your head. You'll notice most of the doors here have a symbol on them. That makes it easier to picture where you want to go. If you know the symbol, you can focus on it in your mind and then you'll end up there. Just start walking and the right door shows up eventually."

"That's cool. But what's the point?" he asked, as we walked over to the buffet.

"To keep the bad guys from getting in and finding their way around."

Tony just looked at me, saying nothing, so I took it upon myself to read his mind.

"Guys like Ben."

Tony rolled his eyes, moving away from me to fill his plate.

I sensed Jared walking up to me before I saw him.

"I think I figured something out," he whispered in my ear. "Sit with me when you're done here."

I quickly filled my plate with fruit and a hard-boiled egg, joining Jared, Finn and Becky at the table. Tony soon followed.

"Spill it." I waited to hear what Jared had to say while I watched Tim walk down my arm to the table where he grabbed some fruit off my plate and started eating.

Jared hunkered down and talked softly. "I decided now would be a good time to work with the elves on doing some team training and recon against the Dark Fae. So I'm going to let the council know that my team of daemons, minus a few changelings like Scrum who will stay back to help out here, are going out into the field for a week-long event. The green elves will join us for part of it."

Finn joined in. "I already talked to Robin. He's good with it."

I nodded. Robin was cool. I knew he'd cover for us.

Jared looked at me. "You think you'll have Chase back in a week?"

"Yes. Unless they run into problems; and if they do, they're supposed to let me know."

Jared nodded. "Okay. It's done then."

"Is the council just going to let you do whatever you want?" asked Becky.

War of the Fae: Book Three

None of us really knew Jared's position here or how much power he wielded, and it seemed rude to ask. Even though he looked like an older teenager, he was really about two hundred years old or something. Whenever there was an assembly he stood behind the council's head table with a couple ogres.

"They trust me to do what's best for our fae family, and that's what I'm doing. Otherwise, this wouldn't be happening at all." He fixed me with a stare, and I knew exactly what he was trying to say.

"Thanks, Jared. Tim and I owe you one."

"Hey!" I heard from the table where Tim was sitting with his strawberry.

"Can it, shrimp."

"What'd he say?" asked Jared.

"He said, 'Tell him I'll give him my new-grown wings later if he wants them.'"

Jared smiled and winked at me. "That's very generous of you, Tim, but it won't be necessary."

Becky giggled at Tim who was stomping around on the table acting all peevish.

The door to the dining hall opened, and I saw Spike and Scrum come in together. Spike's hair looked really messed up but that was normal for him. He was also frowning, though, which wasn't.

"Uh-oh," I said.

"What?" asked Becky.

"Yeah, what's up?" asked Finn, watching me track Spike across the room.

"Spike got a little, uh, frisky this morning and Scrum caught him in the act. It was pretty impressive actually, watching Scrum take him down." I had to give the dork some props. "He threw open the door, issued a warning and then *bam*, pulled Spike into this bearhug of death and knocked his ass out. I mean, like *out* out."

"Well, hot damn," said Finn, his voice full of respect.

"I know," I said, shaking my head slowly, my eyebrows raised. "I wouldn't have believed it if I hadn't seen it with my own eyes."

"Well, good for him," said Becky, smiling like a fool. "He seems really sweet."

"Yeah, but, I don't think Spike's feeling the love right now."

"That's for sure," said Finn, laughing. "Poor guy. He's just tryin' to get some action around here, and he keeps gettin' shot down."

"Oh yeah?" I asked. "Who else is shooting him down?"

Finn shrugged. "Well, you - about a hundred times - Becky, some of the elf chicks I know ..."

I looked at Spike, feeling sorry for him. In the human world, he'd have no trouble at all getting a girl to fall all over him. He was a musician - a good one, in fact. He played guitar in Miami when we first met. He was totally gorgeous in a bad-boy way, which is the best way as far as I was concerned. On top of all that, he was a genuinely nice guy. *So, why did I keep telling him no?*

Spike joined us at the table, slouching over his nearly empty plate.

"Hey, Spike. How're you doing?" I asked tentatively.

"He needs a good pixying," said Tim, giggling.

"Don't even joke about that, you evil runt."

"What'd he say?" asked Finn.

"You don't want to know, trust me."

Spike didn't look up, answering, "I'm fine. Just tired."

"Giving up'll do that to ya," said Scrum as he sat down with us.

Spike scowled but said nothing.

"What did he give up?" asked Becky.

"His will to fight me," said Scrum as if that explained everything.

War of the Fae: Book Three

"I don't get it," said Finn.

"Well," said Scrum excitedly, obviously very happy to be teaching us something, "as a daemon, my job is to protect those who need to be protected - so, like, Jayne for instance. And whenever there's a threat to her safety, I can sense it. So as soon as I get that feeling, I move into action. *Ka-chow!*" And then he did a lame-ass karate chop, slicing the air diagonally in front of him.

I was shaking my head. If I hadn't already seen him 'move into action' I would have laughed my ass off at this point in the story. But he really had put that keg-o-beer body into motion pretty quickly when he needed to. I found myself surprisingly curious about what else he had to say. For some reason the fae didn't get into conversations about each other's race talents or characteristics much, so it was cool when someone revealed something like this. It seemed kind of like a private thing or something, to share too much race stuff. This was not the first time I wished there were some sort of manual that came with this changeling crap.

"Spike was threatening Jayne's safety, even if he or she didn't realize it, so I had to ask him to leave."

This was the part of the story where my face got a little red from embarrassment, and Spike's eyes got a little red from the remembrance.

"He refused to leave, so I had to break his will - his will to resist my orders."

"You mean, everyone has to do what you say? No matter what?" asked Finn, who I could tell was not happy about the idea.

"No, it's not like that. It's just that something inside me tells me when something is right or wrong. And if it's wrong, then my will is going to be stronger than anything else out there. And just like in other parts of life, it's all about the strength of will. A battle of the wills, I guess you could say. The person with the strongest resolve wins. And between a daemon who knows what's right and a guy just ... uh ... you know ... trying to get a little kiss or whatever? Daemons will win every time." He smiled, placing his hands down on the table, looking to each of us for our reactions.

"That's jus' kick butt cool if you ask me," said Finn.

"Chase never told us that stuff before. I'm kinda impressed," said Becky.

"I guess that explains how he's gotten himself hurt so many times so far, since we became changelings," added Finn. "Guy's been shot, pixied ... what's next?"

"Shh!" I whispered. "The pixilation is supposed to be kept on the down-low, dipshit.

"Oh, yeah ... right. My bad. Sorry."

"So what's the deal with that?" asked Scrum. "I heard something about training maneuvers?"

"You're staying here," explained Jared. "The rest of us, minus Brian who will also stay here, are going for a week-long training mission out in the field."

"Who's Brian?" asked Tony.

"You got me," I said.

"He's another daemon changeling," explained Jared.

Scrum looked at me and then Jared. "I understand, Jared. You can count on me."

Jared smiled at Spike. "Yeah. I got that."

Spike looked over and scowled.

"Come on, Spike," I said. "You're not going to be cranky all day, are you?"

He looked at me, refusing to smile. "Yes, I am. Maybe for two days."

"Poor guy needs some loooooove," teased Finn.

War of the Fae: Book Three

Spike raised his eyebrow in challenge. "Better be careful. I'm not discriminating between females and males so much anymore."

Finn got a horrified look on his face. "What? Are you *gay* now?"

Spike laughed; he couldn't help himself. So did Becky and me. It was impossible not to. Even Tim was giggling.

Finn held up his hands in peace, "Not that there's anythin' wrong with bein' gay, don't get me wrong. I'm just askin'."

"No, for your information, I'm not gay. But I can get my needs for energy satisfied by anyone, fae or human, male or female. It's not sex, even though it might feel as good as sex. And eventually I get so hungry, I stop worrying so much about whether the giver is even cute or not. And trust me Finn, you aren't very cute *at all*. Not even a little."

"Well," said a mollified Finn, "that's good news ... that you don't think I'm cute. Not about the gay thing, though. I mean, you can be all broke-back if you wanna be. I don't care. We're friends no matter what."

"I'm not gay."

"Sure, man, whatever you say. I believe you." He turned his head and muttered out of the corner of his mouth, " ... even though you wouldn't catch *me* suckin' no energy outta no *guy*. I don't care how damn hungry I got."

Becky was already giggling but that last comment had her laughing so hard she nearly fell out of her chair. Even Jared was smiling.

Spike threw his fork down. "Oh yeah? Well, just try being an incubus for one day and see how selective you are!"

He stood to go, but I reached out and grabbed his arm.

"Spike, don't go. He's only teasing. I think it sucks that you're kinda like a slave to this need thing. I'd be ... interested in seeing what it's like."

"I'll bet you would," said Finn, teasingly.

"Ooo-hooo," said Becky. "Go for it, Jayne."

"Shut up, you fucknuts. I'm not talking about it like that. I'm just saying ... I don't know ... I'm curious."

Spike got his smile back. "I would be more than happy to indoctrinate you into my world, Jayne. Anytime. You just say the word, and I'll be there." He winked at me, his spirits restored.

"You can count on it." I noticed Scrum getting antsy at the idea, so I added, "And Scrum can supervise."

"Whatever," shrugged Spike. "He can watch if he wants. We can do it fully clothed for all I care - even though ... " he leaned in closer to us and lowered his voice, " ... it's much more fun when you do it naked."

"Oh, geez, Spike ... did ya have to go there? Now I'm gonna have to go wash my eyes out with soap, picturin' you without your clothes on an' with a guy."

"Oh, for shit's sake, Finn, *I'm not gay!*"

We all collapsed in laughter, our worry for Chase temporarily falling away.

"So what are we going to do today?" asked Tony, deliberately changing the subject as part of his constant bid to be the nice guy who worries about other people's feelings and keeps the peace.

"We are going to go talk to Dardennes about you, and then I have to go with Tim to get his blood taken by our healers ... which we have to bring out to the forest for Goose to take back to his lab."

"Who's Goose?" asked Spike.

"Long story ... but he's the guy who's helping fix Chase."

"How come you've got to meet him out in the forest? Sounds like a bad drug deal scene, passing out vials of pixie blood under the cover of trees."

War of the Fae: Book Three

"Just don't say anything to anyone, 'kay? We have to keep this a secret from everyone but us."

"No big deal. I can keep a secret." Spike smiled at me. "Just let me know when you're ready for a test-drive of the Spikester."

Everyone groaned. Test driving the Spikester just sounded so wrong.

"What? She offered! You *know* I'm not going to turn that down."

I stood, motioning for Tony to join me and for Tim to hop on my hand so I could lift him up to my shoulder. "We're outta here. You guys have a good time out in the field. Becky ... see you at lunch?"

"Yep!"

"Save me a seat. I might be late."

"Sure. See you later, tater."

Tony followed me out of the room and towards Dardenne's office. The silver elf hadn't been in the dining hall, so this was the only other place I knew to look for him.

We arrived at the office, and I knocked three times. The door opened to reveal Ivar standing there.

"Is Mr. Dardennes here?" I asked.

"Yes."

"Please show her in," said a female voice from inside.

Chapter Fifteen

I WALKED IN AND SAW that Céline and Niles, the commando dwarf as I liked to call him, were gathered with Dardennes around his desk, looking over what appeared to be a map of the forest. Walking closer, I noticed that it had symbols and markings all over it, but I couldn't see exactly what they were; and some manners learned long ago would not allow me to strain my eyes to get a better look. I wished I could ignore them and act as nosy as I felt, but it just wouldn't happen. *Dammit.*

"Hey, everyone. I think you all know Tony?"

All the heads around the desk nodded. Dardennes smiled.

"Well, anyway, he hasn't heard what race he is yet, so I was wondering what I should do with him today. Can he train with me?"

Céline and Dardennes looked at each other, and Céline gave a slight shrug.

Dardennes answered. "I don't see why not."

Tony and I exchanged smiles before I continued. "I also wanted to know if maybe you thought Tony might be a wrathe?"

Dardennes' eyes opened wider at this question, as did Céline's.

I noticed Niles getting agitated. "What makes you think that?" he asked gruffly.

I shrugged. "I don't know. I don't know much about them, really. But Tony's eyes turned gray after the change, and I heard wrathes have gray eyes."

The three of them and then a fourth, as Ivar walked over to join them, looked closer at Tony's face.

"What color were your eyes before, son?" asked Dardennes.

"Brown."

"Interesting. Tell me ... what other things do you notice that are different about yourself?"

"Well, I'm still able to vibe Jayne; that hasn't changed. But now ... uh ... I'm kinda vibing other people too? I think? And I think I'm hearing voices also. Voices that aren't ... uh ... attached to people."

I looked at Tony in shock. "Why the hell didn't you tell me all this stuff?"

Tony shrugged, looking chagrined. "Sorry. We've just been kinda ... busy. I guess."

I knew better than to ask any more questions. I didn't want Chase mentioned.

"And vibing would mean ... ?" asked Céline.

"Oh, um, it means that I can kinda tell what Jayne's feeling sometimes. Not all the time. And sometimes I know what she's thinking too. Not specific words usually, not details. Just general ideas."

"Hmmm ... " Dardennes crossed his arms and rested his hand on his chin. "Empathic, telepathic maybe ... what do you think?" he asked, turning towards Céline.

"Possibly," she responded, noncommittally.

"He wielded the axe during the test," said Niles.

Tony's weapon that he'd selected during our changeling test was an axe that was similar to a lightsaber, the way it put off blue glowing hums every time he swung it around - at least, when he swung it around provoked and angry. If he moved it when he wasn't mad, it was just a regular axe.

"It's worth a try to send him with Gregale for the day, I think."

"That's a great idea," I said enthusiastically.

Dardennes lifted an eyebrow at me.

"Uhh, if my opinion counts for anything, that is." One of these days I might finally figure out that not everyone was interested in my thoughts on everything. Maybe. But then again, probably not.

"We value your opinion, Jayne. We value all of the changelings' opinions," said Céline. "We have as much to learn from you as you do from us."

"Ain't that the truth," I said, snorting.

Niles frowned at me again. He was grouchy all the time, so it didn't bother me at all. Tony was looking a little worried though, so I nudged him in the arm. "Don't worry. Gregale's cool. He's the one who took me to see you in the Gray."

"Exactly," said Dardennes. "If Tony is a wrathe, he will need to be intimately familiar with the techniques of getting into and out of the Gray."

"We don't need to lose another ... "

"That will be enough, Niles," said Dardennes, cutting him off deliberately. "Would you please show this young fae where he can find Gregale?"

Niles nodded, scowling, immediately moving from behind the desk and heading towards the door.

Tony looked at me, and I could tell from his expression that he was thinking the same thing I was: *Who had gotten lost and where?*

"I'll see you later, Tones. I've gotta ... do something, so ... see you at lunch ."

Tony squeezed my hand before following Niles out of the room. I watched him disappear through the door, a little piece of my heart going out with him. It was like he was my kid brother going to his first day of kindergarten or something. I shook my head to get it back on this planet.

"Where are you going today, Jayne?" asked Céline.

"I have to go to see the healers, and then I'm gonna go work with Gregale and Tony."

"Why are you going to the healers? Are you not feeling well?"

"Oh, no, I'm fine. It's Tim. He's got this wing thing," I explained, being as vague as possible.

"And how are you feeling, Tim?" asked Céline politely.

"I'm in immense pain, and I feel like pixying the lot of you," he answered in his grumpy voice.

"He says he's getting better and thank you for asking," I said.

Dardennes smiled but said nothing.

"That's good to hear. Well, good luck. Please let us know how Tony is getting along, won't you?" Céline asked.

"Sure. No prob." I turned, hurrying out of the room. "Talk to you later."

I closed the door behind me, imagining the clinic in my mind since that was the only place I knew that had healers. It was where Chase had gone when he was shot with the arrow. I had no idea how long it would take to get a pixie blood sample, but it couldn't be an easy process. Tim's veins had to be as thin as a human hair.

We arrived in no time, and I approached the first fae I saw. "Excuse me, but I need to get a blood sample from this pixie." I jerked my thumb towards my shoulder. "Can you tell me where to go for that?"

The guy's eyebrows screwed up in confusion. "You want a what, from a *what?*"

I sighed. I hated repeating myself when I knew I had been perfectly clear the first time. "I need a *blood* sample to be taken from this *pixie* on my *shoulder*. Who does that around here?"

"Uh, I do. I guess. But it's not the easiest thing in the world to do ... "

"Yeah, I figured. So ... where do you want us?"

He hesitated for a second before saying, "Go over to that exam table over there and someone will be right with you."

Huh. That seemed easy enough. Back home I would have needed a referral from my primary care doctor, an insurance card indicating my parents paid a hefty monthly sum for the privilege of having said card, a checkbook ... *You gotta love socialized fae medicine.*

Tim climbed down from my shoulder, using my hand as his delivery vehicle to get him to the white paper stretched out across the exam table. His little feet crinkled it up as he paced back and forth on top. He was muttering under his breath as he walked, but not loud enough for even me to hear what he was saying.

I was pretty sure he knew better than to complain to me. I tried not to feel too much pity for his little wing stumps, one of which was still a little blackened. I needed to harden my heart against his evil pixie manipulations. He could be very convincing when he wanted to be, and I needed that blood sample, no matter what.

A healer arrived at the table - a different one than the one who greeted us. This one looked older.

"Did I hear correctly that you want a blood sample taken from this pixie?"

"Yes, you did."

"I'm sorry, but may I ask what you need it for?"

"No, you may not." *There.* We'll see if the intimidation factor was going to work with this guy.

He visibly stiffened. "Well then, I'm afraid we cannot help you."

"Can't or won't?" I asked angrily. I should have known it wasn't going to be easy.

"Well, I suppose I should have said, 'won't'."

"Why?"

"I should think that would be fairly obvious."

"Well, obviously it's *not*, or I wouldn't be asking." I was rapidly losing my cool.

"Jayne, you may want to chill a little," warned Tim.

"Perhaps I should call someone on the council to discuss this matter. Collecting pixie blood is not something to be taken lightly," said the uptight fae, turning to leave.

I grabbed his arm. "No, don't bother. I'll tell you why we need it - it's not like it's a big deal or anything." I tried to brush it all off, hoping he'd buy it.

"I'm all ears," he said sarcastically.

"I'm going to see the witch, Maggie. She needs the blood for a remedy for the pixie's wing. As you can see he ran into a little problem." I gestured to his back, and Tim was good enough to hunch himself over to display his horrible stubs. "Her methods of getting blood are ... uh ... well, a little violent. So I'm coming to you so that the pixie won't be abused. I know you guys are, like, top notch and all."

"Well, that's a different matter, then." He smiled under the compliment. "See? It wasn't so difficult to answer a simple question, was it?"

I held back my honest retort and just smiled sweetly instead. I didn't trust myself to speak - copious amounts of cuss words were sure to be involved.

"Wait one moment, and I'll get the spike."

War of the Fae: Book Three

Spike?

Tim's pacing increased, and his muttering got loud enough that I could hear it. " ... Just pixie one fae, *one fae*, and everyone gets freaked out. It's just a little unbridled happiness. Why is everyone so down on happiness these days? Chase was boring anyway. All he ever did was look at you. Never said a word. Probably never smiled in his whole life. Now look at him. Happy! Happy, and everyone's all upset ... " and on and on it went until the healer returned. I tried to block out Tim's rants because I didn't altogether disagree with him. A lot of fae could use a little more merriment in their lives from what I'd seen. Drop dead with delirium merriment? ... No. But a little dance now and again and some laughs? Yes.

The healer was standing next to the table with his two hands held out, his thumb and forefinger of each hand pinched together, as if he was about to sit down, cross his legs and do some meditation, mumbling some crazy shit like 'ohm' or whatever. He also had a giant band around his head with some goggles attached to it.

"Let's get started, shall we?" he asked, all smiles now.

He used the back of his hands to pull the goggles down in front of his eyes, looking over at me when he was done.

I burst out laughing, unable to help myself. The goggles were some kind of magnifier, but one like I'd never seen before. His eyes were no lie, the size of dinner plates.

He waited patiently for me to calm down.

"I'll bet you could see a pimple on a pixie's ass with those things on," I said.

"Precisely," he said, all business now. "Could you please hold him down on the table so I can prick a vein?"

I looked at him dubiously. "You're gonna prick his vein? With what?"

"With this." He held up one of his hands that was still in a position like he was about to take a hit off a skinny joint.

"Your invisible spliff?"

"No. The spike I'm holding in my hand. You can't see it without the magnifiers on. It's very thin."

"Oooooh, I get it." I squinted my eyes and thought I maybe caught a glimpse of something. It looked like the finest wisp of a spider's web, but stiff.

Out of the corner of my eye I saw Tim start to run. I could hear the paper crinkling with each little step.

"Oh, no you don't, you little bastard. Get back here."

I snagged him and held him up to my face.

He was fuming. "I don't want to do it! I change my mind!"

I turned around so my back was to the healer, whispering fiercely, "Then I change my mind about pixie colonies!" I had to play it tough with him, or we were going to be here a long time, and it wasn't going to be pretty. Plus, this healer guy was no dummy. He wouldn't stick around to be pixied if he thought there was a chance it might happen.

"You *wouldn't!*" Tim shouted, angry tears glistening in his eyes.

"I would; trust me, little man. Friends help friends. Friends undo their *mistakes*." I turned back towards the healer, my eyebrow raised at Tim, giving him as meaningful a look as I could, while also trying not to arouse the healer's suspicions.

"Fine! But then I'm done helping."

"You're done when it's done and that's it. Now enough of your bullshit. Lie down on the table and man up."

"I'm not a *man*. I'm a *pixie!*" he screeched.

"Well, then, *pixie up*, you little shit."

I could see the healer trying not to smile. I shot him a warning look, knowing full well that if Tim saw us laughing at him, I'd have to start all over with trying to get him to cooperate.

Tim lay down on the table, crossing his arms and pouting.

"Where are you going to stick him?"

"The leg is best. Or the forehead."

I looked at him, aghast. No way was I letting him put that thing near Tim's forehead. One slip and Tim would be blinded or lobotomized or something. "Let's go with the leg." I looked at Tim. "I'm gonna hold you down. Don't you get all feisty on me."

He just glared in response.

I waited until Tim pulled his pants down and laid back, his tunic still covering his nether regions, thank goodness. I gently put my forefinger from one hand across his lower legs and my other forefinger across his chest, over his crossed arms that he refused to move.

The healer leaned over with his giant goggles, and I moved as far to the side as I could, to give him room. He lowered his fingers with the spike in it. I could tell when he touched Tim with it because Tim flinched. And yelled.

"*Ow!* Watch it buddy. Get that thing any higher, and I'm gonna *dust* your ugly ass!"

"Tim says to please not go any higher."

"Tell him the dusting his ugly ass part, Jayne. Tell him."

"No."

"*No* what?" asked the doctor, focusing on his blood-letting.

"Nothing. How's it going?"

"Well." He lifted his hand with the spike out of the way. "So far, so good. Now for the collection."

He lowered his other spliff-positioned fingers from the other hand down towards Tim's leg.

"What are you doing now?"

"I'm collecting his blood in this pipette."

"What the hell is a pipette?"

"In layfae's terms, it's a small glass tube that has a natural vacuum action to it that draws the blood up and into the tube. I'm placing it on the small pool of blood on the pixie's leg, so the blood will go into our tube here. You will take this tube to the witch when I am done."

"How am I going to do that when I can't even see it?"

"I have a carrying case for you to transport it in. The blood will not last long. You must move quickly."

"Oh." I looked down at Tim, who he seemed to be holding up well. He wasn't struggling anymore, although he still looked very grouchy.

The healer stood up, holding the pipette out in front of his goggles. "Very nice. That went better than expected."

"It did? I guess that's good."

"Yes, you never can tell with these tiny veins. But he's a tough one. He'll be just fine. Have him put a little pressure on that spot, will you? Here's some gauze."

He handed me a small gauze packet from his coat pocket. It was about the size of half of Tim's entire body.

I unwrapped it and handed it to Tim, watching as he took it and placed it on his legs. I ignored his renewed grumbling and bitching.

The healer walked away to prepare for the transportation of the blood. I tried not to laugh as he bumped into two tables on his way out, still wearing the goggles.

I looked down at my friend again. "Thanks, Tim."

"Whatever."

"You know, I've never mentioned this, but I've noticed that you speak kinda more modern than the other fae, if you know what I mean. How come?"

War of the Fae: Book Three

"Because I've been around."

"What does that mean?"

"It means that I haven't lived my whole life in the Green Forest, *if you must know.*"

"I don't *have* to know, but I want to. Where have you lived?"

"Around."

"Okay, you're obviously still pissed at me. I get it. Maybe when you cool down you can tell me."

Tim chose that moment to fart, so I decided to stop trying to engage him in any conversation.

The healer came back with a long, thin box. "The blood is in here. You have about an hour or so before it will no longer be useful to the witch."

"Thanks," I said, grabbing it from him, putting Tim on my shoulder, and heading out the door.

"Sorry if I jiggle you too much, Tim, but we gotta hurry."

I rushed down the corridor as fast as I could, picturing in my mind the door that we had gone through with Chase just the night before.

Soon we were out in the Green Forest, near the meadow that Chase had danced in. It was then that I realized I was probably going to be really early and Goose wouldn't be there yet. The blood was going to go bad before he arrived.

I stomped my way through the flowers and then into the forest on the other side of it. I was headed back to the big tree where I'd tried to heal Chase, cussing the entire way.

"Motherfucker, bastard, shitballs, dickbag, fuckhat, ass wanker ... !"

"Jayne!" yelled Tim.

"What?!"

"Are you praying or what?"

"What the hell is that supposed to mean?"

He giggled. "I don't know. I figured a girl like you maybe said her prayers like that."

"You know ... I could send you across this entire meadow with one flick of my finger, buttwad."

"Oooh, that's another good one. Buttwad. I wish I had a pen. I'm learning so much today."

"Yeah, me too. Like how scrawny and pale your legs are."

I heard a little responding sound.

"Fart on my shoulder one more time and you're going to ride on the top of my shoe from now on."

"I have a digestive problem. It's a handicap. You shouldn't bring it up."

"Handicap, my ass. Try eating something other than fruit."

"I have. It gets worse."

"Okay, fine. Stick to the fruit. Not to change the subject or anything because you know how much I like to hear about your intestinal problems, but do you know how to call that Goose guy? I don't want this blood to go bad."

"No way. I'm no Gray walker."

"You make that sound as if being one is a bad thing."

"Well, duh, it is."

My concern about getting the pixie blood to Goose in time was now overshadowed by my worry for Tony. "Why?"

"Too many fae have gotten lost in there. No-thank-you. I prefer the light of day."

"How do they get lost?"

"Dunno. They just do. I never go in there. The Gray is not a good place for pixies. The spirits and fae who inhabit that place are in bad need of pixying, and they know it. They see a pixie and *whammo*, it's all over. Pixie squish."

"Pixie squish?"

"Yes. It's not pretty, believe me."

We reached the old tree that now showed no signs of having been Chase's hitching post.

"So what the hell am I supposed to do now?"

"Wait?"

"Yes, thanks, that's helpful." *Pain in the ass pixie.*

All I could hear was the sound of birds chirping and the breeze gently blowing through the leaves in the trees. I smiled despite my worries. It really was a beautiful place here, wherever we were. We sat there for what seemed like hours just chatting.

"Tim?"

"Yeah?"

"Where are we?"

"Uh ... is this a trick question? ... We're in the Green Forest."

"Yeah, I know that. But where is the Green Forest? Like what country?"

"You mean on one of the human maps?"

"Yeah."

"France."

"I *knew* it!"

"How'd you know it?"

I shrugged. "I don't know. Travel times. Computer." I'd used the computer room at the compound several times when Tony and I were separated. At some point I'd seen a website identifying my computer's IP address as being in France or Europe.

"So where in France are we exactly?"

"Ardennes."

"Is that like a town or something?"

"No. It's a department. A region."

"Oh." I wished I'd paid better attention in geography class. Surely a review of France had been in there somewhere. Maybe back in sixth grade. Then it struck me how similar that name sounded to our mysterious and fearless leader's.

"Sounds like Dardennes. Is that a coincidence?"

"No. Dardennes means 'from Ardennes'. The 'D' used to have an apostrophe after it. It's French. Lots of us are actually from Ardennes, but we don't usually bother with last names like the humans do. Most of us anyway."

I looked up through the trees, trying to gauge what time it was by the position of the sun. I gave up, since I pretty much suck at any type of navigation.

"We are totally screwed. What am I going to do about Chase?" I was trying not to stress too much, but I was losing the battle. I felt tears of frustration prick my eyes.

"Shh!" whispered Tim in my ear, suddenly grabbing a handful of my hair.

"Ouch. What?" I whispered back.

"Quick! Hide!"

I didn't question him; I just followed his order. I ran behind the big tree, to the side opposite of where we were.

"What is it?" I asked as quietly as I could.

"Shhh," was his only response. I could feel his tiny body trembling on my shoulder as he moved sideways to get deeper into my hair.

Sounds of movement through the underbrush deeper in the trees caught my attention. I strained my eyes to see what it was, but it was too dark where the sound was coming from.

War of the Fae: Book Three

I found out soon enough, though, that I didn't need to see who was coming. I could smell them. It was like the stench of rotten meat and horrifically smelly feet all mixed together.

A group of four orcs walked up to the spot near the tree where we'd just been standing.

Chapter Sixteen

I TRIED NOT TO MAKE a sound, reaching out with my mind to tap into The Green. Whatever was going to happen, I wanted that safety net there for Tim and me. I lowered my hand down slowly and pulled Blackie out of its sheath at my leg. It could make even the biggest orc sizzle with dragonfire if need be. *Holy shit,* how I hoped it wouldn't come to that. I was terrible at math, but even I knew that four against one were pretty bad odds.

This was one of those times I wished I had telepathy like the green elves did. I'd be telepathying my ass off to everyone I knew right now. *Help me! Save my ass before it gets eaten!* But for now, all I had was my Earth power and my dragon tooth. I didn't know if pixeying worked on orcs, but I was afraid that if I let Tim unleash *I'd* accidentally get pixied - and that would suck more than being molested by an orc in the long run. And it was also quite possible that a dancing, singing orc was so fundamentally wrong it could somehow throw off the balance of the Earth's rotation and end the world as we knew it. So I decided against considering Tim's help as a possible solution. I was hoping he had followed the same path of reason that I had so he wouldn't take it upon himself to jump out and 'help' me. Maybe, hopefully, his impetuous pixelation of Chase had taught him it was a bad idea to pixie in the presence of friends.

The orcs were grunting to one another, moving closer to my hiding spot. One of them was sniffing the air like a hunting dog. As they got nearer, I took a tentative step to the side, thinking if I could just keep the tree between them and me, they'd never see me and we'd be safe. Unfortunately, I stepped on a dry twig that snapped loud enough to sound unnatural and catch their attention.

Four ugly, black, lumpy heads turned simultaneously in my direction. The chorus of roars and grunts told me, even though I don't speak a word of orcan, that I'd been discovered. I quickly ran around the tree, trying to get back to the more open space where I'd had the conversation with Goose last night. I needed more room to maneuver.

These orcs were faster than the ones I'd dealt with the last time during my changeling test. I had just enough time to get in place with my legs spread wide in fighting stance before they rushed me.

In the instant before they reached me, I thought how totally bogus it was that in the movies whenever the group of bad guys is attacking, they did it one at a time, giving the attackee time to kick each of their asses individually. These orcs obviously hadn't gone to any bad guy school of etiquette, or the movies much, because they were all on me at once in two seconds, like flies on shit - me being the shit, of course.

I swung Blackie out in a wide arc, zero finesse to the move and absolute desperation as my guide. I heard and smelled the sizzle of their black skin as it made contact and burned them with a surge of dragonfire. I was pretty sure I learned the orcan word for *sonofabitch* right then. And then something passed between them that sounded like: '(Roar!) Fargar garnah! (more roars!) Garnah bartor! (more roars!) Loosely translated, I was fairly certain it meant "*Sonofabitch! That bitch has a weapon!*"

War of the Fae: Book Three

They fell back, cursing in orcan and looking down in surprise at their injuries that were now oozing tarry, black orc blood.

"Jayne, run!" yelled Tim.

I didn't wait around to see what else they were going to do; instead, I took Tim's wise advice, running a wide circle around them and then hauling ass back to the meadow.

Please don't be following me, please don't be following me, please don't be following me, I chanted as I ran. It didn't take long before I was out of breath. *Mental note: add daily aerobics to training regimen.*

Then I remembered Tim's blood in the box I'd stuffed in my tunic belt. *"Double fuck!"* I yelled out into the air around me, slowing down to a stop.

"Do I even want to know what that's for?" asked Tim in a trembling voice.

"You're still there? Good."

"Yeah, I'm still here ... hanging on for dear life. I have never missed my wings so much in all my pixie years."

"I hear ya. I think we lost 'em - but I need to go back."

"What?! Are you *nuts?* No way. Just leave me here."

"In the meadow? Where a groundhog could eat you? No, not a good idea."

"Better a groundhog than an orc. Do you know what orcs do to pixies?"

"Shove a stick down their throats and out their assholes and hang 'em over a fire?" I'd actually seen this done to a dwarf by orcs, so I wasn't being sarcastic for once in my life.

"Yeah, if you're lucky. Otherwise, they pick your appendages off one at a time and eat them while you watch."

I shivered in revulsion. Orcs were some nastyass shit. "But I have to get this blood to Goose. Chase is going to be a mental case forever if I don't, and I can't let that happen. Even if I have to kiss an orc on his slimey lips, this needs to get done."

Tim was silent for a few seconds. I turned to go back as he spoke again.

"Fine. But don't just go walking in there. Sneak back in."

"Yeah, okay, sure. But I'm not the best sneaker in the world."

"Don't I know it," said Tim under his breath.

"I heard that. Just tell me what to do or shut up. Either one is fine with me." I picked my way across the meadow, knowing I needed to hurry up, but unable to bring myself to run back towards the orcs. It just seemed all kinds of wrong - must have been my natural instincts kicking in.

"Okay, see that tree on the right? Go there and stand behind it and wait a couple seconds ... listen for orc sounds."

"Or smells."

"Yeah, that too."

I did as I was told, hearing and smelling nothing.

"Now go to that one over on the left ... the one with the low branch hanging down. Do the same thing."

And so we carried on like this for the next fifteen minutes, Tim giving me sneaking instructions, and me trying not to sound like an elephant thundering through the trees. I wasn't sure why I tried so hard; it wasn't like the orcs weren't loud and obvious themselves. The only reason they'd caught me before was because one of them got a whiff of me and got close enough to hear me being stupid. Probably it was Tim they'd smelled. He did have that gas problem after all.

We eventually reached the scene of my orc ass whoopin', but they were gone, just a few puddles of smoking black ooze on the ground marking the scene of the crime.

It felt like it had to be closer to lunchtime by now. I looked around nervously for Goose. As if answering my prayers, I heard his voice come out of the Gray.

"Hello, Jayne. I'm glad to see you here. You're early."

"Yeah, well, not early enough. I got this blood over an hour ago, and the guy at the clinic told me it was only good for an hour."

Goose's faint image appeared before me, eventually becoming whole and no longer see-through. "We will do what we can with what you have brought," he said, holding out his hand.

I reached into my tunic belt and pulled out the box with the pipette in it. "There's this glass tubey thing in here with the pixie's blood in it. I can't even see it. I hope you have some of those fish-eye magnifier glasses that our guy had."

"Do not concern yourself; we have everything we need. I do not know if this will work for our treatment, since as you said the blood is no longer fresh, but we will do what we can. Thank you. I will see you back here in a week then?"

"Yeah. And by the way, if you could *not* send an orc welcoming party next time, that would be great."

"What do you mean?" he asked, a quizzical look on his face.

"The orcs? The smelly, black, lumpy, evil fuckers?"

"Sorry, I do not follow." He cocked his head, examining me as if trying to decide if I was crazy.

"You seriously don't know?"

"No, I am truly sorry. Perhaps it is the stress of your friend being injured that has caused you some ... disorientation."

"Never mind. Just watch your back. There are orcs in this forest."

He laughed in a patient way. "That is not possible."

"Uh, yeah it is."

"The orc are from the Underworld, not the Here and Now."

"Underworld, smunderworld. They're here; I burned 'em, now

they're gone. Look at the blood." I pointed to the ground where there were now just a few scorched areas. *Shit.* I forgot that their blood was like acid and did eventually burn off.

Goose raised an eyebrow at me. "Yes. Well. One week." And then he faded into nothingness again.

Damn Gray walkers. "Come on, Tim. Let's go eat lunch."

"I've lost my appetite."

"Well, then, you can just watch me eat."

"That'll just make it worse."

I broke into a jog, just to piss him off. He held onto my hair extra tight, so I wasn't sure who was torturing who at that point, but we got to the compound in record time. We met Becky and Scrum at the lunch buffet as they were lining up to get their food. I noticed Scrum already had a pile of wiggly meat on his plate, making me think it must be a daemon thing to eat that disgusting crap. I preferred my meat to be good and dead when I ate it.

"So, what happened? Everything go okay?" asked Becky.

"You had trouble, didn't you?" asked Scrum quietly.

"Yeah, you could say that."

"I *knew* it. I could feel it. I should have gone with you. If something had happened to you when I was supposed to be keeping an eye on you ... I don't know what they'd do to me." He was sweating bullets.

"Don't worry, I'm taking you next time. Trust me ... I don't want to be orc food."

Becky's eyes nearly bugged out of her head. "Orcs? You saw *orcs* out there?"

"Shhh! We don't need the entire council on my ass, Beck."

"Oh, yeah," she whispered. "Sorry."

We went and sat at our table. "So, to answer your question, yes -

there were four orcs there. They just stumbled across me. Tim's gas problems gave us away."

"Hey! No way are you putting this one on me!" he yelled from my shoulder.

"Tim has gas problems?" asked Scrum, confused.

"Yep. Farts aaaaall the time," I said, smiling.

I should have known what Tim's response was going to be.

"That's it, punk!" I said disgustedly. "You're on my shoe for the rest of the day. I warned you."

"What did he do?" asked Becky, innocently.

I stared at her meaningfully and then rolled my eyes.

"Oh. Geez. I'm *really* glad I can't hear him."

"Tell me about it."

Tim ignored me, climbing down my arm to get to my plate where a nice, fat grape waited for him. I especially liked it when he ate one of those. He was hilarious, trying to break through the skin while also trying not to get soaked with juice. It was nice, relaxing here like this with my friends and being entertained by a dipshit pixie - way better than fighting creatures out in our forest who belonged in the Underworld.

Tony showed up then, entering the room behind Gregale, a huge grin on his face. He nodded at us before grabbing a plate at the end of the buffet line and filling it up. When he was done, he joined us at the table. Spike sauntered through the door that came from the direction of the dorm rooms and joined us too, skipping the buffet entirely. He looked terrible. His face was pale and drawn, and he had dark circles under his eyes.

"Spike, you look like shit."

"Thank *you*, Jayne," he said, cocking and shooting an imaginary gun at me before putting his head down in his arms on the table. All we could see was the back of his head.

"What's wrong you, Spike?" asked Becky, her face full of concern.

"Hungry."

"Go get some food."

"Not hungry for food," he mumbled.

Becky looked at me, pulling her lips back in a grimace. Then she looked back at him. "Oh. Sorry." She put her eyes down and focused on eating her food.

I made my decision and spoke up before I could chicken out and change my mind. "Spike, after lunch, you and me, my room." I looked over at Scrum. "You too, Scabs."

Scrum smiled. "It's Scrum, not Scabs. And okay. I can supervise."

"Sounds kinda kinky," said Becky, smiling devilishly.

Spike mumbled from his arms. "Never mind, Jayne. I don't need your pity."

"It's not pity. I want to do it. I'm curious, remember?"

Spike lifted his head to look at me. "Seriously?"

"Seriously."

A big grin broke out across his formerly pitiful but now slightly rejuvenated face. "Well, aaaall riiiight."

Tony ducked his head and smiled.

"What're you grinnin' at?" I asked, nudging him.

"Nothin'."

"What'd you do today, Tony?" asked Becky. "Did you find out what race you are?"

"Yep. I'm a wrathe for sure."

"That's cool!" said Scrum enthusiastically. "What can you do? I've never heard of a wrathe. I mean, not even before becoming a changeling. I've heard of elves and pixies and stuff, but wrathes? No.

Not once."

"Would you shut up and give him a chance to talk?" I asked.

"Oh, yeah, sorry." He motioned zipping his lips shut, but I knew it wasn't going to last.

"Gregale's cool. Smart too. He showed me how to get into and out of the Gray. We went all over the place."

"What did he think of your vibing stuff?"

Tony smiled, shrugging his shoulders. "He might have been a little jealous and impressed."

"Vibed his ass, didn't you?" I was so proud of him, giving old Gregale a run for his money.

"Yep. He was surprised. None of the other fae in the compound are empaths."

"What's an empath?" asked Becky.

"Someone who can sense other people's emotions. Kind of like having empathy for them, but at a much deeper level."

"Wow. So can you feel me now?"

"If I focus on it. I used to be able to do this a little before I was made a changeling. Now I can do it with more people and at longer distances. The trick is going to be learning how to focus in on which person I want to read. Sometimes when I'm in a place with lots of people it gets all jumbled up."

"That would get me all discombobulated, I think," said Scrum. "Like, how do you know it's not your feelings you're feeling, you know?"

"It's not the same as my own emotions. Mine are attached to my mind and my heart or something. Everyone's feelings have their own signature. I can tell Jayne's from a mile away."

Spike lifted his chin a little higher, cocking his head to the side and fixing Tony with a red-eyed stare. "What's she feeling now?"

Tony smiled, his face blushing a rosy pink. "I'll let you figure that out."

I smacked Tony on the arm. "That's enough of that talk. I'm hungry; shut up and eat."

Spike winked at me before getting up to leave. "See you in your room, Jayne. I'm going to go lie down and wait for you."

I nodded, saying nothing, trying to ignore Becky kicking me under the table and giggling.

"Sorry, Becky," said Spike as he stood. "I'd tell you to come along, too, but I wouldn't want Finn to get jealous."

She looked up at him and then me, panic in her eyes. "What's that supposed to mean?"

I snickered around the forkful of food I'd just stuffed in my mouth.

"What are you laughing at?"

"Oh, nothing," I said with feigned innocence. She thought she was so cool, but her crush on our green elf friend was totally obvious. Probably the only one who didn't notice it was Finn himself. I put that down not to lack of interest, but to the fact that he was a redneck, and Becky probably didn't know how to perform the redneck mating ritual. I was pretty sure it was something like taking a sexy swig from a beer bottle or something ... or maybe shooting an animal in the forest with a single shot from a crossbow.

"If you're suggesting that I ... and that Finn ... well, you're crazy," she pooh-poohed, overly much. "It's not like that at all. I mean, he's cute and nice, but we're just friends."

"Yep. Whatever you say, Becks. We all believe you."

She sighed heavily at me, trying not to smile. She was attempting to be all firm about it but her carefree attitude made it impossible.

"You water sprites are not tough, like *at all*, did you know that?"

War of the Fae: Book Three

She stuck her chin out. "We can be tough when we want to be."

I scoffed. *Right*. None of them were more then four feet ten. Becky was nearly the biggest one in the whole compound.

Without any warning at all she smacked me on the arm. Before I even had a chance to react, she disappeared, only to reappear on my other side and smack me on the other arm. I turned to grab her, but she disappeared again, appearing on the other side to smack me on the head. I whipped around to grab her but she slipped out of the air once more. I turned immediately, guessing her plan to keep going back and forth, but she was one step ahead of me, appearing again where she had just been, smacking me on the side of the head - this time pretty hard.

I yelled in frustration. "Fine! *Uncle!* Water sprites can kick ass whenever they want!" I was ducking under my arms, trying to protect myself from her next onslaught.

She appeared again to sit in her chair and calmly said, "I'm glad we got that little racial profiling issue straightened out."

Scrum, who had been watching us with a stunned expression on his face, started giggling, and was soon joined by Tony. I scowled at them, but it only made them laugh harder. Tim joined in until he swallowed a piece of grape the wrong way and started choking. I tried to help him by thumping him on the back with a flick of my finger, but it sent him across the table, which made Scrum and Tony nearly screech with renewed laughter. Scrum pushed himself back from the table, and his chair caught in the floor, sending him over backwards to land on the ground - and that was the end of it for Tony and Becky. I wouldn't have been surprised if they peed their pants.

"Come on, Tim. This place is full of juveniles. Let's go."

He crawled across the table on his hands and knees to climb up into my hand and lie on his back, gasping for air. I wasn't not sure if his inability to walk was from the laughing or the failed pixie Heimlich I had given him. Either way, he was getting no pity from me.

"I'll see you dipshits at dinner."

Tony and Becky continued to laugh as they watched Scrum climb up from the floor and follow me out, holding his sides as if he were in pain. The other changelings in the room watched us go out, confusion on their faces. I ignored all of them, refusing to let the grin that was nearly bursting me apart come to the surface. I had an incubus to satisfy, and I had a feeling I was going to need all my strength for this little exercise.

Chapter Seventeen

I OPENED THE DOOR OF my room to find Spike lying on my bed, his hands laced behind his head. His shirt was already off, in a heap on my floor. And *damn*, he looked good. I never thought of myself as much of a tattoo lover. I like one here or there on an arm or a back, but usually not the ones that were all over; but Spike was the exception to that rule. His went from wrist to neck to waist and they suited him perfectly. As I got closer I saw that one of them was a dragon, and that the dragon's mouth was open. It had black teeth.

"Spike, when did you get that tattoo?" I walked closer and pointed to the dragon that wrapped around his arm and across his shoulder, its head ending up on his right chest muscle.

He looked down, raising his eyebrow as he focused in on it. "Few years ago." He took my hand, the one that was pointing to the tattoo, and laced our fingers loosely together. "Why do you ask?"

I reached down and pulled Blackie from its sheath, holding it up for him to see. "Because this is a dragon fang, and it's the only black one around ... or it's one of a pair that is the only black pair around. It's just kinda funny that your dragon has black teeth too."

Spike shrugged. "What other color would they be?"

"Good question."

An awkward silence settled over the room, the only sound being the one made by Blackie sliding back into its holder. I wasn't sure what the proper etiquette was for an incubus feeding or if there even was any. Last time I saw one take place was when Chase got attacked in the forest during our changeling test, and the guy had bitten him on the neck kinda like a vampire but without the actual sucking or drinking of the blood. I wasn't sure I was on board for the biting part.

Scrum cleared his throat, and Tim giggled on my shoulder.

"Alright, first thing's first. Tim, you're going to your room."

I released Spike's hand and walked over, putting my arm on the dresser so Tim could walk down and go to his bed. He had some tiny books sitting on his side table that Netter, our brownie, had procured for him, that he could read while we were doing this incubus thing. I didn't bother to speculate about how Netter had found them or how anyone could even make a book that tiny. I couldn't even see the words.

"I'll just take a seat on the floor over here," said Scrum. "I promise I won't interfere, so long as you don't hurt her."

The red glow in Spike's eyes flared up. "Don't worry. I have no intention of hurting her."

"Yeah, well, even so. I'm not so sure that you can control yourself very well yet, so be aware that if you go too far, I'm going to crash your little party and break your will again."

Spike rolled his eyes. "I hear you loud and clear, don't worry."

"Scrum, turn so you're facing the wall," I said. Even though Spike and I weren't having sex, the idea of someone else watching him feed on me was just a little too kinky for my taste. "Tim, you too. Turn the other way."

"It's my room too, you know!"

"Tim!"

War of the Fae: Book Three

"Fine." I watched him lie down on his bed, his back facing us. His wing nub was still black, but maybe just a little less so, which made me smile.

Spike looked at me, amusement and hunger in his eyes. "Are you happy now?"

"Yes. For now."

"Come on over here and lay next to me on the bed."

I looked at him suspiciously. "I didn't sign up for anything but a feeding, you know."

Spike rolled his eyes. "Yeah, yeah, I know. It's just more comfortable if you relax. Don't worry ... you have your pit bull over there to make sure I don't go too far."

"And no biting."

"Deal. No biting, I promise."

I stood there, not sure what to do until he looked up at me with his pleading eyes and earnest, pale face. "Please?"

"Okaaay." I laid down on the bed, stretching out next to him so we were face to face, each of us on our sides.

"What do I need to do?" I asked quietly. I was really wishing Tim and Scrum weren't in the room. This seemed like it should be done in private - like, really private, not semi-private.

"Just relax and look into my eyes."

That wasn't a hard instruction to follow. The amber and red colors swirling around were drawing me in, and my gaze locked on without me even thinking about resisting. My mind slipped away a little as I watched the amber and red change to red and black, the dark wisps of smoke tangling around the waves of red. It was almost as if the colors were ghosts or spirits, dancing around in his eyes, beckoning me to join them. I couldn't tell if they were flaming spirits dancing in black smoke or black spirits dancing in flames. My body was getting warm all over, especially in certain places, which made this seem like more than just a basic feeding.

"Spike?" I asked, breathlessly.

"Shhh, it's fine. I'm going to start now. Just relax."

The last letter of that word 'relax' dragged out in my mind as a silky, slithering *sssssssss* that made me feel like I was both drifting off to sleep and falling from a great height at the same time. I couldn't feel my physical body anymore. The colors in his eyes grew larger, encompassing my entire visual field, so that now I was inside this red and black world, floating, feeling nothing but warmth and an electric edge of sexual energy. I closed my eyes, and at the same moment, we kissed. Tentatively at first and then more deeply. The visions I had been watching in his eyes stayed alive in my mind.

I soon became aware of another sensation, coming from the core of my body. A gentle tugging that felt neither uncomfortable nor particularly pleasant. It was just a pulling of sorts. The swirling reds and blacks held my entire attention, tricking me with their forms converging and then disappearing to turn into something else an instant later. I found myself mesmerized by the visuals and ignoring the sensation of something leaving me. The kissing was effortless and consuming, enhancing the strange feelings that were threatening to take me over. Whatever they were, I didn't care. I just wanted to figure out what these beings in the swirls were. Why were they trying to hide from me? Who or what were they? The heat generated from kissing Spike's lips and his tongue that danced with mine overtook me.

I was distantly aware of a hand touching my waist, stroking up my back. It blazed a trail of heat that seeped into my bones. I moved languidly in response. I couldn't control that anymore than I could stop the moan from coming out of my mouth.

The next thing I felt was my body being jerked backwards and

War of the Fae: Book Three

Spike's mouth leaving mine. The connection to that swirling red and blackness was severed in an instant. I could feel the cold stone of the floor on my back and cool air brushing the overheated skin of my face and arms. My lips felt swollen and used. I kept my eyes closed, not yet ready to come back completely to reality.

I could sense there was a struggle going on nearby, but I figured it was probably Scrum and Spike duking it out - something I didn't need to worry about. Clearly the feeding had turned into something more erotic than Scrum could stomach. And as good as it had felt, I was glad he had been there to break it up. The last thing I wanted was to know that I'd gone all the way with an incubus in front of my friends. And I might even have done it too; I had been that far gone.

"Is Jayne okay?" asked a worried-sounding Tim from across the room.

Of course no one could hear him, so I answered, "I'm fine. Just relaxing."

"Well, you might want to get out of the way."

I cracked my eyes open to see what he was talking about and rolled over towards my bed just in time to avoid being stepped on. Scrum had Spike in a total body lockdown again, but this time, Spike didn't seem as pissed about it. His face was flushed a healthy-looking pink, and he was smiling devilishly. His eyes were bright red. I looked away so I wouldn't fall into them again. There was a danger in doing that, I knew it for sure now. Unfortunately, it was one of those dangers that a girl couldn't help ignoring since it felt so good and came in such a pretty package. Now Spike didn't just *look* like a bad boy - he *was* a bad boy, in the truest sense of the word.

The guys disappeared out the door, Scrum grunting with the effort the entire way.

I realized how tired I was when I tried to get up off the floor and into bed. I didn't have the energy for it, so I just laid back down on the floor, staring up at the ceiling.

Scrum came back inside the room about a minute later.

"How's Spike?" I asked, not moving my eyes from the ceiling.

"He's fine. I let him go. He's going out to the forest to work off some excess energy, I think."

"Good for him."

"Not so good for you, though," said Scrum, worry in his voice. "Do you need help getting onto the bed?"

"Maybe." I wasn't ready to admit how weak I felt.

Scrum bent down to help me up. "I've seen this before. Usually, when they do it to a fae, the fae passes out. I think you're lucky to still be conscious. But it's weird, because I think he might have overdosed a little."

"Is that why his face was so pink?" asked Tim.

"Tim wants to know if that's why his face was so pink," I said wearily.

"Maybe."

Once I thought about it, I remembered that Spike's face was usually pretty pale when he was feeling normal.

Scrum helped me up so I could lie down on the bed. "Better?" he asked.

"Yeah. Thanks ... for your help today. With Spike and stuff."

Scrum smiled. "No problem. Just doing my job. Being a daemon is the best thing that ever happened to me."

It was hard not to smile back at his enthusiasm for fae life. Being drained of all my energy seemed to make it easier for me not to be annoyed by his eager-puppy personality.

"Where are you from?"

"I'm from California. East Bay. A little town named Tracy."

"Did you like it there?"

He shrugged. "It was okay. My mom died, though, so I kinda stopped liking everything for a while."

"Oh. Well, that sucks." My mom was a pain in the ass, but at least she was still alive.

"Yeah. But now my life is much better." He smiled at me, making me feel like a total dirtbag for being so mean to him before. He was so easy to pick on, though, it totally wasn't all my fault.

"Listen, I'm sorry if I gave you a hard time before."

"You didn't give me a hard time. Really. Don't feel bad."

Boy, this kid must have been treated like shit before, if he thought what I'd said was fine. I vowed then to try harder to have patience with him. Hopefully, it wouldn't be too difficult.

He turned to leave but somehow his foot caught the edge of my side table, causing him to trip and take my furniture down with him. The lamp that was on top shattered into a thousand pieces on the floor, and the tampons that I had in the drawer spilled out everywhere. Scrum looked up, surrounded by shards of broken glass and scattered feminine products, and said, "What just happened?"

Tim laughed his stupid, wingless pixie butt off, but I just sighed. The universe sure did delight in giving me nearly impossible tasks.

"Just clean it up, klutz. I'm going to take a nap. Tell whoever's in charge for me, will ya?" I fell asleep before I heard his answer, and I didn't hear another noise for hours. I dreamed from lunchtime to dinnertime about red demons and black smoky ghosts, reaching out to stroke me and pull me into their world.

Chapter Eighteen

THE FIRST ONE TO SIT down with me at the dinner table was Tony. It was the first time we'd been alone since what seemed like forever. Well, kind of alone, since Tim was now stomping around on the table being goofy. I ignored him.

"You look happy. Tell me what you've been doing," I said. The sense of relief I felt at realizing how content he was nearly overwhelmed me. I hadn't fully appreciated how much I had been worrying about his integration here until I had just said this.

"I *am* happy. I'm not sure I've thanked you enough for doing this for me - for convincing me to come here. So, thanks."

"You're very welcome," I responded, nudging him with my shoulder. "It was entirely selfish, though. You're my best friend, and I needed you with me."

"You can say that, but I know the truth."

I ignored him. I was no saint, that was for sure; but if he wanted to think my motives were unselfish, I wasn't going to argue. "So, what did you learn this afternoon?"

Tony worked to swallow the huge bite of food he'd just taken. If I weren't so sure he was a wrathe, I'd wonder about the amount of food he was eating. He ate like a daemon, minus the squiggly meat.

"More stuff in the Gray. Plus, Gregale invited me to a meeting of the gray elves. We have a lot of common traits, wrathes and gray elves. They let me participate in one of their war strategy meetings."

"Really? That sounds cool. What did you guys talk about?"

"Stuff like numbers of Dark Fae, what they're doing out in the human world, powers their fae have, our training."

"Training. That's interesting."

"How so?"

We were joined at the table by Becky and Scrum who listened in to what we were saying.

"I know there's a war coming and all, but it seems like our training has kinda been disorganized. They don't even realize when I don't show up half the time."

"You're right," agreed Tony, enthusiastically. "I've only been here a day, and I can already see that. We talked about it today, and I gave them some ideas."

"You did? To who? The council?" asked Becky.

"No, the gray elves."

She nodded her head in admiration. "Good for you, Tony. You're smart. They should listen to you."

"Thanks," he said, shyly, blushing a little.

"Our training's not bad," said Scrum, stabbing some wormy thing on his plate and shoving it into his mouth.

"No, the daemon training is in the best shape," agreed Tony. "That's because Jared is directly involved. He's the one who's in charge of organizing the training of all the fae changelings. But he's also in charge of recruiting, so I suggested that he's probably spread too thin. They need someone else to take charge of the training programs."

"Who's it going to be? Niles?" The dwarf seemed to be the most logical choice, if only because he was the most belligerent of all the fae

I knew at the compound.

"No, he manages the dwarves only. He's kinda ... short-tempered with other fae."

"*Pfff.* You can say that again." I liked him, though, even if he was a cranky little bastard.

"They're going to talk to the council and come up with someone. You guys will probably notice a difference in your daily routines after that happens."

"You've really jumped right in, haven't you, Tony?" asked Becky.

He shrugged. "I guess so."

"That's awesome. Really. Jayne totally missed you when you were gone. And she was very worried about you."

"I missed her too." He looked up at me, a suspicious shine to his eyes.

Damn, I was so glad he was here. All would be totally right with my world when Chase was back with us - the regular Chase, not the dancing Chase. And that thought led me to another one.

"Hey, when you go into the Gray, can you find anyone you want?"

"Yeah, pretty much."

"Even a Dark Fae?"

He hesitated. "Uh, maybe. I'm not sure. Why would you want to, though?"

I leaned in closer to him so I could speak softly and still be heard. "So I could check on Chase's progress with Goose."

Tony nodded slowly in understanding. "I could try."

"Tomorrow?" I asked.

"Yes, tomorrow. You can come out to the Infinity Meadow with me, and we'll try."

"Where's that? Have I been there?"

"It's the door with the infinity symbol on it. The figure eight lying on its side?"

"Oh, yeah, I know that door - the symbol that looks like a racetrack." It was the one Gregale had taken me to when he brought me into the Gray to see Tony. "After breakfast, we'll meet there, then."

"I'm coming too," said Scrum.

"Fine."

"And me," said Tim.

I rolled my eyes. "Fine. Anyone else? Beckster? You want to join the party?"

She smiled. "No, I have to work with Naida and the others."

"Party at the lake?" I asked, sarcastically. I'd been allowed to confirm my affinity to Water there at that lake and do a little training, but they'd never let me totally integrate into or explore their underwater world. Regardless of the fact that I had an elemental affinity to Water, I was no water sprite or siren.

"Yeah. Don't be jealous."

"Jealous! Ha!" said Tim. "Who'd be jealous of a bunch of smelly squid-fae?"

"Hell yeah, Pixieman." I held out my finger so he could give me a high-one.

"What did he say?" she asked, suspiciously.

"He said the water sprites are wimps."

"Hey!" she said to Tim, feigning offense.

"Tell her the truth!" he yelled. "She's gonna kick my butt like she kicked yours!"

I stuck my tongue out at him and then looked at Becky, chagrined. "He didn't really say that."

"I know," she said, smiling. "I'm just playing. It's okay to be jealous, though. I would be too if I were you guys." And then she was gone, reappearing over at the buffet - lucky for her, since I was ready to give her a well-placed smack on her bare arm. *Fucking water sprites.*

"Where's Spike?" asked Tony.

"He's doing a night run in the forest," explained Scrum.

"What's he doing that for? And why?" asked Tony.

"That's when the incubi run around like wild fae, running faster than anyone else in the fae world, just for the hell of it. They can be kinda strange that way." Scrum kept eating while he talked, completely oblivious to the pieces of food that fell out of his mouth from time to time.

I got a little sick, looking at him. "Scrum. Dude. Manners ever?"

"Oh. Sorry." He chewed and swallowed, wiping his mouth off with his napkin before continuing. "He sucked down some of Jayne's supercharged energy today, so he's a little high on life right now."

"Like, literally," I said, looking down at my plate as my face flamed up.

"Somebody's embaaaaarrassed," said Tony in a singsong voice.

I jabbed him with my elbow. "Shut the hell up."

"What happened?"

"She practically *did it* with the incubus!" yelled Tim.

I held up my finger in flicking position, aiming it right at him. "Say it again, freak. See what happens."

"Ack!" he yelled, running away from my plate and over to Scrum. "Save me, daemon boy! She's gone rabid after *doing it* with the incubus!" He was laughing maniacally at his teasing, which is the only reason I didn't reach over and give him a good flick on his pixie butt. The really big-hearted piece of me - granted it was a small piece, but *was* in there somewhere - was glad to see him so happy, running around with his little burnt off nubby wing. He had plenty of reasons to be sad, so if my semi-sexual escapades entertained him, then I'd just have to suck it up.

"Stay over there or I'm gonna dunk you in my soup and eat you for dinner."

"*Orc!*" he screeched, pointing at me in accusation.

"*Gnome!*" I responded.

"Oh. No. You. Did. *Not* just call me a gnome," he said, hands on his hips.

"Oh, yes I did. Little *dirt eater.*"

Tim stood there, fuming. Apparently I'd hit the jackpot coming up with that insult. Personally, I didn't think gnomes were so bad. A little dirty, maybe, but friendly. But compared to my sparkly, clean, perfectly coiffed Tim, they were probably considered second-class citizens - at least by him. I wasn't even sure they brushed their teeth, like *ever*, and Tim could be found brushing and flossing away at least three times daily, sometimes more.

"You just wait. Don't fall asleep tonight, that's all I have to say."

I laughed. "What are you going to do? Fart all night? That's no threat - I'm used to it."

"You are soooo lucky I don't have wings right now."

"Yes, I am, aren't I?" I smiled at him devilishly, reaching out slowly to grab him.

He squeaked and ran up Scrum's arm, hiding behind his head. Seconds later, I heard a muffled gagging sound and then Tim yelling, "Holy gnome-head, don't you ever wash your *hair?!*"

He came out onto Scrum's shoulder, waving his arms around his face, as if trying to get a swarm of flies away from him.

"The smell is *on* me! *Ew!* Get it away!"

I stood up and walked over, taking Tim in my hand. "Relax, Tim. Playtime is over. Are you done eating yet?"

"I've lost my appetite. I think there were bugs living in there. I hope whatever he has going on isn't contagious."

"What's wrong with him?" asked a mystified Tony.

"He said he doesn't like Scrum's shampoo."

"Oh, I don't use shampoo," said Scrum.

"Why not?" asked Tony, obviously a little repulsed by this piece of information.

"It's not good for your hair."

"Who told you *that?*" I asked.

"I read it somewhere."

I laughed. "Where? *Homeless Housekeeping*?"

Tony laughed and then quickly tried to cover it up by coughing.

"Is that a real magazine?" Scrum asked.

I walked away, saying, "Goodnight! Tony come see me in my room later." My patience and understanding could only be expected to go so far.

I looked back when I got to the exit door, seeing Tony still laughing behind his fork at Scrum who was now trying to pull his hair out as far as it would go so he could look at it ... but it was too short, so he just kept turning and swiveling his head while pulling on clumps of hair. I shook my head as I opened the door and left the room. The kid was pitiful. If the future of the Light Fae were in the hands of guys like this, I was afraid for my continued existence in this world.

Tony joined Tim and me in our room about twenty minutes later. It was perfectly timed since it had given me enough of a head start to get showered and dressed for bed. Tim took his shower in the sink while I took mine in the actual shower area. I'd ceased being embarrassed about Tim seeing me naked. What was he going to do about seeing a gigantic boob anyway? It probably grossed him out since the boobs he was used to were probably about the size of half a Tic Tac, and those would be the busty pixies.

Elle Casey

Tony sat on the edge of my bed while I got under the covers.

"So you had a good day today, huh?" I asked.

"Yeah, I really did. And I didn't say this at dinner because it might not work out, but the gray elves are going to recommend me to be in charge of organizing the training."

"Whaaat?! That's amazing, Tony? Congrats! How the hell did you manage that?"

He smiled, obviously delighted at the idea. "I don't know. I mean, one minute I was just listening to the meeting stuff, and then I started getting ideas for strategy and ways to make things more efficient, so I started talking. It was like it just was so obvious - problems they'd been dealing with, all the changelings coming in and not knowing what to do with them ... it was just so basic to me. It reminded me of playing chess, you know?" His eyes were bright with excitement, and he gestured with his hands without even realizing it. I'd never seen him so animated. "You have to look at your end goal, winning this war or being prepared to win this war, and then you look at all your resources and how you can capitalize on different strengths, and you see how this move or that move will cause a ripple effect down the line. It's all like the strategies we learned and used in chess club."

"I told you the better name for that group was the 'Rule the World Someday' club."

Tony smiled. "You were right. It's helping me show them how to plan for the war. They really liked what I had to say in there."

"I always knew you were the smartest guy in the world. Now I have confirmation from the smartest *fae* in the world that I was right."

Tony leaned down and hugged me. "Thanks, Jayne. Just ... thanks. For everything."

I hugged him back. "You're welcome. Now stop thanking me

before you get all blubbery. I'll see you tomorrow."

"Okay." He stood to go out. "See you tomorrow, Tim."

"Good night," came the little voice from across the room.

I flipped over so my back was to the door, calling out to my friend. "Tony?"

"Yeah, Jayne?"

"Don't let the door hit you on the ass on the way out."

Chapter Nineteen

TONY WAS LYING ON HIS back on the ground, next to me out in the Infinity Meadow. Scrum sat off to the side, watching us and the edge of the forest that lay not far away. Tim rested on my chest near my neck, quiet for once.

"Just for the record, guys, I don't like this," said Scrum.

I sighed. "You don't like what? Tony going into the Gray? The meadow? What?"

"This place. Something feels ... off."

I probably shouldn't doubt his daemon radar because it had been able to sense when I was in trouble with Spike before, but I'd been out here several times for training and stuff and never had a problem. It was a beautiful day - the sun was shining, the sky was blue, and great, big, puffy clouds slowly drifted overhead. There was even a gentle breeze mussing the hair around my face. Of course, Scrum's hair didn't move since it hadn't been washed in, like, ever.

"Just relax, gnome-head, we'll be fine. Your radar - I mean, daedar - probably has a glitch in it. Just keep your eyes out for the bad guys."

"I plan on it. And just so you know, my daedar, as you call it, has never had a glitch. I'm going to be right over here, and if I tell you to get inside, then you have to agree to just go and not argue." He gave us the most serious look he was capable of making.

"Cross my heart," I said, rolling my eyes when he looked away.

Tony looked at me and spoke in a low tone, "You really shouldn't give him such a hard time, Jayne. He's just doing his job."

I stuck my tongue out at him. "M - Y - O - B, Baloney Head."

"It *is* my business. I could be the new training coordinator."

"Yeah, well, when you get your promotion, maybe it'll be your business. For now, the only thing you need to be worrying about is finding this guy in the Gray."

"Okay, so remind me ... what exactly am I doing?"

"Find that Goose guy. He's a Dark Fae wrathe. Ask him how Chase is doing."

"Where does he live?"

"In the Dark Fae compound."

"Do you know where it is? What it looks like?"

"No."

"Do you have anything of Goose's?"

I frowned at him fiercely. "No, dumbass, I don't. I'm not in the habit of collecting trinkets from people I meet out in the forest."

"Okaaay, chill, I'm just asking. It's easier to find someone if you have some sort of connection. Searching around in the Gray for someone you don't know can be tricky."

"Well, don't do it if you can't."

Tony sighed loudly. "I didn't say I *can't* do it. I just said it can be *tricky*. So tell me what the deal is exactly. If I reach him, what am I supposed to say?"

"Ask him how Chase's treatment is going and if he'll be ready for me to come get him in a few days. Try to get an exact day and time - and verify the place. It's supposed to be at the big tree where he found us the first time."

"Okay," said Tony, squeezing my hand, "here goes nothin'."

I waited patiently, gently holding onto Tony's hand and staring at the clouds in the sky. I saw one that looked like a rabbit and then one that looked like a turtle. *That's funny. Like the fable.* At first they were moving slowly across the sky, but then they moved faster. The rabbit lost its form, becoming smaller clumps and wisps. The turtle turned into an orc. It looked like it was racing across the sky, chasing the bits of rabbit that were left. *Ugh.* The memory of those disgusting creatures was not what I wanted to deal with as I waited out here in the meadow for news of Chase.

The wind kicked up. It wasn't cold, but it felt strange. It was as if a storm were moving in. I heard something near the edge of the meadow, coming from the trees, and turned my head to look at Scrum. "Scrum, did you hear that noise?" His earlier warnings were making me paranoid.

He didn't answer me; he just kept staring.

"Scrum!" I said more forcefully. "Did you hear it or not?"

Still no answer. In fact, no response at all. He was just staring out into the distance as if he were in a fog. Or frozen in place.

I sat up quickly and felt something land in my lap. I looked down and saw that Tim was there, all stiffened in a sitting position, staring off into the distance. A ringing began in my ears, as my brain tried to compute what was happening. I reached my hand down slowly and carefully picked Tim up, lifting him so I could see him better. His body was warm and his skin still soft, but he was definitely not okay. He was all zombied out. I looked back at Scrum and saw that he was in the same condition. I looked at Tony in a panic, but I couldn't tell if this was happening to him too, or if he was just walking the Gray. I was afraid to disturb him, worried it would trap him in the

Elle Casey

Gray or something.

A noise came from the trees again, and I jerked my head towards the sound. Coming from the darkness of the green canopy were a guy and a girl. I nearly pissed myself when I saw who they were. I quickly shoved Tim into the front of my tunic, praying I wasn't hurting him, and jumped up to meet the duo head-on.

Chapter Twenty

"WELL, HELLO, JAYNE. FANCY MEETING you here." The bitchy half-smile she gave me was a straight up flashback from Miami.

"Hello, *Samantha*. Looks like you found a place where you fit right in."

She scowled in response.

I noticed she was wearing a black robe over a white tunic and black pants. I was afraid to think that this uniform meant the same thing it meant in my Light Fae world. If she were one of us, I'd say she was a witch.

Ben smiled at me. "Hello, Jayne. I see you've managed to convince Tony to make the change. Good for you. I'm sure he's making all of you very proud."

"Blow it out your ass, Ben. I'm not interested in your bullshit. You'd better get lost before I call a platoon of green elves in to waste you and Ms. Congeniality here." I gestured with my chin to Her Royal Bitchiness. Samantha and I had met before when we were both runaways hanging out with Jared and his crew in Miami. I had only known her for about two days, but it was enough to see that she had a bad attitude and a massive chip on her shoulder. All of us in Miami thought for sure she'd be invited to take the changeling test with us, but after the interview, she had been rejected - the only one of us. At the time, Jared had been really upset and so had she. Apparently, she'd found a back-up plan ... or it had found her.

"No, you won't do that. Because if you do, your friends here will get hurt." He nodded towards Scrum and Tony on the ground.

"Seems like you've already managed to do that, so I guess I've got nothing to lose." I tapped into The Green, angry with myself that I hadn't powered up as soon as I'd heard the noise that signaled their arrival. I could have been better prepared than I was, and with Tony lying there helpless like that, it was totally stupid to not have had the power on standby. *What had I been thinking?*

"No, they're fine. Just in suspension for a few minutes while we take care of business."

I rubbed my hand slowly over the spot where Tim rested in my shirt. One of his feet was jabbing my boob and I needed to move it, but I didn't want them to know he was there.

"What business?" I asked, trying to distract them from watching me too closely.

"The business of taking you with us."

I barked out a laugh. "Ha! As if *that's* gonna happen. Listen, I appreciate the drama guys, but I'm not going anywhere with you a-holes."

Ben shrugged, still smiling. "It's either you or them. You choose."

"Hmmm," I said sarcastically, putting my finger to my lips. "I chooooose ... *none of the above*." And with that, I threw up a Green energy bubble between them and us, enclosing my friends inside, praying Tony would still be able to get out of the Gray. "Now get the fuck outta here before someone gets hurt. And by someone, I mean *you*."

Samantha looked at Ben, as if seeking his approval. He merely nodded, not even looking at her. He just kept staring at me. His steady gaze and unwavering calm was eerie as shit and making me nervous. He was seriously good at this psychological warfare stuff.

Samantha raised her hand and waved it slowly near the top of my bubble. I felt a glitch in the system - a stuttering of the power. I'd never felt anything like it before and I didn't like it *at all*. I didn't even have to look up to see what she was doing - bending my power shield and getting around it.

"Hey, bitch! Leave my bubble alone!"

"Sorry, Jayne, but she's going to take it down and then take your friends. I tried to warn you."

I felt my protective shield bending and disintegrating in the wake of her power. *How the hell is she doing this?* I started to panic. I drew more power from The Green, but it didn't seem to matter. I felt weak and tired, not sure if it was part of her magic whammy or not. I couldn't hold this bubble and call to the elves at the same time. It was taking all my concentration to hold it up and think through my options. I could tell that no matter what I did, she was eventually going to win out on this, and it was burning my ass. And obviously, my stupid daemon friends weren't going to be any help, considering that at least one of them was under Samantha's thrall. *Fuck and double fuck.*

"Fine," I agreed, angrily. "I give. I'll take it down if you agree to leave them alone."

Ben fixed me with the most intense stare I'd seen since Spike looked at me knowing it was playtime. He nodded to Samantha, without taking his eyes off me. I broke away from under his scrutiny to see Samantha's face as she realized she had been given the order to back off. She looked pissed, but did what she was told.

Something about her made it impossible for me to *not* say

something. "Yeah. That's right. Back the fuck off, *Sam*. And don't think for one second I won't be telling Jared what you did here today."

Bullseye. I knew I'd scored a direct hit when she raised her hand as if to send another spell out, but this one directly at me.

Ben reached up and touched her arm.

She pulled it back quickly as if she'd been burned, a look of surprise and pain on her face.

"Do not let her bait you. Remember our cause."

Samantha scowled at me and turned to go, leaving Ben behind to deal with me. I thought about slamming him with The Green and calling out to my friends, but something told me he would be expecting that. And I couldn't risk having him hurt Tony or Scrum.

I didn't know what to do about Tim. I could leave him here, which would probably be for the best, except that I'd worry about him being wingless and possibly eaten by a ground squirrel or stepped on. And I didn't know how long it would be before they all woke up. If I could have sent a telepathic message right then to Tim I would have said I was sorry, because it didn't take a rocket scientist to know that I was about to be taken prisoner by the Dark Fae, and poor Tim was going to end up one too, by default.

Ben held out his hand. "Shall we?"

Damn him for being so hot. The bad guys were always better-looking than the good guys. I looked at his hand like it had orc poop in it. Like hell was I going to touch it. I didn't care how cute he was. "Take me to your leader or your lair or whatever."

He laughed bitterly. "Why don't I just take you to the Dark Fae compound instead?"

"Do your worst. I'm sure you and Samantha will get your jollies from it. I'm not one bit surprised that she's on your side, you know."

"Oh yeah? Why's that?"

"Because you're all a bunch of Light Fae rejects."

Ben stormed over and grabbed me roughly by the arm. "You might want to learn to shut your mouth once in a while before it gets you in serious trouble."

I smiled, bitterly. "You have no idea how perfect that sounds coming from you."

"Oh yeah? Why's that?"

"Because you sound exactly like my asshole father."

He jerked and dragged me along, saying nothing, until we were at the edge of the forest. It was then that I saw Maggie, the witch.

"Oh, thank The Green, Maggie! You have to help me get away from this douchebag." I jerked my arm away from him and stood on my own. I was so relieved to see her standing there, I felt my knees go a little weak. I wanted to run over and give her a hug, even if she was all bent over and lumpy looking. Now these bastards were going to be sorry. She knew her witch shit - Samantha would be no match for her.

Maggie just looked at me, no expression on her face. Then she shrugged and turned, shuffling away.

I was confused for a second. Did she need more space to cast her kickass spell? Was she going to go get her wand? Did she need a wand? She kept walking, and I freaked out.

"Maggie! Where are you going?! I need your help, *dammit!*"

I noticed another figure standing off to the side. It was Samantha ... smiling. Maggie shuffled past her, nodding as she went.

What the fuck?

"Thanks, Maggie," said Samantha loudly so I could hear, watching me as she spoke. "We appreciate your help."

I was seized by a rage I didn't know I was capable of having.

"You sold me out, Maggie?! You gave me up to the Dark Fae? I thought we were *friends!"* Spit was flying from my mouth as the

venomous words spewed out. "You're no better than a rotten *orc!* You hear me?! A fucking black, slimy, pile of steaming, stinking *orc shit!* I hate you! *I hate you! Do you hear me?!*"

And that's the last thing I remember saying before I saw her beady black eye and everything went dark.

Chapter Twenty-One

MY BACK WAS HURTING - PROBABLY from all the bumpy hard things that were poking into it. I wasn't ready to open my eyes yet and identify what they were. My other senses were telling me way more than I wanted to know. It was cold and damp where I was. The bed or whatever I was lying on was stone, and not very smooth. I could hear water dripping somewhere, and there was a musty smell all around me. I was pretty sure I was underground somewhere or inside a cave. I couldn't hear anything but my own breathing and the occasional tiny splash of water. At least, I hoped it was water.

I moved my hand slowly up to my chest and found that Tim was still there under my tunic. I could feel his warmth, so that meant he was alive. I hoped I hadn't squished him during the transport. There was no doubt in my mind that I was in the Dark Fae compound; I didn't need supernatural skills to figure that out. I was probably in a dungeon. They'd definitely have a dungeon. *Assholes.*

I reached down to my leg and felt the empty sheath where Blackie's solid presence should have been. *Dammit.*

I finally opened my eyes and visually drank in the things around me. I was in a cave room of sorts. The entire space was carved out of stone. There were no bars holding me in here, so it wasn't as dungeony-looking as I had expected. Still, there was a door and it was shut. I was willing to bet it was locked from the outside. There was no bed, just the stone slab I was lying on. It could probably double as a virgin sacrifice altar in a pinch. I turned my head to get a look at the floor, hoping against hope I wouldn't see a puddle of blood there. Luckily there was none. The floor was stone too and damp-looking. One of the lumpy rock walls opposite me had some water trails on it, and I could see that this was the source of the drip, drip, dripping that I'd been hearing.

I sat up slowly, fighting the dizziness that threatened to overwhelm me. Whatever Maggie or Samantha had hit me with had done a hell of a job. I tried to remember one scrap of information after yelling at Maggie, but there was nothing. I could have hooked up and gotten busy with an orc, and I probably would have slept through the whole thing. I squeezed my legs together as the visuals assailed my mind. I wasn't sure I could recover from something like that, and shivered with revulsion just thinking about it.

"Okay," I said out loud to the cave room. "Time to go home."

I tried to pull The Green into me, but there was nothing there. Just a black void. The panic rose up in my throat, but I talked myself down, my voice bouncing off the walls. "Just relax. The Green is out there. You just need to be patient and try again." And so I did. And then again. But nothing happened.

"Fuck!" I yelled out to no one in particular.

"Bugger!" yelled someone back.

"Tim?" I looked down at my chest.

"Would you mind getting me the heck out of your bra, please? It's hot and squishy in here. I'm trying not to vomit, but if you don't get me out soon, I can't promise anything ... "

"You're out, you're out! Look!" I pulled my tunic open as fast as I could and jerked the top of my bra down. Tim wasn't expecting the sudden freedom, so he tumbled out, landing in my lap.

"Oh, crudbuckets, that hurt," he moaned.

I watched him struggle to his feet, trying to get his balance on my legs but failing miserably. I picked him up as gently as I could and set him on the bench next to me.

"What the heck happened? How come I was in your bra?" He looked around as he rubbed his butt with one hand and his head with the other. "And where are we?"

"What happened was Ben and Samantha, helped by Maggie, and we are in the Dark Fae compound. I think."

Tim spun around to look at me. "No!"

"Yes!"

"Oh, this is not good. This is not good *at all*. Jayne, do you know what this means?"

"I'm pretty sure it means we're prisoners. Or at least I am. They don't know you're here."

Tim thought about that for a second. "Are you sure they don't know I'm here?"

"Pretty sure. Why would they have left you in my bra? And I sure didn't tell them you were there."

"Tell me everything you know," he ordered, all business, walking around and occasionally shaking out a leg or bending over to stretch his back. "We need a plan, but first I need as much info as you have. Go."

I filled him in on our sad predicament, trying to remember as many details as I could. When I finished, Tim was shaking his head.

"I can't believe she helped them capture you. That's just typical Maggie. I never should have introduced you to her."

"What do you mean it's 'typical Maggie'? She's always been nice to us."

"Ha! That's what you think. Maggie does what Maggie wants for Maggie's reasons. If it suits her to be nice, she's nice. If she wants your wing, she pulls it off. If she wants to sell you out to your worst enemy, well, she does that, too. Believe me. I know what she's capable of."

"You guys have a history, and I know it's not all good. Tell me what she did to you."

"Other than pulling my wings off more than once?"

"Yeah."

"No. What's in the past needs to stay in the past. Right now we need to figure out how to get out of here. If they keep us too long, we'll end up staying."

I got a super creepy feeling hearing that. "What do you mean? I'm not staying here."

Tim sighed loudly. "Fae who are brought here rarely leave."

"Why? Do they get ... killed?" The idea had me feeling barfy and panicky all over again. I could hear my heart beating in my ears. I had to take a few gulping breaths to keep my stomach contents where they belonged.

"No. Worse. They *choose* to stay. The Dark Fae mess with their minds."

"Not this mind," I said confidently. "I'd no sooner willingly shack up with a Dark Fae than I'd sleep with an orc. Ain't gonna happen, as Finn would say."

"You say that now, but I've seen it. Perfectly rational, intelligent fae. One day they're Light Fae and happily married, the next they're Dark Fae and saying 'See you later, sucker.' Trust me. It happens. And it can happen to you and me. We need to get out." He paced back and forth even faster. At this rate he was going to wear a track in the stone bench.

"Okay, fine. We'll make a plan." I thought for a few seconds and then realized I was fresh out of ideas. "What's our plan?"

"You said we were out there with Tony, but they didn't take him, right?"

"As far as I know, they didn't. Just us - and you only because you were in my shirt."

"I was in your bra, Jayne. Your bra. And let me tell you - your boobs are seriously sweaty and sticky."

"Yeah, well, next time I'll leave you to be a squirrel's lunch, how about that?" I got up and walked around, testing out my legs. "Ungrateful punk."

"Have you seen anyone here yet? How long have we been here?"

"No, and I don't know."

Just then there was a sound at the door.

"Quick, get in my shirt!" I leaned over and scooped Tim up, shoving him back in my bra before he could react. I could feel him trying to get out, digging around and scratching my skin, so I lightly smacked him on the outside of my shirt. "Sssh, someone's coming in," I whispered desperately, "and stop *scratching* me,"

The door opened to reveal Samantha standing in the doorway, smiling her catty smile at me, making me want nothing more than to smack it right off her stupid face. Now that I knew Maggie was somehow involved in messing with my powers, I wasn't as impressed by Samantha's witch status. She was probably a goofy changeling who didn't have a clue, just like all the rest of the newbies.

"Ready to cry uncle and let me out of here?" I asked.

She sneered at me. "Right. You're not going anywhere until Ben's done with you."

"Oh, yeah. Ben. So what ... is he Jared's replacement for your shriveled, black heart?"

"Shut up."

"How long did that take? To forget your friend Jared? A whole day?"

"It's not like that, Jayne. But I wouldn't expect you to understand."

"No, that's good. Don't expect me to understand how you could sell all your friends out for a lying demon just because he happens to be good looking. I'll never understand someone like you."

"So, you think I'm good looking?" said Ben, stepping out from the other side of the door to stand next to Samantha. "That'll be all for now, Sam. I'll meet you at lunch."

"But ... "

"I said that's fine. Please leave us."

"Don't you think ... ?"

"Samantha. Go." He glowered at her.

She shot me a look of hatred and then stormed off, leaving Ben and me almost alone, Tim still hidden in my bra. Thankfully, he had stopped struggling. I could feel his tiny body moving with each rapid breath. I prayed Ben wouldn't see or hear it. For all I knew, this turd had supersonic hearing powers.

"So what's the plan?" I asked, irritated. "Torture? Dismemberment? Death? Just tell me; the suspense is giving me a rash."

Ben smiled and walked in, shutting the door behind him. "None of the above."

"So?" I threw my arms out. "Why'd you bring me here?"

Ben shrugged. "It's a necessary part of the plan."

"Your plan for world domination?"

He laughed humorlessly. "Hardly. But call it whatever you want, it makes no difference. I will get what I want; I always do."

I stuck out my chin, unable to help myself. "You didn't get Tony. And I know you wanted *him* pretty badly."

Ben smiled at me pityingly. I didn't like that look one bit. "If it was Tony I wanted, don't you think I would have just snatched him up like I did Samantha?" He must have read the surprise on my face because he continued, "Yes, I did take her as soon as you and your friends got on that plane. She's been here even longer than you've been Light Fae. We don't require our recruits to go through any ridiculous tests."

"Yeah, that's right. I hear you'll take any mentally deficient shitforbrains that comes along. Samantha's not the only proof of that."

Ben's look went from looking condescending to annoyed. "You are patently incorrect, but it makes no difference to my plans. Continue to be ignorant for all I care."

"Astute observation is not ignorance." I had no idea where that had come from, but I decided to roll with it. "All I've seen is deceit and tricks. You lied to Tony and you hurt my friends. You're willing to kill humans and fae to get what you want. That tells me you need people of questionable morals to build your army. Samantha is a perfect example of that."

"And what has Samantha ever done to you?" he asked, folding his arms and leaning back on the door.

"Nothing, other than being a person who hangs out with losers."

"I'm sorry, but you must be mistaken. You're looking at the soon to be winners of the fae war. You'd be doing yourself a favor to join us."

"In your dreams. Send me back now, and I'll tell them to go easy on you."

Ben shook his head slowly. "You really don't have any idea what you're saying." He pushed himself away from the door. "But that makes no difference. You will serve your purpose and then you will be released. Or killed. Whichever suits my needs at the time."

The hardness in his voice chilled me to the bone. There wasn't even a hint of potential remorse in his expression. I believed him when he said he would kill me if it was convenient, and it had a tempering effect on my words.

"Why me? Why did you take me instead of Tony?"

He looked at me, searching my face. "You really don't know, do you?"

"Know *what?!*" I asked, exasperated. I was already tired of his games.

He took two steps towards me.

I backed up until my legs hit the stone bench behind me. The closer he got, the more I was able to feel his warmth; it came off him in waves. I stared at his face, unable to look away. His hair was gently tousled, a shock of it falling over his forehead. It was dark, dark brown, nearly black. His deep green eyes penetrated my resolve as he stared at me and spoke again.

"You will be the one who starts the war," he said coldly, calmly.

I felt the blood drain from my face. "Me?" I said weakly. "How can I possibly start a war locked up in here?" I licked my lips in nervousness, my entire mouth having gone bone dry.

Ben smiled, almost sadly it seemed, slowly reaching up and touching a finger to my face. "So soft. So cool to the touch," he said, almost as if to himself. Then he blinked his eyes a few times and his expression hardened. He dropped his hand to his side. "They will come for you. And when they do, we will be ready."

He spun around and strode from the room, slamming the door shut behind him.

I was frozen in place for a few seconds, digesting his words and weighing them for their cost. I had to get the hell out of here before they could become fact instead of just a madman's ramblings. I didn't have the same faith he did about my level of worth to the Light Fae as a group; but I knew my friends would come for me, and I didn't want any of them to get ambushed.

I could feel a wiggling in my shirt, and I placed my hand over its source. "We have to get the hell out of here, Tim."

A muffled, "Agreed!" came from within.

I ran to the door and pulled on it, expecting it to be locked, but it flew open and slammed into the wall. I lost my balance a little but quickly regained it, running from the room into the hallway. I looked in both directions, deciding to go to my left. I reached back in, shut the door behind me, and ran. There was no rhyme or reason to my decisions now, just survival instinct.

I ran down a hallway that looked disturbingly similar. I passed door after door, wondering when I'd come to the end or to a turnoff. Eventually out of breath, I stopped, placing my ear to a nearby door. I heard nothing, and gently tried the latch. The door opened bit by bit to reveal a room of stone, like my cell. I opened the door wider and saw a stone bench just like the one I had been sitting on. I threw the door open the rest of the way and saw that I was standing in the doorway of my original cell. I could see the trail of water that had dripped down the wall.

"*Fuck* a fucking *orc!*" I yelled out to the room, clenching my fists in frustration.

Tim's head poked out of my shirt, his hair sticking out in all directions. "What happened?" he whispered hoarsely.

"The hallway's spelled. I ran for five minutes and got exactly nowhere."

"Cuss word!"

I paused in my ranting, looking down at him. "What did you just say?"

"Cuss word?"

"Is that your idea of swearing without swearing?"

"Obviously." Tim used my buttons to climb up to my shoulder. "Put your hair down so I can hide when they come back."

I yanked out the rubber band holding my hair in a ponytail, sliding it onto my wrist. I was fresh out of ideas and full of pissed off.

"Can I complain some more about how much my lack of wings is hindering our escape?"

"Go ahead. I'm right there with you. But maybe you should keep it quiet in case this place is bugged."

"Oh, it's not."

"How can you be sure?"

"Pixies can sense stuff like that."

"Stuff like what?"

"Well, electronics or anything that acts like electronics - like bugging spells."

"And why haven't you told me this stuff before? Don't you think I might have wanted to know about it?"

"What? I'm supposed to tell you about *all* of my amazing abilities? That could take a very long time, you know. I have piles of them."

I knew for a fact that if he had wings right now, he'd be brushing them and preening. He is inordinately proud of them and his general pixieness. I was too, normally, but now all I was doing was worrying about how to get him and his wing nublets out of here alive.

Chapter Twenty-Two

I DON'T KNOW HOW MUCH time had passed before someone finally came to the door. Maybe it was just a few hours or maybe it was a whole day; it must have been a while though, because I was getting hungry, and I seriously had to pee.

The door opened and a small guy stood there, wearing the clothing of a sprite - possibly a wood sprite from the looks of it. Tim had been sitting on my shoulder, so luckily he was able to jump into my hair as soon as he heard the latch moving.

"It's about time," I said irritably. "I have to go to the bathroom."

"Please follow me."

I went behind him down the corridor to another door. He pushed it open to reveal a bathroom.

"There is a toothbrush and other items you might need on the shelf."

I tried not to be mad at this guy. I knew it wasn't his fault that I was here, but that didn't make it okay that he was going along with my imprisonment.

"I'm not staying here, you know."

He just looked at me without expression.

I brushed past him to do my business, surreptitiously putting Tim in the stall next to me so he could do his thing without the sprite seeing him. The guy stayed outside, giving us the privacy we needed. I ran the water after, so he wouldn't hear Tim and me whispering to each other.

"Is this place bugged?"

"No."

"Did you see any way to escape on our way here?"

"No."

"Me neither. Keep your eyes peeled. Look behind us while we're walking and see if you spot anything."

"Okay."

We walked outside the door, Tim hidden once again in my hair.

The wood sprite pointed to the symbol of an arrow on the door. "This is your bathroom. You will be able to find it by image-seeking this symbol."

So that's what they called it here - image-seeking. Same spell as our compound. I filed that information away in my head for later.

"How do I find the way back to my room?"

He smiled without humor. "You will only be able to find one room - your room. No symbol needed."

Dick. I withheld from saying anything out loud. This guy would get what was coming to him one of these days, when the Light Fae came and kicked all their asses.

He delivered us back to our cell where I found Ben waiting, sitting on my stone bed. The door closed behind me, and I stepped a couple paces in before stopping in front of him.

I smiled with fake cheer. "How *not* nice to see you."

Ben smiled back, but it looked more like a grimace. "You might as well get used to it. Me visiting you. I can't seem to help myself."

"Oh, goody."

War of the Fae: Book Three

Ben got a distracted look on his face and said, "Enter!" at the door.

It swung open to reveal a tall, thin male fae wearing a dark gray tunic. He stepped inside, nodding to Ben and acting like I wasn't standing directly in front of him.

Ben stood and looked at me, all pleasantness gone from his expression. "Jayne, this is Leck. He's a wrathe. His job is to get information from you, and your job is to give it to him. I suggest you cooperate. It will be easier for everyone that way."

I looked at him in confusion. *What the hell was he talking about? What information?*

Ben gave me one more intense look and then moved to the corner of the room. He nodded at Leck. "Proceed."

Leck moved forward, his eyes now focused on me. I didn't like the blank stare I saw there. It was like he was an empty-headed zombie or something. It was scary seeing eyes the color of Tony's in a face like that. I backed up, slowly raising my hands without even thinking about it.

"Listen, Leck, you'd better stop right there, because if you so much as touch me you're gonna get hurt."

He stopped about a foot in front of me. "Sit down."

"No." I stood my ground, my chin lifting slightly in defiance. This guy Leck could kiss my big white ass as far as I was concerned.

That was the last clear thought I had before the headache started.

"Please sit."

I grabbed my head, trying to stop the pain that was shooting through my skull. "Go ... fuck ... yourself ... !" I gasped out.

"The pain will not stop until you comply. Sit down."

I didn't want to sit. I refused to sit. But the agony was almost unbearable. I felt my knees giving way and my legs buckling. I crumpled to the floor, some deep part of my brain making sure I didn't squash the poor little defenseless pixie in my hair.

As soon as I hit the ground, the pain receded and eased off to a dull throb. It was still awful, but nothing like the needles of misery that had just been skewering my gray matter. I took short, shallow breaths, trying to move past the pain and nausea.

"What kind of evil sonofabitch uses torture to get a person to sit down?" I looked at him through my veil of pain and saw that I was appealing to the wrong person. He cared nothing for my complaints. I looked over at Ben, still standing in the corner of the room. "What is *wrong* with you?"

He shrugged, casually. "You have information. I need it. You will either give it to me willingly, or I will take it from you. It's up to you. Just know that the end result will be the same."

"I won't sell out my friends," I growled at him.

Ben nodded at Leck.

The pain began again, just a slight increase, but it was enough to cause me to draw my breath sharply inward. I tried not to focus on it, but it was nearly impossible. It was consuming my every thought.

Leck spoke again in his empty voice. "Tell us where to find the nearest entrance to the Light Fae compound."

I just stared at him, giving him the dirtiest look I could manage.

He waited a few moments and then just blinked ... slowly. Before his eyes completely opened back up, the pain blossomed across my forehead.

A moan escaped my lips before I could clamp my mouth shut and stop the sounds from coming out. I put my head down, squeezing my eyes closed, listening to the sound of my breath panting in and out on hyper drive. I couldn't tell them. *Neverneverneverneverever ...*

"Tell us where the nearest entrance to the Light Fae compound is," he said in a louder voice. It cut through the pain and drove what felt like steel daggers right into each hemisphere of my brain.

"*Gaaaahhhhh!!*" was the only sound that would come out of my mouth.

Somewhere I heard Ben's voice saying, "Ease up, I think she's going to tell us."

He sounded confident and as assholey as a guy possibly could, and that just sealed the deal for me. I'd keel over from a massive stroke before I gave him anything he wanted. As bad as this felt, all I could think about was how he could have just as easily done it to Tony or any of the others. He had no conscience. I prayed to the universe and anyone else who might hear me that they wouldn't find Tim in my hair.

The suddenly pain eased up, and there were no more stars shooting across my visual field.

"Look at me," said Leck.

I lifted my head, but my eyes refused to open.

"Open your eyes."

"Can't," was the only word I could manage.

He grabbed me by the hair on the top of my head, lifting me halfway up and forcing my eyes open with his other hand. They started watering immediately, even the dim light in the room too much for them at this point. This dickbag had somehow forced a seriously ass-kicking migraine on me. It would serve him right if I stroked out right here on the floor.

"Where is the entrance?"

I whispered the answer to him, but he couldn't hear me.

"What? Speak louder."

I gathered up all the energy I had left and shouted the answer. *"IT'S IN YOUR ASS, YOU FLAMING FUCKBAG!"*

The pain blew up behind my eyes as he let go of my hair and

released another torrent of punishment on my brain. The room went dark, and I fell all the way back down to the floor, landing on my side in the small puddle created by the drip, drip, dripping of that leaky cave. The pain came and went in tortuous waves, over and over, along with nausea that may or may not have turned into vomit on the floor. I was too far out of it to really know or care. I felt myself convulsing and then a sweet, sweet release as my mind let go. My last conscious thought was that I couldn't wait to sink the Dark of Blackthorn into this guy's vile, black heart. He was going to be one sorry motherfucker if I ever got out of here alive.

Chapter Twenty-Three

I FELT A GENTLE TAPPING on my cheek.

"Jayne. *Jayne!* You have to wake up."

Tim's voice. It sounded worried. Why was Tim so worried? Was I late to breakfast? Had I slept in?

I slowly became conscious of the sensations I was experiencing in various parts of my body. My neck was kinked. My shoulder, ribs, and hip ached from lying on a hard, unforgiving surface of some sort. *Stone?* Why wasn't I in my bed?

And then I remembered. And then I smelled the odors. I opened my eyes and saw that I was looking up at the room from my position on the floor, and there was a rancid puddle of what smelled like dried up barf right in front of my face.

"Fuck *balls*, what happened?" I asked as I sat up. "Arrgh! *Shitshitshit*, what the hell? Why is my head exploding?" My brain was pounding as if Tim and a few of his friends had started a rock band in my skull - and they were a mostly percussion group.

"They tortured you," cried Tim softly. "It was the worst thing I've ever seen in my life. I can't believe a fae would do that to you." My poor pixie friend was really broken-hearted. "You've been out for a long, long time. I was afraid you weren't going to wake up."

I took a few deep breaths, trying to convince the pain to go back into the recesses of my skull. "I don't remember everything too clearly. Who was that guy that was in here?"

"Leck. A wrathe."

"Yeah." Hearing his name helped my memory return. "And what the hell was up with the whole migraine brain-melting power, anyway?"

"I don't know, but I thought you were dying. It was horrible. I wanted to pixie him, but I wasn't sure if I could do it without hitting you, and I was worried they'd kill us both if I tried."

"No, I'm glad you didn't. Don't do it unless I tell you to. I don't want them to know you're here; they'll just use you to force me to tell them stuff."

"You can't tell them, Jayne. No matter what, don't do it!" he said in a panic.

"No shit. You think I don't know that?" I reached up to hold my head in my hands. "*Fuck me*, I need an aspirin." I massaged my temples thinking it might help, but they felt so bruised I gave up quickly. I wondered what a CT scan of my brain would show right now - probably a lot of dead spots. I seriously thought it was highly probable that they had disintegrated parts of my brain.

"We've got to figure out how to get out of here," I said, looking around, wishing I'd somehow missed an escape route in my previous examinations of the room. "I don't know how much of that torture stuff I can take before I resort to killing myself." I wasn't kidding, either. I decided after this encounter, that I was officially a wimp. Insult me all day long and I'll manage, no problem; but bring the pain, and I'm ready to check out. And I'd rather check out that sell out any day of the week.

"I won't let you do that, Jayne. If I have to, I'll pixie you so they won't be able to hurt you. All you'll feel is happiness for the rest of eternity, or at least until you die of exhaustion from dancing and singing."

"Well, let's save that for our Plan Z, okay? I'm not suicidal, and I'm not ready to give up my occasional defeatist view of the world quite yet."

"And none of us are ready to have you give it up, either. There's a special charm to your fatalism."

"Shut up and help me figure this out, would you?" I got up carefully, waiting until I knew my legs were steady enough before moving back to the stone slab. I had to get away from the disgusting yack on the floor.

"We need a brownie or someone in here to clean up this shit. There's not a hell of a lot worse than looking at your own upchuck after suffering the world's most excruciating migraine."

"Yeah there is ... being forced to look at a giant puddle of someone else's."

I gave him a withering look, but I couldn't really argue.

He walked across the floor to join me, and I reached down to give him a lift up, wincing at the throbbing pain that started again in my head. We sat there like that on the cold bench for what seemed like hours, with me doing an occasional deep breathing routine to try and manage the aftereffect echoes of pain that still pounded across my head. I laid down, drifting in and out of sleep, choosing to rest on my sides as much as I could because lying on my back intensified the headache.

At some point in the night someone delivered a plate of bland food just outside the door. I noticed it when I got up to use the bathroom. I felt a little better after eating and washing my face. Tim also ate a few bites of the tasteless garbage that was our dinner.

Neither of us knew if meals were going to be offered with any regularity, so we ate even though we didn't feel like it. I used the small napkin they included with my plate to cover the grossness on the floor.

"These Dark Fae are animals," I said with disgust as I sat down on the stone slab, my back against the nearby wall. "We would never treat fae like this."

Tim cleared his throat and gazed up at the ceiling, looking guilty as hell.

"What?" I asked.

"Well ... that's not exactly true."

"What the hell are you talking about? We don't torture fae, Tim."

"You haven't seen *all* of the rooms in the compound, have you?" he asked me mysteriously.

"No, have you?"

"Not all of them. But more than you have. More than the council knows I have."

"Tiiiim ... fess up. What do you know that I don't?"

He shrugged. "Just that the Light Fae have rooms like these and that they're in the middle of a war, too."

I felt a little sick to my stomach. I couldn't picture Dardennes or Céline ordering someone to be tortured like Ben had done. "Did you see anyone being ... tortured?"

"No. But I heard some things."

"Torture stuff?"

"Maybe. I was outside this door one time. Whoever was inside wasn't happy."

"When was this?"

"A couple days ago."

"Why didn't you say anything?"

"I don't know," he shrugged, looking down at his clasped hands.

War of the Fae: Book Three

"I don't want you to think I'm making excuses, Jayne, but I'm older than you. I've seen a lot of things in my time, and I know that when anyone's at war, certain rules are bent. Some are even broken."

"Yeah, but we're *Light Fae*. We're the *good guys*. We don't torture fae."

He shook his head sadly. "It's not that simple, Jayne. Good guys ... bad guys ... the lines are a little blurry, don't you think?"

Everything he was saying disgusted me and pissed me off. He reminded me of Ben. "No. I don't think they're blurry at all. Good guy means you don't torture or kill. Bad guys do that stuff, but we don't. It's simple."

He fixed me with stare. "You need to dig a little deeper."

"No. I don't."

Just then the door rattled, and I snatched Tim, throwing him up on my shoulder. I tried not to wince at the pulling and yanking of my hair as he frantically hid himself.

"Were you talking to someone in here?" asked Ben, looking around suspiciously.

"Yes. The army of green elves who are on their way here to kick your sorry ass."

He smiled patronizingly. "There is a very strong blocking spell surrounding this cell. None of your friends can hear you and neither can The Green."

"Spells were made to be broken," I said as fiercely as I could manage.

"No, it's rules that were made to be broken," he responded, staring at me intensely.

"Something you're obviously quite good at - for example, the rules regarding basic decency towards others."

"I didn't come here to argue with you."

"What *did* you come here for then? To torture to me some more? Because that was just plain fun. Let's do it again. Maybe we can do some on you, too."

Ben's eyes flashed red. "Do you have any idea how frustrating you are?!"

"Do you think I give a shit about that?!" I yelled back.

"You should, Jayne, you really should! Because I hold the key to your survival. One word from me and you're done here, headed on a one-way trip to the Otherworlds."

I took two steps towards him. "Let's get one thing straight, Ben," I nearly spit the words out. "I'm not afraid of you. I hate you with every ounce of my soul. I'm not going to help you hurt my family or anyone else. You can burn in hell for all I care."

Ben took a step towards me, the two of us now just a few inches apart. I could feel the heat of his body, tied to Fire, sending pulses of electricity up and down my whole body, and not all of them completely horrible. His eyes burned bright, and I knew I should be afraid - I'd seen him nearly on fire before - but for some reason, I wasn't. I felt the purity of The Green in my veins, even if I couldn't call it to me right now. It was out there, somewhere, waiting for me to link in again. The thought of it filled me with a confidence I didn't know I had.

"Be afraid of me, Jayne. Please." He reached out as if to take my hand, but then stopped himself. He was nearly pleading. Had he given me any other attitude, I probably would have spit in his face. But the way he said it? It was as if he were begging me to be afraid of him, and that totally didn't make any sense.

"Why? Why do you want me to be so afraid of you?"

"Because ... " His eyes scanned my face and my shoulders, as if he were memorizing my features, coming to rest finally on my eyes. " ... I don't want to destroy you." He reached his hand up slowly, touching my temple with his finger, drawing it down my face to my neck, leaving a trail of fire that didn't burn as it went. "But I will, if you force me to."

I felt my breath catch in my throat. Everything he was doing, and every vibe he was sending, was in total contradiction to my imprisonment and torture he had personally ordered just a few hours before.

"Why are you doing this?" I whispered.

His eyes hardened and he jerked his hand away, stepping back, his eyes returning to their flaming, angry state. "We are at war, Jayne. The sooner you accept that and yield to me, the sooner your situation will be made better."

His abrupt change of heart pissed me off. I threw my hands out, gesturing around at the ridiculous cell I was being forced to sleep in. "Oh, so until I yell *uncle*, I get to sleep on a stone bench surrounded by my own vomit?" I folded my arms across my chest. "Well, you know what, Ben? You can go fuck an orc for all I care. I'd rather swim in this shit before giving you the satisfaction."

The red glow built up around him in an instant. He was on the verge of losing his cool, and even though I didn't know him that well, I knew the temper tantrum of this Dark Fae demon guy would be epic. I doubted that I'd survive it. Probably this whole compound wouldn't. My arms dropped to my sides and my panicked mind went into overdrive ... and that was when the idea hit me. I could detonate this whole damn place with Ben's help. All I had to do was make him angry enough. I didn't even consider the sacrifice I was making of myself and my friend Tim. All I thought about was the end result.

"Yeah, go ahead. Blast me, Ben. Send me to the Otherworlds with your fire. You know the only reason you can do it is because you've totally cut me off from my power down here. If we were up there in the Green Forest, I'd kick your ass to the Underworld and back. I'd take your Fire and shut it down with my Water! I'd take your Wind and snuff it out with my Earth! You're *weak*!" I stepped up until I was close enough to smell the brimstone that was like an aura around him. "You're a user and a torturer. You have no code of honor. You don't *deserve* to be fae."

That last bit was what did it, maybe. It was the worst thing I could think to say at the time. Even though I wasn't born fae, I did have a natural talent for making up good insults. Apparently the whole 'deserving to be fae' thing was a hot button for him - a truly inspired shot to the heart.

The fire burst forth and surrounded him in a giant, flaming ball. I stumbled back, getting as far away from him as I could, but the heat was nearly unbearable. I hoped he was angry enough to burn this whole place down. I didn't want to get roasted for nothing.

I had a few seconds as he was being consumed in the flames to think about my moment of sacrifice and death. I should have been more afraid, terrified even. But there was nowhere for me to go, and I knew that. It was pointless to fear now. There were no windows to jump out of ... no way to get past him to the door ... no Green power to cool me off and protect me. I was just sorry that Tim would be caught up in it.

"I'm sorry, Tim!" I yelled.

I felt a responding tug in my hair at the exact same time the door to the cell flew open and a great roar of displeasure filled the room.

Chapter Twenty-Four

THE ROOM WENT WHITE - ALL white. Not only the colors in the room, but the sounds and the temperature. It was as if we were all suddenly transported to a completely blank place with nothing on the floors, walls or ceiling but emptiness. A strong wind whipped past and over me, sending my hair flying around my head. Just when I thought it was going to be strong enough to lift me up and take me away, the noise of the wind disappeared and was replaced with a faraway tinny sound, like a television channel that wasn't getting a signal. My hair settled back on my shoulders. I didn't know if I was still in the same room or somewhere else. *Dorothy must have felt like this when she was swept away to Oz.*

Then it came to me - maybe this was what the Otherworlds were like. Maybe I was in a waiting room for the Overworld. *Oh, pleasepleaseplease let it be the Overworld and not the Underworld.*

The only problem with this theory was that I could still feel Tim in my hair, and I was pretty sure that when I died, I wasn't going to be able to take hitchhikers with me. I slowly reached my hand up to place it on the back of my head. Tim was there, trembling. Somehow he'd managed to hold on and not get blown to kingdom come. He was being quiet now - probably in a state of shock. I hoped he hadn't peed on me.

I shifted the weight of my legs from one foot to the other, feeling around a little bit with the toes of my moccasins. I was still standing on the ground of the cell; I could feel its uneven surface below me.

The white receded into a light gray. Slowly, the stone floor, walls, and surfaces in the room took on their natural hues. I saw that I was still in the same spot in the cell, but now Ben was gone and in his place stood another fae - a female wearing a silver robe. She had white hair and silver-gray eyes. She looked so much like Céline, it was freaky. I almost called her Céline before stopping myself. I didn't need to give these fae any intel at all, and I decided this included names.

I convinced myself that the first one to speak automatically had the upper hand. "Who are you?"

"I am Maléna of the silver elves. And you are Jayne, the elemental of the Light Fae."

I just tilted my head, refusing to confirm or deny who or what I was. "That your light ball that came in here?"

She looked at me, a question in her eyes, before she caught on to my meaning. "It was the wind that came, not light."

"Seemed pretty bright to me."

She examined me as if I were a rat in a cage doing something curious. "You are amusing."

"No, actually, I'm pissed. I want to be let out of here. You have no right to hold me against my will."

"According to whose law?"

I hesitated. "According to the law of the Green Forest." I was pulling stuff out of my butt now, but it sounded good to me.

"There is no such law."

"Well, there should be. I'm not sure who's in charge of making them around here, but obviously they've been asleep at the wheel.

War of the Fae: Book Three

They missed the whole 'torture is inhumane' thing, too."

"We are not humans, and so we are not bound to act humane. We act as fae and therefore do what must be done to protect faekind. You may leave once you have answered our questions. I believe you have been given enough demonstration of our methods. Do not force us to send you to the Otherworlds. Tell us what we want to know, and we will send you back to the Green Forest to find your way back home."

"Why? So you can destroy my home and everyone I care about? No. No thanks. I'm not cool with that." This was one cold-hearted bitch. She made Ben look evil-lite. "What happened to Ben?" I was wondering if he'd been blown up by the tornado that came through. It had seemed designed to put his fire out. It would have been awful convenient for the Light Fae if the Dark Fae just extinguished each other. Maybe I could orchestrate another one of those little catastrophes.

"Ben is none of your concern. You should be more worried about yourself."

"I'm not *concerned*, I'm *curious*. Big difference."

Maléna just looked at me for a few more seconds and then left the room. She kept the door open, so I wasted no time going over to it and looking out. She was nowhere to be seen. I ran a few paces down the corridor and tried to open another door, finding myself once again in my own cell.

"Sonofafuckface," I said disgustedly, sighing as I entered the room, shutting the door behind me. "You okay, Tim?"

"Yeah," he said weakly from my hair.

"Want to come out?"

"No. I'm gonna stay in here for a while."

"I don't blame you. I wish I had a giant hair nest I could hide in."

I laid down on my side on the stone bed, wondering what time it was, thinking it must be pretty late. I was exhausted. Despite the terrible hard, coldness of the bench, I found myself drifting off. As my brain tried to unwind itself, my sleepy thoughts floated over the events of the day - or days. I really had no idea how long I'd been here.

I thought about Ben and warred with myself. Part of me hated him down to his very essence, but another part of me was curious about him. I tried to deny and ignore it, but things weren't adding up with him, so it kept my brain interested and wondering, damn traitor that it was to me sometimes. Ben was cruel and did terrible things; he was willing to do anything to reach his goals - even kill me. But he was also showing flashes of compassion or mercy. He could have taken Tony, but he didn't. He could have killed him in the meadow, but he didn't. He could have tortured me more, but he didn't. None of this was making any sense, and it frustrated me. I placated myself by imagining what type of torture I could do to him to get answers to my questions. First, I'd make him sit and listen to Scrum for six hours straight. I'd have a witch do a spell on him so he couldn't block out the sound of Scrum's voice and couldn't fall asleep. Then, I'd feed Tim an entire plate of fruit, and lock Ben and him up in a very small, enclosed space ...

My happy thoughts were interrupted by another sound at the door.

Leck entered the room, alone this time.

Fuck me, not again. My brain was weeping in fright, but I refused to let it show on my face. "Oh, boy. Lucky me," I said, sitting up and fixing him with a bold stare.

Leck stood in the doorway, saying nothing.

"You won't beat me at the staredown game, Leck. I rock at this."

He still said nothing. He just kept looking at me, and it was creeping me out.

War of the Fae: Book Three

"Anyone ever tell you that you have the personality of an ogre?"

I saw a slight, almost imperceptible lifting of one of his eyebrows, but nothing else. I knew I was getting closer to pissing him off, and for some sadistic reason, I really needed to do that - make him angry. I couldn't use The Green or Blackie against him, but I could use my razor sharp wit. At least, that was what I told myself.

"No, wait. That would be in an insult to ogres everywhere. I think it would be more accurate to say that you have the personality of an orc ... "

Leck's lips thinned.

" ... an extra stupid one."

He took three long steps towards me and then gave me the evil eye. The pain exploded in my head. I had time to get a few words out before it became too much to bear.

" ... orc ... fucker!"

I rolled off the stone slab, cradling my head in my hands as I fell onto the floor. I panted, some part of my brain telling me that it could be possible to breath through the pain, like women did when they were having babies. A few seconds later the only rational part of my brain that was still functioning decided that anyone who says you can breathe through intense pain like that has never tried to do it before. *Lying bastards.*

The agony was so great, it overwhelmed my thinking. Tim was no longer my concern. Ben blowing me up? *Okay, fine.* Whatever. Tornados carrying me off to never-never land? *Sure. Whatever floats your boat. Just get this awfulness out of my head, and I'll agree to anything.*

The pain receded. My tightly closed eyes fought to open. I wanted - no *needed* - to see if Leck was still there. My desperate hope was that he was gone again and I could fall into a deep, dark sleep where the stinging, slicing barbs would no longer be able to reach me.

One eye opened and my hopes were immediately dashed. Leck was still standing there, only now he had a slight smile on his face. He didn't have to say it; I knew what he was thinking. *Now who's laughing?*

I felt like he'd nearly knocked me out with that last hit. Maybe that was the key - piss him off enough to overdose me, and then I could sleep through it. I looked up at him, now with both eyes open.

"Not bad," I groaned, "for an orc fucker."

I had expected my torture to continue with the brain melting, so I was totally unprepared for the kick to the face that I received. It snapped my head backwards and caused me to roll halfway over. I tried to keep my head lifted off the floor a little so I wouldn't squish my friend, but it was taking all of my concentration. If this guy was going to start physically kicking my ass like this, Tim wasn't going to make it. So even though the pain from my eye was distracting me from the pain in my head, it changed things. I could no longer afford to bait him and hope for a blackout.

"*Shit!* What'd you do that for?"

"Tell us what we want to know and it will all stop."

"Yeah, I got that. And maybe I'd be willing to talk, but I have to go to the bathroom, first."

"No."

I lifted my head and locked eyes with him, giving him the most withering look I could muster. "Are you seriously going to torture me by making me shit myself? I'm not the only one who will suffer with that one, you know."

Leck got a look of extreme distaste on his face, which made me very happy. I tried like hell not to smile. I really didn't have to go, but I was struggling to think of any way I could both delay the inevitable and also find a place to stash Tim so he wouldn't get taken down with me in a beating.

"You may use the bathroom. If you take too long, I will send someone in after you."

I bit back the retort that was ready to fly out of my mouth, not wanting to push my luck. I knew this guy was the real deal - a truly black-hearted Dark Fae. It was like someone had taken away his soul. I shivered thinking about it. Tony could have been made into one of them.

I stood up slowly, trying to ignore the pounding in my eyebrow where Leck's foot had caught me. I could feel something warm trickling down the side of my face; I wasn't sure if it was sweat or blood. I walked as casually and as confidently as I could, stumbling only once. Leck moved to the side, allowing me to pass.

I pictured the bathroom in my mind and got there way too soon. I wanted to stall as long as possible, even though he'd threatened me about hurrying up. I stood in front of the mirror, noticing that the stuff dripping down my face was indeed blood. He'd split a section of skin above my eyebrow, so I not only had a gaping, bleeding wound, I also had a puffy, swollen knot above my eye. At least it wasn't the eye itself. I slashed some water on my now not so pretty face, trying to rinse the blood away, but it only served to make the bleeding worse.

Tim tiptoed out onto my shoulder and just watched me, saying nothing. He had a very sad look on his face. I didn't say anything because I couldn't handle his pity right now. If a single traitor tear came out of my eyes, I'd probably turn into a Neanderthal and punch the mirror or something.

There were paper towels near the sink, which I used to try and stop the worst of the bleeding. I'd already stained the heck out of my tunic, but at this point it was hopeless. I wasn't sure why I even bothered with the towels. I was covered not only in blood but also dirt, drool, and I didn't want to know what else. *Please don't let it be barf.* I threw the wadded up, red-stained papers in the sink and grabbed some more. They soaked up the blood too quickly, and every time I took them off, it pulled the dried blood away and started the bleeding again. *Is it possible to bleed to death from an eyebrow cut?*

I stared at the huge pile of bloody paper towels in the sink. Then I looked up in the mirror, seeing the toilet behind me in its reflection. I stood there for a minute doing nothing, wondering why my brain was nudging me. I couldn't figure it out, so I gave up and grabbed the paper towels to throw them into the trash bin; but I changed my mind at the last second and threw them into the toilet instead.

"What are you doing?" asked Tim.

"I don't know." I stared at all the bloody towels in the toilet, watching them sink and become soaked with toilet water, my mind racing. "I was going to leave you in here, but this place is spelled and you can't fly. You'd starve to death before you could get away."

"So don't leave me here. I want to stay with you."

"He's going to beat the piss out of me, Tim; and if he does that, you'll get hurt too. They'll find you and kill you, I know they will. I can't let that happen."

"So what's with the towels in the toilet? Do you have an idea?"

"I think I do. Maybe." *Do I? Do I have an idea?* It was a long-shot, but even a long-shot was worth trying at this point. "Just be ready to jump ship and find a place to hide until your wings grow back and you can fly the hell out of here."

"I'm not going to leave you, Jayne."

"Yes, you are. Trust me ... I'd leave your stupid ass."

"No, you wouldn't. I know what you're trying to do, Jayne. Don't try to make me mad so I'll go."

I sighed. "Tim, if you love me, you'd do what I'm asking you to do."

"That's dirty pool, Jayne, dirty pool." I could feel his frown burning into my neck. "But I'll think about it."

"Fine. That's good enough for me."

I walked back to the sink and pulled out all the paper towels from the dispenser, shoving them into the toilet until it was stuffed. "Okay, Tim. Time for Operation Clogged Shitter to begin."

I walked over and stuck my head outside the door of the bathroom. "Um, excuse me!" I said loudly out into the hallway. "Is anyone out there? I'm having a little bit of a problem in here!"

A door opened down the hall and the wood sprite dungeon warden came out, obviously irritated. "What is the problem?"

I looked at him sheepishly. "Actually, it's a little embarrassing." I gestured for him to come inside. He looked at me suspiciously, but followed me in.

I pointed to the toilet. "I guess I must have used too much paper last time I was in here because it won't flush. And I really need to go now, but I can't unless it will flush, if you know what I mean. Is there another bathroom I could use?" I tried to look as embarrassed as possible and not devious, which was how I felt inside - devious and hopeful. *Come on, you stupidass wood sprite ... fall for my mad escape plan!*

He took a few steps over and peered into the toilet, his face getting a disgusted look. "What did you put in there?" he asked angrily.

"You're fucking kidding me, right?" I could tell my reaction surprised him a little, so I decided shame was the right track. "What? You Dark Fae don't ever shit? Get periods? What is that? A Dark Fae thing? So if I join up, I'll never have to take another dump again? Never have to find a tampon in the forest? Because that's tempting, let me tell ya."

He looked at me in horror, his mouth moving but no sound coming out. His eyes went back and forth from me to the door and then over to the toilet. He was in full panic mode. These wood sprites were no good at verbal confrontation, lucky for me.

"Listen, just bring me to another bathroom so I can take care of business, okay? I won't tell anyone I know your secret about pooping and periods okay? But honestly, you should put it in the brochures. You'd get a lot of female recruits that way."

"We don't have ... there are no ... everyone ... " He closed his eyes and took a deep breath. "Fine." He opened his eyes back up and fixed them on me calmly. "Let's go. And hurry up. Leck is waiting for you."

"Yes, and I sure can't wait to get back to him, too. You know how he's doing that torture thing? Wow, is that ever fun. He's even started kicking me in the face now, did you notice?" I pointed to my bloody eye, but he refused to look. "It doesn't seem to bother him at all that he's twice my size and I'm a girl. You Dark Fae are so modern-minded. Do you beat your wives, too?"

He ignored me as we walked down the hall. I tried like hell to notice any kind of distinguishing feature on any of the doors as I chattered away, but so far, no joy. They all looked the same.

The sprite stopped in front of another door. "Here," he said testily. "Use this one. And don't use so much paper this time."

I gestured for him to come closer and leaned towards him, whispering conspiratorially, "F-Y-I? I know you haven't pooped in a long time, but sometimes, a lot of paper is just necessary, you know?" I left him sputtering outside the door. I had to hurry up and figure out what the hell to do next - I had no time to enjoy my bodily function humor torture.

This bathroom was much like the other, if not a little nicer. It had two toilets and two sinks, plus a small metal boxy thing in the corner. I quickly moved over to it, realizing when I got closer that it was an old fashioned heater of some sort. "What the hell?" I said, running my hands over it, looking for a way to open it.

Tim came out of my hair. "What is it?"

"A heater thing. You could hide in here."

"Yeah, it'll be perfect until someone starts a fire," he said sarcastically.

"Listen, it's warm out. Summer's here. No one's going to light a fire in this place anytime soon. Your wings will be back in three weeks or so. You just need to find a way to get some food. Maybe if you crawl up in that pipe that goes into the ceiling you could find a way out, or at least find the dining hall or kitchens."

Tim climbed down my arm to get closer. "It has possibilities," he conceded, grudgingly.

"Well, check it out while I go get this stupid blood off my face." The cut was oozing again.

I left Tim at the heater and walked over to the sink, turning the tap on and letting the water run over my hands as I stared at myself in the mirror. I looked like shit. My hair was a giant ball of knots. My face had dirt and blood on it. My lips were chapped and thinking about cracking. I closed my eyes and took a deep breath, letting my mind drift to the place in me that held memories of The Green. *Man*, how I wished I could pull its healing power into me right now and fix myself up.

I felt a tingle in my fingers. At first I thought it was the temperature of the water changing, but then it became stronger. I opened my eyes and looked down, worried this place was spelled with witchy faucets. Maybe the water was poisoned.

But the feeling coming through the water wasn't a bad one. Once I focused on the sensations, I found they were actually pretty nice.

Very nice. It felt like ...

"No ... ," I whispered, afraid to be too hopeful.

"What?" asked Tim.

"Tim!" I whispered excitedly, "I feel something!"

"Yeah, me too. Desperate ... hungry ... sad ... hopeless. Pick your adjective."

"No, stop screwing around, I'm serious! There's something in this water!"

"Quick! Come get me, come get me!" He was jumping up and down anxiously on the heater, gesturing with his hands and waving me over.

The wood sprite's voice came through the door. "Are you almost done in there? Leck wants you back."

Yeah, I'll just bet he does. "Out in a minute! I'm a little constipated right now!"

I reached over and grabbed Tim. "Stand here on the edge of the sink and put your hand in this water. Tell me if you feel it too."

Tim and I let the water run over our hands. There was no mistake - something was going on here.

"I feel nothing. It's just water," he said, disappointment lacing his words.

"No, Tim. There's something there. I can feel it. It's strong."

Tim stared at the water on my hands and then he looked up at my face, meeting my eyes. "Jayne. You're an elemental."

"Yeah, so?"

"You have ties to Water."

I thought about that for a second. Flashes of Naida and Becky ran across my mind. "What does that mean?"

"I don't know!" he said feverishly. "Maybe you can connect! How does it work?"

War of the Fae: Book Three

"I have no friggin idea, Tim!" I said, panic lacing my voice. "I've never communicated using water before! That's Becky's thing, not mine!"

"Listen," said Tim, holding out his hands in a calming gesture, "just relax. Reach out to the water - through the water. See if you can find anyone out there ... a water sprite, a siren ... a frog, a tadpole ... *something!*"

I took a deep, wavering breath and closed my eyes. I figured I had about two minutes before the wood sprite busted down the door to drag me out of here. I had to give it a shot.

Chapter Twenty-Five

I REACHED INTO THE SPARKLY sensation that was flitting across my hands where they rested under the water still flowing from the faucet. At first, my connection was almost imperceptible, just a fluttering; but then I sensed a stretching - a reaching out beyond this place where I was right now. *This is what it must feel like to be a beam of light in a fiber optic cable.* I was zipping along a current, going with a flow I could not see, images and flashes of feelings flickering by and almost tickling me as I went along. I focused on the two fae I knew who were associated with this element - Becky and Naida, the siren from the Lake of the Green Forest.

At first I had nothing to grab hold of, just a jumble of pictures and bits of sensation. But slowly things took shape and gained focus. I could sense that what I sought was out there ... if only I could reach it. Tim was saying something but I couldn't concentrate on him very well. I was absorbing the things I was seeing and feeling in the water. A few of his words broke through my concentration ...

"... like The Green!"

Hearing those three words made me realize that this moment I was having with the water was not unlike the ones I'd had with The Green. Tim was right. There was a network of beings out there, all connected to each other through these elements. I was connected. I was linked to both networks - the ones of Water and Earth, and they were connected to each other ... *weren't they?*

I decided that attempting to make some sort of cross-link between the two was worth a try. Either I was going to bring The Green in to me and somehow at least protect myself from the worst of the torture, or I was going to cause some sort of cataclysmic event. Maybe the elements were never supposed to mix. I didn't have enough time to sort it out or consult the wise and wonderful gray elves, so I decided to fall back on my standard philosophy: *what the fuck ... might as well give it a shot.*

I called through the water to my friends. I focused every ounce of energy I had on recalling their faces, their personalities, and our shared history. I conjured up the feelings I had when we were experiencing those events together. I pictured Becky's laughter and easy smile. I remembered Naida's stoic face, luring my friends into the water during our changeling test. I saw it all; and through all these visions, I felt them, their fae energy surging through our Water element, reaching back out to me.

I knew Becky was feeling me there now. She was worried and scared but relieved, too. I tried to let her know where I was and that Tim and I were going to try to escape. It was harder for me here using the water link. I didn't have enough experience with it. I didn't know if she was getting the message or not.

Naida was there too. I felt a calming presence from her, and anger. I knew the anger was not for me; it was reserved for the ones who held me here. Man, how I wished I could see her float in here and sing them all to death.

I moved away from the link with my water friends and focused on working out a connection between Water and Earth. I knew it was there somewhere.

I thought about the Green Forest and the trees ... the leaves and the vines ... everything that had touched me and others before, when I needed them. I thought of the roots of the Ancients, digging down into the soil, reaching out for the water that nourished. And it was there that I found my connection. It had been waiting for me all along.

I stood in the bathroom, connected through Water, and pulled The Green to me. It rushed in, filling every part of my being with its cool, healing light. I felt the spot above my eye tingle, and knew that the skin was pulling together, the scar tissue weaving itself over the once-bleeding gash. I felt my energy restored, and my sense of hope soared until it swelled my heart with happiness. Now we had The Green, Tim and I. Now we were going to get the hell out of this nightmare.

I sent a silent thank you out to Water, grateful for its assistance and link to The Green. I pulled my hand out from under its flow, testing to see if the connection remained, relieved to find that it did. Even the Dark Fae creatures helped my connection here. Even their Dark Fae hearts couldn't hide from the power they fed with their life forces. I turned the faucet off and opened my eyes to look at Tim.

"Did that go as well as it looked like it did?" he asked, smiling hesitantly.

"Better. I'm linked to The Green now."

"I *knew* it. I could feel the hum, even without my wings. Pixies can do that you know ... sense The Green."

I smiled, so full of joy right now I couldn't give him a hard time about his pixie posturing. "I know, you're the awesomest. You're the man ... the pixieman. Now let's go kick some fae ass."

Tim jumped into my waiting hand and ran up my arm to get into my hair. "Giddyup, you elemental fae butt kicker!"

Elle Casey

I reached up, gently flicking him in the ass for yanking on my hair and treating me like a horse, but I didn't have time to properly scold him because someone was banging on the door.

"Time to come out!" shouted my wood sprite jailkeeper.

Time to test my strength, you mean, asshole. I put up a field of Green power in front of the door. "Come on in and get me, gnome head!"

I could hear some grumbling on the other side of the door. The latch moved. It went still for a second and then jiggled again, before more silence followed.

"How did you lock this door? These doors aren't lockable. Open up right this instant!"

He sounded like my mother. I tried not to laugh. Escaping the clutches of the bad guys was supposed to be serious business, but I was so full of the power of The Green right now and the idea that I could be possibly escaping, that I couldn't help but be happy.

"No!" I was high on life or something. I was gushing light and joy. It was so not like me, but it felt oh, so damn good in this miserable place.

I heard the sprite's angry, striding footsteps receding down the hall. The Green was amplifying all the sounds around me. I could hear Tim breathing fast, showing me he was as excited as I was. Soon I was able to hear several sets of feet coming down the hallway towards the door.

Leck's voice seeped in through the wood, sending a creepy sensation up and down my spine. It was a bit of a wet blanket on my happiness; hearing it caused me to lose some of my optimism. I knew he was on the other side, less than a couple feet away, trying to figure out how to get in and hurt me. That kind of evil was hard to totally block out.

"Open the door, Jayne. We aren't done talking."

War of the Fae: Book Three

Tim was trembling again. "He's going to come in, Jayne," he whined quietly.

"No, he's not," I whispered. Then I shouted at the door, "Go torture your mother, Leck!" I hoped insulting someone's fae mother was as rude as insulting someone's human mother. Maybe if they got mad enough, something would break around here and I'd be able to find a way to get out. Hopefully the thing that broke wouldn't be me.

"I'm giving you five seconds."

"Give me whatever you want. I'm not coming out until the Light Fae arrive to kick your asses."

I considered testing the power link for communication, but I was worried about my ability to do too many things with it at once. Could I hold them off with my giant Green power bubble shun and talk to the green elves at the same time? It was worth trying, but I was afraid to do it with Leck standing right outside. I knew now that as a wrathe he could do things like walk the Gray and send excruciating pain into my body, but I had no other clues about his remaining powers. Wrathes were some scary shit. I was glad my friend Tony was one. Once he had it all figured out, no one would ever mess with us again.

I felt something pressing against The Green. It didn't feel right; it felt dark and dangerous. It had to be Leck trying to do something, or maybe Samantha again. Although this time it felt different, more ominous. Maybe Leck was trying to get in here through the Gray. I had no idea how The Green and The Gray were connected, or separated for that matter, and I really didn't want to know, either.

"Whatever you're trying to do, it's not working. Go torture someone else. There must be a small child or an old lady around you could mind melt for fun."

I could hear a couple of subdued voices on the other side of the door, but it was difficult to figure out what they were saying. I could tell that they were pissed, though. *Good.* At least I wasn't totally inept at this fae power shit.

The pushing on my power bubble had stopped, so I quickly reached along the connection I was holding to see what else or who else I could find out there. Finn was my most likely candidate since he was a green elf, and I knew I could reach those guys through The Green. But he was out on training maneuvers for I didn't know how much longer. I wasn't even sure where he was or how long I'd been in here. But still ... it was worth trying to find him. If I could talk to Finn, he could let Jared and the council know what was happening. Unfortunately, I'd have to tell them about Chase, because if anyone was going to come here for rescue purposes, I wanted him taken, too. So far none of the fae here had mentioned Chase, which told me they either didn't know he was here or they didn't know about our connection.

I pictured Finn in my mind, hearing the redneck accent flavoring his speech. I saw his reddish hair and freckles, the sinewy forearms that flexed as he drew back his arrow and sent it whistling through the air to hit its target. I saw him smile at Becky, always amused at her happy comments. I waited to see if I came across him in my connection, but before I could go far enough, I heard more sounds out in the hall.

"Jayne." It was Ben.

I said nothing but dropped my attempts to reach Finn.

"Jayne, I don't know how you managed to lock this door, but you have to open it up. I won't be able to protect you if you resist right now."

I had to say something to that. It was too ridiculous to leave unanswered. "Protect me? If setting that pitbull Leck on me is your idea of protection, you can go suck a duck butt. He nearly killed me."

"You're being dramatic."

"Have him liquefy your brain for a few minutes and see if you still agree with that statement."

"Jayne, listen to me. Maléna will come." His voice had an urgency to it that made me nervous. Mostly because *he* sounded nervous, and I was pretty sure that this wasn't an emotion he usually suffered from.

"Let her come," I said cockily, even though I had plenty of misgivings. She had pretty much completely shut Ben down and sent him out of my cell - either with a simple command or with some blast of that tornado wind she had sent in - which told me she was a badass. I just didn't know how *much* of a badass she was. I wished I had spent more time with Céline learning about the silver elves. First thing I was going to do when I got back was talk to Tony about the gray elves' plans for fae training. If it wasn't too late, a primer course in fae basics was definitely in order. Those fools didn't realize how much the changelings' ignorance was hurting all of the Light Fae as a whole and risking our safety.

I heard nothing for a minute or longer, so I assumed Ben had left and I was alone again with Tim, but then I heard a light tapping on the door. A voice was talking to me from the other side, but it was too faint to hear. I moved closer.

"What did you say?" I didn't even know who it was. I put my hand at the door and could feel warmth, and it wasn't just the wood. Ben.

"Jayne. Please. I'm begging you. You're going to break Tony's heart by getting killed in here."

"Ben, why don't you just leave me alone? I'm not coming out."

I jumped back in fright at the loud bang that issued from the door, shaking it on its hinges. I'd heard a sound like that when my mom and boyfriend would get into fights. That would be right before we would have new holes in the walls, courtesy of Rick the Dick.

"Did you just punch the door?"

"Yes."

"Wow. Mature."

"I'm frustrated, okay? Tony is my friend ... *was* my friend. I know how much he cares about you. You're going to die and he's going to blame me."

Ben was making my head spin again. Could he be any more ridiculous? He orders my torture and then begs me to save myself by submitting to more of it? If this situation wasn't so life and death, it would feel like typical guy shit. Say one thing, do another. Lead a girl on, making her believe he cares, and then dump her after she gives it up. It wasn't like I had a whole lot of experience in the area, but I'd had my heart cracked once or twice by careless boys. I knew when I was being played.

"You don't need to worry about Tony *or* me. I'm not going to die, and you walked away from Tony's friendship when you brought me here."

I heard the low roar that told me Ben's burning fury was getting the better of him. I pulled more of The Green into me, hoping I wasn't going to have to battle through the elements with him. I didn't have the fighting experience and definitely not the confidence. I was on the wrong turf, too. Maybe if I had my fae peeps behind me, I'd feel differently. But here, all I wanted to do was hold the bad guys off until I could make my getaway.

I heard more noises in the hallway and some shouting. Ben's warmth disappeared from my radar and was replaced with a cold silence.

"What do you think they're doing?" whispered Tim.

"I have no idea. But it's creeping me out ... the silence."

"Me too."

We moved away from the door, sitting down on the bathroom floor next to each other.

"If things go badly for us here, I just want you to know how much it has meant for me to be your friend," said Tim, looking down at his tiny hands.

"Same here, Tim. But we're getting out of this. Alive. Our friends are going to come."

"Were you able to contact them?"

"No. But I'm going to try again in a minute. I'm just a little afraid of taking my concentration off the big power bubble I put up around the bathroom."

Tim look around and up at the ceiling. "We're in a bubble right now?"

I shrugged. "That's what I call it. I imagine a giant bubble of power made out of The Green and it just goes there."

Tim smiled. "I feel better already." He looked at the bathroom door, yelling happily, his tiny middle finger held out in front of him, "Screw you, Dark Fae! You've been bubble shunned!"

The smile immediately left both our faces when we heard the answering wind. My mouth dropped open, and all of the blood drained from Tim's face at the same time. Maléna was back, and she was doing something inside the wind, just outside the door.

Chapter Twenty-Six

THE HOWL OF MALÉNA'S TEMPEST was getting louder and louder. I wasn't sure if it sounded like a total level-five storm to me because I was hearing things more acutely, or because she was really brewing up something that powerful for us. I could see the door to the bathroom shaking from the force, but inside our power bubble, we didn't feel a thing. The wind didn't touch us or anything nearby. It was as if the bathroom were in the eye of her hurricane.

The Green hummed continuously, neither fading nor wavering in its strength. The winds outside the door were wailing, making Tim and me very nervous. He climbed up my sleeve and sat on my shoulder, clutching a fistful of my hair just in case. It wouldn't take much of a breeze to send him into the wall.

"How long can you hold her off?" Tim asked.

"I don't know. Forever? It's not like keeping it up is tiring me out or anything. I can feel the shield, and it seems strong." I didn't want to tell him my theories or fears out loud, but I had a sneaking suspicion these Dark Fae were using the wrong weapon against me. Maybe I was totally out in the weeds, but it seemed like the only way to fight an elemental was to use the other elements. My theory was that Samantha and Maggie had gotten to me before by coming at me right through the power I was using, and having the ley line there to help. It was possible I was wrong; but if I wasn't, I hoped like hell Ben didn't figure it out. Apparently, Maléna could control the wind to some degree, but not like Ben could. I'd been calling him a Dark Fae demon all along, but that wasn't what he was. I knew that now. He was an elemental like me.

I remembered that one night when Ben came riding into Tony's room *on* the wind. It was a totally different sensation than the one Maléna was creating here. She could control some wind by traveling in it, but the element Wind did Ben's bidding - the way Earth did mine through The Green. None of the other fae could do that. This I knew from what Dardennes had said, and because when I was in my Element, doing what I do, I knew I was alone there. I was aware of the other fae and creatures who were connected in through their own unique abilities, but none of them controlled the Element itself.

"So how do you see us getting out of this?" asked Tim, interrupting my thoughts.

"That's a great question. I guess I imagine being rescued. I can use The Green to shield us, but I still can't get out of this spelled compound. Unless someone comes to get us, how can we possibly escape?"

"We could take a hostage."

I laughed humorlessly. "With what? My scary breath? No, wait ... I'll tell you what - I'll grab that wood sprite next time he comes near the door, and you can fart in his face. That'll put him under your spell and then you can order him to show us the way out."

Tim pulled my hair. "Very funny. I had a more *realistic* plan, like having Chase come get us, but if you're going to be a comedian ... "

"Chase? As in the recently pixelated Chase?"

"Yeah. Maybe they've fixed him. He's here somewhere, right?

They must not know about him or they would have already used him against you. Maybe that Goose guy can help, too. He didn't seem so Dark Fae-ish to me."

The way he said that sounded funny. I twisted my head to try and get a look at him, but he hid behind my hair. "How many Dark Fae do you know, anyway?"

He didn't answer right away.

"Tim ... ?" I said threateningly. Now was not the time for him to be coy.

"A few, okay. I know a few. Some better than others."

"Who exactly do you know, and how well? And don't play games with me. We need to explore every option."

Tim sighed heavily, right by my left ear, giving me goose bumps all down my arm and leg on my left side. I reached up and grabbed him, holding him out in front of me. I bent my legs up so that he could stand on my knee and be at my eye level.

"Spill it, Tim. I know you have secrets. It's time to share."

"Fine." He sat down on my knee with his legs folded. "I might have a ... *mumblemumblemumble* ... " The rest of his sentence faded out so low I couldn't hear it.

"Say that again? And at a volume that someone other than a dog could hear, please?"

"I *said* that I *might* have a *wife* hanging around in here somewhere."

I almost sent him flying across the room without the use of wings when I heard that priceless little nugget.

"You *what?!*"

Tim just folded his arms across his chest, saying nothing.

"And why are you just now telling me this? Don't you think it might have been important to share that fact before?"

"Why? It's not like she would do anything to help us. She's Dark Fae!"

"Was she Dark Fae when you married her?"

"No. She changed sides."

I looked at him in shock. "Tim, that's terrible."

"Tell me about it."

I looked at him in mock pity, still not very happy that he'd kept this from me. "Was it your gas problem?"

Tim threw his hands up. "I can't believe you'd joke around at a time like this!"

I slapped both hands down on the stone floor. "Well, I can't believe you'd hide this from me!"

We both sat there, staring each other down.

"Give it up, Tim. You know I'm gonna win this."

"No, you won't. I can stare until a fae's eyeballs fall out."

"All I have to do is lean in and blow my gnarly breath on you and it's gonna be all over."

Tim held up his hands. "Okay, okay, I surrender. Keep your vom breath to yourself, woman. You win."

"So, tell me what happened ... because I know she didn't leave you for another pixie. You're too hot for that."

"I know, right?" Tim shook his head. "That she-pixie was nuts. She never had it better than when she was with me. Her name is Abby. I rubbed her feet, stroked her wings, made her breakfast every day ... " he sighed. "And then one day she was gone. *Poof.* A couple weeks later I found her at Maggie's. Maggie had taken Abby from the forest - who knows what the heck she was doing out there, she never told me. Maggie was using her wings in one of her brews ... some sort of deal they'd made. I stayed with her, giving up my wings in exchange for Abby's release. After Abbey's wings grew back, she left, promising to

War of the Fae: Book Three

come back and get me when mine were grown in again. I waited an extra three days for her to come. And let me tell you, being at Maggie's with wings? *Scary.* She's always eyeing you, waving that wooden spoon around. I was sure one day she was just going to knock me over the head and take my wings all over again."

"So what happened next? Did Abby come back?"

"No. She never showed, so I left. Then I flew around everywhere looking for her. Eventually I met up with some other small fae and they told me where she was. About two months later I saw her in the forest. She apologized but told me she was staying. She tried to get me to go, too, but I told her *no way*. This pixie is no Dark Fae."

"Wow. That totally sucks." I couldn't think of anything else to say.

"Yeah. She dumped me after seventy-five years of wedded bliss."

I nearly choked. "Seventy-five years? Holy bat balls, Tim. That's a long time."

"Not really. Not for fae folk."

"It is in my book. Did she ever tell you why she went over?"

"She tried, but I refused to listen. It's all a bunch of propaganda anyway."

"Alright, so I guess we scratch her off the list of possible helpers."

"Yeah. Way off the list. If she tried to help I'd refuse to go with her."

"Well, let's not get crazy. If she offers, we're taking her up on it. Then we'll tell her what a ho-bag she is for leaving you."

Tim smiled at me. "Okay. Deal. But run really fast after you say it. She'll pixie you for sure if you call her a ho-bag."

"Oh, yeah. I forgot about that part - the pixelation stuff."

"Do you hear that?" asked Tim, his head cocked.

"Hear what?"

"Nothing. That's my point. That howling wind is gone."

I listened, and sure enough, he was right. It was silent.

I put Tim on my shoulder and then stood, walking cautiously over to the door and putting my ear to it, trying to detect any sounds coming from the hallway. There was nothing, and no heat either. I got down on my hands and knees and lowered my eyes to the floor, attempting to see under the door. There wasn't enough of a crack to be able to tell if there were any feet there, so I stood back up.

"Is anyone there?" I called out. I wasn't sure if anyone would actually answer, but figured it was worth asking.

"Do you think we're all alone here now?" asked Tim.

"I don't know. It's not like we need a guard; we can't leave the hallway. Do you know what time it is?"

"I have no idea. I'm not sure if we've been here half a day, a whole day, two days ... without windows and regular mealtimes, it's hard to say."

"I know. Well, they've been pretty much constantly harassing us for hours. Maybe we can assume it's nighttime since they've finally left us alone. That means we have several uninterrupted hours while they sleep to try and contact our friends."

"Go for it. And then we need to try and sleep, too. Who knows what tomorrow will bring."

"Agreed," I said. "You stand here on my shoulder. If you hear anyone coming, signal me. But don't pull too hard."

"I wouldn't dream of it." He giggled.

"Tim, I'm not playing."

"Oh, me neither."

I sighed, giving up on having a serious conversation with him. And then I blocked out all thoughts of Tim and his hair pulling from my mind. I needed to focus through The Green and find my friends.

War of the Fae: Book Three

We had an SOS signal to send and a rescue to arrange.

Chapter Twenty-Seven

I FINALLY FOUND FINN, BUT he was really far away. He was able to contact green elves at the compound, but there weren't enough of them there to do anything for me now. He sent me images of groups of green elves and daemons working together in preparation, but I didn't have any idea how far in the future these forecasted images would actually become reality. I sent him visions of Tim and me in the bathroom. He seemed confused by it, but I didn't know what else to show him. I flashed him mental pictures of Ben, Maléna and Leck. I hoped he understood that if he saw any of them, his job was to shoot first and ask questions later.

I found Becky again and tried to let her know I was okay. All I could get from her was a feeling of panic and anxiety. My water communication skills needed a lot of work. I severed the link, frustrated that I wasn't getting anywhere with it.

Tim's snores distracted me from my attempts, so I decided to give up for the time being. I'd done all I could anyway. I made myself as comfortable as possible, piling up a bunch of paper towels under my head on the floor as a pillow. Eventually, I drifted off to sleep, thinking about how hungry I was.

My mind was a whirlwind of sleepy dream sounds and fuzzy

images. Fae and people from my past mingled together, talking to me, yelling, crying, and eating even. It was like I was having a life review and there wasn't enough time to get it all done in order. Someone had taken my cookie jar of memories and shaken it up really good, throwing the crumbs out on the floor. Now I could hear Tony's voice.

"Jayne! Jayne! Is that you?"

Of course it's me. This is my dream.

"Jayne, it's me, Tony. I'm in the Gray. Can you hear me?"

Tony was here? In the Gray? Am I in the Gray?

"Tony?"

"Oh, thank God, you answered. I'm projecting across the astral plane right now. I can see you; can you see me?"

"No." I had no idea if I was answering out loud or just in my head. *This is so confusing.*

"Where are you? This looks like a bathroom."

"It is a bathroom. I'm in the Dark Fae compound somewhere, but I have no idea where. Their hallways are spelled. I've only seen one cell carved out of rock and two bathrooms. I have The Green protecting us in here. I couldn't channel the power in those other rooms. We're in here due to some ... uh ... technical difficulties."

"What do you mean? ... Never mind, you can tell me later. It's not safe for me to stay here. I just wanted to tell you that Chase is coming for you. He's coming. Just sit tight."

"What do you mean, Chase is coming? Is he okay? I don't want him to get hurt!"

"Listen ... oh crap, I have to go. Just go with Chase, okay? We'll fix the problems later. I'll see you ... "

And then he was cut off. I wanted to yell, *What problems?!*, but he wasn't there anymore. I started to talk to Tim about Tony but realized that I was still seeing wacky images, and my body felt like it was in cement. *Oh. I'm still sleeping.* I roused myself and stretched for a second, looking around the bathroom as my unconscious mind caught up to my waking mind.

"Tim," I whispered loudly. "Wake up. I have to tell you something."

He ignored me completely, still snoring away. I decided to leave him alone and go back to sleep. If Chase did come tonight, I'd hear him. I needed to get some rest or I wouldn't be able to function when my rescuers arrived, whoever they turned out to be.

No sooner had that thought crossed my mind than I heard noises outside the door again. My ears pricked up. Would it be Chase or Ben? Maléna or Leck?

Whoever it was, he was laughing. And then coughing. *Okay, so none of the above.*

There was a knock at the door. "Jayne? Are you in there?"

I got up slowly and crawled over to the door. "Who is it?"

"It's me. Chase." Then another giggle.

"Who's with you?" I asked, confused. I didn't recognize the voice of the giggler.

"No one."

"Who's laughing out there with you?"

"It's just me. Hurry up and open the door. We need to get you out of here."

I was afraid this was a Dark Fae trick. Maybe someone was projecting Chase's voice. "Prove it's you."

"Don't you recognize my voice?"

"Yeah, but not that fucked up laugh."

"Okay. Uh, remember when we went into the fourth obelisk? And we had to say what our fondest desire was?"

"Yeah?"

"I still have that same desire. So let's go." He started laughing again, only this time it was more of a snort. But even so, I knew this was Chase, no doubt about it. During our changeling test at the end, we had to speak our fondest desire out loud to enter into the compound. His was to take care of me. And now, even though he was sick and almost as much of a captive as I was, he was still doing it. *Talk about dedicated.* My throat hurt with the devastating emotions that got suddenly clogged in there.

I weakened the shield I'd put up and grabbed the handle of the door, pulling it open.

Chase stood in the doorway, his hand on the frame, a huge grin on his face. "Jaynie!" he exclaimed, stepping in and grabbing me around the waist, spinning me around. "Oh, I'm so happy to see you!"

I quickly put the power back up and bubbled him in with us. Then I pushed off his chest as hard as I could. This guy was Chase, yes; but he was acting about as un-Chase-like as a guy possibly could. He was still pixelated, apparently.

"Put me down, you big dope."

"You look beautiful," he said, grinning his fool head off, but releasing me gently to the floor.

I went over and scooped Tim up off the ground where he was sleeping. "Wake up, sleepy. We have a problem. A big one." Not only was Chase mentally crazed, he'd obviously lost his sense of sight. That was the only explanation there could be for anyone to be calling me beautiful right now.

Tim sat up, scrubbing his eyes so he could see. His hair was a mess, and I didn't have the heart to tell him; his 'do was so important to him.

"Oh, hey, Chase. How are you?"

"Excellent, my little pixie friend, how have you been? Long time no see." He laughed at that and put his hands on his hips, apparently waiting for an equally enthusiastic response.

Tim looked at me sadly. "Still not fixed, I see."

I shook my head, saying nothing.

"So, I guess I need to get you guys out of here. Goose tells me you're in a bit of a pickle."

I opened my mouth to speak, but I couldn't. I was picturing Chase selling some useless shit on a QVC infomercial. I'd bet he could sell the hell out of it too with that smile.

"Oh, you're so adorable, I can hardly stand it!" he squealed, grabbing my cheeks between his hands, squeezing them together and leaning in to kiss me smack dab on the super-puckered lips. "Come on, kids, follow me. Bring your mighty green power parade with you, Jayne. You might need it."

Tim and I exchanged looks and shrugged at each other, shaking our heads sadly. It took an awful lot to strike both of us simultaneously speechless, but Chase had managed.

He moved towards the door again, so I gathered my wits about me as best I could and surrounded all three of us with The Green. I sent the message out that I needed this power bubble to move with us, keeping all of us inside at all times without letting anything or anyone else in. I did it as fast as I could because Chase was already moving out into the hallway. I included a small addition to my instructions, asking The Green to block any noise we made from reaching outside the bubble. I had no idea if it would work, but it would sure make it easier to escape if the Dark Fae didn't hear Mr. Chatterbox on the way out.

"I've sure missed you guys. This place is boring with a capital *B*. All they ever talk about is getting ready for the war, starting the war, defeating the Light Fae in the war. It gets old pretty quick."

"Why are they saying all that stuff to you? Don't they know you're Light Fae?"

"Oh, I'm not Light Fae anymore. I'm Dark Fae now."

"*What?*" the word came out strangled. I was instantly sick to my stomach. "Chase?" I grabbed his arm and made him stop walking. "What do you mean, you're Dark Fae? Did you ... change sides?" I almost couldn't say those last two words. It was inconceivable.

"Had to." He shrugged. "Don't worry about me, though, Jayne. I'll always have your back." He grinned spectacularly at me, like he was modeling for a toothpaste commercial.

Tears sprang to my eyes, and I started crying. "No, Chase, *no!* I don't want you to be Dark Fae! I won't let you!"

He smiled as if he felt sorry for me, patting me on the shoulder with his great big hand. "Ssshhh, don't cry. I'm fine. I'm happy, see?" He gave me a heart-stoppingly handsome smile and pointed to his face.

"No you're not! You're *pixelated*, you idiot, there's a *difference!* This is not *you*. This is a maniac, crazy, drugged-out version of you. You'll be better soon, back to the old Chase, I know you will. If they can't fix you here, Maggie will fix you. Tim will give her more wings, won't you Tim?" I looked at him, desperation on my face.

Tim's expression looked no better than mine. He nodded his head furiously. "Sure. As soon as they grow back, they're yours, Chase. All yours." He kept nodding, now at me. He looked as freaked out as I felt.

"Come on, sweet thing," murmured Chase in a calming voice. "We have to get moving. Someone's bound to come see what's going on. I don't have a lot of time to get you to the door."

"But you're coming with us, aren't you?" I pleaded, pitifully, even to my own ears - and I totally didn't care. This couldn't be happening.

War of the Fae: Book Three

It was like losing another Tony.

He gave me a playful frown. "No, silly. I'm staying here. This is my home now." He walked briskly again, looking back to make sure I was following. "But I want you to know if you ever change your mind, you can come be Dark Fae, here with me. I'll be your daemon again and things will go back to the way they were." He laughed really loud and then coughed, almost as if he were trying to control his laughter with it.

The tears continued to flow down my face, and I choked on sobs that rose up from deep inside my heart. All I could think about was how I'd really fucked things up ... *big time*. I'd hand-delivered my daemon - the toughest, most solid, dependable, loyal guy in the whole world - to the enemy. The pixelation had messed him up, and obviously their treatment wasn't worth a shit. I'd totally fallen for Goose's line of bullcrap. And on top of all this, I'd handed over a vial of Tim's pixie blood to the Dark Fae, which the healers had warned me could be used in very dangerous witch spells. The idea of Tim's blood being used to conjure up weapons that could be used against my friends made me physically ill. My head was spinning, making it necessary that I stop walking and hold onto the wall for support.

"Chase!" yelled Tim. "She's going down!" He had a slight edge of panic to his voice, which probably stemmed from the fact that he was on my shoulder, and if I went down, he was going down with me. Stupid pixie never seemed to remember that I was the only one who could ever hear him.

"Whoa, there, Jaynie-girl. Just relax. I've got ya." And that was the last thing I remembered - Chase picking me up in his big, thick, strong arms, the smell of his delicious body drifting up into my nose, the warmth of his embrace enveloping me, and for one moment, making me feel safe.

Elle Casey

I lost consciousness and slipped like a worthless coward into the welcoming blackness.

Chapter Twenty-Eight

I FELT THE WARMTH NEXT to me and moved closer to it. I didn't want to wake up from this nightmare, especially now that the physical torture part was over and had been replaced with this ... comfortable whatever it was.

"She's moving."

"Are her eyes open?"

"No."

I could hear the concerned voices of my friends, and the familiar soft blankets under my fingertips told me that I was in my own bed in the Light Fae compound. I was happy about that and wondering what this warmth next to me was. It felt like a golden retriever or something - warm, soft, and heavy. But I still didn't want to face the reality that was surely waiting ... my world, turned all upside down.

"Bring me over there."

"Tim, maybe you should just let her sleep."

Yeah, Tim, just let me sleep. Somehow Tim had conned someone into getting close enough to him to be able to hear him and do his bidding.

"No, she's faking. I can tell. Her eyelids moved. Bring me over there so I can see her better."

Elle Casey

I heard footsteps moving from the dresser to my bed. Soon enough there were little footfalls moving up my body towards my face.

Fucking pixie.

"Time to wakey, wakey, Jayney-poo," said his annoying voice. I felt a tiny tapping on my cheek.

"Go away," I croaked.

"She *is* awake!" exclaimed Becky.

"Foof! And she's got the bad breath to prove it!" yelled Tim, making exaggerated gagging sounds.

Idiot.

"You can't pull a fast one on Mr. Tim," said Finn's deep south voice.

I turned my head so it was facing where I thought Tim might be standing, breathing out as much as I could as I talked. "Go away and leave me alone. All of you." I didn't want any of them there. I wanted to be alone in my misery.

I felt Tim fall down on my chest and heard him continue his gagging act.

"No deal, babe. You gotta get up." This was Spike, and now I knew who it was that was lying with me on the bed.

Someone took my hand and tugged on it a couple times. "Come on, Jayne. Come back to us." It was Tony, and he had given me just what I *didn't* need to hear - his kind and patient voice, with no judgment in it.

I felt the tears coming again, and I flung my arm up over my face. "Just leave me alone, would you please? Get out." I tried to yell it, but I didn't have the strength. Too much of my energy was focused on the sadness.

"We're not going anywhere," said Tim in one of his sassiest voices. "Now get up and stop feeling sorry for yourself. And brush your teeth,

Jayne, Dragonbreath of Blackthorn."

I waved my hand around where I thought he was standing, trying to brush him off of me. "Get out of here, you pain in the ass," I growled angrily. It was on the tip of my tongue to blame him for Chase's predicament, but I knew that wasn't fair. I clamped my mouth shut, just letting the tears flow down into my ears. I hated crying lying down; it made my ears all squishy.

I cracked my eyes open and turned my head to the side. I found myself about two inches away from Spike's gorgeous face. He cracked a sexy-as-hell grin at me, flashing me my favorite smile. "Hi beautiful."

It should have made me happy to hear that, but instead I started bawling. It made me think of Chase saying it earlier. I covered my face with both hands and struggled to turn over under my tight covers so I wouldn't be facing Spike anymore, wishing they would all get out of my room and leave me the hell alone.

"I know you want us to go, Jayne, but we can't," said Tony. "We need you to get up and talk to us. There's a lot of stuff happening right now. You've been asleep for about eighteen hours."

I barely heard what he was saying. I tried to block it out so I could wallow in my despair.

"Let me give her a little kiss. That'll get her up," said Spike, his smile still blazing in his voice.

"No!" said four voices all at once.

"Okay, okay, sheesh ... I'm just trying to help."

As sad as I was, I couldn't help but laugh a little inside at Spike's attempts to get some sexytime in, under the guise of 'helping' me.

I felt Spike's bodyweight leave the bed. "Time to take serious measures in hand."

"Spike, I'll get Scrum if I hafta," said Finn, a warning in his voice.

"He won't hurt her," said Tony, calmly, confidently.

I was still crying silently, but my gasps for air were fewer and less forceful. I didn't feel as though I were drowning in the darkness quite as much.

I felt the covers being drawn back and Spike's hands sliding under my legs and back, lifting me from the bed. My arms stayed at my sides. "Don't hate me for what I'm about to do, love. I'm helping you." He leaned over and kissed my neck, inhaling strongly, giving me chills. My cries dialed back even more, but I kept my eyes shut, resting my head against his chest. I didn't care what he did.

He walked. I blocked out the sounds of those around us, hearing only some whispering and the drawing back of curtains.

What the?

And then the sound of water shooting out of the shower head hit my eardrums. Two more steps taken by my friend Spike and suddenly I was instantly awake.

"What the hell?!" I fought him, trying to get away. "Let me go! *Let me go!"* I was squirming and lashing out at him as hard as I could. The water from the shower poured down over both of us, soaking through my clothes and spattering into my nose and mouth.

"I'll let you go when you calm down!" yelled Spike. "Jayne, chill." He held on tight, doing nothing to protect himself from my violence.

"I'm *not* going to calm down! Do you hear me! I'm not! I'm leaving! I'm leaving here!" My struggles mingled with my cries and slowly weakened. I couldn't do both at the same time; I didn't have the strength for it. I gave up on the struggling and just sobbed instead. "Do you hear me, Spike?" I said weakly, "I'm leaving this fucking place."

"Shhhh, I heard you, but I'm not buyin' it. Just relax." He dropped my legs, but held onto my shoulders, pulling me firmly against his chest and gripping me in a not unpleasant bear hug.

I put my arms up against his chest, meaning to push him away, but he held me tight.

He lifted one hand to pet my head, over and over, while he murmured comforting words and sounds. "Shhhh, everything's going to be okay. Just give it a little time."

"Nothing's going to be okay anymore. Chase joined the Dark Fae. Did you know that?"

"Yeah, we know. Tim told us everything."

I choked on a random sob. "Then you know it's my fault. We lost Chase because of me. He's totally changed."

"I don't know that at all. I know that he was doing what he wanted to do - taking care of you - and he got accidentally zapped by a pixie. And you tried to help him and the Dark Fae got to him. It's no one's fault that it happened, but theirs."

"I did it," I whispered.

"Jayne, babe. You know I love ya. And if you'd let me, I'd show you just how much. But that doesn't change the fact that looking at this objectively, it's not your fault. You do not control the fates, ... " he chuckled almost to himself, " ... just the elements."

He continued to stroke me as the water poured over us. My crying gradually dissipated in the face of reason. I wanted to hold onto the pain, but my brain wouldn't let me. And my temper wouldn't let me either. I wanted to get back at those Dark Fae bastards, especially Ben. If I couldn't blame myself for this shit, then I was going to blame it all on him. If he had left Tony alone, we wouldn't be in any of this mess. I didn't care if it made sense to anyone else; it made sense to me, and now I had a nice big fat target for my anger.

Spike's petting slowed down, and he pulled away from me a little to look at my face. I lifted up a hand to wipe my nose. I was certain this moment was one of the ugliest of all time for me. It was hopeless, really, but the idea of standing here in the shower with Spike while snot dripped out of my nose ... was too much for me to manage.

"Better?" he asked, searching my eyes for confirmation.

"No."

He smiled, pulling me to him and squeezing me tight. "Better. Good. Take a shower. Becky will bring you your stuff."

I put my hand on his face as he moved to pull away.

He stopped instantly, a question on his face, hope in his eyes. His hand dropped to my waist and held on.

"Thanks, Spike. You got soaked for me. You probably have my boogs on your shirt, too."

"Anytime, babe, you know that." He leaned in for a kiss, but I dropped my head. I was embarrassed about what I'd done ... my tantrum ... my runny nose ... everything.

He grabbed my chin, forcing my head up and giving me a very chaste, close-mouthed kiss on the lips. "Later, when you're feeling better, we'll finish what we started here." He raised an eyebrow and then looked pointedly at the shower.

I cleared my throat, embarrassed and a little aroused. "*A-hem*. No promises."

"I don't need any," he said, winking. He released me and walked out of the bathroom, yelling to Becky on his way, "Hey Beck! She needs clothes and a towel!" The door swung shut behind him.

I leaned against the wall, letting the water wash over me, still fully dressed. The water felt good, but it couldn't do what I needed it to - wash away the memories and the feelings. Unbidden images of Chase's happy face kept coming back and flashing through my mind's eye, making me miserable all over again.

Becky walked through the door with a load of my stuff in her arms. As soon as she saw me, she instantly looked sad. "Oh, honey, don't let this get to you so much. We're gonna fix it ... I promise!" She looked so hopeful, I couldn't keep crying in front of her. *No reason to torture everyone else with my shame.* If she wanted to have false hope, who was I to take that from her?

"Thanks for bringing in my stuff, Becky." I worked like hell to keep my voice from catching on the giant lump that wouldn't leave my throat.

"You're welcome. Can I ... help you or anything?" She looked like she was at a loss.

"No. I'll take it from here. Just give me a few minutes."

"Sure, hon. No problem. I'll be just across the hall in your room with the guys."

"Where's Scrum?" I wanted to talk to him about Chase.

"He's out training, but he'll be here soon. We sent him a message that you're up."

"Okay. Thanks."

Becky left me to my shower, and I used the time to get out of my clothes and clean off every speck of Dark Fae dirt that might be hiding on my body. No matter how hard I scrubbed, I felt like there was still some there. I only stopped when my skin turned bright red and threatened to bleed.

I dried myself off and dressed in the white tunic and jeans that Becky had brought. Under the pile of clothes was my sheath and, miraculously, Blackie too. I pulled the weapon out, dragging my fingers along its length. *Chase.* He had to have been the one who made sure I got it back. *What had I done to deserve such loyalty?* He'd changed sides, and yet he still took care of me - a stupid Light Fae girl. I took in a big wavering breath and let it out slowly. Time to face the music. I needed to be someone who deserved that kind of dedication.

I left the bathroom and joined my friends, hoping like hell they'd still want to be my friends when all was said and done. If our roles were reversed, I wasn't sure I could or would be as generous with them as I was hoping they'd be with me. Hopefully, they were better fae than I was.

Chapter Twenty-Nine

I WALKED IN AND NOTICED right away that Scrum had joined the party. I expected him to judge me harshly, so I was a little surprised when he perked right up with, "Hi, Jayne!" as soon as he saw me. I gave him a half-hearted wave and avoided looking at Spike, focusing on Tony instead as I went over and sat down next to him on the bed.

"Hey," he said, moving over to give me more room.

"Hey." My voice was rusty from all the emotion that had ravaged my throat in the last hour.

Tony looked at everyone. "Okay, so as all of you know, I've been made the new training coordinator for the Light Fae."

He glanced at me, and I acknowledged the pride I felt with a nod. I was so glad he could feel me right now with his wrathe vibing talents. I was too wiped out to say the right things.

"The gray elves have met with the council, and now, after taking Jayne and Tim's kidnapping into account, you will notice several changes around here." Tony turned his gaze to me. "Jayne, the gray elves and the council want to meet with you as soon as possible." He looked up at Becky. "Can you let them know we're ready and find out where and when they want to see us?"

"Sure," she said, a second before disappearing into thin air.

"What kinda changes should we be expectin'?" asked Finn.

"Well, first of all, there will be several cross-training exercises. The green elves and dwarves will be working with all the other fae on battle tactics. The silver elves, gray elves, and I will be collaborating together to share our work with the wind and the Gray with all of you. The witches will be giving some lectures and demonstrations on the most common spells we're likely to see during wartime." He paused, looking at all of us in turn. "And each of the high-value targets in our compound will have constant guards and additional training duties."

"And who would those high-value targets be?" asked Finn.

"Well, Jayne for one. Me for another. Naida."

"Why us?" I asked. "What was the selection criteria? 'Cuz obviously it wasn't those who are the best fighters, or Finn would be on the list. And if it included the fastest or most dangerous, Spike and Tim would be on it."

Everyone nodded in agreement.

"No, those weren't our criteria. We've done a full analysis of our resources, and those that are both vulnerable and valuable are on the list of those needing extra protection and work - to help them be not quite so vulnerable."

"Ah," I nodded. "I'm not worth a shit at fighting off the bad guys, and I'm dangerous to let loose. I get it. I'm on the short bus."

Tony frowned at me. "Don't say it like that."

I held up my hands, "No, no offense, don't worry. I got myself kidnapped by the bad guys and couldn't get myself out of it. I deserve to be on that list - except I'm not sure I agree about the high value part."

"Don't underestimate your powers, Jayne. The gray elves have some theories about you that I think will surprise everyone."

I sighed, knowing that while it sounded romantic, it wasn't very likely. Even while getting my ass kicked and feeling like I was on death's doorstep, I still couldn't pull that rabbit out of my butt. Weren't a person's most awesome skills supposed to come out in moments of stress? The only thing I found out in my moment of stress with Leck was that I had a low tolerance for pain and no skills to get rid of it.

Becky reappeared, interrupting my one-woman pity party. "They're ready for you now. The meeting's in the assembly hall," she said, nervously.

"What does that mean?" I asked, looking at her and Tony.

"Don't freak out," said Tony. "I know they want to hear from you about what happened, even though they know most of it from Tim already. There are a lot of important decisions to make, so they're probably involving everyone. It'll be faster that way."

I sighed. That was all I needed - to be in front of the assembly *again* ... for the third time. These fae were probably getting sick and tired of seeing me up there. It reminded me of being called to the principal's office, only this was worse because I had a couple hundred witnesses. I thought I'd left public humiliation behind me in the human world at high school.

Spike stood up from his spot on the floor. "Don't worry. We'll be with ya."

"Yep. All of us," said Scrum cheerfully. "And if Chase were here, he'd be with you, too."

Everyone groaned at him but me. Finn threw Tim's tiny bed pillow at Scrum's head. I just fought the urge to cry.

"Who invited this kid here, anyway?" demanded Tim.

I waved his anger away. "He's right. Chase would stand up for me. He's that kind of guy." I cleared my throat to push the frog that was in there back down. I would not allow myself to cry in front of the Light Fae. If they were going to roast me, I was just going to have to take it.

Chapter Thirty

WE ARRIVED AT THE ASSEMBLY hall much quicker than I would have liked. There were only a few seats left, but knowing I was going to be called to the front to testify to my own stupidity, we didn't bother taking them. My friends had reaffirmed their intention to stand with me and show their support as we walked the hallway to the meeting.

I looked up at the front and saw that the council was already in place on the raised platform of seats set in a semi-circle in front of the audience chairs, some of the members talking to one another, others just looking at the crowd. Jared was in his usual spot behind them with Ivar and Niles.

Dardennes raised his arms up, standing in the front of the room behind his council seat, calling out to everyone to take their places and quiet down. His eyes scanned the gathering group, stopping when they reached us. He gestured for us to come forward. As we walked down the center aisle, the noise in the room dropped to barely discernible whispers. Everyone was watching us. A few latecomers scrambled to get to their saved seats as quietly as they could. By the time we reached the front, everyone was in place and observing us with undisguised curiosity. I was in the center of my group of friends, Finn and Scrum on either side of me, Spike and Becky behind me, Tony in front, and of course, Tim on my shoulder.

Dardennes began his opening speech while we stood there trying not to feel totally self-conscious. "My fellow Light Fae, thank you for gathering here today. We asked you to come because we have some information to share, and the council has requested that your input be considered before certain important decisions are made." He paused a moment to let his words sink in before continuing. "The changelings you see before you today are here because we have asked one of them, Jayne the elemental, to tell you a story about her recent kidnapping by the Dark Fae."

Murmurs broke out across the crowd, signifying to me that maybe not everyone knew about what had happened. I was surprised at this, considering how small our compound community is.

"On a related note," Dardennes paused to point at Tony, "just a general announcement. The changeling Tony, who is our one and only wrathe here in the compound, has been working with the gray elves and is now officially our newly appointed changeling training coordinator. I understand that this appointment was well-earned and has been unanimously approved by all of the gray elves, who as you know, are head of our war strategies group."

Heads around the room were nodding and fae were turning to one another to whisper comments. This piece of news, at least, seemed welcome. I had my fingers crossed, hoping the parts that I had to contribute would at least not make everyone want to vote me off the island. I didn't know if that were even possible, but if I were in their shoes, I would want to have that option.

Dardennes looked at me. "Jayne, if you will please relate your tale to the group here, that would be a helpful lead-in to our next topic. Just begin with your initial contact with the Dark Fae."

I nodded at him and then turned to face the crowd. Tony stepped to the side so they could see me better.

"A couple or few days ago ... sorry ... I'm not exactly sure when it was, the days have kind of blended together ... I went into the Infinity Meadow with Tony and Scrum ... he's a daemon ... and Tim ... the wingless pixie, to do some training stuff." I hoped that little fib wasn't going to get me in trouble, since technically we weren't doing any training. I noticed some smiles at my description of Tim. He probably didn't appreciate it so much, but at least he didn't yank my hair.

"We were lying in the meadow grass when I heard a noise. Then I saw that Scrum and Tim and maybe Tony too, were frozen - not moving." I looked over at Dardennes and he nodded his head at me, so I continued. "Then two Dark Fae came out of the forest. Ben and Samantha. Samantha's someone I knew in Miami, when I was a human; a girl who Dardennes and Céline had rejected as a changeling recruit."

There was some murmuring in the crowd, and I took a quick moment to glance over at Jared to see his reaction. He was frowning, but I couldn't tell what that meant.

"Ben told me they were bringing me to the Dark Fae compound. I refused to go, so they did something that knocked me out. The next thing I knew, I was in the Dark Fae compound with Tim, in some sort of cave room."

Someone shouted from the crowd, "Why didn't you use your power against them or at least attempt to protect yourself?"

I looked at Dardennes and he nodded again.

"I tried. I actually did use The Green for a little while, but Samantha is a witch and she started damaging my protective cover, and Ben threatened to hurt my friends if I kept resisting."

Someone from the witch group spoke up then. "She would have to be a very gifted witch to be able to affect your power as you describe. And you say she's a changeling?" The implication was obvious. I was going to have to fight to prove the truthfulness of my story. I shouldn't have expected anything less, and a little piece of me was happy about it. I wanted the Light Fae to be tough, now that I knew how ruthless the Dark Fae could be.

"She had help. At first I thought it was just her, and since I have no experience with the witches, I didn't know what was normal and what wasn't. But then I saw that Maggie the witch was involved."

That got the witches really hyper - they were all talking to one another and gesturing wildly. I noticed a lot of angry faces.

"Please, fellow fae, let her continue. We will discuss the ramifications of the details after she finishes."

The group quieted down in response to Dardennes' request, so I began speaking again. "Maggie has been my friend in the past and has helped me a lot ... and some of my friends, too. But I have since learned that Maggie helps whoever she wants. She doesn't discriminate between Light Fae and Dark Fae. I'm not sure what her motivation is for helping one and hurting another, though. Her decisions don't make a whole lot of sense to me."

I could see that this struck a chord with a few others in the audience. Some heads were nodding, some in agreement and some with what looked like a willingness to at least consider it.

"Jayne, will you please tell us what happened in the Dark Fae compound?" requested Dardennes.

I took a breath and continued. "Well, I was tortured by a guy named Leck, a wrathe, on the orders of Ben, an elemental, I think, who controls Fire and Wind. I also had a confrontation with someone name Maléna who is a silver elf." I looked over at Céline to see her reaction, and I wasn't surprised to see her face go white - whiter than it normally is. This confirmed for me that at least there was some connection between the two of them. I so hoped we were going to hear what that connection was during this meeting.

"Why were they torturing you?" shouted one of the gray elves. "And what about the pixie? Where was he?"

"The pixie was hiding in my bra ... ," this got some laughs from the crowd, " ... so they never knew he was there. And the reason they were torturing me was for information. They wanted to know how to get into the Light Fae compound."

The roar of unhappy fae voices rose up so loud it was impossible to continue. I scanned the crowd, trying to pick out individual reactions. The green elves as a group seemed to favor retribution - they all had their hands on their bows and looked angry. I glanced to my left and saw Finn doing the same. I looked over at Niles, and he had his axe out of its holster, swinging it a little at his side. He was ready to chop some kneecaps, that was obvious from the axe and the murderous expression on his face. Becky just seemed scared. I looked for other sprites in the assembly, and they appeared to share the same feeling. I wasn't sure if they were all a bunch of wimps or the only smart ones in the group. The witches were very animated and talking amongst themselves. I knew the reason the Dark Fae couldn't find our compound was because of the spells those witches had made, so the pressure was on them, probably.

"Did you tell them?" shouted a green elf. The entire room went dead silent. The sprites in the crowd that I had noticed looking scared seemed especially interested in my answer.

"No. I did not."

More murmuring and even some distrustful looks.

"I find it hard to believe that a changeling held out under threats of torture and did not provide the information demanded." This came from a gray elf.

Tony stepped forward and opened his mouth to defend me, but I stopped him by putting my hand on his arm. "Let me," I said softly. I needed to do this. I had a lot of rage built up inside me from what had happened - not just to me but to Chase, too. This was going to make me feel better.

"Just because you're a complete wuss who would crumble at the slightest threat doesn't mean I am. And just so we're clear, it wasn't just *threats* of torture, it *was* torture. The wrathe went into my head and tried to melt it. And just so you know, a brain melting is a very unpleasant, *very* painful experience. I was also kicked in the face by this guy. You can't see my injuries because I was healed by The Green, but trust me, they were there."

Tim stood up on my shoulder and yelled, "You guys are lucky it was Jayne there and not any of you! I've never seen a braver fae in my four hundred years of life!"

I smiled, warming at his compliments, but said quietly to him, "I appreciate the vote of confidence, but no one can hear you but me."

Céline stood at the council's table. "The pixie corroborates her story."

My head whipped around to look at Céline. *Could she hear the pixie too? Since when?* I looked at her questioningly, meeting her eyes. She just bowed her head to me, no other expression on her face.

"She can hear me?" whispered Tim.

"Maybe." There were too many mysteries in this place, especially where Céline was concerned. I was trying to decide if I should call her out right here in front of this entire assembly, when Dardennes started talking again.

"How did you get out of the Dark Fae compound?"

And so here I was. The moment when my indiscretions and bad choices were going to be revealed to everyone. This was like the worst type of confession ever - too many people to see my shame, too many bad things to say. I felt like I was laying my inner self out there, raw, for everyone to see and criticize ... and turn away from. Had Tim told them everything? About the pixying too? Would they send him away? I didn't know what to say and what to hold back, and I couldn't ask Tim without Céline knowing.

"Uh ... I plead the fifth?" I looked over at Dardennes, ducking my head as I said it, but he frowned and shook his head at me. He was probably the only one out of all these fae who even knew what that meant.

"Jayne, just tell the truth - all of it. Good or bad, it'll be okay," said Tony.

"The truth shall set me free, Tony? Is that what you're saying?"

He shrugged.

It seemed ironic to me that this same phrase had come to me before, when I stood outside the fourth waypoint after the changeling test, deciding whether to enter the compound or not. The truth had set me free then, at least inside my own blocked mind; hopefully, it would do the same today.

I took a deep breath and squared my shoulders. "Okay, so I'll tell you what happened, and it will be the truth. But I'm warning you - some of it will probably piss you off, and I'm sorry about that. I never meant to hurt anyone ... "

And so I told them the story about Chase and how he ended up there, and how The Green came to me through Water, and finally how Chase delivered us back, even after declaring his loyalty to the Dark Fae.

The entire time I talked, everyone stayed completely silent, hanging on my every word. I could see that some of the things I said surprised them, some things made them upset, and others just made them look more curious. When it was all over, I looked at Dardennes and then back to the assembled fae.

"So that's the story. I don't really know how I got back here, since I blacked out when I was still in the Dark Fae compound. But Tim can tell you the rest."

"I don't think that will be necessary, Jayne, but thank you for your honesty and forthrightness. We do appreciate that." He nodded to me and then looked back to the crowd. "The council considers that this act against one of our own is an overt act of war and that we must respond in kind. Therefore, we bring this notion to your attention for your deliberation. The topic is now officially open to debate for anyone who would like to submit a comment."

I raised my hand immediately, not sure what the protocol was. But a gray elf beat me to it, leaping to his feet and talking right away.

"The gray elves have done a significant amount of planning with regard to this war, and we all agree that we need more resources." He looked at Tony and nodded. "The changeling Tony has been a very welcome addition to our ranks and has proven himself to have a sharp mind when it comes to developing strategy and considering various battle scenarios. He suggests that we need to train our changelings in an accelerated fashion so we can include them as resources in our planning models. This will help, but it's still not enough. We need to bring in the others."

This last comment brought a chorus of cries from the fae, and not just from the audience. The council was also in an uproar.

Dardennes held up his hands for silence. "Are you saying that we need to call in *all* of the others? Because that would be a logistical nightmare I'm not sure we could manage, especially in such a short time frame."

"No, of course not," responded the gray elf. "But we could bring in a couple hundred who have the skills that we need to fill the holes in our arsenal."

One of the council members stood, this one being the werewolf guy I encountered during my changeling test. Today he looked like a regular, muscley guy. He spoke in his deep, rumbling voice, "You say that we will have what we need to defeat the Dark Fae with the addition of two hundred more?"

Another gray elf stood to join the first and responded, "Yes, so long as they are the specific fae we have identified."

"Why not just get three hundred then, and end it faster?"

The gray elves looked at each other in confusion. Then the first one answered, "Because that wouldn't be the most efficient use of our assets."

That got a few laughs from the crowd, but none from the gray elf group. I had to smile too. They were so anal about their numbers and plans. No wonder they liked Tony so much. He was totally awesome in math. I was with the werewolf guy, though. Seemed like more was always better. Maybe I'd get Tony to explain their logic to me later.

I raised my hand again, still not comfortable with just talking out of turn.

A witch stood and said, "The witches of the Light Fae would like to speak to the changeling Jayne and the pixie about the spells used in the Dark Fae compound."

Dardennes responded without even looking at me. "Jayne and Tim will be made available to all fae groups that need her input in their planning."

I propped my raised hand up with my other hand now, getting tired of keeping it up in the air.

"Why does the changeling Jayne stand with her hand in the air? Is this a side effect of her torture?" asked a wood sprite out in the assembly. I was starting to get the impression that wood sprites on the whole were not the sharpest knives in the drawer.

"Jayne, do you have something you want to say?" asked Dardennes, sounding a little confused himself.

"Uh, yeah. That's why I have my hand up. Anyway, I just wanted to say that they told me the reason they kidnapped me was to start the war. They figured you'd come and get me and that would be what got everything rolling."

I could tell right away that the gray elves were eating this shit up. I could practically hear their brains calculating from here. Tony was getting antsy too, so I knew he was right there with them. His first stop after this meeting would probably be war-planning central. Even though I'd never seen it, I'd bet they had some sort of war room somewhere in this place. Tony was probably going to drag his mattress over and sleep there. This was like the biggest and most complicated chess match ever, and with real life and death stakes, too.

A dwarf stood and yelled out, "This is the proof we needed! They are deliberately calling us to war. I say we answer the call!" Several roars of approval rang out, especially from all of the fae under four feet tall. But there was also some agreement among the others, especially the green elves and some of the witches. I wasn't sure that they all had the same motivations, though, and that concerned me.

I realized that hand-raising made no sense in this forum so I just talked really loudly, hoping they would listen to me. "Hey! I was just wondering!" That intro got the roars down to murmurs, so I continued without yelling. "I mean, shouldn't we all be going into this thing for the right reasons? And shouldn't those reasons be kinda the same?"

The dwarf answered me. "We go to defeat the Darkness!"

A witch yelled, "We fight to assert the superiority of Light over the Darkness!"

War of the Fae: Book Three

A green elf joined the fray, "We fight to protect our own!"

Shit. After hearing this, I knew we were in trouble. "I know I'm just a changeling, and not a very good one either, and I realize I kinda got myself in hot water and that caused us all some problems ... and I'm really sorry about that ... but I have to say that it just seems like none of you really agree on what this war is supposed to be about. And I can tell you that the Dark Fae seem to have a very solid plan, and they all seem to agree on what it is and why they're following it. The winner of this thing is probably going to be the one that's the most organized."

"Organization is important, but it is *strength* that wins wars, young changeling. But you would not understand this. You are too young and inexperienced," said the outspoken dwarf in the crowd. His friends all nodded, impressed with his wisdom.

But me? Not so much. I fixed the little twerp with my hardest stare. "I may be young, but I know stupid when I see it. Trust me - I've done plenty of stupid things in my very short lifetime. What you all fail to realize is that they *have* strength - the same as us. They have green elves, they have dwarves, they have witches doing the same spells on their compound that ours do here. They have daemons now too, thanks to more of my stupidity. So the only thing that sets them apart from us right now, is they're more organized. And that means they're gonna win if we don't get our asses and our priorities figured out."

The dwarf looked like he wanted to say something belligerent back, but he gave up, turning to look at his friends. I was saved from another verbal assault by a gray elf.

"The changeling is correct. We must be united in our efforts and we must organize. The gray elves are prepared to meet that task, if our Light Fae brethren are willing to work with us. But we must warn you

- we do not have the luxury of time. We must begin today. The Dark Fae are ready to attack at any moment, and we must be prepared."

Dardennes looked out at the crowd, scanning all the faces there. Everyone was looking at him, waiting for him to speak.

"The council will now take a short recess to discuss the comments you have thoughtfully provided."

He stepped back from his chair to visit with Céline who had stood to be next to him. Niles was off to the side listening in. Jared was talking to Ivar, while the werewolf conversed with Naida and the old witchy-looking guy I remembered from my last grilling - the one who didn't want Tony to be a changeling. He was probably sorry now about that stupid recommendation he made to turn Tony away. The other council members were speaking with one another in hushed tones.

The fae in the room were all talking to their neighbors in low tones as well. I took it as a sign of respect that they didn't interrupt the council or speak very loudly. I turned to my friends. "So, what do you guys think?"

"I think you hit the nail right on the kisser," said Finn. "We gotta get our butts in gear here or they're gonna smear us, plain and simple."

"Yeah. It's kinda scary that we could actually be involved in a war ,though," said Becky, her usual dopey smile replaced with a frown.

"I don't think you have to worry about it so much, Becky. I'm not sure the sprites are going to be in the middle of the action," said Scrum.

"I hate to be so callous about this whole thing, but I'm looking forward to the training," said Spike. "Valentine's cool and all, but my training can be pretty boring sometimes."

"Yeah, all that suckin' on guys and stuff," said Finn, mockingly.

Spike punched him in the shoulder. "Better watch it before I start getting a craving for ginger elf energy."

War of the Fae: Book Three

Finn punched him back. "Don't call me a ginger." He thought for a second and added, "And you keep your suckin' ideas to yourself. I ain't on the market for none o' that guy-on-guy stuff."

I saw that Spike was thinking seriously about being offended by Finn's continued ribbing, so I got between them. "Listen boys, we have a bigger problem than Finn's homophobia and Spike's denial, so let's just simmah, okay?" I smiled at both of their fish-out-of-water faces.

Becky giggled. "Good one, Jayne."

Scrum spoke up, "I don't get it. Is Spike gay? Not that it matters, I'm just curious." He looked at Finn, "And are you really afraid of gay guys? 'Cuz in my experience, they're usually pretty nice."

I rolled my eyes.

Finn looked at Spike. "Are you gonna do it or am I?"

"Let's both do it."

Scrum looked at the two of them, suspicion in his eyes, as they advanced on him. "Hey guys, I don't know what you're planning, but you better stay away. I can take you both down, you know. And not like you're probably hoping either, Spike, cuz I'm not gay."

Just as Finn and Spike were about to reach out for Scrum's arms, Dardennes cleared his throat loudly and began speaking again, foiling their plans for the mighty pantsing or wedgie-ing they had in mind.

"Thank you for your patience ... ," announced Dardennes.

Everyone in the place stopped talking and sat forward, listening in rapt attention. Spike, Finn, and Scrum immediately stopped messing around and got serious as they waited to hear Dardennes' next words.

" ... The council has discussed the matter at hand and has the following directives for our community." Dardennes looked around and made sure everyone was paying attention before continuing. "First, each fae here will be expected to join with those of his or her race, to begin an enhanced and accelerated training program, as outlined by the gray elves. Please send one representative from each group to get your schedules. There will be some crossover, with different groups training together and different groups conducting training. At times you will be the trainers and at others you will be the trainees. I expect *all* of us can agree that we could use a refresher course in some areas, so even our elder fae are expected to comply." Dardennes shot some looks out at the witches and then over at the old coot on the council, who returned his look with a frown.

"Second, we must all be aware that the Dark Fae are actively working towards starting this war, and we know they will do things we wouldn't consider doing as part of their strategy. Therefore, the council finds it must insist that no one go into the forest without at least one partner - and this partner must be highly skilled in the art of combating Dark Fae magic." He heard the grumbling coming from the witches, so he finished with, "Note that as we conduct this training, more and more fae will fit that description, so if any particular fae group feels burdened by this directive, please understand that its effects will only be temporary."

I looked over at the witches, and they seemed to be a bit mollified by his last statement.

"Last, the Dark Fae obviously want access to our compound. Our witches have done a fine job of spelling it, but we cannot assume it has not been breached or will not be breached in the future. Please be vigilant. Keep your eyes and ears open. If you see or hear anything that seems suspicious, please contact someone on the council immediately. We ask that you not engage any Dark Fae directly unless you have adequate resources at your disposal." I noted his eyes scanned the room and locked on various changelings who were scattered around. The message was clear: *changelings, don't even think about it.*

Heads were nodding all over the room. The sprites in the assembly looked around in fear at all the other fae. I wouldn't be surprised if they all jumped ship and went to live out in the trees and lake until this was all over, being the 'lover not a fighter' brand of fae.

"This meeting is now adjourned. Please send your representatives to Tony and the gray elves for assignments."

The noise level rose as people got up out of their seats and headed towards the door. The gray elves were immediately surrounded by well-meaning fae following the council's order. I looked at the head table and saw that Dardennes and Céline were both coming over. Céline's gaze in particular was very focused on me.

Chapter Thirty-One

I TOOK HOLD OF THE hand nearest to me. Spike looked down at me warmly, the amber and red gently swirling in his eyes. I hoped he understood this was not meant as a girlfriend thing - it was my need for reassurance. Dardennes and Céline didn't look mad, but they definitely looked *something*, and their intensity was freaking me out a little.

Tony had left us as soon as the meeting was over to join the gray elves who were gathered near the exit door; a quick glance in his direction told me he was busy coordinating the training of various groups. Everyone wanted to talk to him, and he looked very businesslike. I was so friggin proud of him in that moment, my heart felt like it was going to burst. My joy was short-lived, however, when I sensed the arrival of the two silver elves. I tore my eyes away from Tony to greet them.

"Jayne, thank you for coming here today and telling your story. It could not have been easy for you," said Céline, searching my eyes.

"You're welcome."

"I know you don't feel like what you did was anything special, but it was. You proved to all of us where your loyalties lie and the depth of your commitment to us. This will not be forgotten."

Her praise made me uncomfortable. It wasn't like I was a saint or anything. If I were being honest with myself, I wasn't sure that my refusal to give up secrets was a matter of commitment to the Light Fae, or my distaste for Leck and my stubborn nature refusing to give someone I don't like something he wants.

"Ask her about Maléna," said Tim.

I looked at Céline to see if she'd heard him. All she did was raise her eyebrow a fraction of an inch, and then turn to Dardennes. "Shall we go talk to the gray elves? See what they have in store for the council members?"

"Yes. Go ahead, I'll be there momentarily."

Céline nodded to all of us and walked away. I watched her back, suspicious that she was hiding something and that Dardennes knew exactly what it was. I was now officially on a mission to figure out who Maléna was to Céline and if Céline was hiding that connection from me ... and why.

Dardennes spoke to me then. "I want to echo Céline's sentiments and let you know that all of the council members are grateful to you. We understand that you suffered for your family here. If there is anything you need, to aid in your recuperation, I hope you know that you may ask any of us. We are all happy to help."

"I have my friends," I said, looking at each of them in turn, seeing their loyal smiles. "That's all I need right now for my, uh, recuperation. But I do have some questions I'd like answered."

"I would be delighted to answer them; however, right now I believe we all need to focus on our new training regimens and schedules. Why don't we agree to meet later in my office to go over your questions? Would that be agreeable to you?"

He was being so formal, I couldn't tell if he was messing with me and putting me off, or if he was just being polite.

I shrugged. "I guess."

"Splendid. I will see you at dinner. Please bring your food to my office and we will eat together."

"Can I bring anyone?"

"As you wish," he said, smiling. "And now, I will take my leave. I believe the gray elves would like to speak with all of you." He bowed his head and turned to go, leaving us standing there.

"Well, I guess that's that," said Finn. "You got yourself a date with the boss t'night."

"I guess so," I said absently, watching Dardennes walk away. I squeezed Spike's hand in a silent thank you and then pulled my hand away. "You guys ready to do this thing?"

"As ready as I'll ever be," said Becky, for once not smiling.

"Buck up, little camper," said Finn cheerfully. "Now you get to come shoot some arrows with ol' Finn!" He reached out and tweaked her ear.

"I don't like shooting things," she said, frowning despite his teasing.

"I'm looking forward to it," said Spike, "even if those wood arrows do make me a little nervous."

"What's with the wood arrows, anyway?" I asked. "I remember that Valentine guy saying something about it when Finn shot him during our test."

"Yeah, well, incubi have like an allergy to certain types of wood."

"An allergy?" I asked. "What? Do you, like, break out in hives or something if you get shot? Because I notice it didn't kill Valentine."

"No, it's more serious than hives. You nail us in the heart and that can be the end of the Here and Now for us; then it's off to the Otherworlds. But if you miss the heart, we can usually recover from it. We're fast healers - a benefit of the fae blood, I guess. I think most fae are ... fast healers, I mean."

"What if we nail you in the leg or somethin'?" asked Finn.

"Nothing. It only hurts and pisses us off."

"What about the neck? What if I shoot you *right* in the artery in your neck?" Finn nodded as if this should be enough.

"Nope. We're not big bleeders."

"What about the eyeball? Can I kill ya with an eyeball shot?"

"Geez, Finn! Bloodthirsty much?" I asked.

He shrugged. "I gotta know what can kill the enemy. You said them Dark Fae got incubusses too. I don't want none o' them Dark Fae incubusses suckin' on my neck if I can help it."

Spike rolled his eyes, "It's *incubi*, not incubusses, you goofy redneck."

"Listen, I'm proud of my heritage. Call me whatever you want. But when them incubi come outta the woodwork durin' this war, I'm gonna shoot 'em, dead center in the heart ... or the eyeball if you tell me the eyeball's a kill shot. If it's just a 'piss 'em off shot', well then, I'll just stick with the heart."

Tony came walking up in time to hear the tail end of the conversation. "You see, this is the stuff I've been talking to the gray elves about," he said. "We need to have these give-and-take sessions where we discuss race characteristics like weaknesses and strengths. This will help us."

"Yep, I agree," said Finn. "Now I know how to shoot to kill." He smiled evilly at Spike.

"Yeah. And I know whose energy to suck out first," said Spike, turning his blazing red eyes on Finn.

Finn had the brains to look a little disconcerted. He smiled tremulously at Spike. "Easy now, incubus. You know I was only messin' with ya."

War of the Fae: Book Three

Spike just raised an eyebrow at him, saying nothing. He didn't need to; the swirling red and black in his eyes said it all. Even I was a little nervous at this point. I'd seen Spike's blazing speed before, and Finn's quick draw was no match for it. And I was pretty sure Finn had already done the calculations in his head too, from the look on his face right now.

"Okay, boys, put your weapons away," said Becky smiling, completely unafraid of Spike's rising heat. "So Tony, what are we supposed to be doing right now?"

"I have all your schedules, so if you guys want, I can give them to you now."

"I don't even know what time it is," I said. "How much training time do we have left today?"

"Well, we have to eat lunch soon, right?" asked Scrum, his stomach taking that moment to growl loudly, causing all of us to giggle. He patted his belly. "Down, boy. Don't worry, I'm going to feed you soon."

Becky kept giggling and couldn't stop, her laughter turning into snorts as she gripped her stomach. Finn watched her, shaking his head and patting her shoulder.

Now that all the pressure was off of me, I was hungry too. "Can we get lunch? I'm starving."

"Yeah, come on," said Tony. "Let's eat and I'll tell you your schedules at the table."

We walked to the dining hall, and I let Tim's yammering away about his list of top ten fruits distract me from all the questions swirling around in my head ...

" ... I'm not sure which is better, grapes or blackberries. Do you think they'll have those on the buffet today? On the one hand, blackberries are tangier, but they're so much messier, especially if we're comparing them to green grapes. Those are easy. But then again, messy. You really can't beat the apple though ..." and on and on it went, keeping me occupied with worry-blocking nonsense until I was actually sitting at the table watching Tim wrestle with one of those green grapes he likes so much. I stabbed it for him with my fork to keep it from rolling away, and he sent me a look of gratitude, right before he grappled with the skin, trying to strip it off so he could get to the pulp beneath.

" ... are you listening Jayne? This is important, you know."

"Yeah, sorry, Tony. I'm listening. I have to be where? With who? When?"

He shook his head. "I knew you weren't listening. You're going with the green elves, first. Your job is to learn their hunting and tracking skills."

I looked at him, confused. "What? I'm supposed to start carrying around a bow and arrows now?"

"No," he said, frustrated, "you are *supposed* to figure out how to avoid the green elves and keep them from hitting you with arrows."

The light bulb went. "Ooooh, I see. And what am I supposed to do for them?"

He smiled. "I'm glad you asked. Your job is to show them any vulnerabilities you may have noticed in ... uh ... others of your kind."

I looked at him sternly, my eyes narrowed. "You mean Ben, right?"

Tony's face reddened. "I guess, yeah."

"So you want me to tell them how to get a kill shot on Ben?" I didn't know why I said it like this. Maybe I wanted to see how far Tony would take this strategy when it involved someone he knew.

"Yeah." His voice caught and he cleared it with a cough. "Show them the kill shot."

War of the Fae: Book Three

"Wow." I was impressed and not so much in a good way. "You've sure turned into a bloodthirsty bastard, haven't you?" I should have been happy that Tony had integrated so fully into our new life, but something about it bothered me.

"Listen, don't make this harder than it already is."

"I'm just saying it like it is, Tony. You need to be aware that what you're telling people to do will end up killing someone down the line. And, I'm sorry, but I'm just a little worried that you're not going to be okay with that when it happens."

Tony stood up, visibly shaken. "I know what you think and what you feel, Jayne. I don't need you to tell me like I'm a little kid."

I grabbed him by the forearm to keep him from leaving, beseeching him with my eyes. "I'm not doing that. I'm just saying something I think you need to hear because I'm worried, that's all. Don't get all pissy about it, 'kay?"

Tony sighed. "Fine."

"BFFs?" I squeezed his arm.

He rolled his eyes. "Whatever."

"No. You have to say it or I'm not letting you leave to go plan the evil empire's downfall."

"Okay, fine. BFFs. Can I go now?"

"Yes. Go rule the world. Come see me when it's all over."

"Just go see the green elves after lunch. I'll see you at dinner."

I saluted him. "Yes, Captain! Jayne Sparks, reporting for duty!"

He walked away shaking his head, carrying his plate with him. I watched him visit several other tables, talking and smiling as he gave out his instructions to the different changelings. He was a natural at this leadership stuff. It was going to be up to me to keep his head on straight and make sure he didn't forget who he was. And I was happy to do that because who he was, was pretty damn special.

Chapter Thirty-Two

TIM AND I REPORTED TO the green elves training grounds as ordered by Sergeant Bossypants Tony. Over the next three straight hours, Finn and his group showed us how they do their tracking and hunting. Tim lamented on several occasions about how much he wished he had his wings back, since he was stuck on my shoulder the whole time. The wings were more than nubs now, but still only less than a third of the way grown back.

I learned some of the basics about not breaking off branches or disturbing the underbrush when I was walking, and how to recognize signs that the green elves were in the area. Apparently, they used some temporary markings on the trees and along the ground that only they were able to recognize, to communicate with one another. I also learned the arrow feather markers for each of the elves. They all had their own unique feather patterns that made their arrows easy to tell apart. Well, easy for them anyway. After a one-hour lesson I was just beginning to get a grasp on all of it, and then it was time to change positions. Now it was my turn to talk to them about the vulnerabilities of an elemental.

During lunch, Tim, Finn, and I had tried to concentrate on the couple of times we'd seen Ben in action, to figure out if he had any weak spots. The problem was, the only fae we'd ever seen him fight with, was Tim. And within about a second of Tim's threat, Ben had lifted a finger, shot out a laser bolt of fire, and blasted Tim's wing off, sending him into a death spiral.

I knew from standing near Ben that he could get pretty hot - literally - but I wasn't sure what he could do with that heat, other than channel some of it into a destructive beam of light. Probably, he'd throw it in a giant fireball at anyone who pissed him off ... but what else?

It seemed kind of unfair, really. If I got mad I could throw a big ball of glowing green stuff at someone and send them into a coma-like oblivion. Ben could incinerate them with a focused beam of fire from hell. It reminded me of grade school kickball games - he'd be the first one chosen for the team, and I'd be picked dead last.

I looked at the green elves gathered around me and wondered if they were bummed that they'd gotten stuck with me instead of Ben. None of them seemed disappointed, though, and it made me want to work harder to make them happy. They looked at me in rapt attention, waiting to hear whatever it was I had to say - even Finn who already knew pretty much everything about me. I knew they were expecting me to prepare them for the war that was coming.

The idea that Ben could do something to hurt these men and women, who were depending on me to keep them safe and teach them skills, was beyond stressful. I had such a heavy mantle of responsibility hanging over my shoulders right now, it was hard to concentrate. I kept worrying that I was going to screw it up. I could totally picture the sneer on my mother's husband's face. I pushed that sickening vision as far away as I could.

"I wish I had more to tell you. I never saw Ben do anything really but power up with fire, zap a pixie, and travel with the wind."

"What do you mean 'power up and zap a pixie'?" one of the elves asked. The eyes of all the elves went to Tim, sitting on my shoulder. I didn't even have to see him to know he was preening over his badass self. Yes folks, he had been zapped, and he had survived. Superhero, anyone?

I explained, "Well, when Ben got angry at me, he started to build up what looked like an inferno around him. It got very hot and strong and eventually fully covered him. And then Tim was going to attack him, so Ben shot off one of his wings."

Some of the elves cringed, sending looks of sympathy Tim's way.

"Didn't he burn?" asked one of the younger-looking elves, earning him a punch in the shoulder from one of his friends. Finn didn't even look over at him, he just rolled his eyes.

"Who? Tim?" Seemed like a silly question. He hadn't tried to hide his blackened nub the whole time we'd been back. In fact, it would be more accurate to say he showed it off, like a little black badge of courage.

"No, Ben."

"No. I could feel the heat, but I wasn't burned either. Neither was anything near him, other than Tim. I think he can control whether it burns or not - anyone and everything, not just himself."

"Did he torture you with fire?" asked another elf.

"No." And he could have, which was something that was also bothering me. I felt like I needed to say something about that, even though it seemed as if I were defending him. "He could have for sure. But he didn't. He seemed to hold back from doing that. I got the sense that ... he didn't want to hurt me."

"I thought he was the one who ordered your torture," said Robin, the head of the green elves.

"He was ... he did. But I'm not sure that he's the one in charge over there. I think this silver elf Maléna was calling the shots, and he was doing what she told him to do, at least in the cell where I was being kept."

There was some grumbling about that. I could tell from some of the looks I saw passed around that she wasn't unknown to at least some of them.

"Who is she, anyway?" I asked.

"You do not know?" asked Robin.

"Uh, no. Should I?"

Robin rubbed his chin, thinking about his answer. "I think you should talk to Céline or Anton about Maléna. They are better equipped to give you the information than anyone here." He cast his eyes out to the group, and they all looked down.

I could tell that meant I wasn't going to be getting any intel from these guys. *Dammit.* I hated talking to Dardennes. But maybe I could track Céline down when she was alone. I would have to talk to Tim later and see if he had any ideas. Or maybe Tony would know who Maléna was and I could avoid the council members entirely.

I shook off that line of thought and continued with my lecture. "Of all the Dark Fae I've met, the only one who struck me as really evil was Leck, the wrathe."

"Why only him?" asked Robin.

"Because he was the only one who seemed to enjoy hurting me. And I'm not sure, but I think he paid me a visit after my official questioning and torture was supposed to be over, to do it some more ... just for fun, or for extra credit or something."

I saw the young elf lean to his friend and say in a low tone, "What does she mean 'extra credit'?"

The older elf shoved him, whispering loudly, "Shut up, Falco, just listen!"

Elle Casey

I looked at Finn who I could tell was trying not to laugh, stretching his face into as serious a shape as he could. It made him look like he had gas pains. I hoped I would remember to tell him that later.

This eager Falco guy reminded me of Scrum, so I took pity on him and answered, "I think he was hoping he could get some sort of information from me that he could take to his bosses and then maybe they'd think he was really great or something. You know, like being an extra good tormentor."

"Ohhhh, I see," said the elf, ducking as he saw his friend coming at him again.

I decided to voice my thoughts on this whole torture scenario to the oldest and wisest green elf I know. Maybe he'd have an explanation I could be happy with. "Robin, what do you think about this thing with the Dark Fae, how only one of them actually tried to hurt me? All the others could have, but didn't. What does that mean ... to you?"

Robin shrugged. "The gray elves are wiser than I in the ways of war."

"I know they're the brainiacs, but I want to know *your* opinion."

Robin raised his eyebrows at me in confusion, as if this were a foreign concept - someone really wanting his opinion. But after a few moments of consideration, he replied, "Well, it is curious. But there are many possible answers. One could say they wanted to keep you alive and conscious so as to gather as much information from you as possible. Or that they were going to do more to you, but that you escaped before they could." He hesitated before giving me his last theory. "Or maybe they did not torture you because they did not see the value in it."

And that was what bothered me; because I had the same theory.

"That makes them sound a lot like us."

Robin shrugged. "They are like us. After all, we are all fae."

"Yeah, but aren't they supposed to be the bad guys? All fixated on world domination?"

Robin inhaled and exhaled slowly before answering. "They have different opinions about what our place in the world should be, but I'm not so sure that world domination is a proper description of their goals."

"Well, I wish someone would spell it out for me then, because I'm just confused."

"Talk to the gray elves. They can explain it better than I."

"I plan on it." Added to my mission of figuring out the Maléna mystery, was now the dilemma of figuring out what exactly these mofos were really after.

Tim fake snored really loudly in my ear. Apparently, I was getting too boring. He was probably happy that my next question was interrupted by the eager Falco, once again unable to control himself and act like a proper, reserved green elf.

"When are we going to see your powers and try to work with them?"

"I'm ready whenever you are." I fixed Robin with a stern look. "But I hope this doesn't involve being shot with arrows, because I'm not sure I'll be able to keep from sending all of you to your happy places again."

Robin cracked a rare smile. "I assure you - I will not be giving any orders to shoot today. I specifically asked the witches to provide us with a safe training ground for our work this afternoon."

I looked around. "Are they here now?"

"No. But if someone tries to tamper with their spell they will come."

"Okay then," I rubbed my hands together, "what do you want me to do?"

"Zap 'em! Send their sorry elf butts into The Green!" yelled Tim, gleefully.

"Shhh!" I said out of the corner of my mouth, immediately smiling afterwards at the group so they wouldn't think I was nuts. Even though they were aware that I could hear Tim, I knew it still looked weird to them ... like I was always talking to myself.

Robin was too distracted to notice. He was trying to act all cool, but failing miserably. "Well, we had all been hoping, that you might work with us to find a way to use your power over The Green to enhance the work we do." His eyes were bright with expectation.

"Liiiike, in what way?"

"Well, our work focuses on hunting, tracking, and fighting with bow and arrow. We do all of our work in the forest ... and your power is focused in the forest. So maybe there is a way to perhaps enhance our skills through your connection to The Green."

I wasn't really sure what he was getting at, but I felt like I needed to clarify a couple things. "Just so you know, my power isn't necessarily focused in the Green Forest. I draw power from the trees and stuff, but the connection is with everything, everywhere. The greenery, the creatures, the spirits, the memories - here and everywhere. I think it's more attached to the Earth as a whole system, rather than just the forest itself."

Robin and many of the others were nodding as they considered this. Falco spoke up, "That's a lot bigger than I thought. How can you handle that much power? Seems like you'd explode or be absorbed into it."

Both his friend and Finn dropped their heads, shaking them slowly from side to side. Apparently, Falco was a lost cause.

War of the Fae: Book Three

I smiled at him. "It *is* big, and I'm not sure how I handle it. I'm not sure that I've ever handled more than just a little bit of it. I pull in what I need. Honestly, I don't know how I do it or how I regulate the amount. It just sort of happens." I shrugged, a little embarrassed. "I'm sorry I can't describe it any better than that. I'm new at this."

That earned me a few smiles from the elves, especially Falco. He probably felt better knowing he wasn't the only dumbass in the place.

I looked out over the sea of eager faces in front of me. "I worked with Céline once, and I was able to isolate her energy in the mix. Would you like to try something like that?" I asked.

"What do you think we could achieve with isolating energy?" asked Robin.

"I don't know. Maybe if I can find you in the links, I could channel some of my power into you?" It was an idea anyway.

Robin shrugged. "I am willing to try. But I do not know that it is wise to involve the entire group. Just in case something goes ... not as planned."

"Wrong, you mean."

Robin tipped his head to me, remaining quiet. He was nothing if not polite.

"Okay, so who's going to be the guinea pig?"

"Pardon me?" asked Robin, confused. "You want someone to be a pig?"

"No, it's just an expression. Not a pig. Who is the elf who's going to try this with me?"

Falco took three giant steps forward so he was standing in front of Robin. "Robin, I would like the honor."

Falco's friend came pushing through the elves to grab him by the shoulder and pull him back. "My apologies, Mother, he does not know his place."

I reached out and grabbed Falco's hand, pulling him back towards me, temporarily engaging in a tug-of-war with the elf. "First of all, don't call me that, or I'll have to slap you silly. And second of all, Falco can do it just as well as anyone else, unless Robin has a problem with it."

Robin raised his eyebrows but stepped back, nodding his head at me again. The other elves took his cue and also moved back a few paces.

I could tell Falco was totally psyched. He was practically bouncing with enthusiasm.

"Just let me zap him once, Jayne," said Tim. "Just one little pixying ... "

I turned my back on Falco for a second to whisper-yell at Tim, *"Pixie anyone in this group and you'll get a one-way ticket to the pixie colony that is farthest away from me!"*

"Okay, okay, geez, lighten up there, dragon slayer."

I turned back around to face Falco again, clearing my throat. "A-hem ... how about if we start with you holding my hands? Maybe ... I don't know ... it'll be easier for me to find your energy source that way."

Falco looked happily terrified at the idea. "Oh ... uh ... okay." He reached his hands out in front of him and I noticed immediately that they were shaking.

I stepped forward and took his clammy hands in mine. They were soft in places and hard in others. He had callouses in a couple spots corresponding to the weapon he used every day. I looked up and noticed a sheen of sweat on his forehead.

"Don't worry. I'm not going to hurt you."

"I know," he said softly, with barely contained excitement, "it's just that this is the single most exciting moment of my life!" His voice raised up to a squeak at the end, which he tried to recover from by coughing lightly. Poor kid looked like he was about to have a heart attack.

I tried not to be too flattered by his compliment, otherwise the universe would surely cause me to lose control and send him to la-la land as punishment for me getting too cocky. I pulled some of The Green into me and sent it through my hands to Falco, just enough to help him calm down. I could see the effect immediately, as his eyes first widened and then his lids dropped a bit, his face now looking much more relaxed and mellow.

"Wow. That's ... nice."

"Yes," I smiled back at him, "it is, isn't it?" *So far so good.* I took a deep breath, preparing myself for the next experiment. "Now, I'm going to open up this field of energy to include everyone here. I just want to get a feel for all of you, to see if I can pick Falco out of the group."

Robin and the others nodded their acquiescence.

I reached out through The Green, bringing the elves into the fold and then searching through our connection to find their energy signatures. During my work with Céline, I learned that every creature has a unique presence, and once I knew that creature's signature inside the connection, I could find it again. Now, I could sense the group of elves with me, all of them linked up to every other thing here and beyond.

If I were to put into a visual image everything I felt whenever I touched The Green, it would be like a picture of a tangled ball of string that had no beginning and no end, turned around and in on itself, sometimes touching, sometimes just passing by another piece of itself. And all of the living things on this planet were a part of that string. *We* were the string. I could never understand 'string theory' in physics class, it was beyond my mental capabilities. But my own string theory? The Green String Theory? Now, that was easy. It was based on one simple premise: we are all part of the same thing. We are all part of the One - a giant ball of cosmic, tangled up stuff.

I heard a little noise by my ear, a tiny squeak, then Tim saying, "Ooopsy, 'scuse me. I think it's the grapes from lunch."

Nothing like a pixie fart to bring a girl's head out of the ether. I reached up to flick him, but he moved nimbly to the back of my head, grabbing onto and swinging from my ponytail as he giggled maniacally. I gave up on my retribution and got back to the task at hand. "Okay, can everyone feel the connection?"

I saw smiling elf faces and nods all around.

"Okay. Now, Falco, I want you to push back on the connection."

"Push back?" he asked, a bemused expression on his face.

"Yes. You're holding my hands right now. If you have to, use my physical connection to help you get the feel for it. Push on me."

He shrugged his shoulders, "Okay, you're the boss." He pushed on my hands, but I felt no difference in the connection.

"You have to push mentally, not just physically."

Falco's eyes rolled up into his head a little as he chanted quietly to himself, "Mentally not physically, mentally not physically, mentally not physically..."

I felt the gentlest push against our connection.

"Good! Keep doing it. I can feel you now."

His chanting continued as I felt his energy's presence grow, "Mentally, mentally, mentally not physically, mentally, mentally, mentally..."

I dropped his hands, and he didn't even notice. There was no glitch in the link. He just continued to push on our connection, his signature now coming through loud and clear.

"Okay, now, stop pushing back. Just relax for a minute."

War of the Fae: Book Three

He complied, and I closed my eyes so I could concentrate better. I could feel all the elves near me, their energies melding into the mass of others that were here with us in the forest; but now I could also specifically feel Falco's signature. It was so easy now that he'd temporarily separated himself out for me with that mental pushing. His pulsating energy reminded me of a bouncing puppy, eager to go outside and play. My lightheartedness got the better of me, and I accidentally let a little of it slip into The Green. I heard a few gasps of surprise from the guys in front of me.

"Whoopsy, sorry about that. Just a little happy is all." I opened my eyes and noticed many sets of closed eyes and a few slack jaws. "Oh shit, you guys aren't going into comas, are you?" *Motherfucker*, I was going to get an F on the gray elf report card if I kept doing this shit. For the first time in my life, I cared about grades ... and of course it was when there were no grades actually being given out.

Robin opened his eyes and spoke. "I'm still here."

Other eyes around the circle opened up, and the elves chimed in. The last was Falco who finally closed his mouth and opened his eyes, saying, "Whoa, am I *here!* Yes, I am still here! *Whoot!*" His joy was palpable. I could feel the waves of it coming through The Green, multiplying and spreading out like the ripples on a lake after a stone is dropped in. The smiles of his cohorts told me that they could feel it too. This connection was what they used for their telepathy - The Green. I wondered if they even really knew how it worked.

"Wow, this kid is really excited. Better step back. I see a green elf make-out session on the horizon," said Tim.

I ignored him, knowing that Falco and probably all the rest of them were too damn intimidated by my weirdness to want to kiss me. It might have bothered me if I hadn't already decided that all the green elves I'd met so far weren't my type. They were too nice, too serious, and too damn polite.

"So, what does this mean?" asked Falco, breathlessly. He took a respectful step back and stood next to his friend.

"Well, I guess it means that at least I can identify you, no matter where you are out here." I looked around at their faces, hoping someone would jump in with suggestions or something. "I don't know if that's helpful or not ... "

"Do you think, once you have identified one of us, that you could send power just to that individual?" asked Robin, a thoughtful frown on his face.

"Maybe. What did you have in mind?"

"I would like to try ... an experiment."

"Sure. What is it?"

"He wants to be Super Elf!" yelled Tim.

"Shut up."

"Excuse me?" asked Robin, confused.

"Ignore that. Just tell me your idea."

Robin frowned for a second and then continued. "I would like you to identify my signature, and then when I am ready to take my shot from my bow, you send me a boost of the power. I have some theories about what might happen, but I will wait to share them with you; I fear that your knowledge of my hypothesis might affect the integrity of the outcome."

"Geez, Robin, are you totally channeling my biology teacher right now or what?"

"I am sorry, but I do not follow you ... "

"Never mind. Let's just do this. Just give me a second to find you in the energy mix."

I reached out through the low-level hum that surrounded us and felt for something that reminded me of Robin - serious, stalwart,

War of the Fae: Book Three

intelligent, dedicated - everything that was this noble green elf warrior.

"Gotcha. Can you feel me?" I sent him a small up-charge of The Green and he nodded.

"Yes. I felt that."

"Okay. Go ahead then, and tell me when you want the power boost."

Robin turned, and in one smooth, well-coordinated motion, slipped the bow off his back and pulled out an arrow from its quiver, notching it in the bow's string. He drew back the arrow, and from my position beside him, I could see that he was squinting at some far off target through the trees.

"Please send me the force now."

I reached into the power base and pulled some into me and then sent it out to Robin, filling his connection with the essence of it.

Robin released the arrow, sending it whistling through the forest. I lost sight of it immediately, but the gasps of the other elves had me searching their faces for clues of the outcome.

"What happened?" I asked in a hushed voice.

"Looks like you surprised the potatoes out of 'em," suggested Tim.

Robin's bow arm lowered, and he turned to me, smiling. This time, it wasn't my green energy release causing it, either.

"Did it work?"

"Yes, I would call the experiment a success and my hypothesis proven."

"What happened?"

"Come and see for yourself," he said, turning and walking in the direction of the arrow's flight.

I followed along, looking down most of the time, trying not to trip on the fallen branches and tangled vines on the forest floor. I'd hate to have my awesome reputation as this kickass elemental suffer from the realities of my klutziness in front of all these green elves who were a hell of a lot more skilled in this forest than I was.

After a minute or so of walking, we reached a tree. I noticed a green elf mark on it, one of the types that we had learned about earlier when they were teaching Tim and me. There was an arrow sticking out of the center of that mark.

I looked back from where we had come. I couldn't even see that spot from here.

"Holy shit, that arrow went a long way."

"Yes, it did," he agreed, smiling first at me and then at the arrow.

I got the distinct impression he was waiting for something - for me to say something else. I looked back up at the tree and at the mark that was still visible under the arrowhead.

"Isn't that the symbol for safe passage?" We had learned before that there were symbols representing safe passage and various other things, including danger ahead, areas to avoid, food storage nearby, etcetera. I'd only learned a few of them. This particular symbol had seemed important, though, so I definitely remembered it.

"Yes, exactly." He beamed at me, in a very un-Robinlike way. It really lit up his face, and I couldn't help smiling back.

"So you put an arrow through a 'safe passage' symbol. What does that mean?"

"What do you think it means?" he asked, his face going all serious on me now.

I grimaced a little, afraid of sounding stupid. "That it's not a safe passage anymore?"

Robin nodded. "Exactly. Very good, changeling. You are making excellent progress."

Relief washed through me. I didn't know why it was so

important to me that he felt that way, but it was. I really, really didn't want to screw this up and make any of them hate me. "So what exactly did that extra boost of power do for you?" I had never really watched them fire their arrows at things so far away, so I didn't know how out of normal this was.

"It enabled me to shoot farther and with greater accuracy."

I nodded, thinking about the ramifications. "That could come in handy."

"In many ways," agreed Robin. "I would like to know if you could do this for more than one green elf at a time. Would you be willing to try?"

I shrugged. "Sure. Why not?" I looked around the immediate area. "Where? Here?"

"No, let's move to our shooting range."

Tim and I followed the group of elves to a large, grassy meadow, filled with large tree stumps set out at various distances from the tree line surrounding it. A gentle, late afternoon breeze set the grasses swaying and brushed past the flushed skin of my face. It felt nice to be out in the sun again, feeling the movement of the air around us. The forest blocked many of these sensations, even though some part of me knew they were still out there somewhere.

"Normally, when we stand at this distance, we can hit the targets in the second row of tree trunks with great accuracy." He pointed to targets out in the distance that showed heavy use with chips taken out of the front and lots of arrow holes. "As we move out to the targets farther away, our accuracy suffers. Obviously, it is safer for us to hit our intended target from a greater distance."

Tim took this moment to add to the commentary. "What he's saying is, that unlike pixies, the green elves need to hit the enemy from as far away as possible because they're the biggest wimps in the forest."

He squeaked when I was finally able to land a finger flick on his tiny butt. It wasn't an easy target to reach either, so I was pretty proud of myself. *The green elves've got nothin' on me. Accuracy, my ass.* I'd bet they couldn't flick a pixie butt without even being able to see the target. But to be fair, I'd had lots of practice.

Robin could see that he'd lost me, so he stopped talking for a moment. I suddenly realized it had gone quiet and my face turned red as I noticed him standing there patiently waiting for me to catch up.

"Oops. Sorry. Lost me for a second there." I pointed absently to my head. "... Tired."

He nodded. "This will be the last exercise, I promise." He turned to his group, signaling to them with some sort of wave that apparently meant *spread out and take aim*. It reminded me a little unpleasantly of the day he'd ordered his friends to shoot me, so I looked at him suspiciously; but he seemed oblivious to my fear and kept talking.

"We will aim for the farthest targets. I would like you to try and tap into all of our connections and send each of us the extra power - everyone but *one* elf. You choose the one who you do not give the power to, and do not tell us which one that is." He leaned in and whispered in my ear, "But do not select your friend Finn, because I fear then that this test will be of no value. He can hit the farthest target without your ... shall we say ... help." He nodded, staring me intently in the eye.

I nodded back, trying like hell not to look at Finn and give the secret away. He'd been hanging in the back of the group the whole time, never letting on that we were friends. I didn't want to blow it for him and screw up his rep as a sharpshooter, so I vowed to myself that I'd make sure he wasn't the one singled out to miss.

Robin walked over and joined the others, dropping his bow off his shoulder and into his hand, simultaneously loading an arrow as he went.

I stepped far back from and slightly behind the line of elves. I didn't like the idea of The Green being involved and arrows going all wonky on us. The last thing I wanted to do was personally test Spike's theory that all fae healed fast and were hard to kill. So many of the other rules didn't apply to me - I'd hate to find out that this was one of them.

"Ready?" asked Robin in a raised but controlled voice, glancing over at me for a brief moment before turning his attention back to the targets sitting off in the distance. A line of tunic-covered arms lifted bows horizontally and pulled bowstrings back, elbows jutting out behind them in a fierce showing of controlled strength.

I didn't hesitate - I drew extra folds of vibrating green energy into me and then wrapped them around the elves I sensed standing nearby, feeling each of their contributions to our pulsing link of power. I could especially feel Falco's signature since it tingled a bit with his enthusiasm for the connection. Next, I pulled one elf out of the fold, the one who had given Falco such a hard time. My inner bitch smiled deviously, looking forward to the turning of tables this was sure to cause. I tried to school my outer features so no one would know who my victim was.

"... Aim!"

The line of elves raised their bows in unison until they pointed halfway to the sky. The soon to be deadly discharge of weapons filled me with awe and more than a little bit of fear. *Man, I was so glad I wasn't going to be on the receiving end of that firing squad.*

"... *Release!*"

I watched as thirty or so wood shafts tipped with arrows and finished with feathers sailed out from the line and through the air, all

Elle Casey

but one headed out towards the farthest targets.

Chapter Thirty-Three

IN LESS THAN A SECOND it was all over. The elves lowered their bow arms, once again in unison, to hang at their sides. Robin separated himself from the group, slipping his bow over his shoulder as he walked towards me.

"What happened?" I asked. I could see that the arrows had hit the far targets, but my eyesight wasn't good enough to see details.

"I'm not exactly sure." He reached me and gestured towards the targets. "Come. Please."

He looked back and signaled the rest of the elves with a jerk of his head so they would follow us to the targets.

The first thing I noticed was a single arrow, stuck into the ground about fifty feet in front of the farthest targets. The group of elves walked up to it one at a time, and after studying the feather pattern on the end, looked over at the elf I had singled out who was trailing behind the others. His face got redder and redder by the second as the realization of his shame took hold.

Falco reached the arrow and smiled, pointing. "Hey, look, Dav, it's yours! You missed!" The smile on his face wasn't malicious, but it earned him a punch in the arm nevertheless. "Ow," he said, rubbing his shoulder and moving away to locate his own arrow with a barely concealed grin on his face.

Each of the elves was walking up to a target and pulling an arrow out, some of them having to use knives from their belts to dig out the buried tips. Falco searched all of the targets and the areas behind them before turning to Robin, who was busy examining the tip of his arrow before placing it back in his quiver.

"I can't find mine. It's not here."

Robin frowned, surveying the targets here and then closer to our starting point.

Sure enough - even I could see that there were no more arrows. Everyone's but Falco's had been accounted for.

"Where did you aim?" asked Robin.

Falco looked a little nervous. "For the ... targets?"

"Are you telling me? Or asking me?" asked Robin, a bit severely.

I was starting to have the same misgivings I think Robin was having. Falco had stepped in shit again. Poor kid couldn't seem to help himself.

"This guy makes Scrum look like a genius," said Tim, giggling.

I hated to say it, but I kind of agreed with him. They had the same personality - eager, happy, likeable - well, with Scrum it had taken me a little longer for the likeable part, but still, likeable was on the list. But when it came to doing his job, Scrum was pretty damn good, I had to admit. Even though he looked like a harmless beer keg with legs, he could lock up a dangerous incubus like nobody's business.

"No, I'm not asking; I'm telling. But ... uhhh ... ," he cleared his throat, " ... I might have been thinking about another target ... at the same time?" He shrugged and ducked his head, embarrassed. I noticed his friend looked a little less ashamed and a bit more chipper. Apparently, misery loves company in green elf society just like it does with humans.

"What target, Falco?" said Robin, sighing with the sound of infinite patience.

"Um ... the Ancient One? ... Possibly?" The last word came out more like a whisper.

All the other elves looked at him in shock, some with even a bit of fear mixed in.

"You? ... Took aim? ... At *the Ancient One?*"

Tears sprang to Falco's eyes. All he could do was nod.

Even Falco's friend seemed stupefied. I was no body language expert, but if I were reading this whole scene right, someone was knee-deep in shit without any waders. I'd heard Finn say that once, and at this moment, I could fully appreciate how in certain situations, those redneck sayings just totally worked better than anything else.

Finn was nodding his head, mindlessly. I knew he was thinking the exact same thing as me, and it wasn't any supernatural power making me able to do that either. I could tell it from the look on his face.

Robin got all serious. "We need to call in a witch and go investigate. We must ... make this right."

One of the elves spoke up, "Robin, he may have been aiming at that, but that doesn't mean he hit it. It's too far away! No one could see it from here, not even a bird."

Several of the other elves nodded. Falco brightened a little, but then he looked at Robin and his face fell again.

Robin wasn't buying it. "He was hooked into The Green. He had Jayne's link. I am afraid that when we have her with us ... well ... let us just go and see. We will manage the consequences as we must."

I had the urge to ask him who the Ancient One was, but I almost didn't want to know. I was going to find out soon enough, so I held my tongue, focusing instead on not tripping over tree roots. I just hoped no one was dead because of me.

We walked through the forest for a distance that seemed way too far for an arrow to travel, even one riding The Green power waves. The sun was beginning to go down, the air getting cooler and making my sweaty skin feel better with its gentle touch. This walking all over the place and watching my every step to keep from falling was a lot of exercise. On the one hand, I totally hated it like I hated all forms of exercise. On the other, I was thinking about how rock-hard my legs and abs were going to be, and that made me happy. *No pain, no gain, I guess.* Now I just had to think of a silver lining for all the hair pulling I was getting from Tim as he tried to hang on. It made it a lot more difficult when he occasionally yelled out, "Giddyup donkey! Mush! Yah!"

"Keep it up, turdmonkey, and you're gonna be riding on my shoe."

Robin looked at me sideways, but said nothing. I didn't bother explaining myself since that would have taken precious breath, and I needed all of it for the huffing and puffing that was keeping me conscious.

I recognized my surroundings. We were coming to the place where the gargoyle door opened up, and I was instantly on my guard. The last time I'd seen Maggie she'd delivered me up on a silver platter to the Dark Fae. I stopped walking and grabbed Robin by the sleeve, making him stop next to me. I searched his eyes for signs that he was delivering me to our enemy, but I saw nothing there but curiosity.

"Why are we stopping?" he asked. "Are you tired? Do you need to rest?"

"No. I'm just making sure you aren't going rogue on me."

"Rogue?"

War of the Fae: Book Three

"Yeah. Making sure you aren't handing me over to the enemy."

"Why would I do such a thing?"

"I don't know. Why would you order a bunch of elves to shoot me? Maybe you're under a spell."

Understanding dawned in his eyes. "Oh, I see your meaning. No, I have not ... gone rogue. I am bringing you to the Ancient One ... to see if Falco's arrow has reached its target."

"And where exactly is this *Ancient One?*"

"Just there." He pointed into the woods on the other side of the meadow.

"That's where Maggie the witch lives."

"Precisely."

"Uh, she and I don't have the best history, actually. Maybe I should just sit this one out."

"Don't worry. We have someone coming to ensure your safety. And you have us." He gestured to the other elves.

"Yeah, I appreciate that, but what I'm more worried about is me managing my temper. Because I'm pretty sure if I see her ugly ass face again, I'm gonna zap her into next year with The Green."

He looked at me, shocked, but it didn't sway me in the least.

"She deserves it, Robin. She handed me over to fae who tortured me. For no reason." I thought about her past bargains with me and the volume increased in what was quickly turning into a rant. "Or maybe she did it because someone traded her a pixie wing or a friggin mushroom for my ambush, I don't know."

Robin held up his hand to stop me. "Yes. I understand your feelings. If you wish to stay behind and go back to the compound, we will not fault you for that."

All their eyes were on me. I felt justified in my anger, but at the same time, I didn't want their opinion of me to diminish. They seemed to think I was someone special, and if I ran away or acted like a brat, they might change their minds. I should have gotten the hell out of there and let them. High expectations were a trap. They caused you to reach too high ... and that just made the fall down that much farther and a lot more painful. But I decided to keep going with them anyway. I didn't want that cranky old bitch to think she'd scared me away.

"Fine. I'll go. But she'd better not start any shit with me."

Robin nodded. "I will endeavor to keep her from doing anything to displease you."

The other elves were nodding at my decision. I tried not to feel too warm and mushy inside over their obvious approval.

We were soon joined by a witch carrying a staff. I'd seen this guy out in the crowd at our latest assembly. He seemed to be one of the more subdued of the group. I didn't recall him being one of the yellers or stick wavers. Robin walked with him, explaining the situation to him, the witch nodding off and on as he took in the information.

"Do you think there's going to be a showdown?" asked Tim. I couldn't tell if he was excited or worried about the prospect.

"I hope not. I'm not sure that I'd be able to control myself."

"So don't bother trying. Just let her have it."

"I'm not sure that would work. You were knocked out so you don't remember, but she was able to bend my green power shield before."

"Oh, that's right. She was able to defeat the bubble shun."

I felt a little offended at that comment. "Well, I'm not sure I'd say 'defeat', but yeah, she was able to bend the bubble shun."

"She's powerful, Jayne. Don't underestimate her."

"One of these days you're going to tell me all your secrets and all *her* secrets, Tim."

"I know. I'll tell you all of hers when we get back. I think you should know now."

He conveniently ignored my demand to know his personal stuff, but I'd get them out of him eventually.

"Cool. It's a date. We just need to survive this part so we can get to that part."

We were interrupted by our arrival at the edge of the forest. Everyone quieted and gathered into a group.

"We are going to see the Ancient One now. Please stay close and remain in sight of the witch. We are going into Dark Fae territory, as you all know, and the council has been clear about our need to be on alert and to be cautious." Robin looked around at everyone until he was sure they had all agreed to his conditions. "Let's go."

We followed the witch in, walking two by two, until we arrived at Maggie's house, stopping about thirty feet in front of it. The mighty tree rose up out of the forest floor, its branches spreading out over our heads to reach deep into the forest. It wasn't a redwood or sequoia, but it was as big as that kind of tree - maybe bigger. The base of the trunk was as big around as a giant truck, or even a house. In fact, the base of the tree was a house. Maggie's house. Its front door was an arch that was carved right into the wood.

And that door had an arrow sticking out of the middle of it.

We all stared for a few moments, our eyes and brains digesting what we were seeing. Robin motioned for Falco to step forward, and he did so, shaking. I could feel his nervous signature sending vibrations through The Green. I had pulled the power into me without even thinking about it. My survival instincts were on high alert. The ley line that ran under this giant tree made it that much easier for me to use my powers without effort.

Robin and Falco approached the door, walking quietly. The Light Fae witch stood off to the side, scanning the area left and right, as if he were watching for Dark Fae to jump out of the trees at any second.

Falco looked at the arrow and then turned to Robin, nodding. Robin gestured with his head and Falco reached up, grasping his arrow by its shaft and pulling it out of the wood. A branch overhead moved and caused a groaning to echo out through the forest. Every elf in the place involuntarily ducked slightly, looking up at the giant tree that was obviously not happy.

I tapped into its energy without even thinking twice. The feelings and images I got back sent me reeling.

Power. Majesty. History. All of it wrapped up in this being ... this living thing that was connected to the forest, the elves, and even *me*. Everything. Flashes of things - awakenings, death and violence, storms, the cries of babies and of angry men. All of it was mixed up in the waves of energy that battered away at my brain.

Why? Why were these images coming to me like this? I reached out to this old tree, this Ancient One who the elves spoke of with such reverence. What did it want from me and what could I possibly do for it?

The hum of our connection increased in both tenor and volume. It tried to consume me and carry me away, but I resisted. I didn't want to be pulled under. I wanted to stand here as equals and communicate. I sensed through my resistance that the tree had never encountered this type of rebellion before. The humming built up even more, and I had to resist the urge to put my hands over my hears. I knew it wouldn't have helped anyway because the sound wasn't coming to my senses through my ears; plus, I didn't want to show any signs of weakness. I reached out to the ley line under my feet and tapped in. Two could play this game.

I pulled The Green into me, more than I'd ever pulled before, and felt the welcoming coolness and love it always brought. My heart soared with an experience that I was never able to feel in my regular human life. No friendship, no mother's hug, no soft purring kitten had ever inspired this kind of connection with the world before. But now was no time to wallow in the wonderfulness. I had to show this tree who it was messing with.

I sent my message to the Ancient One, my message being the power of ... *what?* I didn't know what it was. I felt a hand gently take mine, and I cracked open an eye to see Falco standing there looking at me in a panic, worry written all over his face. It made me smile. I had friends here in the Green Forest. Fae who cared about me. An idea formed in my mind then ... perhaps I knew what my message could be. *The power of love, maybe?* But how could it be possible that love was more powerful than any of the things it had showed me, or any of the things I had so far experienced that had scared me or hurt me? I didn't know the answer to those questions, but I was pretty sure that this pureness that rushed through me and around me from The Green *was* love - the power that connected everything to everything.

With the first awareness of my message, I knew the tree wanted to resist. Its branches shuddered and stiffened. I opened my eyes fully and witnessed this reaction taking place while my ears heard the ominous cracks that rang out and bounced off the neighboring trees. The ground undulated beneath our feet as the tree's roots fought the incoming power threads amplified by the ley line energy conduit.

The elves standing nearby all had looks of panic on their faces, including Robin who was usually pretty hard to intimidate. I released Falco's hand and held up my own in a message of reassurance, telling my friends silently to wait and see what would happen. I felt confident that my plan was going to work and that they were in no danger.

The Ancient One pushed against me with its will, insisting that it keep this veil of darkness over itself and everything around it. We were in the Dark Forest, and I could tell from the tree's reticence that there had been no light here for a very long time. I knew, better than any of these elves who had been lucky enough to be born to the Light Fae of the Green Forest, how someone can just learn to live with unhappy circumstances and stop noticing how much it sucked. This tree was a lot like me in that way; it had adapted itself to its circumstances and just accepted them ... allowed them to become a part of it. But I'd found another way to look at my life, and so could the Ancient One - assuming someone bothered to show it an alternative and that it would have the strength to resist the constant pull towards complacency and darkness.

I pushed back, sure now that the veil must be lifted and the light be let in. Heat and strain and anger and might - all of it bombarded my soul through the connection we shared. And still I held firm to The Green that surrounded and protected me. Still I held firm to the idea that it was time for the Darkness to cleave to the Light.

The giant tree gave one more groan of resistance, the earth bucked one more time - so hard it sent several elves to the ground - and then the Ancient One capitulated, finally, willingly, accepting the message I was sending.

I received a responding stream of images and sounds - warm sunshine on leaves, babies cooing and responding to smiles and gales of laugher from their mothers, the whistling rush of birds suddenly on the wing, and the vision of lazy pollen motes floating through a glorious, flowered meadow. The joy of it lit my face and set it to burning. I looked out at my friends, the elves, and saw them staring at me, their faces at first registering shock and then tentative pleasure. Leaves rained down on our heads and a gigantic lower branch of the tree moved slowly towards me.

War of the Fae: Book Three

The elves and witch quickly gathered together, suddenly afraid again. I reached up to take Tim off my shoulder, holding my hand out towards Falco. "Tim, hang out here for a second, okay?"

Tim said nothing, hopping into the outstretched hand of Falco.

I gestured with my chin for them to leave me. "Go. I'll be right back."

The giant branch reached my feet, and I knew exactly what to do. I climbed onto it, grabbing a small but sturdy connected limb to steady myself. As soon as I stopped moving, the branch began its upward climb, extending until it reached the next branch up. One by one, the tree's arms elevated me higher and higher, to the top of the forest canopy, until I could see out above everything.

I felt the breeze now and saw two large hawks, circling above the nearby meadow, drifting on the currents that rose high above it, pushing against their wings and keeping the birds aloft. I could smell the flowers and grasses and the wood of the trees, the soft loam of the forest floor and the fungi and mosses on the fallen and rotting tree parts. I pulled energy up from the ley line and shared it with this tree, and watched in delight as small, baby leaves on its nearby branches unfurled to welcome the fading sunlight.

We stayed that way, the tree and I, for a while. I watched a blazingly beautiful sunset begin in the distance as the Earth turned towards night. A piece of me wanted to stay there forever; it was so peaceful and I was so connected to the beauty. None of the ugliness of the real world could intrude up here.

But I knew that there was beauty and love waiting for me down below, too. And I couldn't abandon those who would never abandon me. I'd had my time out, but now it was time to get down and back to the business of living and learning and caring and fighting and maybe even dying. Hopefully, though, the dying part was a lot further out in my distant future.

I thanked the tree for sharing with me and asked it to bring me to my friends. It obliged and I soon found myself on the ground again. Everything was the same as I'd left it, and at the same time, it was totally different.

The witch was pretty much stunned, staring up into the tree with his mouth hanging open. The elves were all smiling and Falco was getting nudged by his friend, who he turned and punched in the chest. The friend just rubbed the spot, frowning but not retaliating. I was happy to see that the pecking order had maybe seen some adjustments today. The sense of unity and peace that I had gained by communing with the Ancient One faded a bit, but its essence remained in my heart. I was going to guard that beauty with everything I had.

Robin walked up and nodded at me, waiting for me to speak.

Time for me to get my head out of the clouds and back into the real world. I took a big breath, letting it all out in one big sigh, smiling at my elven friend. "So, what's the deal with the arrow then? It was Falco's right?"

"Yes. I will have to discuss this with the gray elves, but if my guess is right, this means that in some cases, maybe with all green elves or maybe with just some," he spared a glance for Falco and then looked back at me, doubt in his eyes, "our aim has become something more than just line of sight. It has become connected to our inner eye."

"Wow. Inner eye. Freaky."

He smiled absently. "Yes. You could say that."

Falco walked up with Tim standing on his shoulder and hanging onto a lock of hair near Falco's ear.

"Next time I'm going with you," said Tim, firmly. "No fair leaving me with gnome-head here. I think we've got another one of those 'I don't believe in shampoo' fae here. *Ew-yuck.*"

War of the Fae: Book Three

I smiled. "Deal." I held out my hand for him to jump into, glad no one but me could hear him now.

I saw the look of shock on his face at the same time I heard the noise coming from the front of the tree.

"What's going on out there? Is that you, pixie? I can hear you, you know. I was trying to sleep!"

Maggie's voice.

"Oh, *fuckbuckets. It's her!*" I said in a panic. "I didn't know she was here. Damn, after all that and she's just now waking up? She must sleep like the dead."

"Who?" asked Robin, momentarily confused.

The witch in our group finally spoke up. "Maggie ... " He appeared to be steeling himself for an encounter, his legs spread apart and his staff held up in front of him with both hands.

"Oh, shit. This is not good." My mind raced. *Whattodowhattodowhattodo?*

"Do something, Jayne," hissed Tim in my ear. "If she comes out here, she's going to spell us all! She's going to know you messed with her tree! ... And she *hates* it when fae mess with her tree ... worse than she hates lying!"

"Shut up! I'm trying to think!" I could see the front door opening, a loud creaking signaling the angry witch's imminent arrival. The panic Tim was creating in me made it impossible for me to concentrate.

And then the idea came to me. With no time for inner debate or worry of regret, I sent a message to the huge tree, whose legs were her home. *Please let this work.*

The door ceased its forward motion and abruptly reversed direction, slamming shut with a loud bang.

"Hey!" came the cranky, haggy voice from behind it. "Who's touching my door?! Step away, before I make you sorry you were ever born!"

I turned to the Light Fae witch and elves who were now staring at me in horror and yelled, "*RUN!!*"

Chapter Thirty-Four

THE GROUP OF US SPRINTED through the Dark Forest back to our compound as fast as our legs could carry us. Tim held onto my hair for dear life, shouting in my ear the entire way.

"Mush, you thoroughbred donkey, mush! She's coming! She'll feed me to her rats if she catches me! She'll burn your eyebrows off! She'll put burrowing beetles in your ears! She'll ... "

I blocked out the rest of his litany of horrors. It was stealing precious skipped heartbeats from my suffering cardiovascular system, and I needed all of its strength right now to move my slow-as-molasses ass to the compound.

The wind kicked up behind us, throwing rotted leaves and small twigs into the air to sting our skin and blur our vision. Tears were streaming down my face, my eyes working like mad to get rid of all the dust and dirt. I could feel Maggie tapping into the ley lines running through the forest to work whatever magic it was that was affecting the weather. I experimented with jumping onto the line while I ran, finding that I was able to block her flow as I fled for my life.

Take that, you old bag! I'd gotten stronger than her in that respect. I knew now that I could control who had access to the lines. I could feel her frustration with me and then the success of my efforts when her fighting against my hold on the ley line ceased and the winds died down.

We reached the door of the compound in record time, everyone pushing to enter the hallway at once. Someone slammed the door shut behind us, and I let the hold on the ley line drop. As soon as we were in, we stopped running and just stood there for a moment. The corridor was full of sweaty, dirty, out of breath elves, a gasping girl, a wheezing witch, and a petrified pixie. I don't know who started laughing first, probably Falco, but within seconds of that door shutting, we were all laughing and shouting - even Robin. *Man, did it feel good to be alive* ... and not just alive, but having fought to stay alive and having won.

Finn threw his arm across my shoulders and squeezed me tight to his side while he laughed. "You were amazin', Jaynie girl. I'm so glad you showed up at that warehouse in Miami that day."

I reached across and playfully punched him in the chest. "Me too, Finnster, me too."

The laughter eventually died down, and we all headed back to the more populated areas of the compound.

"Finn ... Tim and I have to go to Dardennes' office with our dinner. You wanna come? I'm going to ask him some questions about some of these Dark Fae and stuff."

"I wouldn't miss it for nothin'."

"Okay. I'll see you there, then. I'm going to go get cleaned up first."

"Sounds like a plan. I'll walk with ya to the rooms."

We parted ways a few minutes later at my door. Tim and I spent the next half hour getting decent before going to dinner, chatting in the room after our showers.

"So, what exactly happened back there, anyway?" asked Tim. "I was so busy hanging on for dear life I think I missed some of the details." He paused for a second and then continued, "You should ask Netter to get a saddle for me."

I raised my eyebrow at him. "You must have pixied your own ass to think I would let you saddle me."

"Just 'til I get my wings back ... "

"How 'bout this: I'll wear a saddle when you stop using shampoo."

Tim looked at me, aghast. "And become a gnome-head? *Never!*"

"Yeah. So, you know what you can do with that saddle then. And to answer your question about what happened, I'm not exactly sure of all the details myself really. I was just working on instinct."

He snorted. "That's a scary thought."

"Yeah, no kidding. I think what I did was open the tree's eyes kinda. Well, not that it has eyes ... its mind? I'm not sure if it has a mind either." I sighed at my inability to express myself. "Anyway, I let it see what it was hiding from. There's a lot of darkness there in that part of the forest. It's like a blanket lying over everything. That tree hadn't seen the light in a long time."

"That's why it's called the Dark Forest, duh."

"Yeah, I guess I knew that. But why is it like that? I mean, why choose the darkness when you can just as easily choose to be full of light ... ness?"

"I'm surprised you would ask that. Don't you already know the answer?" Tim was looking at me all serious-like, and I tried to avoid his eyes. Good thing he didn't have his wings totally back yet, otherwise I know for a fact he'd be buzzing around my face, refusing to let me look away.

"Whatever. I just showed the tree the other side of the coin."

"Maggie's going to be mad," he said carefully.

"Yeah, so what? She sold me out to the Dark Fae. I hope the tree kicks her saggy ass out."

"It won't."

"Yeah, I figured. What's her connection to that tree, anyway? How is it that she gets to live there, inside it like that ... that the tree lets her?"

"You'll have to ask her that," Tim answered mysteriously.

I wasn't sure if he meant he didn't know or that he just wasn't telling. "No way. I'm not going near that old cranky bitch. Not in this lifetime."

"You forget ... that's a really long time now that you're fae."

"No, I didn't forget. That's how long I really meant."

Tim sighed. "You don't mean that. Maggie may have sold us out one time, but she's helped us, too."

"So? She's just a stupid witch. I'll find another witch friend to help me."

Tim got on his bed and started jumping up and down on the mattress. "Whatever you say, boss." He looked like a miniature spastic three year old, bouncing diagonally, forward, back, sideways - straining his body to get as much height as he could, trying to do splits in midair.

"What in the hell are you doing?"

"Practicing."

"Practicing for what? The circus? Do they even have a pixie circus?" The image of Tim in a tiny clown suit was almost too much. I wondered if I could get Netter to find us a tiny clown costume, complete with itty bitty round red nose and floppy shoes ...

"No, smarty ass pants, I'm not practicing for the circus; and *no* there aren't any pixie circuses. Pixies aren't into gratuitous idiocy."

"You coulda fooled me," I mumbled under my breath.

War of the Fae: Book Three

"What?" he said breathlessly as he continued to jump like a maniac.

"I said, are you ready for dinner?"

"Yeah ... just ... let me finish ... this one move ... "

I watched as he took one last ferocious bounce off his mattress and launched himself into the air, trying to do some sort of flip or something. But I could see halfway through the maneuver he wasn't going to make it. And I was too far across the room to help him.

I watched as his body arched in slow motion, over the bed, and over the dresser, putting him into a direct trajectory to land on the cold, stone floor. I knew in that second that he was about to go splat, and there was nothing I could do to stop it.

My heart cried out some sort of crazy desperate prayer into the ether; I didn't even know what it was, it happened so fast. The Green surged through me and shot from my outstretched hands that were frozen in place, involuntarily reaching out to try and save Tim from across the room. My chest felt like it was almost bursting with the stream of energy that was coursing through me.

It hit Tim like a laser beam, capturing him in midair and suspending him above the stone. He was broiling around in a radiant green bubble for a few seconds until he seemed to balance himself out, his hands up in front of him as if he were feeling the edges.

The look on his face was classic Tim. For a split second there was panic ... and then absolute joy. I could see his mouth moving but could barely hear his words. He sounded like he was underwater. He kept making bouncing movements inside the bubble as if he wanted it to go somewhere. It stretched and moved to accommodate his changing positions.

My hands were still out in front of me, more due to instinct than anything else. I had no friggin' idea what I was doing now or what I was supposed to do next. I just kept watching Tim and his crazy antics inside the bubble. He gestured towards his bedroom set on the dresser.

I finally found my voice again. "You want me to move you to the dresser?"

He nodded his head furiously and bounced up and down some more, all while yelling his fool pixie head off.

"I can't hear you, dumbass, just wait a second." I was afraid I was going to drop him. I had no idea where this power had come from or how I was managing it. *Am I controlling it, or is it controlling me?* I didn't recall asking The Green to come in, which was normally what I had to do for something even remotely like this to happen. I looked at the green light coming from my hands and the path of it leading to Tim. It wasn't hurting me or wearing me out to keep it flowing, but I had no idea how I got it started or how to turn it off. I focused inwards, connecting to the source of that stream of light, trying to figure out how I might control or at least influence it.

I sensed something different there in The Green this time. I couldn't quite put my finger on it, though. It wasn't darkness, but it wasn't the clear, pure light of The Green either. It reminded me of something old ... something ... profound and mysterious ... like the Ancient One.

Had something from that tree rubbed off on me? Or had it somehow entered The Green when I had connected them together? *Damn, I wish I hadn't trapped Maggie in her house and totally pissed her off, so I could go ask her. Sigh.* Another bridge burned. I was going to have to stop doing that at some point in this life of mine, especially now, since it was going to be so damn long. *Hopefully.* There was always that chance that my complete lack of knowing what the hell I was doing could come back and bite me in the ass, making me one of the shortest-lived fae ever. I was just hoping that it wasn't going to be today.

"Hang on, Tim. I'm trying to figure this thing out." I focused on that deeper essence that was with me now. I thought of how before I had to kind of strong-arm the Ancient One into doing what I wanted and accepting what I saw as the inevitable truth. This new flow that I was feeling needed a stronger hand than I was used to using in my links.

Sure enough, once I decided to bend the light to my will, it responded. I moved my hands slowly to the left, guiding the pixie bubble over to the dresser. Soon, Tim was suspended above his bed. He was jumping up and down in excitement, stretching the bubble lengthwise, completely clueless about the fact that I was worried I could possibly fry his little butt into oblivion with my every move.

Okay, so now what? I could feel that The Green wanted to stay there with me. It was like an eager puppy, straining at the leash. I pushed back the thoughts of how much work and trouble an eager puppy can be. I had to tame this bastard here and now, or I was going to be a walking nightmare for the Light Fae; as if I weren't enough of that already, putting people into comas and sending arrows around the forest like unmanned military drones.

I wrenched back on the green light in my mind, straining with the effort. I could see the bubble getting thinner, but Tim still remained trapped inside.

There was a knock at the door, but I didn't want to risk breaking my concentration, so I ignored it. I could hear the door creak open and then Becky's voice.

"Whoaaaahh, that's awwwwesome. How'd you do *that?*"

"I have no idea. I can't shut it off," I said, nervously.

"Oh. Well that's a problem, isn't it?"

"Yeah, no shit. Any ideas?" I looked over at her briefly as she walked up to stand at my side, alternating nervous glances between Tim and me.

"Maybe you could just, I don't know, put your arms down or something."

I started to move my hands to my sides and the bubble bounced wildly, knocking Tim over inside. He struggled to get up, all cranky now because I'd messed up his hair. He smoothed it down while shooting me the stink eye.

I put my hands back up, making sure Tim was once again suspended over his bed. "Got any other great ideas?"

"Hey, don't put your hate on me, I'm just trying to help." She stuck her tongue out at me.

"Try harder, H-two-O girl, my arms are getting tired."

"I'm gonna go get somebody. I'll be right back."

"Who are you going to get?!" I yelled, but she was already gone, disappearing into thin air, probably just to piss me off. She knew I was jealous of her mad teleporting skills.

Becky was back in less than a minute. "She'll be here in a sec."

"Who?" I asked, suspiciously. But then I knew. My room, which was totally closed off from the outside world, was suddenly full of wind. *"What the hell did you do, Becky?"* I whispered angrily.

A mini tornado appeared out of thin air up near my ceiling and then touched down next to me. Its revolutions slowed until I could see the form of Céline taking shape.

I frowned at my friend. "This was the best idea you could come up with? Tattling on me?"

Becky rolled her eyes. "I didn't tattle. Céline will help you, not punish you. She *likes* you, dummy." Then Becky tried to blind me with a smile so bright it could out-shine the sun.

War of the Fae: Book Three

I just shook my head at her. "Whatever." *Friggin happy-ass water sprites.*

The Green was holding strong and true. Even my nervousness about Céline being here didn't have any effect on it. Tim sat down in the bubble with his legs crossed. I could totally picture him in there holding a box of popcorn in his lap. My screw-ups? ... Total pixie entertainment.

"Jayne," said Céline, looking a little taken aback, "hello."

"Uh, hi."

"What exactly do we have here? Or do you not know?" She glanced at Becky who I could see out of the corner of my eye was shaking her head and mouthing the word 'no'.

"Well, what we have here, is me saving Tim's ass and then me getting stuck in savior mode."

"Uh-huh. I see. And so you need assistance in ... shall we say, shutting off the power?"

"Yes. That's exactly what I need." I felt better already, having defined the problem.

Céline looked at the bubble and then back at me. She was staring at my face, and I tried to smile at her in return, but I was too worried about Tim being forever trapped in one of my screw-ups to do much better than a grimace.

"Let's try this ... can you try to focus on something else, maybe? Instead of thinking of The Green, think of another thing or another person - like your friend Tony, for example."

Saying it was easier than doing it. I tried to think of something else, but my panic would rise up as soon as I saw the bubble start to move. I was afraid Tim was going to start zinging around the room and go splat into a wall or something. "I can't. I keep thinking the bubble's going to get away from me, and then I won't know how to get it back. Or Tim."

A knock at the door took her attention away from me. I sensed Becky leaving my side, and the door opening behind me. The sound of Spike's voice filled the room.

"Well, well, well ... what do we have here?"

Becky spoke in hushed tones. "She's stuck. She can't let go of it."

Spike came up behind me and talked softly in my ear. "Got yourself all up in the shit again, didn't you, Trouble?"

"Yeah. You could say that."

Spike addressed Céline. "So, what's the scoop? You getting her out of this mess?"

"I'm trying," she responded, frustration in her voice. "I'm afraid I'm a bit out of my element. I am merely a servant to the wind. I do not command it. She has a much greater control going on here than I am familiar with."

"Why don't I give it a shot?"

I looked at Céline, wondering if she would be okay with an incubus changeling stepping in where she had failed. I probably shouldn't have worried because Céline wasn't about ego or status.

"By all means," she gestured towards me, "see what you can do."

Spike stepped around to where I could see him. He was so ridiculously good-looking I could hardly stand to look at him. All the sexual tension set the bubble to bouncing again, and Tim got a little panicky looking. He held his hands straight out from his sides, steadying himself against the curved green glow as he cast worried glances at us.

Spike smiled at me. "Hey, babe. You okay?" He reached up and stroked my upper arm, sending shivers down my spine. The green glow intensified.

"I'm not so sure that's the best approach, Spike," warned Becky.

War of the Fae: Book Three

"You're making it worse."

"Shhhh ... I'm just going to guide you through a little exercise the incubi use to help us focus, okay?"

I nodded my head, not trusting myself to speak. If this focusing exercise included him getting any closer or touching me anymore, we were going to have a problem.

"Okay. Now, look at the green light in your hands. Block out visions of anything else. Just focus on that light."

I did my best to do what he was saying, but he was standing too close. Visions of green lights warred with visions of Spike without his shirt on ... Spike leaning over me ... Spike kissing me.

The green glow got brighter again and the bubble darker. Tim was waving his hands in front of him, gesturing for me to stop.

I sighed in frustration. "This isn't going to work if I can see you or hear you, Spike."

Spike stepped away and whispered something to Becky. I heard her say, "Be right back."

"Becky's going to get Valentine," said Spike. "He'll be able to help you."

Oh great. Spike's mentor. The last time I'd seen him in action, he'd nearly drained Chase's life energy from him.

Spike stayed out of my visual range, but I knew he was still back there. It kept my light burning brightly.

My bedroom door opened with a bang, and then I could hear Valentine behind me.

"Oh. My. Goodness. What have you gotten yourself into *now*, sweetness?"

"I'm a little stuck. Spike says you can help me focus and get this thing wrangled."

Valentine addressed Spike, "How come you couldn't do it, lover?"

Spike cleared his throat, embarrassed, "She can't focus on it right when I'm around."

"Tsk, tsk. Young love. Always interfering in the flow. How many times have I told you? There is no room for love in the life of an incubus."

Before Spike could reply to that interesting tidbit of information that I was trying not to let bother me, Valentine arrived at my shoulder.

"Okay, cutie pie. Here's what you're going to do. Focus on that adorable green light you have coming out of your hands. Focus on that and nothing else. Hear my words but then do it without thinking about me. I know, I know ... how are you going to stop thinking about Valentine? How could anyone? Believe me, girl, I hear what you're saying. But try. Try very hard."

Becky snorted behind me, and it made me smile.

"Get yourself all joined up with that pretty light. *Mmm-hmmm*, that's right, it's just you and the power. Nothing else matters. Commune with it. Meld with it. Welcome it in. It is you and you are it. You are one."

As his words droned over me, I felt myself slipping into a more focused realm. Now I could sense the power flow and how it continuously coursed through me without actually leaving.

"Once you are fully connected mentally, grab that flow and pull it back into you. Show it who's boss. Make it go. You're in charge, sweetie, you're the captain of this ship. Show it your fierceness. Hold nothing back. You are the queen of the green light. This is your house."

I am the boss, I am the boss. Get your ass back in here green light. Don't make me put orcs back in your damn trees.

I didn't know if that last thought is what did it, but suddenly I felt a shift in the power. Now The Green wasn't flowing through me ...

War of the Fae: Book Three

I was flowing through it. Overwhelming. Controlling.

I moved my hands until Tim was suspended just a pixie-foot above his bed. Then I visualized myself grabbing the flow and shoving it back down through my feet and into the floor below.

As if I had turned off a light switch, the green glow snapped off, taking the bubble with it. Tim was dropped down onto his bed where he bounced once and then sat, cross-legged and wild-eyed. That lasted for about a second before he jumped up and started whooping.

"Whooooo hoooo! That was *awesome! Do it again!"*

I stepped over quickly, fixing him with an angry stare. "Stop jumping around you crazy-ass pixie before you light a fuse to another nuclear bomb."

Tim stopped jumping and pouted at me. "Party pooper."

"Party pooper, my ass. Don't you realize how serious that was?!"

Becky came over and touched my arm. "It's fine now, Jayne. Relax. Tim is fine."

"Yeah, but ... " I couldn't put into words what I was thinking. I couldn't shake the images of Tim being fried or exploded by a power flow that was coming through me that I couldn't control. My other mistakes with The Green were different. The power seemed more passive. It just made people oblivious and happy. Now it was almost aggressive. I was afraid of what it would do to someone when it backfired.

Spike grabbed my hand and pulled me to him, causing me to land smooshed up against his chest.

Céline spoke up, "Well, if I'm not needed here, I'm going to head to dinner. I believe, Jayne, that you will be joining Anton in his office? Will I see you there?"

I nodded my head, unable to speak now that I was breathing in Spike's scent and he was staring down into my eyes with a sexy smile on his face. I could see his teeth glistening from behind his lips.

Valentine broke into my getting-too-warm daze, saying, "Okay, babies, I can see that you don't need me anymore. I'll leave you to your star-crossed love. Toodles."

I shook my head to get it out of Spike-land for a second, looking at Valentine's retreating form. "Thanks, Valentine. I appreciate your help."

"Oh, it was nothing. You did well. I think you would have been an absolutely *divine* succubus. So much control ... tsk, tsk ... " And then he was gone, the door shutting behind him.

"So guys. Time for dinner, right?" said Becky, injecting a bunch of fake cheer into her voice.

"Yeah!" agreed Tim. "Time for dinner, not for swapping spit!"

I turned and frowned at him. "One more thing, Tim. Just say one more thing."

He stuck his tongue out at me and then sat down on his bed, putting his moccasins back on. "I'm hungry. Am I allowed to say that? Or are you going to bubble-ize me again?"

I rolled my eyes and took a deep, calming breath.

Spike was grinning at Tim and me. "What'd he say?"

"He's hungry. And he gets cranky when he's hungry." I looked over at Tim as I finished. "So I'm not going to flick him in the ass like he deserves."

I was rewarded with a pixie fart.

I pushed Spike away, now totally not in the mood for romance. "Thanks for everything, Spike."

He reached out to grab me back. "How about a kiss for ... success."

I looked at him like he was crazy. "Uh, no. For some reason - thank you, Tim - I'm not really in the mood."

War of the Fae: Book Three

Spike frowned at me playfully.

"Maybe later."

His smile came back.

Becky grabbed my hand. "Come on, lover girl, let's go."

"Wait a sec." I pulled her with me towards the dresser. "Hop on, Tim. The dinner train is leaving."

He jumped up from his bed and ran over to get on my shoulder, grabbing a handful of hair a little too hard.

"I'll do it, Tim."

"Fine." His hold loosened.

"And don't even think about what you're thinking about, or you're gonna be riding the shoe." I'd never actually made him do that before, but tonight I totally would. One more pixie toot and it was all over for him.

"*TThhhpppt.* Maybe you *should* do a little lovey, sucky, woo-woo with Spike. It might cheer you up."

I didn't dignify his suggestion with a response, possibly because a part of me agreed. But right now I couldn't trust myself to handle it well, and I didn't even know if it was safe for Spike anymore. Who knows? I could accidentally put him in a bubble and then not be able to get him out. He'd die of starvation in there.

I tried not to think about it anymore as we headed out the door to get some food to take with us to Dardennes' office.

Chapter Thirty-Five

BY THE TIME I HAD my plate of food and had arrived at Dardennes' office, the room was full of my friends. Finn was sitting next to Becky on a small couch. Dardennes and Céline were at his desk together. Spike and Scrum were standing while eating from plates on a small table - Scrum's was full of wiggling meats and other gross things, Spike's nearly empty. Tony waved a bread roll at me from a single chair positioned across from Becky and Finn.

"Hi, uh, sorry we're late. It's Tim's fault."

"Hey!" he yelled in my ear, but I ignored him. A little revenge was just what the doctor ordered to cheer me up, and I had no problem with self-medicating.

"Not at all," said Dardennes, a smile in his voice. "We were just chatting. I suggest that we get started now, though, and all of you should feel free to eat as we talk. I know you've been working hard and you need to make sure you have the necessary energy for your continued training."

I didn't see any sense in beating around the bush, so I took a seat next to Tony and immediately started asking questions.

"First, I'd like to know what Céline's connection is to Maléna." I looked down at my plate, acting like I was interested in my food. I didn't want her to think I was challenging her or anything, but I was more than just a little curious.

"Céline?" said Dardennes. "I will leave this one to you, dear."

Céline cleared her throat. "A-*hem*. Well. Maléna? She is ... my sister."

I looked up at her, saying, "I *knew* it. I totally nailed that one. Are you guys twins? Because you sure look like it."

Her mouth turned up slightly at the corner, but it looked more like a grimace than a smile. "No. We are not twins. She is younger than I."

"So why is she ... ," started Becky, but then she stopped, her face turning red.

I looked at Becky, realizing that she wasn't going to finish, and said, "I think what Becky wants to know is ... how is it that Maléna's Dark Fae and you're Light Fae?"

I looked over at Becky and she nodded at me, her face still flaming.

"We used to both be Light Fae. Then she ... met someone. A Dark Fae silver elf. She fell in love and then ... she left. She joined him and the Dark Fae."

"Bummer," said Scrum, half-chewed food showing in his mouth.

"Yes," agreed Céline, clearing her throat again. "Bummer, as you say."

"Who was the guy?" asked Spike, a sly look on his face as he stared at Dardennes.

Céline looked at Dardennes. "Anton? I believe this one is for you." She looked down at the table, but not before I saw the sadness in her eyes.

Dardennes didn't answer right away. He sighed, staring off into space for a moment. Then he looked at us, one at a time. When his eyes fell on me, he answered, "The Dark Fae silver elf who she fell in love with ... was me."

The responses erupted around the room.

"What?!" I said, shocked out of my gourd, even though a little piece of me wasn't that surprised.

"How could that ... ?" asked Tony, confused.

"Whoopsy," said Becky, shrugging her shoulders.

Spike just smiled, all crafty-like. He must have already had it all figured out. He and Valentine were the gossips of the compound. I made a mental note to talk to him about it later and find out what else they knew.

Finn just looked at his food, chewing and not making eye contact with anyone.

Since everyone seemed too uncomfortable to continue, I decided to take charge of the interrogation. "So, she was a Light Fae, fell in love with you, joined the Dark Fae, and then what? You left her there and came here?" *Man, that sounded totally cold-hearted.* I looked at Dardennes' face, but he didn't seem angry - more like resigned or something.

"Essentially, yes. But there is much more to it than that."

"Much more, like what?" I pressed.

"The Dark Fae council ordered me to do something that I would not agree to do. I was found in dereliction of my duties to the Dark Fae and asked to leave."

"What was it that you refused to do?" asked Finn, now looking as if he were paying closer attention to the conversation.

"I was told to kidnap Céline and bring her to them."

"Whoa. Bad soap opera drama - pitting lover against lover and lover's sister," said Spike.

I shook my head at him. Sometimes he scared me with his

Valentine-ness.

"Why didn't Maléna come here with you? I mean, her sister's here," said Tony who had completely abandoned the pretense of eating, all of his attention now focused on the conversation.

"We were together as Dark Fae for many years. But there were ... other Dark Fae who had different fundamental beliefs than I, and after many years, I realized that I could not continue to support a mission I so strongly disapproved of. Taking Céline was, as they say, the last straw for me."

"But Maléna didn't feel that way?"

"No. She did not. And she had ... other reasons to stay."

It sounded like my parents' marriage - stressful and unhappy. I wondered if fae could get divorced.

Céline jumped in. "My sister is a very headstrong and brutal person. She believes very firmly in the superiority of the fae as a species and thinks that our position should be asserted over the human species for the good of all fae, regardless of what methods are used. She justified her actions through any means possible. Neither she nor ... her compatriots ... can see how their philosophy will actually hurt all fae."

Finn jumped in again. "I guess I ain't exactly crystal clear on the differences between us an' them. All I ever get is they're the bad guys, we're the good guys, now go get ready for battle." He paused, looking at all of us changelings. "You know, this reminds me of civics class in the sixth grade, you know? When we studied the Civil War an' all? There were families torn apart then; some brothers fightin' for the South, some for the North. All because of their philosophical differences an' all."

"Finn's right," said Tony. "I think I understand what the different philosophies are from my work with the gray elves, but I wouldn't mind an official explanation from you, Mr. Dardennes, about what they actually are."

Dardennes smiled at us patiently. "I think perhaps that this clarification is long overdue. I know it was mentioned to some degree when you were first offered the opportunity to make the change. But so many things have happened in your lives since, and it has all been a bit overwhelming. I would be happy to explain in more detail." He looked at Céline. "Feel free to add to my discourse at any time."

Céline nodded her head.

Dardennes turned to face us. "As a former member of the Dark Fae, and follower of their creed, I can explain it to you thusly: the Dark Fae believe that fae are a superior species. They have supernatural abilities, are connected to the magic of the universe, and have intimate relationships with the elements. Some can even walk between our world of the Here and Now and the Otherworlds." He paused to look at Tony and then continued. "Humans do not have any of these talents, cannot do any of these things. In addition to this natural sense of superiority, the fae have needs that can, or in some cases must, be met by the humans. These needs include the need for sustenance - for example, the incubi and succubi use human sexual and life energy to feed themselves - and also the need for their resources. There are many fae in the world, but even more humans. We depend on them for their manufacturing, banking, farming - as many of us eat foods that are not human. We even need their artistic expression. Some fae thrive in more creative environments. Humans help them to stay grounded and stable."

"So if this is true for all fae, where's the difference between the Light and the Dark?" asked Becky.

"The difference is in the way we believe humans should be treated and the role we should play in their society. The Light Fae believe our best chance for survival and to have access to the resources provided by the humans is to stay hidden ... to continue to operate in their shadows and dreams, not in their realties. However, the Dark Fae do not agree. They want to be out in front of the humans, living in the open, no longer hiding who they are and what they do. They want to exert their power over the humans and assert their fae domination."

"Okay," said Finn, "I get that. What I don't get is why they don't just go do it. Why fight the Light Fae at all? It ain't like they need our permission."

Céline joined in the conversation now, and I noticed Tony nodding his head at what she was saying. "They do not have enough Dark Fae to fight a resisting human species. There are millions more humans than fae. The balance was different many years ago, but even then, there was a concern about the Dark Fae's ability to not only meet human resistance but also the opposition of the Light Fae who would join the humans. They assume rightly that we would unite with the humans in fighting them, because we believe that it would be the only way we could live through it. Once the humans became aware of the fae, they would naturally want to exterminate them. We are a different and alien species in many ways and therefore a threat. We would have to pretend to *be* human and fight the Dark Fae just to survive the aftermath."

"Yeah, but with the faes' supernatural abilities, it wouldn't matter that the humans have bigger numbers. One fae is worth about ten humans in terms of strength. Or in some cases, more," said Spike, looking directly at me.

"Nah," said Scrum, once more in mid-chew. "You hafta factor in the human fear. That makes 'em stronger. Plus every human can have firepower; all they need is a gun."

"Or a bow and arrows, I guess," said Spike, shooting a look over at Finn, who tipped his head in recognition.

"The daemon is correct," said Dardennes. "The fear of the supernatural is incredibly powerful. Humans may think they'd be happy to know that vampires and werewolves actually exist, as a romantic notion, but if they were ever really confronted by one that was trying to suck the life out of them or even eat them, they would feel differently."

I laughed at that. "I know my first meeting with a real werewolf didn't go exactly as I'd always imagined."

Becky smiled. "I know, right? Where are all the bare-chested Jacobs anyway?"

The guys just looked at us with question marks floating above their heads.

"Never mind," I said, looking back at Dardennes. "So, their plan is to what? Defeat us? Then how are they going to accomplish their goal if we're all gone?"

"Their plan is not to defeat us," said Tony. "Their plan is to make us join them, through intimidation and fear. But there would be loss of life. It is unavoidable if we engage them."

"Oh." *Bummer*.

"That's just ... wrong," said Becky, "going after your own faekind like that."

"According to them, what we are doing is wrong - hiding in the forest and walking away from what they say is our legacy," explained Céline.

"So why are they called 'Dark' and we're called 'Light'?" I asked. "I mean, isn't that them agreeing they're evil by aligning themselves with Darkness?" I couldn't imagine who would actually call themselves the friends of Darkness, unless they were Satan worshippers or something.

Dardennes smiled. "Now we're getting into the theoretical realm. Darkness, according to the Dark Fae, is merely the absence of Light. It is, to them, the ultimate expression of who they are and the strength of their beliefs. They are a strong and proud group of fae. None of them calls their brethren 'dark' as in 'evil'. They all claim to be the only fae who are truly fae, unfettered by human emotions and human influence. They consider our 'lightness' to be our concern for the humans and our need to protect them from our kind. They see it as a weakness and turn from it." He looked at Céline for confirmation and received an answering nod. "Think of Dark Fae as those who have remained true to our original beliefs and can trace them back over many centuries ... and Light Fae as fae whose ideas and values have shifted with time, adapting to the realities of sharing our world with the humans and their changing beliefs and customs."

I tried to grab hold of what they were saying, but it was pretty much as clear as mud ... which wasn't surprising considering who was telling the story. I wasn't even sure I was getting the basic concepts, but I decided to take a crack at it anyway. "So what you mean is that Dark doesn't mean evil, it just means 'old school fae'?"

Dardennes smiled and jabbed a finger at me. "Exactly!"

"And when you say Light, you mean like, 'enlightened'?"

"Yes! You understand perfectly," said Céline, proud of me for some nutty reason.

Whatever. This shit didn't sound like a good reason to go to war. And a war that wasn't really meant to eradicate anyone but to change their minds about their philosophies? *Weird.*

I shook my head. "Well, you guys can call it whatever the hell you want ... as far as I'm concerned, they're the bad guys and we're the good guys. That's all I need to know for now."

"Telling it like it is ... Jayne is never one to disappoint," said Tim, laughter in his voice.

"Thanks, Tim. Just trying to keep it real."

Our attention was immediately grabbed by the sound of the door being thrown open and the voice of Gregale ringing out across the room.

"Anton! Céline! Come quickly. We've had a breach! The Dark Fae have come!"

Céline's lips closed together in a thin line, turning down at the corners in worry.

"Where? Has anyone been hurt?" demanded Dardennes.

"Near the gargoyle door. And yes, a witch was hurt."

Dardennes came out from behind his desk. "How many are here?"

"We do not know, Anton. We think at least two, and one of them for certain is a witch."

"Are you thinking what I'm thinking?" asked Tim.

I whispered back, turning my head to the side so he could hear me over the commotion, "If it's Maggie, I'm gonna put her in a green power slingshot and shoot her sorry ass out over the top of this forest. Maybe all the way to Spain."

"Now *that's* something I'd like to see," said Tim.

"Yeah, well, let's pray that you don't." I moved to join Dardennes and the others gathering around the door.

"What do you want us to do, Mr. Dardennes?" asked Tony.

I reached out and grabbed Tony's hand, and he squeezed mine reassuringly. Spike caught my eye and gave me a nervous nod. I could see Becky sidling up close to Finn.

"Go to your rooms and await further instructions ... with the exception of you, Tony. Please report to the strategy room to meet with the gray elves."

"Thank you, sir," said Tony before squeezing my hand one more time and then letting it go. He rushed out of the room, trailing behind a fast-moving Gregale.

Dardennes and Céline left in a hurry too, abandoning the rest of us in the doorway.

"So, we goin' back to our rooms?" asked Finn, his hand on his bow.

"*Hell* to the *no*," I said, offended that we were being told to go hide. "I'm going to the friggin gargoyle door."

"Jaaayyyne ... ," warned Tim.

"Shush, Tim. I'm going. If you want to take your pansy ass to the room, go ahead. But you'd better watch out so you don't get stepped on, because I'm not taking you back there."

"First of all, how dare you suggest that I *walk* to the room." He sniffed in disgust. "Pixies do not walk. We either fly or get taken places. And second, I wasn't suggesting we split up. I was merely reminding you that you recently messed with a certain someone who lives just outside that door, and that this certain someone might not be all that excited to see you right now."

"Yeah, well, that certain someone can kiss my big white butt."

"Who can kiss your big white butt?" asked Becky.

"No one." I looked over at Spike, and he appeared as if he were about to say something sexy, so I held up my hand. "Put it away, Spike, put it away."

"Put what away?" asked Finn, now as confused as Becky.

Scrum leaned in and looked at each of us. "I think she's telling him to put away his ... "

" ... And that'll be enough from you, daemon boy," said Spike, smiling and clapping Scrum on the back, throwing him forward and off balance. "So, what's the plan, warrior boy? Gargoyle door or room? Where're you going?"

Scrum shrugged. "Where Jayne goes, I go."

These words that I'd heard uttered more than once by Chase made my heart spasm uncomfortably for a second. I missed him and his strong, silent, dependable presence. His amazing biceps and chest didn't make him easy to forget, either. I looked at Scrum, and there was just no comparison. Adonis or the beer keg with legs? *Yeah. Easy.* No offense to Scrum, because he tried like hell and usually did okay, but I really needed Chase right now and wished like hell he were here.

"Let's go, then," said Finn. "I'm tired of shootin' at targets and playin' around. I wanna go at the real deal."

"You mean, you want to shoot someone?" asked Becky, disbelief and censure in her voice.

Finn frowned. "No. I mean, if them assholes're gonna come here to our home and try to mess with us, I ain't gonna take it lyin' down. And neither should you, little non-violent water sprite, 'cuz this is your home too. If you don't fight for it, you ain't gonna have it for long."

Becky swallowed hard. She squared her shoulders and said, "Fine. I'm with you. But if I disappear, I don't want any of you complaining and calling me a chicken. Sometimes ... I can't help it. When I get scared and start thinking about somewhere I'd rather be, I just sometimes end up there, okay?" She looked at each one of us for confirmation that we wouldn't rag on her.

"*That* is the most lame-ass excuse I think I've ever heard. 'I can't help it? I disappear by accident'? Man, you water sprites are total wusses." I tried to look at her all serious, but the outraged expression on her face had me laughing. "Chill out, guppy-girl, I'm just messing with you."

She closed her lips and blinked her eyes a few quick times. "Fine. Let's go," she said, pushing past me and out into the hallway.

Elle Casey

I stepped forward and grabbed her hand, getting ahead of her and then pulling her along, refusing to be shunned and ignoring her continued attempts to stay mad at me. We followed Finn, who had taken his bow off his shoulder and loosely notched an arrow in the string. I'd seen him in action before, so I knew if someone appeared around a corner, he'd have that thing flying in no time at all. It made me feel a small measure safer. But not much.

Chapter Thirty-Six

WE ARRIVED AT THE GARGOYLE door and saw no one and nothing out of the ordinary. It seemed strange to be gathered again at this place we had not so long ago rushed into, escaping the imagined anger of Maggie.

"Should we go out?" asked Finn.

"Just open it," said Spike, "see if there's anybody out there."

"Oh, for shit's sake, people ... get out of my way." I shouldered my way to the door and grabbed the ring handle, pulling it in towards me and forcing everyone back. At first I saw nothing, so I turned to tell my friends they were overreacting ... but then I felt it. A buzz on the ley line.

I turned back to the entrance in time to see a figure coming towards the door from the edge of the trees. A witch with a black cloak on.

"It's Samantha! *Get back!*" I yelled, shoving them with my butt, pushing the door shut as fast as I could. Just before the edges made contact and closed completely, a force began pushing it inward.

"Shit! Help me! She's got the door!"

Scrum and Finn rushed to my aid, bracing their shoulders against the wood and pushing with me as hard as they could. But it was no use; the door continued to open. There was an ominous creaking sound coming into the hallway as the two forces battled to win control.

"She's ... using ... magic," grunted Scrum.

"Spike, get in here!" yelled Finn. "I'm gonna shoot her!"

Becky screamed, "Finn! You can't shoot Samantha! She's our friend!"

I looked at Becky like she was crazy. "She's no *friend!* She joined the Dark Fae! She's trying to get in here to hurt us!"

The door was open about a foot now, but so far no one was coming in from the outside or standing in the opening. I could see the muscles in Scrum's and Spike's arms and backs straining against Samantha's force.

Becky grabbed my arm, squeezing as she begged. "She's only with them because she was rejected by Dardennes." Tears filled her eyes as she pleaded with me silently.

I pulled my arm back, shrugging her off. "Whatever the reason, she is who she is, and she's doing this to attack us. You think she wants to come in for tea? You think she's not going to blast us right between the eyes when she sees us? You've conveniently forgotten, I guess, that she was one of my *kidnappers.*" I shot her a look of anger so strong, it was possible she actually felt it.

Becky flinched at my emotion, dropping her hands to her sides. "It's not ... it's too ... " And then she was gone. Disappeared into thin air again.

"Fucking water sprites!" I yelled out into the air.

"Jayne, let her go! You have bigger things to worry about," advised Tim, nervously, pulling my hair like crazy. "You need to power up and blast that witch to smithereens!"

The door was now open wide enough for a smallish fae to fit through. I had about five seconds before it was fully open. Scrum and

War of the Fae: Book Three

Spike were losing their momentum, their feet sliding along the stone floor inch by stuttering inch as they lost the battle, and their faces were showing the strain of their efforts. Finn stood off to the side, arrow notched and bow up at the ready. He was waiting for the right moment to pull back on the arrow and let it fly.

I plumbed down into the depths of the nearest ley line, drawing up its power and letting it roll over me, while also blocking Samantha's access. I heard sounds coming from outside the door now, but I ignored them in my bid for focus over my control of The Green that was now flooding up from the earth and filling my every cell.

The door opened more, and the sight of many bodies greeted our eyes. It was no longer just Samantha standing out there, and we were no longer alone at the gargoyle door.

The door opened the rest of the way, the witch's power finally overcoming the strength of my friends. It flew back and hit the wall, revealing the battlefield beyond.

Finn rushed out, his arrow drawn back. Scrum moved to be near me, standing at my side. Spike dropped back, too, taking up a position on my other side. Tim was my eyes and ears, better able to see what was going on, since so much of my concentration was taken by my attempt to accumulate and channel my energy. We stepped out into the grasses and entered the fray.

An entire company of Light Fae elves was battling a motley crew of Dark Fae. Standing in front of the Dark Fae contingent was Samantha, a thin, gray haze surrounding her. I watched as several arrows bounced off of it and landed on the ground, useless. There were a couple Dark Fae on the ground near her with arrows sticking up out of their bodies - ogres by the looks of it. Big ugly fuckers.

In the dying light of evening, I saw Falco off to my left and then farther away Robin and many others I recognized from our training in the forest earlier. Was it only today that we had been there? It seemed so long ago. The orange and gold bands of the fading sunset gave the battle a surreal feeling, as if this was all just a bad dream.

"There she is!" yelled Samantha. "Take her down!"

Her meant *me*, apparently, since about fifteen sets of weapons turned to point in my direction. I threw up a green bubble around me, Tim, and my two bodyguards without even thinking. I sent an image out through The Green to Robin and prayed like crazy that he was communicating it to his elf buddies. They all raised their arrows, each choosing a target.

Everything had come down to this one moment. This was my last ditch effort to use the powers I had not yet learned to harness, to save my friends and keep the Dark Fae from entering our compound ... from taking over our lives and forcing us to adopt their fucked up view of the world.

I sent my power into the green elves standing next to me, whose signatures I could feel, pure and light in The Green ... giving their minds' eyes the energy and magical connection they would need to find their targets, no matter how far away and no matter who they were.

Samantha lifted her arms, and I noticed one of them held a staff. She was only a changeling, but she looked like one of the older, more experienced witches. I knew that force she had used to physically push our door open and was using to shield herself from the deadly arrows was no small spell, and the fact that she did it while being cut off from the ley line was seriously impressive. She knew her shit and wasn't afraid to use it. I had to protect my friends from her ruthlessness by showing no mercy.

I couldn't put the bubble around the elves, or their arrows would bounce off the inside and allow their attackers to come at them and surround them. Instead, I strengthened the one around the four of us - Scrum, Spike, Tim and me. Then I faced Robin, nodding my head. Time to launch those badass mindseye arrows and let the chips fall where they may.

I saw Robin's mouth moving, the sound of his voice muffled by the humming force of green light that kept us protected. The words I knew he spoke - *Ready? ... Aim! ...* - resulted in a line of arms being lifted and arrows being drawn back.

Samantha stole a glance at them, finally breaking her concentration for a second as she gestured to her ogres to attack.

I saw my opportunity and took it. I shot a message out to Robin and watched as he changed his trajectory to aim at her.

His last command was issued - *Release!* - and a shower of arrows launched up into the air and soared over the open space between us and them.

Samantha turned back to me, but she was too late. I didn't know if it was her loss of focus or the special force sent behind that arrow that did it, but either way, Robin's arrow found its target.

Part of me flinched at the vision before me, the aftermath of the green elves' volley. Ogres fell to the ground with arrows sticking out of them, some of them looking like giant porcupines they had so many. Samantha stood completely still, staring down at the arrow that was sticking out of her chest. I knew without getting closer that the feather on the end would identify it as Robin's. It wasn't in her heart, it was on the other side. Robin must have deliberately not taken the kill shot, and I wasn't sure if I was happy about that or not.

Three Dark Fae elves remained standing just behind and to the side of Samantha. They stepped forward awkwardly, arrows notched in their bows and pointing to the ground. They kept their eyes on us, while trying to steal glances at her.

She lifted her head and fixed a malevolent gaze on me. I stared right back. I was standing ready to deal her the last blow, when a sudden movement out of the corner of my eye caught my attention.

Becky. She had appeared between Samantha and me suddenly, materializing in the middle of the field. I let some of the Green power drop away because I needed to get to her before she did something foolish, and I couldn't do it trapped in this stupid bubble.

"Samantha!" Becky shouted, running forward with tentative steps towards her. "You've been hit!"

Samantha lifted her arm and yelled, "Now!"

A beam of white light streamed out of her staff and hit Becky right in the chest, sending her flying backwards to land in a tangle on the ground. Her right leg was bent at an unnatural angle, and she laid there motionless in the grasses, her eyes open and staring up at the sky.

"Becky!" I screamed, turning to run to her.

Scrum and Spike both grabbed me by the arms. "No! Jayne, you can't go! Stay inside where it's safe!" yelled Scrum.

"No, Jayne, stay!" yelled Tim, pulling my hair as hard as he could.

Angry tears coursed down my face. *"Fuck that!"* I pushed desperately at Scrum's hands that were trying to grab hold of me. I wrestled with Spike, too. "Spike, let me go! I need to help her!"

He held onto me with a grip of iron. "No!" growled Spike. "Samantha's hoping that's what you'll do. She's trying to kill you. Stay here!" Then he squeezed me extra tight. "Look! Becky's not there anymore! She's gone!"

I looked up from my attempts at escape and saw that, sure enough, Becky's body had disappeared. I hoped like hell that meant she wasn't dead. I didn't think a water sprite could teleport without being alive, but at the same time, I worried that she had gone to the afterlife or had been teleported by Naida or someone else from the murky depths of their watery home.

A movement near Samantha pulled my attention back to the battle. I watched as three arrows sailed out from behind her, towards the green elves that had since reloaded their weapons and were pulling them back to finish the job they had started with their last volley. Everyone but Falco. He was staring at the place where Becky had just been, his mouth hanging open.

I watched in horror as an arrow flying faster than I could have imagined pierced him in the chest and threw him back three unsteady paces, before I could do a single thing about it.

I screamed, throwing my hands up to my face in horror. "Nooo! Falco!" I reached out to him, but my feet were rooted to the ground in fear and dismay.

He looked up at me and then down at the arrow protruding from his body, sinking slowly to his knees. He turned his head back to me, giving me a weak smile before falling slowly to his side, his eyes remaining open as his head hit the grass.

The anger welled up in me and took over. I felt the power of the Ancient One pouring into my connection, filling me with a dark fever that rushed in and started burning me from the inside. I turned my attention to Samantha and fixed her with a threatening glare, letting the protective bubble drop completely.

She stood there for a moment, facing me with an arrow sticking out of the left side of her chest, blood staining the front of her clothing crimson. Then she took two steps back towards the forest, looking down so she wouldn't trip on any of the bodies littering the ground around her.

"Where are you going?" I growled at her, taking several steps forward. "Running back to Ben? Going to tell him how you killed your old friend Becky in cold blood?"

"It's not like that, Jayne," she barked out at me.

"Yes! It is! It's *exactly* like that!" I screamed at her. Then I lowered my volume, dropping my voice into its most menacing tone. "But I've got some bad news for you, you evil bitch. You aren't going anywhere. Your days as a Dark Fae end *here. Now.*"

A green light tinged with the old darkness of the Ancient One surged up out of my body and into my hands. I held them out in front of me and turned my palms to Samantha.

She lifted her staff and muttered words under her breath. I felt a prickling along my neck, as if there was a lot of static electricity in the air.

"Jayne, stop!" yelled Tim, pleading with me and pulling my hair like crazy.

I didn't even flinch. I was beyond hearing or obeying.

I released a stream of green power out of my hands, and aimed it directly at her. I expected it to blast her to kingdom come, and couldn't wait to see it happen. But instead, a ray of red-lit flames came from out of the trees behind her, intercepting my bolt of energy and sending both beams skyward in a swirl of red and green light.

What the fuck?

And then I heard his voice.

"Jayne. Let it go! You cannot win this."

Motherfucker. I'd know that voice anywhere.

Ben.

Chapter Thirty-Seven

BEN, THE GUY WHO COULDN'T seem to stay the hell out of my business and out of my life. Always sticking his head in where it didn't belong. Now he was going to be sorry.

Even though the sound of our combined and battling forces seemed loud to everyone standing around us in the meadow near the trees, I knew that he would hear me perfectly when I said in a calm voice, "She killed my friends ... my people. An eye for an eye, Ben. It's you or her. I'll let you decide."

"Jayne, I'm not going to let that happen. We're here to enter the compound, and you're going to let me in. You're going to let *us* in."

My nostrils flared with the anger that continued to rise up inside me. I drew two deep breaths into my chest, filling my brain with oxygen and preparing myself for what I was about to do. Only once so far had I managed to combine the powers of the two elements that did my bidding. I was going to do it again, right here in this meadow outside the gargoyle door to the Light Fae compound, and snuff Ben's light out forever. He refused to choose between himself and Samantha, so I was going to make the choice for him. First he was going, and then her - a two-fer.

"Spike," I said calmly, "take Tim and back the hell up."

"Jaaayyne," he said, "whatever you're thinking, you might want to re-think it."

"Spike!" I yelled, my tone brooking no argument. "Get Tim *now!*"

Spike said nothing in response, but I soon felt the weight of my small pixie friend leave my shoulder.

"Notch an arrow, Finn," I said, my hands never wavering from their position, channeling the power of The Green out of the earth and into a stream that was still all tangled with Ben's fire, both of them shooting up into the sky, separating the clouds that gathered there and lighting up the night that quickly gathered in around us.

I glanced over to see that Finn was doing as I asked.

He lifted his bow up and drew back the string. "What am I aimin' at?" he said, his voice slightly muffled by his shoulder.

"Samantha. Kill shot."

I watched as Finn's eye squinted, putting Samantha in his sights.

"Jayne!" yelled Tim's voice from behind me. "Wait! Don't do this!"

"Shhhh!" hushed Spike.

"You're going to get hurt!" Tim continued to whine.

"What do you want me to do?" asked Scrum at my shoulder.

"Carry my body back inside if I fuck this up."

"You got it." I could feel his steady presence there, not questioning, preparing for anything.

And now I was ready. I had my sharpshooter in place, my peeps at my back, and Becky off hopefully somewhere safe, no longer lying in the grass all twisted up and staring at the sky.

I drew it in - power not only from the ley line here, but several off in the distance. The soil led me to the roots, the roots led me to the trees, and the trees to the leaves and vines. I communicated through the living things and touched all of them that touched the water. I pulled it all to me.

The stream of power that was coming from me changed slightly. It went from pure green to a lighter green and then to a flow that changed and glistened, first green then blue then turquoise and back again. I had to force myself not to get lost in the kaleidoscope.

The flow was thicker and stronger. I had to physically control it now, not just mentally. My arms felt like they were holding something heavy. I tried not to let them shake with the effort because I still needed more.

I called out to the moisture in the air - the invisible sheen of humidity that the water sprites traveled in. I brought it into my field of control and sent it towards Ben.

Slowly, slowly, the balance of power changed. My light was snuffing out the angry red of Ben's. I smiled maliciously, angry and exhilarated with the power that surged through me.

The wind started to kick up near me. The ends of my hair stood up, pushed by the currents of air that rushed around me and threatened to push me off balance. What was first a slight breeze quickly became a gale.

"Jayne!" yelled Finn, "I don't know if I can shoot in this!"

"Mindseye arrow, Finn! Just imagine your target, and I'll take care of the rest! Get ready to let it fly!"

I yelled out into the tempest of fire, wind, water and earth, "Last chance, Ben! Walk away or die!"

I heard nothing in response. I hoped that meant he was struggling to contain my onslaught like I was battling to contain his.

"Get back into the compound, Spike! Take Tim with you!" All I needed was my little buddy launched into this maelstorm.

"Are they in?!" I yelled to Scrum.

"Yes!"

"In five, Finn ... ready?!"

"Yeah," he said, his bow up and fighting the wind, his eyes closed as he sent me the vibe of his signature through the mess of energy surrounding us.

I focused enough to find him, and once I had his signature, sent some of the green energy into him. I saw him flinch as it hit. Then I started my countdown.

"Five ... four ... three ... two ... *one!*" The arrow left Finn's fingers at the exact moment I pushed the last bit of extra power I'd been holding back into him.

It was aimed directly at Ben's heart.

Hate Cliffhangers?

Not to worry! Just go to Amazon, find the next book in the series, click on the "Look Inside" cover of the book, and you'll be able to read the first several chapters of the next book for free. I know, I know ... cliffhangers make you crazy, right? Sorry. I just can't seem to help myself. :)

Other Books by Elle Casey

War of the Fae: Book One, The Changelings
War of the Fae: Book Two, Call to Arms
War of the Fae: Book Three, Darkness & Light
War of the Fae: Book Four, New World Order

Clash of the Otherworlds: Book 1, After the Fall
Clash of the Otherworlds: Book 2, Between the Realms
Clash of the Otherworlds: Book 3, Portal Guardians

Apocalypsis: Book 1, Kahayatle
Apocalypsis: Book 2, Warpaint
Apocalypsis: Book 3, Exodus
Apocalypsis: Book 4, Haven

My Vampire Summer
My Vampire Fall

Wrecked
Reckless

About the Author

Elle Casey is an American writer who lives in Southern France with her husband, three kids, Hercules the wonder poodle, and Monie the bouvier. In her spare time she writes young adult novels.

A personal note from Elle ...

If you enjoyed this book, please consider leaving feedback on Amazon.com, Goodreads.com, or any book blogs you participate in. More positive feedback means I can spend more time writing! Oh, and I love interacting with my readers, so if you feel like shooting the breeze or talking about books, please visit me. You can find me at ...

www.ElleCasey.com
www.Facebook.com/ellecaseytheauthor
www.Twitter.com/ellecasey
www.Shelfari.com/ellecasey

Acknowledgments

As my portfolio of titles grows, I've started to notice that I'm thanking a lot of the same people. Regardless, their contributions should continue to be recognized because without them, my stories would suffer or perhaps not even exist. So ... onwards and upwards. First, thanks to Beth Godwin and Margaret for the editing. I have proven time and again that I'm not capable of editing my own work, so thank you for your red pens and eagle eyes. To the reviewers and book bloggers who have featured my book on your sites, thanks ever so much. You have allowed me to see my books through different eyes and it's just an amazing view. Thanks to those who have left me reviews on Amazon.com and Goodreads.com – and to those who have sent me emails or blog posts or joined me on Facebook, please how much it means to me to hear your kind words. They are my drugs, and I am addicted! Thank you to Samantha Young, fellow indie writer who's never hesitated to give me encouragement and something to shoot for. To Ashley Delgado at WhatsYourStory book blog tours for arranging my first ever book blog tour. I love your entrepreneurship and positive attitude! Thanks to Amazon for giving indie authors like me a platform from which to share our work. Thank you to Facebook for connecting me with readers and long ago made friends who I thought I'd lost. Thank you to France, a lovely place to live and raise a family amongst friends. Thank you to my girlfriends in France, especially Caroline, Joy, Patricia, Isabelle, and Béa, the DDG you-know-whats. To my husband and children who allow me the time to write and encourage me every step of the way. And to my mom, who captured Abby in a bell jar and sent her to me, even though I hate surprises.

Made in the USA
Lexington, KY
26 November 2016